Sleeping DADDY

NICHOLAS WESTERFER

Copyright
© 2024 Nicholas Westerfer

All rights reserved.
No part of this publication may be reproduced, distributed, or transmitted
in any form or by any means, including photocopying, recording, or other
electronic or mechanical methods, without the prior written permission of the
publisher, except in the case of brief quotations embodied in critical reviews
and certain other noncommercial uses permitted by copyright law.

Sleeping Daddy
Published by Nicholas Westerfer
USA

ISBN: 979-8-9913267-0-4 hardcover
ISBN: 979-8-9913267-1-1 paperback
ISBN: 979-8-9913267-2-8 ebook
ISBN: 979-8-9913267-3-5 special edition

This is a work of fiction. The characters, events, and settings portrayed in this
novel are the products of the author's imagination and are not based on real
people or actual events, except where noted. Any resemblance to real persons,
living or dead, or to actual events is purely coincidental.
The author and publisher have made every effort to ensure that the content is
accurate and engaging, but the events and characters depicted should be viewed as
fictional and intended solely for entertainment purposes.

For information about this book, visit: www.nickwesterfer.com

I can, and I will.

The love between a father and his daughters cannot be broken.
The day I became a father, is the day I really started living.
It was the day I experienced true love, in its rarest, most beautiful form.
It was the day the past no longer mattered, and the only things of
significance were my little girls and their dreams.

For Evangeline and Isabelle, my daughters.

Sleeping DADDY

Prologue—Present Day

Dear Hope,

When you were little, I told you a story about a king and a princess. The tale came about on a night the world threatened to swallow us whole, on a night I wasn't sure I knew how to keep going.

That night was heavy with thoughts of your mother and sister, an unbearable tension that thickened the air and clouded the sun. You, clad in cute powder pink pajamas, were determined to stay up all night and play with Peter Panda. Tired and numb from trying to fix everything in our lives, I felt hopeless, bound to a life where only pain would rule.

You refused to sleep. True to self, you were rambunctious and wild, full of life, and ready for adventure. I lost my temper, covered my face, and grunted angrily, just wanting to slink into sleep without the nightly battle.

To my surprise, a warm press of lips fluttered on my cheek: a kiss you placed there on your own. Drawing back my arms, I saw your smiling face. It was mostly gums with sprouting teeny-tiny teeth, and a look of pure childish appreciation on your face, a yearning affection. It was love, in the cleanest, purest sense. It was trust in the way humanity was intended to develop. Strength sang in my bones, because surely, right then…I knew exactly how to keep going.

Cradling you close to me, I started talking, and the words formed the story.

We called it "Sleeping Daddy," and if you can't remember, it went like this:

Once upon a time, there lived a handsome King,
Who loved his Princess even more than the flowers of spring.
That King worked hard all day and all night,
To run his kingdom without a fight.
The wind blew heavy, and it was hard to dream,
But the Princess could always find a way to make him beam.
The sky tumbled and rumbled as he fell asleep,
No noise could wake him from counting sheep.
All the land could hear those snores,
They were loud and rumbling like the mighty shores.
He became known as *Sleeping Daddy* by all,
Because no one could wake him, no noise big or small.
Then, one day, his Princess came along,
She gave him a kiss that made him feel strong.
The King awoke with no more fright,
And smiled always, day and night.
So, every day from that day on,
The Princess scurried to the King at dawn.
She was fast and speedy, and never late,
For she knew her kiss would decide his fate.

Whispering the story, holding your tiny hand, you would fall asleep, warm, safe, and forever protected in my arms…and I yours.

You've changed me. Finding someone who can love you, even with all of the imperfections and craziness that weaves your existence, changes you.

You've restored the fundamental fabric of my thoughts, reestablished faith amid the clouds of doubt. As time pushes forward with its forceful hand, take our story and hold it in your heart.

Love,
Daddy

Part 1

January, 44 Years Ago

Chapter 1

The frigid air claims the room with an unwelcomed force, chasing the morning cobwebs of sleep away without the necessity of caffeine. The bitter bite of dawn runs its fingers down my spine, teasing and mocking as I fight to rise before the impending alarm.

Pulling the comforter tighter around me, the distant moan of Boston hums in an omnipresent melody, contradicting the absence of sun. I search for the strength to pull myself up. *The clock. Any minute, the alarm clock will ring and wake her too.*

Weakness wins. It's too hard to move when the world outside this comforter bites, when outside these cotton walls, you become a puppet on the strings of life.

The cacophonous ring booms, violates the quiet like an explosion. The alarm clock blinks, the sirens hitting the wintery air like cannons in a war.

5:00 a.m. Rise and shine.

Before the noise prompts my exit from bed, Ella stirs. She groans, turning, her warm hands sliding gently around my torso, her breath meeting the back of my ear.

"Morning," she mutters, gruff with sleep.

I turn to face her, the unexpected embrace making it even harder to leave the nest.

"Can you skip work today? Let's sleep in while we can," she whispers, shivering against the cold.

I run my hand under her shirt, warm skin meeting my icy palm with a jump. "Sounds like a dream."

She smiles, and I wish I could see better in the darkness. I imagine her long black hair unkempt, spilling free from its normal home behind her ear. The dainty freckles under her eyelashes scattering back into place before the morning light begins its claim. Those eyes a dangerous shade of blue, dark as the sea, breaking with waves of baby blue and white.

"Jesus, shut that alarm off," she mutters, pulling the blanket over her head.

"It's too cold to move."

Pulling the covers over my head, I move to kiss her. My hands go for the dimples on her back. She wiggles, giggling into my mouth.

"The alarm, Keith, it's so loud," she says, pulling away.

As I begin the climb out of bed, she whispers, "You're forgetting something."

I nod, shuffling my feet to the dresser. Flicking the alarm off and the light on, I head back to the bed and pull the comforter down to reveal the bulging baby bump hiding underneath. I kiss her swollen stomach, once, then twice, a kiss for each growing pumpkin. I move my chin up and down, purposely tickling her with my scratchy face. "Morning, little blueberries."

"They're pineapples now!" she corrects, squishing her face.

"Ouch! Easier to pass a couple blueberries."

She rolls her eyes. "Dr. Stacey said twins generally don't come on their due date. Always a little before," she says. "Knowing our luck, I'll have the rare set of twins that decide to stay put till after."

"I'm fine with after."

"Keith, you're not him." She purses her lips.

I tense, knowing the "him" that she's referring to. "Who? Frank? I know. I know that, but this world is tainted. At least they're safe in there. And warm."

I never thought I would have kids. Always tried to picture what it'd be like but couldn't. Then the doctor told us to think pink, and then to think double-pink, and the picture is moving closer and closer toward developed. Twins. Two little girls who will bring me to my knees with a single tear.

"You are gentle, just like the sunset. You are alive, just like raging fire. You are careful and kind. You are reckless and passionate. You teach me. You show me. You are a champion. My champion," she says, reciting our vows. Reciting what she wrote for me years ago.

Ella has a way with words. Whether those words are kind or pointed, they're powerful. I'm horrible. I never know what to say until it's too late.

"After you left last night, I was thinking about the names again. Hope and Faith," I say. "Feels right."

"Yeah?" Her eyes beam.

"Hope and Faith Higgins, I like the sound of it."

Twin girls are bound to drive me gray, and if they look like their mother, I'll need an immense amount of hope and faith not to be senile by the time they're teens.

I go to leave, but she stops me with a hand on my forearm.

"Don't forget your new plant. I left it on the table."

I grin in response. Ella buys me plant after plant for my desk. I somehow seem to kill every last one of them. Every other month, she purchases a new one and leaves it on the table. She thinks it's good for my eyes to look at something green in contrast to the computer screen all day. It's become a game for her, like: *How long will this one last? I give Keith a month before killing this.*

"Thanks. I won't forget, and I have a good feeling about this one. It looks like a fighter."

She rolls her eyes.

Jumping out of bed, I move for the bathroom. On entry, the temporary smile Ella drew on my face disappears.

My eyes find *his* in the mirror, my reflection bringing a sadness. For in those eyes—my eyes—breathes the lacking. The outward absence from the presence I swear I carry. Staring too long reveals the stranger, the naive soul not yet knowing of the world. Seeing in the mirror, divulges the truth: *I am Frank, nothing more.*

The light flashes, his face twists and melds itself to mine, his features covering my own. He becomes a part of me and I him.

Fear, overwhelming and stark, surges…*and I him…*

I look to the faucet, avert my eyes so he can't hurt me again. I'm becoming the man I fear most.

I hesitate to move, waver at even turning the sink on, hating that feeling when cold fingers submerge into warm water, the burning and tingling that starts in the fingers and then crawls up the entirety of your hands. I turn it on anyway, scrub my skin fire engine red, to get the ingrained paint from my hands and from under my nails.

Ella went out with a girlfriend last night, and I spent hours held imprisoned by canvas. Painting invades my brain like a welcomed fog. It's the one thing in life I do that I don't overanalyze. The strokes come naturally, my brush seeming to move without effort. If I was meant for anything in this world, it's to paint. The burnt orange meeting the yellow of a summer sunset infects me. Color and texture ignite me.

With stinging hands, I pull on the gray suit with the dark green, button-front shirt, the cotton material all too familiar. Looking to the mirror, cautiously, it's me that's not familiar. It's me that's becoming someone else. Some other Keith…the Keith that's more of him and less of me.

I'm becoming my dad. The circles and lines digging into my face are turning me, changing me, into him. And if I look like him, what's to stop me from acting like him?

Ella doesn't know everything; she doesn't know the full story. She's optimistic, yet no matter how hard I try to convince myself I'm worthy, I have a little voice murmuring, *She's your life, but you don't deserve her.*

I think she knows it too. Some days, I look at her, and when she looks back…it's like I don't know who my wife is. Not truly, not deeply. There is this quiet, an absence of words. A sense building in the way her eyes refuse to connect with mine. A tenseness I am accumulating from the apprehension in her shoulders.

She senses the internal wound I carry. Realizes that, if the wrong rock gets overturned, weakening the pressure to stanch the bleed, I'll never stop leaking on the inside.

A gray morning light fills the sky, the delicate shades of a rosy summer sky still months away. I make my way down the stairs and into the dining room. The plant rests atop the expensive mahogany dining set. The table, which was a gift from Ella's parents, seems to cry out for help when arranged against the tacky laminate floors and other half-priced IKEA furniture clogging the space.

"Lucky Bamboo. Hard to kill," the note fixed to the healthy bundle of green stalks claims.

A challenge.

I'd believe that Ella purchased the plant to combat my black thumb, but as I turn the card stock over, I see the true reason. "Get that pro-motion!" it reads, claiming that Chinese tradition believes you'll get one year of good luck and prosperity, albeit only if the plant doesn't die off, in which case be prepared to kiss the next twenty-nine years of your life away.

Ella wants me to get a promotion. She's always complaining that I need to stand up for what I deserve. That I need to fight for what I want. But, honestly, I don't want a promotion. I want to get in and get out, real quick and dirty. I want to keep my head down while doing the bare minimum it takes to collect my paycheck.

It's hard to effectively communicate that laziness, and the problem is, I keep finding myself working for it anyway. When those who love you believe something of you, you start believing it too. And Life at Your Reach is an incredibly popular place to work. It's consistently praised in the *Boston Business Journal* for its remarkably fast climb in contracts. It's the only advertising company that specializes in marketing green and environmentally safe products that doesn't take any shit for having a huge carbon footprint.

I should be proud to work there. Instead, I dread the full fifty minutes it takes to get from Mission Hill into downtown Boston. And it's not only because I'm uninspired, or because I'd rather be painting. It's because I don't necessarily see eye to eye with my boss, Richard.

Richard is rough, crass, and he finds a sick joy in making life hell for the people reporting to him. He's miserable, and it fills him with childish glee to taint and draw another human into his misery.

I make my way to the kitchen, grabbing my phone from the charger and scampering out the door into the connecting garage. I tuck the bamboo plant on the passenger seat, wondering briefly if I should cover its leaves to give it a fighting chance. Twenty-nine years of bad luck sounds like something I should work to avoid.

The garage door rumbles open, exhaust meeting the crisp winter air in bellowing clouds as I back from the driveway. The highway is void, empty of cars and people. Cold earth and the vast desire to turn around and head home are the only obstacles standing between me and Richard.

I delay the inevitable with a brief stop for coffee, but soon enough, I arrive at the office, park in my standard spot in the aging parking garage, and clumsily carry the bamboo through the Beltwhile Enterprises building, while balancing coffee and my briefcase.

At the elevator, I hesitate before pressing the call button, but then sigh, per usual, tighten my butt cheeks and finger the key for Life at Your Reach. It's a fast elevator, the whir of the motor inaudible against the uncomfortable tickle in your belly.

The door groans open, and with no surprise, Richard's the first thing I see. Scowling, and shoveling a powdered donut into his mouth.

He's a stocky man with thick eyebrows and whiskered nostrils. His smell is a putrefied concoction of stale coffee and cigarettes. His brain is made of cement. I know this because he has body hair stretching out from every visible surface, yet he's completely bald on his crown. The back of his neck looks like you could poke a fork into it, put it on a bun, and then eat it for lunch—if hairy sausage-neck was your thing.

His eyes catch mine, and he goes from famished and starving to locked and loaded in seconds. He waddles closer, huffing and puffing like he wants to blow the place down. "Keith!" he yells, checking his wristwatch. "It's already ten after! *I've* been here a good twenty minutes!" His cheeks are red, and his hands are gesticulating a message I don't compute.

He's well-dressed, wearing a black pin-striped suit with a black shirt and silver tie. Stylish, but sloppy, with his shirt wrinkled and untucked around the belt. His shoes are untied, and I can see at the bulging buttons of his gut that he isn't wearing an undershirt.

"Sorry," I sing, putting extra effort into sounding like I love life. "The traffic was backed up today. Plus, I stopped at McGregor's Bakery. I picked you up your favorite sugar cookie. It's a special day today, you know? It's been three amazing years with you leading Life at Your Reach," I lie.

I got the cookie for free when I bought my large coffee. I sip that coffee, hoping he hasn't heard about the special.

"Bullshit! I got this donut there this morning," he says, chunks of said donut shooting out of his mouth and across my jacket. "There wasn't a car on the road!"

"I figured I had a 50/50 shot with that excuse."

"Keith!" he hollers, straight into my face in that obtuse way only he can pull off. "Green Games! You've got to get me Green Games!" he says, moving back into the office.

I follow him toward my desk, taking mental notes as we go, trying not to hyper-focus on that godforsaken neck of his.

"Get Mikey Sigs on the phone! Get them all on the phone!" he demands, scooping the rest of the donut into his mouth and snatching my cookies. "Green Games has to sign today. Got it?" His eyes sharpen. "Or we move you to the mailroom."

"We're just about ready to close," I say. "I'll try to arrange a meeting for first thing this afternoon."

"Don't try. Just do it," he growls. "And why the hell haven't you shaved your face yet? You're looking more and more like an abandoned dog every day."

I force a smile. "You sound like my wife."

"I talked to HR regarding acceptable shrubbery display too. They said I can't do jack-shit about you prancing in with a new plant every other day. But, just so you're aware, I want to slap that bush right out of your hands."

My pocket dings before I respond, vibrating with an incoming text message. The sound puzzles me, makes me freeze in my footsteps, because I generally have all sound shut off, per Richard's orders.

He growls, turning on me "Shut that damn thing down and get me Green Games!"

"Okay, okay!" I say pulling out the phone, then cringe at the shirtless picture of Justin Bieber on the lock screen. It's Ella's phone, I must have grabbed it by mistake.

"Are you queer now too?" Richard asks, seeing the picture.

I ignore him, my eyes reading the message: *Call me about last night…* *-Ethan*

I drop the lucky bamboo, my breath rushing out as it crashes to the ground next to my desk. The thought of twenty-nine years of bad luck washes together with some unknown face named Ethan.

Chapter 2

Pebbles of soil speckle the gray tile, the earthen smell of the potting mix replacing the sterile chemical scent of the office. *Call me about last night?*

"Shit!" I drop to all fours to examine the mess.

Richard chuckles from above. "On second thought, screw HR. I'm sending out a memo today banning all plant products. Safety protocols!"

The soil pebbles break and smear under my hands as I move to make small anthills out of them.

Ella went out last night. Caught a movie with a girlfriend before life gets too crazy with the babies' arrival. I wasn't invited, but I didn't care. Instead, I stayed home, lost in my painting. When she arrived back, she trotted right upstairs, the hum of the shower coming only a few minutes afterward. I had assumed that was for my benefit. She knows I don't like to break concentration when I'm inspired to paint.

I shake my head, start sweeping the rubble back into the cracked plastic pot.

"Get this cleaned up, and get me that contract," Richard says, chuckling. His shoes knock into two of the piles, spilling the dirt further as he moves toward his office.

I work faster, shoveling fistfuls back into the pot, surprised to see that the stalks of the bamboo are undamaged, the sturdy green pillars still upright and steady.

"Great…" I mutter, packing the soil tight with my fingers. "Twenty-nine years of bad luck."

An unexpected giggle startles me. The light chuckle grows louder as a woman—the new girl—crouches down to assist with the sweeping. She greets me with a smile, her blond pixie-cut tucked untidily behind her ears, her cheeks rosy.

"Oh…you don't have to do that; I can get it."

She shrugs, her big eyes saying hi, the peculiar mix of seafoam green and brown shimmering like two emeralds bending the light, the hues swirling and dancing so complexly that picking one defining color would be impossible. She laughs.

"You're laughing at me?"

Her lips tighten against her soft complexion. Her nose, thin and small, in the center of her face, crinkles as she tries to control her giggle. "I'm not laughing at your misfortune, I promise. It's just, do you realize that you talk to yourself all day? I just started two days ago, and I feel like I know more about you than I probably should."

My cheeks warm. "I've heard that once or twice," I say, smiling. "Name's Keith Higgins. Sorry I haven't stopped by and introduced myself yet."

She shakes her head reassuringly. "Oh, I know your name. I've had the pleasure of hearing Richard yelling it," she says. "I think…he might hate you."

I nod. "You catch on quick."

She drops a pile of soil pebbles into the cracked pot, shimmies further out to gather more. "The self-muttering…I haven't decided if that means you're crazy? Should I worry that I sit next to a crazy?"

I chuckle, shrugging.

"Uh oh! You're the crazy in the group?" she asks.

"Well, Rich gives me a run for my money."

She smiles, shows off her perfect teeth. Little dimples form just past her lips, as she deposits the last of the pebbles. "Lucky bamboo?" she asks, picking it up and climbing to her feet to examine it more closely. "It's a survivor."

"Yeah. My wife," I say, gathering the rest of my belongings and getting to my feet. "She likes to test my cultivation aptitude. I can't kill this one too."

She grins and considers this. "We can save it." She hesitates. "Let's give it a name. I've read that plants have similar feelings and emotions to humans."

"Name the plant?"

"My votes for Sasha. It looks like a Sasha to me," she says. "That's sort of my thing; I sense names."

"Sasha? My plant's a female?"

She laughs. "No, it's a plant, silly. Besides, Sasha can be a boy's name too. Gender norms are fascist. It just looks like a Sasha." Her fluorescent pink heels click across the polished tile floor as she moves toward the sea of gray cubes.

I examine the bamboo, seeing only a plant, but playing along. "It really does look like a Sasha!" I walk around the cubicle and to my desk. She heads the opposite direction, but pivots at a cube that's directly adjacent to mine.

She hefts Sasha up over the divider. "Lots of water," she directs. "Maybe a new pot first, but you better get to work. I sense the impending return of Mr. Beltwhile."

"Yeah, I smell him coming too." She moves to sit down, and I remember my manners. "Oh, I never got your name."

"It's Jennifer. Jennifer Clark."

"Nice to meet you, Jennifer."

"Same," she says, making her voice deeper and official. "How long have you been here?"

Ella's phone vibrates again, a message from "Hubby": *I think you took my phone?*

"Too long," I mutter to Jennifer. "Hey, I should make some phone calls. Thanks again for the help."

"No problem."

As I sit, I see her blond head drop below the wall, the *click-click* of a keyboard starting seconds later.

I unlock Ella's phone, opening the message. I respond, *Sorry, I must have grabbed it by mistake.*

Three bubbles of a response show instantly. Then: *No worries.*

A half-second later a vibration, from the mysterious Ethan: *Sorry, wrong number.*

"Keith!" shouts Richard from behind, breaking the silence.

"Shit!" My cheeks warm.

Richard's panting and red-faced. "Did you get in touch with Mikey Sigs yet?"

"You mean within the three seconds I've been at my desk? No. No, I haven't."

"Call him now!" His meaty hands go to his hips.

I swivel in my chair. "Yeah! Yes, I'm on it," I say undocking my desk phone and opening my planner to find the number. I hear Rich storming off as I press the keys.

"Good morning," answers the gruff voice, thick with Boston accent. "It's Mikey."

"Hey, Mikey. It's Keith calling from Life at Your Reach."

"The Dorchie!"

I laugh. "I was born in Detroit."

"Yeah, but you still got that Dorchester blood in you. You catch the Pats game?"

I lie out of necessity. "Yeah. Brady's moves—wicked."

"Dude's untouchable! The best there this...everything else is just gahbidge."

"Hey, I'm calling about the contract. Hoping we can get those papers signed today?" I ask.

He groans. "Ah, shit. You still doin' the biddin' for the Southie?" he asks.

"You know the game; it's a rich man's world."

"Ain't that the truth? They'll sign today, I can guarantee that. Bastards will want something in print though. And ain't no way you're gonna catch Green Games doing the printing. Can we have something sent?"

"Not a problem. I can come there myself."

He laughs. "You're just trying to skip out on the Southie. I tell you what, grab me something from Dunkies on the way, and I'll make sure you get those signatures quick."

"Done."

We bullshit back and forth for a few more minutes, until I manage to weasel my way off the call. As the phone cracks back into its home, I pull up the contract and send it to the printer.

After picking up the contract, I deliver the news to Richard. "Green Games will sign today, but they want something in print. Can I go get the signatures?"

He scowls and gives me the you-are-a-piece-of-shit pout. "Make it happen."

I swing back to my desk, grab my coat and bag, while attempting to down my barely drunk coffee. It's hotter than expected, and I burn my tongue. "Shit!"

"We have got to work on that!" Jennifer says, poking up from behind the divider. She rests her chin on the metal bar between our desks. "There are so many other words in the world, dude."

I laugh.

"Heading out?" she asks.

"Account's ready for signatures." I slide the contract into my bag. "Thanks again for the help earlier, Jennifer." I motion to Sasha.

"Sure, but do me a favor, call me Jenny."

"Is that the name you sense for yourself?"

"Sure is," she says, smiling. "By the way, you're leaving, and you haven't watered Sasha yet." She stands, handing over a porcelain serving bowl. "Just went and stole this for you."

I grin, surprised.

"And water," she says, handing over a brimming paper cup. "You have to soak it."

I quickly move the plant to the new bowl and douse it with the water. "If this plant lives, we'll have you to thank."

"Here," she says and tosses a fun-sized bag of peanut M&M's. "Congrats on Green Games."

"Thanks! At least your day will be peaceful now...no crazy, self-muttering neighbor."

She chuckles. "Ya know, if Richard wasn't constantly screaming, 'Keith!', I'd have sensed your name was...Frank."

Chapter 3

The driver's door slams, thudding closed with an echo that shakes the maturing Honda.

Eyes shifting, they lock onto the rearview mirror, two shit brown footballs—vast, yet empty—studying the situation in a pathetic show of feebleness, looking for him, because his name, with the sound of any door slamming, is enough to cause terror. The eyes looking back are not only my own, but his too.

Why do I look like him?

Frank… She had sensed Frank in me, and I had almost locked up. Had almost turned to the window to look for him in my reflection. I want to revoke the name Sasha from my plant now, her naming talents are offensive.

I start the car, rip the bag of M&M's open with my teeth and pop three in my mouth.

Frank…

I shiver. His name, even today, makes me shiver.

Fumbling to get situated, the phone vibrates again. A text from "Hubby" via Ella: *Did I get any messages? Can't do anything with this dinosaur version of IOS you have.*

I hit dial. Wait for it to go to voicemail, then hang up. Her text follows immediately: *Can't talk. At my OB-GYN appointment.*

I plug in the address for Green Games on the phone and pull from the parking space. The dingy darkness of the garage doesn't help settle the nerves rooting from Frank, and my mind keeps looping back to the phrase: *Call me about last night.*

Ella had gone out last night. There's a silence in her eyes lately, and something in my bones whispering that I don't know who she is. The absence of words, that disconnect of eyes, the tenseness in her shoulders— it's all there. I've been using the pregnancy the same way a child uses a Band-Aid...pretending that what you can't see, can't hurt.

I shake my head, hit the brake at the exit, and slip my parking ticket into the machine. The arm moves up.

I'm ridiculous. Not trusting Ella is the consequence of not trusting myself. It's the Frank in me that I've suppressed and locked away. The result of sweeping my past into a cannon that's bound to explode, the results of...of sweeping Mom away.

My mom tried hard, but life with little to no education in Detroit was a losing battle. She spent days scrubbing houses clean for little pay, only for Dad to steal the money and buy his booze. Her hands were ruined from the work, creased and cracked to the bone.

That never stopped Frank from taking what he was owed.

It was summer that day, the air moist and thick. Mom got Dad to leave, gave him forty dollars, thinking it was enough to have a full-weekend binge if he went to all the right bars.

After he left, she turned to Scott and me. "We're leaving! Pack a bag and bring only the necessities."

"What the fuck are you talking about, Ma?" Scott shouted, his tone sounding more like Dad the older he got.

She planned to leave, to package us up, and rid ourselves of Frank. Leave without a word, taking a bag, without a trail for him to follow. Move out to Boston and live with her friend, Meredith, from grade school. Meredith's husband, Mike, owned a landscaping business and he needed the extra help.

"I'm not leaving without Dad!" Scott moaned.

"Scott, he's only getting worse. I've let this go on long enough. Now let's go! Get upstairs and pack a bag." She grabbed him by the arm and tried to pull him up the stairs.

He blew up, raising his fists, threatening to strike at Mom.

I stood. "Don't touch her!"

He moved from Mom to me, grabbed me by the shoulders, and shoved me into the wall. "What are you going to do about it, pussy?"

Unwanted tears sprang into my eyes, and I pushed them under.

The way he hit, the way he hurt, the way he spoke—it reminded me of Frank. *Like father, like son.* He was becoming the man we usually fought back against together.

Mom screamed, "What's wrong with you? We *have* to leave him!"

"No…I'm not…I'm not leaving without him," Scott whimpered, his eyes threatening to show weakness. He turned and ran from the house, slamming the door in his wake.

I wanted to leave, and it wasn't because I didn't love Frank. It's because he *knew* me. He knew me on a level no one else could understand, knew that I was a piece of his evil. I wanted to run from that idea as much as I wanted to escape him.

I understood that this was the strongest thing Mom had ever done. She was being courageous, so I helped her pack. Shoveled clothes for Scott and me into separate duffels and lugged them down the stairs.

"What if he went to tell Dad?" I asked.

"He won't. He's good. He'll come to his senses any minute now, and we'll get moving." She smiled, slipping the bus tickets into my front pocket for safekeeping.

I reached out, hugged her, giddy with the excitement for a new adventure.

Those minutes turned to hours, our pacing feet starting to grow sore. Mom looked worried we would no longer make the midnight departure.

Around 8:00 p.m., the cops showed up, with flashing red and blue lights, telling us with somber faces that Scott was dead. He had jacked a car, stolen a handle of vodka, and then wrapped himself around a telephone pole. Dead on impact.

The pain was like a bullet, harsh and crippling. A scream lodged in my throat. Mom crumbled to the floor, hysterical, sobbing.

Nevertheless, I was selfish, selfish and tired of being a punching bag.

"Mom, we should go. We should leave, the two of us. Dad will blame this on us. On me!" I was crying just as hard as she was, but I felt it, felt it in my bones that Dad always loved Scott more than me. This sudden loss would only kill me too.

Harboring that sadness, I was still able to remember the sound his fist made, cracking into my skull, and the blinding pain that followed. Still remembered all the times I'd cowered on the floor beneath him, pleading for him to stop, the noise the belt made when it finally made contact with skin, the smell of blood that filled the air after his assaults, tinged with the faint smell of leather.

And the screams, the screams between him and my mother fighting. The screams of her crying after he hit her. The way she screamed for him to stop when he was hitting us. The screams Scott choked out from under a brutal, drunk father. *And me.* The screams that *never* came from me but stayed hidden inside. I couldn't scream. *I wouldn't.* My only defense against his fists were the tears I wouldn't shed in front of him.

But Mom's face was confused, weary. Like she'd forgotten all of that.

I pulled her up. "We can do it. We can go…together."

She was blinded, her face wrecked with trails of tears. She curled over in sorrow, pulled herself into a ball, and wailed.

"Mom!" I cried, needing to throw up. "We have to leave."

It hurt, the tears being ripped with fumbling fingers from my soul, but I didn't give up. I pulled at her. "Please!"

Her eyes were gone, not there, lost in some haze of a world where Scott was still alive.

Then the door handle jiggled, and the house fell silent. It rattled again, and my heart grew in frantic measure.

Boom! The front door opened, slammed into the wall.

9:09 p.m., the clock said.

The entire house shook. Forty dollars hadn't gone nearly as far as Mom hoped. The smell was instantaneous: chemical and feral. Yet his eyes were not as gone as they should have been. His movements were not as sloppy as an all-day bender called for.

My heart raced. I watched as he kicked at the packed bags with his booted foot. "The fuck is this?" he hollered. Shaking one of the twenty-dollar bills, an evil grin showing his teeth.

He knew.

Mom rose from the floor, broken and forlorn. "Frank! Frank, Scott… It's our baby…Scott."

She went to him, fell against his body, wanting his embrace. I couldn't understand why, why she would want his touch, when all of this was his doing.

You always hear how drunks regret their latest binges. How they wake up the next day, spinning and sick with regret for whatever shit they got into the night before. How they apologize and promise they won't hit you again, that they won't fight and scream like that in public again. That they didn't mean it, this isn't them. That they will try harder and stop drinking.

"This time's different, this time I'll change."

That is not Frank.

He didn't apologize. He didn't swear that the next time would be different. He didn't hide his swollen, puffy face in shame. That wasn't him.

I wanted him to try, to say that he would stop drinking, and that he was sorry he was such a cruel drunk. To admit he had a problem and show some sort of regret for his drunken tirades. I wanted him to be human enough to lie and say he'd get better.

He never did. He never pretended to care or tried to apologize. He just accepted himself as right. He just stole the power by not giving one ounce of a shit about us. Even in his early morning sober moments, he never showed remorse. He never swore to try. He never said, "Give me one more chance." He just took it without asking, and I wanted him to ask. I wanted him to beg. I wanted him to be that dad. The drunken loser that made a last-ditch effort to pretend to love us.

He wasn't one to beg his wife to stay. He was one who made *her* stay. Because how could she leave him? How could we leave him? We owed him. The world owed him.

I tightened my shoulders.

His eyes bore holes into mine while she wept in his arms. He patted her and stroked her hair, as if he actually cared, while he studied me with malice. Like this was my doing. As if I'd been the one to kill my brother. Something in his glare told me he wished it had been me instead of Scott.

Finally, he had had enough of her pussy-bullshit, took two hands, and pushed her body into the wall with a sickening crack. "Enough," he said, turning and slapping her across the face. "I knew you were up to some bullshit. Handing over forty dollars like it was no big deal? What, you been whoring yourself out now?"

She quieted, went still, her eyes shifting back to reality.

He pressed her to the floor, and then moved for me with swift feet.

I startled, fled, went for the stairs in a gallop, only for him to have my ankle before I could make it to freedom.

"You planning to leave?" he hollered.

My feet went out from under me, my hands smacking wood before my face could crack into the stairs. He pulled, yanked and sent me crashing down.

"Where you going to go, huh? Ain't nobody gonna take in a bitch with a pussy son!"

He squatted on me, his eye glittering, not only with anger and disgust, but also with some sick need for retribution. Like I was stealing something that belonged to him.

His hands went around my neck and squeezed. Squeezed and squeezed until life wanted to leave. Until, finally, he'd had enough, and flipped me over, kicking me while he freed his belt.

Mom's face came into focus. Slack, awake, staring at me.

She was not screaming his name. *She always screamed his name.* She wasn't fighting. She was watching, and I will never figure out what was worse...hearing her screams or hearing nothing at all.

When he was finished with me, he stumbled up the stairs, drunk and tired. I stayed on the floor, nearly broken, aching from head to toe. Then, I heard the clock ding at the half hour.

9:30 p.m.

I stood, wobbly on my knees. I went to my bag, picked it up, and slung it over my shoulder. Put my hood up and combed my long hair forward to block my battered face.

"Let's go," I muttered to Mom.

She looked dumbfounded.

"Get up, Mom!"

She flinched, going inward on herself...like she didn't even trust *me* anymore. Her voice small. "No..."

The beating hadn't made me cry, but tears were coming now. "Mom?"

"Keith...no."

Anger and pain twisted my insides. "Why?"

She said nothing, turned her face, closing her eyes.

"Why?" I screamed it this time.

"Shhh! Jesus Christ, your father's right...you never know when to shut the hell up."

My world shifted, tilted, and I felt like I was falling. She was choosing him. "I hate you," I said, my voice broken and tears bubbling out. "That's what you want?" I cried, pointing up the stairs. "Him?"

She was quiet.

"You watched him..." I steadied my shoulders and tightened my jaw. "You really are..." I trailed off as I started to realize the words coming out of my mouth were my father's, but I finished the sentence anyway. I finished it, blubbering like an idiot, tears flowing hot and wet on my face, and hating Frank even more for putting words like that into my head. "You really are a weak, disgusting whore, aren't you?"

Weak.

Disgusting.

Whore.

Dad's favorite words to spit in her face with his fists.

I watched the words leave my mouth in slow motion, and I wished I could pull them back, wished I could reach out and grab them so that they never reached her.

Wishful thinking holds no power.

She looked sick. Her eyes were like a wounded animal about to be finished off by a careless hunter. Raging waves were beating the inside of my body, knocking me back and forth, but I pushed forward.

I took a bus ticket from my pocket, chucked it in her face, shaking my head as if I was disgusted. I opened the door, walked slowly, never turning around, no words of protest in my wake.

A fresh fifteen years old, I got on that bus, and I showed up on the doorstep of a stranger, who had no reason to take me in, but did...Mike and Meredith embracing me as their own.

Mom never even called.

Ella's cell phone vibrates now, rings with a loud jingle that slices through the quiet of the car. For a second, I think of her, of Mom, and I wonder if maybe she's making that call now.

That's a fools thought. The phone vibrates again with an incoming call from Hubby.

"Hey."

"Keith..." Ella says. Her voice nervous, unsure. "My water just broke."

I go cold. How can I admit that, *no,* no, I am not ready for this?

Frank is me. I am made of him.

Chapter 4

"Good afternoon, this is Jennifer Clark with Life at Your Reach."

I clear my throat as the nerves from Ella's proclamation root deeper, as the fear follows my veins like a roadmap to grow branches of dread. "Hi, Jennifer—Jenny. This is Keith."

"Keith Higgins?" she asks, her voice rising.

"Yeah." What am I doing? Why would I call her? There's got to be someone else that can help. Stuart? Trent?

"I nearly jumped out of my chair. It's the first time my desk phone has rung."

I roll my neck and wait for the stubborn stoplight to turn green. Each minute is growing shorter. "I'm in a pickle," I say, trying to force a calmness, but my words stagger, go unmeasured.

"Okay?" she says. It seems cautious, the suggested smile easing from her tone.

"I need your help. I know you're new and have no reason to help, but my wife called. She's at the hospital." I lick my lips, the void of moisture making my tongue like sandpaper.

"Oh?" she says. "Is . . . Is she alright?"

"Yes, sorry. I'm sorry, she's fine. She's pregnant; her water broke."

She sighs. "Well, good. Great!" She sounds semi-confused, off beat. "Are you, like, freaking out?"

"Just a tad," I say, looking at my hands and wondering why they look so delicate all of the sudden. Will my kids have delicate hands too?

She clears her throat, like she's unsure how to move forward. "Well, just remember to breathe and count."

I smile, despite the growing panic. "I'm not calling for parental advice. I'm calling about Green Games."

"Right! I assumed. What do you need me to do?" she asks, her lively nature snapping into place.

The clock ticks, another minute gone. "I'm sorry, I know we just met, but…can I please ask you to collect the signatures and close out the Green Games account? They're expecting me today, and Rich—"

"Really?" she asks, her voice rising an octave.

"Well, if you don't mind. Do you mind? I was panicking, and I couldn't think who to call."

"Yeah! I mean, no, of course I don't mind. I've literally been sitting here looking at my phone for hours. Richard has yet to throw me anything challenging." There is a rustling sound and then her voice comes in a whisper, "You think it's because I'm a woman? Did I accept a job from a misogynist?"

It feels wrong to laugh, but I can't stop the chuckle. "Rich is a lot of things, but he isn't one to harbor work. It's your first week. He's probably just breaking you in slow. Besides—ah shit, what am I saying? Yes! Yes, you accepted a job from a misogynistic asshole."

The car rumbles, the light still saying no.

She sighs. "Thanks! It's better to know these things right off— Oh!" Another rustle, followed by whisper chuckles. "Oh, my word! He just walked by; I saw his head."

"Count the sausages, it helps."

"What?" she whispers.

"Never mind."

"Congratulations, BTW. Boy or girl?" she asks, voice moving out of a whisper.

"Girls! Twins!"

She gasps. "Awesome."

"Scary," I correct.

"Are they your first?"

"Yes."

"How do you feel about kangaroo births?"

I clear my throat. "Wait, what?"

She laughs. "They're disgusting!"

"Why?"

"I've seen one! Trust me. They come out looking like hairless rats, covered in this oozing plasma. They almost look like a sticky gummy bear," she says, amusement in her voice.

"Okay." I chuckle.

"I have it saved on my DVR. So, I can be the noble gatekeeper of the quite graphic video, if you're interested."

"Maybe *I* sit next to the office crazy?"

"You'd regret watching it, but it would have prepared you for this moment."

"So, my babies are going to look like sticky gummy bears is what you're saying?" I ask.

"I don't know. They haven't shown a human birth on Animal Planet yet."

A car horn blares from behind, signaling that the light finally switched to green. I let off the brake, ease forward.

"Higgins, are you driving on the phone? That's stupid; you're going to get yourself killed."

I flip to speakerphone and accelerate to speed. "You're on speaker."

"That's not any better!"

"Jot down my cell phone number," I say, calling out Ella's number. "I'll text you the address for Green Games. You'll have to meet Mikey Sigs—I apologize in advance."

"Why?"

"Because you're female, and he'll notice."

There's a flicker, a flash in my eye. A moving object in the road. I'm hurtling toward it. One, two, five seconds go by before I jerk awake, slamming on my brakes to avoid hitting it. For an instant, I think it's a child, a kid in the road, but no it's dark, fur-covered. The car lurches, the tires squeal, smoke against the asphalt.

A damn animal.

A plump raccoon perched on his haunches, black nose twitching, his beady little eyes staring me down with confidence, as if he has all the right in the world to be in the middle of downtown Boston in the height of daylight. Tires screech from behind, the following car stopping a breath away from my bumper.

"Shit!"

"I told you! I'm hanging up before you die!"

SD

The pink and blue sign reads "Labor and Delivery." After ringing the bell, two massive wooden doors open without sound, granting access to the birthing unit. The overly clean, whitewashed tiles lead the way forward, emitting a strange sense of danger. The sterile, chemical smell reminds me of alcohol.

I take a breath. *I am not Frank.*

"Hello!" the receptionist chirps. She's friendly, pleasant in voice and appearance, as she goes through her protocol. After signing required paperwork, she fastens a bracelet with—oddly enough—a cartoon picture of a raccoon around my wrist. She directs me around the corner while claiming, "Your wife has been anxious for your arrival."

I want to clarify why it took so long, explain that I lost an extra ten minutes because a rabid raccoon hijacked the road, tell her I laid on the horn. Explain that I had to roll my window down in the chill of January to holler at it to move along. But that would be a waste. The coincidence of the bracelet would render me a liar.

I suppose I would be anyway, because what is the excuse for the ten minutes I spent tapping my hands on the steering wheel after I arrived? For the five I spent turning my eyes back and forth to the rearview mirror, wondering if Frank's were somehow there too.

I could blame the new girl—Jenny. It took two minutes to text everything she needed to know to close my account.

I hurry along the corridor, searching for the door marked "Higgins." When I find it, my hand touches the strong wood, and I move to push it open, but stop. Two voices stream from the room, so I hold my breath and listen for words.

"How much longer?" asks Ella.

It seems like no one will answer, but then a woman responds. "Now that you've changed into the gown, try and get some rest while you can. You have some time yet; it's a slow process."

"When will…the doctor be in?" There is a strange pause in the question.

"Soon enough. You're all checked in, so we'll get all of the standard procedures moving."

I lean my head against the door, take a few deep breaths, then push it open.

The nurse's eyes flick to mine, and she smiles in a wide grin. "Looks like your man decided to show up."

Ella goes to grin, but it rinses as she winces and fingers her side.

"Are you in pain?"

The nurse chuckles. "Men!" she says to Ella, shaking her head. She turns back to me. "It ain't gonna feel pretty."

Ella's face lights up with the start of laughter, like the initial spark of a burning match. Then it's extinguished, and a puzzled look takes over.

Her expression twists, contorts. "Oh!" She throws her head backward, grunts, the rest of her body seeming to turn in on itself. Her hands hook onto the bed rails, the knuckles turning white with pressure.

"Ah, looks like we got one!" the nurse says.

Ella coils, flips, and pivots. She lets out a gasped little scream before going still and seeming to mellow out.

"Breathe. Gotta remember to breathe, sweetie. We'll check that cervix within the next ten minutes."

Ella nods, forcing her breath.

"We'll get the doc in shortly, and hopefully, by then, that other little nugget will have decided to flip. I just know she's breech."

Ella turns to me, her eyes showing discomfort and fear. "She thinks one of the babies could be breech."

"What does that mean?"

The nurse chirps in. "I've been doing this for half my life, and I can tell by the shape of that belly that one of them babies is head up. A head under the rib cage, instead of being turned down and ready for flight. That's a no go. We need the babies to come out headfirst. If she doesn't turn, it would mean she would come feet or butt first. That's dangerous. Generally, if a baby's breech, we have to schedule a C-section because of the dangers a natural birth would present."

I see the panic in Ella's face and then my own fear returns with sledgehammer force.

"But we aren't panicking," the nurse says. "We still have plenty of time to get the baby to flip. We see this all the time, and I know a few tricks we can try to get the baby to move." She reaches for Ella's hand to comfort.

I move to the bed, go to sit on the edge, then hesitate.

Ella notices. "You can sit, Keith."

"I'm going to go, dear, but I'll be back. We need to get a fetal heart rate monitor on you ASAP." She pats Ella's hand and smiles before leaving.

Even after it is just the two of us, there is this need to whisper. "She's nice."

"Her name is Elizabeth."

I nod, forcing a smile and reaching for her hand.

"I was at my appointment, and my water broke right in the waiting room. At first, I thought I was peeing my pants, but another woman in her first trimester started jumping up and down, cheering."

"I can't believe it's finally happening."

She takes two breaths before responding. "It's happening."

I stand back up, start to pace.

Today, I'll be a dad. Not just to one baby girl, but to two. Two little things to love and cherish, to show right from wrong. I am sick with nerves, there is a fear so gripping it's like I can't breathe, but there's exhilaration too. To hold them, to see what a part of me and a part of Ella makes…it seems a little like magic.

"What do we have to do to flip the baby?"

"I don't know." She fidgets as if she is suddenly angry. "Elizabeth keeps saying she thinks I'm breech, and that they have tricks, but she hasn't shown me anything." She focuses on her breath again. "I just want…the doctor to get here already."

"Want a massage? Maybe it'll distract you," I say. "Help you relax."

The onset of another contraction shows on Ella. Tension builds in her shoulders and sweat ripples at the edge of her hairline. Small tears fall from her lashes and fade into her nightgown. She tightens like a bow, and then, just as quickly, her body relaxes, calms like whatever was about to come decided to spare her.

"I wish I could take the pain away."

Her eyes darken and she smiles. "I don't. This experience is what makes me a mother. It's painful, but it's…beautiful. This pain, it means nothing, knowing I'll get to hold the angels inside," she says, she takes a measured breath, flattens her hair with her palms. "But, yeah, distraction—I need a distraction. Turn that TV on," she says, pointing to the outdated flat screen.

I move across the room, reach up, and flick the TV on. As the screen begins to light, a weird feeling comes over me. On the display, two raccoons sit on their back paws, their front hands reaching out and popping man-made bubbles. The news anchor laughs, reaches for a wand, and starts blowing more bubbles.

"That's weird," I say.

"Aww, I think they're cute."

"Cute, yes, but weird, because I almost killed a raccoon on the way here. It was just chilling in the road." I look toward my wrist, at the bracelet with the protruding cartoon raccoon on it.

"That's not that weird, Keith."

"Yeah." I shake my head, agreeing.

I fake a grin, try to revert the energy in the room before it shifts to something heavier.

Ella's phone starts buzzing, the word "Mom" displaying on the screen.

"Christina's calling. Does she know you're here?" I ask, handing her the phone.

She nods. "Hello," Ella answers.

The door swings open, and Elizabeth returns, carrying an armful of supplies. Ella tries to use her as an excuse to hang up with Christina, but Elizabeth assures her that she can work around it. There is a special strap that she puts around Ella's belly. She tucks, pulls, and fastens it around her swollen stomach with a practiced ease.

She hooks the wires to a nearby monitor, and then approaches me. "That will graph the contractions, and we'll be able to watch the mountain crest at the top and then make a gradual descent when finished. Keeps a record of how close they're coming."

She points to the numbers at the top of the screen. "These numbers are the babies' heart rates. Just tracks and makes sure they aren't in distress." She points to the first number, smiles. "Nice healthy heart rate." Then she moves her finger to another number. Goes to speak, but suddenly pales.

"What is it?" I ask.

Her face pales even more, making my heart drop into my stomach.

"Baby B..." She hesitates. "It's nothing. I'll be right back. I'll—I have to page Ethan," she says.

My first thought is yes, go, and please get Ethan. Then...Ethan?

Ethan? The text from this morning flashes in my head: Call me about last night.

I am unable not to ask. "Who is Ethan?"

"Dr. Stacey. I have to go get Ethan Stacey." She moves with haste, her quick pace like a dash for the hall.

Ella isn't speaking to Christina anymore. She's looking at me, nervous. "Keith, what did she say?"

"She's going to get…the doctor."

"About the baby! What did she say about the baby?"

"Nothing! She pointed to this number, muttered, 'Baby B.'" I point to the same number, and it reads 80. Then I move my finger over to the other number that made her smile: 155. What does it mean? It's the heart rate, but 155 sounds high, right? But she smiled at *that* number. It was the 80 that caused the panic.

My insides shake, tremble, and I suddenly want to vomit. I hear her say that name again: Ethan. It plays in my head repeatedly. Ethan. Ethan! Ethan! Then that damn raccoon's muzzle is twitching in my mind's eye.

80? 80. It's 80!

My head throbs, and I'm furious. Why am I furious?

"A baby's heart rate should be between 110-160 beats per minute. 80 is too low! It's too low, Keith!" Ella shouts, and it's only then I realize she's on the phone, doing a search for the answer. Her face drains of color.

I want to reassure her. I should go to her and tell her it'll be okay, but it's like I can't breathe. It's like all the oxygen was sucked from the hospital, and my head is being squeezed. I want to speak, but the only words I know are "Ethan" and "80."

She screams, her belly tightening, the next contraction coming, despite her need for reassurance. I move to the end of the bed, grab her foot, and start massaging. "Good job. Breathe…" I try.

"Don't," she says, yanking her foot away, her pale complexion pinking.

I move away, and then someone else is there. Thick, meaty hands are leaning Ella forward and pressing palms into her lower back. "Breathe. Deep, controlled breaths, El."

He is tall and broad-shouldered. His chest is wide, and his arms are heavy under the white lab coat. He's perfectly pressed, no wrinkles on his clothing or face. His wavy brown hair is styled to the side, not a strand out of place.

She seems to rest against him comfortably. He rubs in circles, putting her body at ease, moving his hands up and down her back with an undisclosed intimacy that makes me nauseous.

I say one of the only words I remember, "Ethan?"

The contraction crests, drops back down, and Ella relaxes, forehead damp with sweat. The room is silent, empty of noise. I go to break it, then hesitate.

"That was quite the contraction for so early in the process," the doctor says, his voice even and deep. He stands, moves to the wall, and snags latex gloves. He notices me, grins with a practiced manner. "Hello, I'm Dr. Stacey," he says. He doesn't move to greet me, but, instead, slips his hands into the gloves.

He gave no first name, but doctors generally don't. The thing is, I've said it already. I put it out there.

Did the doctor text Ella? Does it even matter if he did? *Let's not turn coincidences into conspiracies.*

It's nothing. It could be anything. Maybe she had stomach pain? Perhaps she was concerned that something was wrong?

Something *is* wrong.

"80. The heart rate is 80, is something wrong?" I ask.

"I don't want you to worry just yet," he says, addressing Ella. "One of the girl's heart rate is lower than expected. I have the nurse bringing an additional Doppler, and I ordered an ultrasound just to put us at ease. This could be an electronics issue. Faulty transducers are always causing unneeded stress." He presses on her belly. "Baby B is certainly breech, though—we'll have to address that. I'll need to check the cervix to see where we're at first." He directs her to spread her legs, his voice calm and professional. "I'll do this quick. Stay relaxed," he says.

Ella's eyes study me while he performs the check, her breath forced and practiced.

My cheeks burn.

"El was my first patient here in Boston," he explains, breaking the silence that seems to be required for such an intrusive measure.

"Wait, what? You've never delivered a baby before?"

He chuckles. "I've delivered hundreds of babies. Just meant she's the first patient I met after moving here from Florida." He withdraws his fingers, removes the gloves, then crosses his arms. "Your body is moving right along—faster than expected. Your cervix is just under eight centimeters dilated."

"Is that bad?" Ella asks.

"Could be the reason for the lowered heart rate. I'm going to send for some meds to slow the contractions down. First things first, let's get you repositioned. It's going to sound strange, but I want you to kneel on the bed. Get into the cat position on all fours and then gently tilt the pelvis back and forth." He demonstrates with his hands.

"Okay," Ella says, swinging her feet to the side.

I move to help her, work to keep the aging nightgown from exposing her backside. I notice Ethan looking away, granting her privacy to shift into a new position.

When she is repositioned, he walks around to study the monitor, and I study him again. His face is smoothly shaven and perfectly distributed. A buzzing noise comes from his pocket. He steps back, pulls his phone from his lab coat, and answers. A few seconds later, he's nodding, mumbling his thanks, and hanging up. "The ultrasound technician is en route," he declares.

The idea comes in a flash, and despite the wrongness, my eyes start searching for Ella's phone. If I find it, I can call that number back. I can see if that phone buzzes. But what would that solve? Would it prove something?

"The heart rate is still low, but that made an improvement," he says.

My stomach lurches. My baby is in distress, and I'm focusing on the fact that the doctor's name is Ethan. It's stupid. Shame makes me lower my head. "What are the next steps?" I ask. I move to Ella, put my hand on her lower back and start massaging.

"Ultrasound," he says, and, as if on cue, a knock comes at the door.

A female technician comes in, smiling big and broad, pushing a cart stacked with monitors. She goes to Ella, puts her hand out to greet her. "Hello, Mama. Almost time to welcome you to the motherhood club, I hear."

"Hi, Ally. Baby B is breech, and the heart rate is questionable," Dr. Ethan says, bypassing any routine introductions.

"Oh no," she says, her voice soft. "Let's get a look inside." She unwraps the wires and sets up her machine. "I'll need you to flip back down, sweetie," she says, helping to move Ella. "This gel might be a little cold, so brace yourself." She squeezes a clear substance into a neatly configured pile above the belly button and then places the probe on her stomach. "Okay, so here is Baby A. She looks great, steady heartbeat, and head and cord are positioned perfectly for delivery."

My face warms, this tickle taking root in my tummy. This ultrasound is different than the first one we had. I can actually see her little nose and mouth. It's a fuzzy picture of the little girl I will get to meet and hold soon.

"Let's find Baby B," says Ally. She repositions the tool and moves to the second baby.

I'm instantly relieved to see another healthy baby with the same little nose and mouth.

"Their noses, lips. They're beautiful," Ella says.

I squeeze her hand and smile, turning to look at Ally, but my stomach plummets, the smile falling off my face after meeting her expression. She's serious. Concerned and quiet, her eyebrows showing trouble. Her scarlet red lips are pursed, eyes turning sympathetically to Ella. Then to Ethan. "Dr. Stacey, can I have a word in the hall?"

"Absolutely. Please excuse us," he says.

They walk hurriedly to the door with tight shoulders and arched brows, the entire chemistry shifting back into a daunting concoction of worry and fear.

"What's wrong? Is something wrong with my baby?" Tears start streaming down Ella's face, a panicked tension building in her body. "What did they see?"

I stroke her hair, try to calm her. "Nothing, there was nothing. I saw two perfect little girls, that's all."

She snaps her eyes to mine, a sudden anger there, pointed at me. "Did you not see her face?"

Her voice wavers, the anger in her eyes melting into concern.

The door opens, and Dr. Stacey pushes in, walking swiftly to Ella.

"Ethan, what's wrong?" Ella demands.

The chemical smell of the hospital is suddenly too much. Nausea grabs me, and I study the cold white tile below me to steady. She said his name...no, breathed it. Exhaled his name in a way that settled something inside of her.

"I need you to remain calm for the babies' sake," he says, and it infuriates me. Calm? How can she possibly remain calm?

"Remember I was telling you I suspected that one of the babies was breech?"

Ella nods. "But we can fix it right? You have techniques that will help flip her."

"No, not this time. The ultrasound showed that the baby's umbilical cord is wrapped around her..." He hesitates, steadies himself. "The umbilical cord is wrapped around her neck. This could cause issues with the blood flow to her heart. We need to do an emergency C-section. I know this isn't what you wanted, but this is the best option for you and the girls right now."

She whimpers, a shaking sob threatening to break. "Will she be okay?"

Ethan reaches for her hand, rests his gently atop it. "Those babies will be here sooner than we were thinking, and I'm going to make sure they get here as quickly and safely as possible. Her heartbeat falling is a bit of a concern," he says. "I've asked Ally to book the OR, and I am going to go get prepped and scrubbed in. Just relax and trust me. The nurses will be bringing you to meet me upstairs soon."

I move to her, reach out and take Ella's other hand.

Ethan hesitates, takes his hand from hers, and leaves the room with a forced smile. Ella watches him leave, her expression compounding with fear and anxiety.

"Hey…everything will be okay. Everything will be just fine," I tell her.

She turns, looks at me with her big blue eyes, the waves raging and painting a dangerous picture. Every muscle on her starts to shake with nerves. I put the cover over her and crawl in bed. "It will be okay. Everything will be okay."

SD

I think she's having these babies, right now.

Pacing the room, Ella's pained face is getting harder to look at. I check the clock and what feels like an hour has only been five minutes. Time is slow. These people are moving too slow. But Ella is fast, her body is throbbing, contracting. She's a petal blossoming before my eyes.

Another contraction hits. They've been coming more frequently ever since Dr. Stacey left us almost fifteen minutes ago.

"Breathe, baby. Breathe," I say, massaging her feet, watching her squirm in the bed.

The graph keeps going up, higher and higher, with no crest. The mountain's too tall; it's not easing.

"Breathe."

"It hurts, it hurts," she cries, turning to her side. She clinches her stomach, eyes wider and bigger than two fists. "Make it stop!"

Panic grabs me by the throat, the blood draining from my face in a violent, dizzying rush. Stars dance at the edges of my vision. I hesitate, my heart beating in my ears.

She's sobbing, crying, tears streaming hot and wet down her cherry face.

Something's not right. This can't be right.

The door opens, and a fleet of nurses flurry into the room, moving and surrounding Ella. They start taking her vitals and checking her cervix.

Ella's hysterical, crying, screaming, and then yelling. "It hurts!"

"You have to calm down. You have to breathe," a nurse says to her. "Sir, can you calm her down?" She looks at me, and I look back. I can't move.

The doctor rushes in, the nurse from before, Elizabeth, exclaiming, "She's having the babies. The first baby is in the birth canal."

Dr. Stacey's face whitens for only a microsecond, and then he's moving. "Okay. Okay, Ella, change of plans again. This baby is ready, and we can't transport you like this. When I say go, I need you to push for a count of five. Okay?" He raises the bed and positions the foot hooks, so her feet hang comfortably. "It looks like you'll be getting half your wish today. We'll deliver one baby naturally, and then we'll need to rush to the OR," he says.

Ella nods. "It hurts."

"I know. But you can do this, on the count of three, I need you to push. One…two…three."

On three, Ella pushes with everything she has, her face turning purple, her veins protruding from her temples. Little grunts and screams escape her lips, and she apologizes for them. A briny, metallic smell fills the air.

The top of the baby's head appears, crowning. A dome of dark hair making butterflies dance in my stomach.

"Take a breath, Ella. One or two more pushes on my go, and the baby will be out. You're doing great," the doctor says. "Okay, go."

Ella pushes. Through blood, sweat, and tears her body opens with grace to give life. The cervix unwrapping under the pressure of the baby's head. Primal instincts force her to push until her body breaks and tears open.

"Okay, Ella. This is it. You can get her out on this push. I know it," says Ethan. "Go."

Ella's eyes burn with determination, a need so strong to purge herself of the enduring pain, convincing her to split herself open. She lets out a scream, pushing with her soul, and the baby's head and shoulders are out. Once the head and shoulders appear, Ethan slides the baby the rest of the way.

She's tiny, only a little bigger than my hand, and blue, just like a blueberry. Ethan rests the baby on Ella's chest.

"Why isn't she crying?" I ask.

"Oh, she's beautiful. Look at her. Perfect, healthy baby girl. Time of birth 11:48 a.m.," he says.

Overwhelmed, time shifts from slow to fast. Suddenly, she's crying, and I'm relieved to hear her voice. The nurse rubs her with warm towels, wiping away the red and white liquids coating her skin.

My eyes stay on her…she's…my baby.

She has a perfect squishy nose and powerful lungs. Her deep, dark eyes are open and wide, pulling in snapshots of the new world she was just born to. Her wet head is shadowed with chocolate hair.

My insides shake, this thing I never knew existed blossoms: instantaneous love.

"I'm freaking out," I say to Ella. "I'm, like, really freaking out!"

Ella manages a smile. "Hope, this is Hope."

"Hope! Hi! I'm your daddy." Smiling down at her for the first time, wet tears fill my eyes.

"Keith, will you be cutting the cord?" Ethan asks.

Without hesitating, I nod, reaching for the scissors. He directs me to cut between the clamps. It takes two tries, but I make it through the chunky cord.

I'm a…dad.

"Ella, the nurses will take Hope and give her a routine checkup. I need to get you to the OR. We need to take care of Faith. We only have a short window," says Ethan.

"Keith, stay with her. She needs one of us," Ella says, her eyes on Hope.

I hesitate but can't imagine leaving Hope all alone. "I love you. I love you. Okay? I love you," I say, swallowing hard.

The nurse takes the baby, and Ethan resets the bed, getting prepped to move Ella. I watch him, in the vortex of his job, focused on his patient. I'm suddenly grateful he's the one taking care of her. He looks at me and nods reassuringly, as if to say he would protect her with his own life. "We will keep you updated," he promises.

Faith. Faith is in there, and he'll get her out.

I kiss Ella again and watch her leave. We share a glance that seems to slow the commotion of the room. A small part of me can't help but feel like I just handed her over to Dr. Stacey. I just put two things I love in somebody else's hands. It's all on him to protect them.

When they're gone, I cross the room to watch Hope. The nurse rests her under a heater, the light glowing orange. Hope seems comfortable and content. I get my first real look at her: an adorable bundle of pink skin and wrinkles, little hands and feet, an abundance of silky hair. I feel those beautiful butterflies again.

The nurse puts eye drops in Hope's eyes, and then gives her two needles. My baby girl was just born, and she already knows pain. This irrational need to protect her fills me.

She's weighed and measured, and the nurse scribbles the number illegibly on the paper. "Five and a half pounds and seventeen inches," she says.

After her bath, they dress her in a warm hospital one-piece, slip a powder blue and pink cap upon her head.

Hope's warm and happy, and I finally get to do what I haven't stopped thinking about for the last nine months...I get to hold my five-and-a-half-pound little girl for the first time.

She's tiny in my arms when I take her, small and fragile in size, yet her eyes stronger and wiser than her minutes here should allow. "Hi, baby."

Those eyes meet mine, and I feel life change.

Chapter 5

The cold winter air needles its way under the safety of my blanket and wraps around my exposed chest. I clutch the fabric closer, covering the lower half of my face with the worn cotton. The familiar musty smell helps to calm my rapid breathing.

They're arguing again.

Panic is working its way into my gut, as it always does when I can hear him. I can hear the gruff and slurred words of a drunken Frank. I know Scott's awake too. I can hear him, rustling around, listening, readying himself across the room.

It's bound to happen, at some point—he knows it, and so do I. *It always does.* When Frank gets this angry, when he fumes this hard, he uses the things my mother loves the most to punish her.

My legs tremble. They want to leap, jump, run to find safely. They want to move, but I can't allow them. I lock myself here, in my bed, under my blanket, and wait. I wait for my turn.

"Frank!" she hollers. "You were with her again! You were with that slut, weren't you?"

Frank growls, then a glass shatters. Mom lets out a high-pitched scream of pain in answer. I sit up, unable to stop myself, listening closer, harder, for the sound of heavy footsteps on the floor.

"Lay down," Scott whispers. "Are you stupid or something?"

"I heard Mom. She sounds hurt."

"Shh," he says. "Shut your mouth."

Another thud, then a moan from Mom. He sits up now too. I see his face, lightly illuminated from the glow of the outside streetlight. He's listening. He turns his head to the side, straining for more sound. Then we hear him. We hear him coming. Louder, closer. He's thudding his way up the stairs.

A blast of motion to my left. I jump, startled at the unexpected movement. Scott flings himself from his bed, silent, and unheard. He bolts for the door. My mind scurries to catch up. *He's running? He's hiding?* I look around. I look for my own place to hide, but, no, Scott's not hiding. He shoves a chair under the doorknob and makes his way hastily back to bed. "Lay down!" he hisses.

The drumming feet have made it to our door now. I lay down, pulling the covers over my face. I hear the doorknob jimmy. My heart races. My heart pounds. Then more pounding. Not my pounding, but his. He's pounding his fists into the door. *Bang, bang, bang!* The noise rings in my ears, the vibration shaking the room.

"Boys!" His voice booms in the quiet night air.

I jump, unable to stop myself. I roll to the wall, covering myself completely. My body shakes with fear.

"Open this door!" he hisses. He bangs on the door, violently and uncontrolled. Again and again and again, banging and thumping as he slams himself into our safety net.

"You wanna do this the hard way? Fine!" he screams.

A moment of unnerving silence covers the room, then nothing but the sound of smashing, splintering wood. The door buckles open, the chair squeaking its way across the room.

A noise. *It was my noise.* Unwillingly, a whimper slipped out between my lips, which means he'll take me first.

I stiffen. All of me stiffens as I wait for his hands. He doesn't speak, he doesn't yell, but his ragged, uncontrolled breathing moves closer. I shut my eyes tighter, squeezing myself into a ball, trying to become invisible.

Then, I smell him. His rank chemical odor fills my nostrils and mixes with the smell of my unwashed blanket. Beer and liquor swirling together in the air, making me tremble with nausea.

His course hand grabs the back of my neck, yanking with a vehement jerk, ripping me from bed. The light from the hallway fills the dark room, blinding my unadjusted eyes. "Piece of shit!" he bellows. "You fucking piece of shit! Funny game you're playing."

He slams me to the floor, the air rushing from my lungs. Then his hands are in my hair, yanking me toward the door. I scurry on my knees to follow, trying to lessen the pain. "Let's go see that *bitch*!" he hollers.

Pulling me by the hair and into the hallway, he puts his booted foot on my shoulder and kicks. I land hard, a brutal vibration crawling its way up my spine. My head whips back, smashing into the floor.

There's no time to register pain. I'm jerked back into motion. His hands are around my ankle, pulling. He's muttering, "Bitch…bitch, she always has something to say, always! Worried who I'm fucking? I'll show her. I'll show her!"

At the stairs, he doesn't slow, but pulls me without sympathy down the uncarpeted treads. My back slams into every stair, the floor burning my bare skin on contact.

When it's over, he pushes me to my stomach. "Don't move…don't you fucking move!"

Another moment of silence, then the muffled clatter of a dragging object. Frank grunts. My eyes shift to see him across the room. He's pulling my lifeless mother. He heaves her next to me, her moan letting me know she's still alive.

He takes her face, shaking her awake with forceful slaps across the cheeks. Her head is bloody, her eyes bruised. "Wake up, Lily! Wake the hell up!" he says, the drunk intensity in his eyes making me want to vomit. "This is for you. This is for *you* to see!"

Her eyes open, confused sleeping unaware. Then, sluggishly, she looks around, her eyes falling on me. She wiggles to life, moving more. He lays her on the floor. I hear the swish of leather. Then I hear her voice before I even feel the first blow.

"Keith!" she screams. She starts to cry. She tries to move for me. "Stop!" she bellows. "I'm sorry!"

The belt slashes into me.

I startle, my insides jumping from the past pain. My head jerks aggressively, looking for him, but the moldy remnants of my childhood home dissolve. The sterile white of the hospital room emerges, the wave of chemical odor from the cleaner assaulting me instead.

"Sorry, sir," the nurse says. "Did I frighten you? Just checking to see how the baby's doing." She's a young nurse, stethoscope hovering just inches above Hope's chest.

"No…" I mutter. "No, it's fine. Just a chill." I watch as she listens to Hope's heartbeat, her little face serious as she sleeps peacefully in the hospital bassinet. "Any news on Ella?"

"Don't worry, Mr. Higgins. It takes time," she says. "Soon enough, I'll be wheeling in your second little bundle."

I smile, excited for that moment, but despite her consistent chanting not to worry, I have a lump lodged dangerously in my gut. An uneasy tingle eating at my spine.

Hope will have the "I'm older" bragging rights to hold over Faith.

Hope. Hope's rhythmic breathing, the gentle rise and fall of her chest, it helps to tame the mounting anxiety. There are these butterfly movements under her eyelids, a little pout on her lips. Her forehead wrinkles when a noise disturbs the silence.

Watching her doze reminds me of something I heard years ago. Mom said we're made of the same matter that fashions the stars. That we are complexly connected to everything in this universe. The smallest molecule is a part of the largest. Parts of her and parts of Dad grew with parts of the Earth to make another life inside of another life.

I find some paper and a pencil to draw Hope.

I start with the outline of her arms. Both hands are raised and pressed to her cheeks, her left fist escaping the bundle of fabric to rest below her eye. I sketch the tiny hand and all of the wrinkles on her newborn baby-fist. Then, I move to the arch of her chin and work up. I shade the soft curve of her lips, and the slight dimple at the top of her mouth leading to her nose. Then the subtlety in the curve of her eyelid.

Mom held me when I was this small. She cradled me to her, kept me safe, and loved me. Did Frank? Was there ever a moment when he loved me? Was there a day, or a week, or maybe even a year, where he didn't regret me? I can't remember the first time he hit me. It's just something I always knew he did. But there had to be a first time. There had to be a start. How old was I? What did I do to provoke it?

And there's the problem: what did I do? Logic tells me that I did nothing, but years and holes in self-worth, continually convince me that I'm merely paying the price for my own faults.

A gentle knock on the door draws my attention, the curious face of Christina—Ella's mom—poking around the corner. "Ella?"

She's wearing black skinny jeans and an oversized black sweater, with black leather boots. Her hair is shorter, chopped off right below the ears. Her hair is dyed dark brown with the gray peppering her temples.

"Hey, come in," I say.

Paul, Ella's dad, follows close. He's dressed in baggy sweatpants, his full head of gray hair sloppy and sticking up in the back, a goofy grin plastered on his chubby face. He's holding a gift bag, the colorful tissue paper poking out of the top. Everything about him contradicts his wife.

Christina and Paul beam seeing Hope. Their faces glow, smiles stretch from ear to ear.

"Well done, son," Paul says, coming for a closer look. "She's beautiful."

Christina's eyes fill with tears. "She's stunning."

"This is Hope."

There's a stillness in the room, then Christina makes subtle eye contact with me. I smile and nod. She reaches into the bassinet, cradling the baby close to her. "Where's Ella and the other baby?" she asks.

"There were some complications," I start, not knowing how to explain it without causing panic.

"Complications?" Christina's head snaps up, her voice shifting.

I hold up my hands. "Everything is going to be fine! It's just, Hope was ready to come out, and Faith wasn't. Faith was breech," I explain. I leave out the heart rate, unable to vocalize that threat. "So, she is having Faith via C-section." Nerves dance in my stomach.

Christina's face pales. "Any updates?"

I shake my head, no, check the clock again. Why is it taking so long? I count the time. It's been close to an hour since Hope was born and they took Ella. Is that too long?

I glance at Christina, who looks worried.

"It's been over an hour," I whisper. "I don't know how long it should take, but the doctor promised updates, and I haven't gotten any."

"Let's trust the medical system," Paul says, and I look at him and notice that on the front of the gift bag he's clutching is a cute, furry raccoon.

It's like a sledgehammer hitting me in the stomach. Breath is pushed out of me in a violent torrent. Something feels wrong. My brain is screaming it, and the air is crackling in some way I've never felt before.

"Why is there a raccoon on your bag?"

Paul's eyebrows collide, perplexed. "Because it's cute."

I look at the bag again and shudder. Am I losing my mind? Is this what it feels like to go insane? The raccoons, they…they have to mean something. One in the road, on the bracelet, the TV, and now…the bag. It means something. Why does it mean something?

I suddenly want to scream. My patience and stupidity finally crack open, all of my anxiety and worry spills free. But, as my eyes shut and my mouth opens to release, I hear myself lying, "Everything will be okay."

I stumble backward, confused. Then I'm tripping, falling, and landing on my ass, my head falling backward. The light above burns down, filling my eyes, and for a second…I wait for Frank to grab my ankle and start pulling.

Christina sucks in her breath.

"Keith?" Paul questions. "What's going on?" He comes to me, offers a hand, and all I can see is the eye of the raccoon taking me in.

I take his hand, shutting my eyes again. "I'm worried. I want Ella in here now."

"Everything will be okay," Paul says, and it's my lie from before.

I sway on my feet. *Everything will be okay.*

But then he's here, the handsome doctor, Ethan. He's letting himself in, his face to the door, back toward us. His shoulders slump in an unnatural proportion. He isn't the same stoic being as before.

"Are you the doctor?" Christina asks.

My words don't come, but dance inside: *Everything will be okay.*

The doctor…Ethan, turns around, his face painting a picture that I don't want to see. A picture that looks both black and scary, before he's even muttered a word. A chill cuts through me.

"Faith?" My voice croaks out.

His eyes deflate. Something in them tells me how wrong everything has gone. I fall to my knees, the marble floor stony under my palms.

"What's going on? Where's the baby?" Christina questions. A wild panic shivers in her words.

Ethan's voice is unrecognizable when he finally speaks. "She…" he mumbles, then straightens. "She didn't make it."

My whole body turns cold. Thick chunks creep up my throat. She didn't *make* it? She didn't make it! She didn't make it… She? She.

Christina doubles over in a surprised pain. She's standing over the bassinet and rests Hope inside, her arms clutching the rim. Paul rushes to her side.

"Faith wasn't strong enough for the surgery, and Ella wasn't stable," the doctor says.

My insides slam against my heart. A rushing in my ears makes my head spin.

"I had to do what I could to save Mom," he whispers, fighting something invisible. "Mr. Higgins, Faith didn't make it."

My teeth clench together, and a shattering fall brings my heart to my stomach. Out of every emotion and feeling tearing through my body, the only one I can control is this sickening urge to throw up. I keep swallowing vomit, forcing it back down and in.

Then, this doctor is on his knees next to me, and without warning, his hand is on my shoulder, squeezing. I start shaking uncontrollably, weak and dizzy, feeling like someone else is breathing for me. Like I'm a stranger to myself, like I'm watching it all happen.

Except…I'm not watching, I *feel* it. Someone took something from inside of me, and it's something I just know I'll never get back. Something that, no matter how hard I try, I can never fix. A chunk was torn from me, and everything that's left behind is scattering in a shifting frenzy to avoid the emptiness.

As if she knows what happened, Hope begins to cry. An unknown primal urge to comfort her forces me to my feet. I stand and go to her, unfolding myself from the foreign man I've become on the floor. I pick her up, hugging her, and her newborn smell both calms me and breaks me. I weep in painful sobs. It's like Hope gave me my first breath, and now Faith is asking me to breathe under water again.

Nothing in life prepares you for this pain. I have lost my child. I have lost Faith, and it's wrong on so many levels.

I lost Faith. My daughter. Hope has lost her sister. She'll never have bragging rights about being older. She'll never have her best friend by her side.

"Ella will wake up soon. You should be there," the doctor says.

It's now, for the first time, that I'm realizing I still have Ella.

I remember his words. *"I had to do what I could to save Mom,"* he said. His focus was on Ella. He saved her.

"What happened to Ella?" My voice sounds strangled and distant.

He wipes his palms on his blue scrubs. "Her vitals…" He takes a deep breath. "They dropped before we even made it to the operating room. She hemorrhaged and was losing an excessive amount of blood. We worked to stop it, but even after the bleed was controlled, her blood pressure was dropping." He shakes his head like he doesn't understand. "I had this instinct to check her lungs. Sure enough, they were filling with fluid. Pulmonary edema." His eyes dart around the room. "I was worried it was an amniotic fluid embolism. It wasn't, but I had to assure the situation," he says.

Did he let Faith die?

For one hot second, rage sets fire to my insides, but then this heavy sadness absorbs everything, and I'm left floating above my body.

Chapter 6

The muted glow of the lights; the sterile, pungent smell; the constant beeping; and the endless rotation of nurses...the crying. A good-natured joke that doesn't bring a smile. All of it's exhausting. All of it's a persistent reminder that my little girl is dead, and I have to be the one to tell my wife. We are leaving the hospital with one baby and two car seats.

Everything will be ripped out from under us, and we'll be left to fall. Two scrambling bodies fighting to land on their feet, scratching and clawing to hold onto each other in the midst of impossible winds.

How can two fragile people not break when they're dropped?

How can anything ever be the same again?

Ella lies there, her hair finger-combed to one side of the hospital pillow. Her face pale, still, almost peaceful, yet tension in her eyebrow makes me wonder if maybe she senses the danger in waking. The hum of the machines...it seems to vibrate the room, aiding in the discomfort of the temperate air flow. Christina and I have been resting in these chairs, waiting for Ella to wake, counting the seconds till she decides to come back to us, but dreading the arrival.

The specialist assured me that they did everything they could, but Faith wasn't strong enough to survive. Her heart was weak, and the stress of birth would have killed her regardless. If the doctors had focused on Faith, then Ella's blood pressure may have continued to tank, undiagnosed late-onset preeclampsia being the root cause of the fluid in her lungs.

Christina yawns, she pushes herself out of the chair, arches her back in a stretch. She moves closer to the bed, strokes and then takes Ella's hand in hers.

"She's still so pretty," I say.

She turns to me, the tears in her eyes. "She's fragile," she whispers. "Even the person who is a piece of you, grows away. Grows into their self, and then the world happens to them, and you just have to…watch it."

I picture life outside of the hospital carrying on, everyone going about their daily routines like nothing even happened.

"I guess, for some things, all we can do is be a witness."

"You aren't just watching. It hurts you too," I say, and for a moment, I sound angry. I guess because I *am* angry. My daughter is dead. Faith is dead, and she can't come back, and that hurts so deep, so far inside of me that…that, all I can feel is black. I'm angry…at the world…at the universe. Angry, because I can't fix any of this.

I want to cry. I want to scream. I want to run.

Anger, darkness…it's a symptom. A symptom of death and turmoil, the obscurity that follows. It's almost like I can feel a coil opening inside me, a perpetual twilight looming. A void. Or an abyss calling to me. A curtain wanting to close, hiding the world, shielding me inside, refusing to part.

Something like this infects you. It ruins you.

Ella spent thirty-three weeks preparing for how to lose the baby weight post-delivery. She never prepared for what to do when you lose more than you thought was possible. What if she questions the point? If there's death, if we all die, if there's an end with no after, then what's the point of dragging out the misery? What's the point of anything?

"Wake up, sweetie," Christina says, patting Ella's head. "Keith and I are both here. Just open your eyes. Hope is safe with your dad. Can you wake up for me?" Her voice cracks a little.

"She'll need time," the doctor has already warned. It's normal for women to suffer postpartum depression, or even post-traumatic stress, after a loss like this. Her body is shattered, both physically and spiritually.

"I was thinking about your tenth birthday. How you wanted that puppy so badly. Daddy said yes, but I was absolutely against it. I thought dogs were smelly and dirty, and I didn't want to clean up after it. You opened all of your presents, and afterward you smiled. You smiled and said thank you to everyone in the gentlest voice. Do you remember that?"

She pauses, almost like waiting for Ella to answer.

"I had to leave," Christina continues, "because I could see that hidden disappointment. Do you remember me crying? I was crying, and you came to comfort me. I told you I was just upset that my little girl wasn't so little anymore. That was a lie. I wasn't upset that you were growing up. I was upset that I was the reason you had that disappointed look on your face. I was the one that was holding you back from really smiling. The real smile that is as bright as the sun and makes my whole world spin," she whispers.

"So, later, I went out. I went to every pet store in a thirty-mile radius looking for a white puppy. Just like you wanted. It took a while, but I found one. He was all white, with just a spot of black on his nose. Patch...with his little black nose. I bought a red ribbon and tied it around his neck. By the time I got home, it was late. You had gone to bed early. It was just after nine, and you were so confused when we barged into your room. I flicked on the lights and said, 'Rise and shine, sleepyhead. You forgot one of your gifts.' You saw that puppy and I saw my sunshine," she says with tears streaming down her face. "That night I went to my room, and cried, again. All night. Because I made you happy, and that's all I've ever really wanted." She sits on the bed, drapes her arm across Ella. "I'll just be here, forever, for as long as it takes for the sun to come back out."

The lump grows in my throat.

A low moan comes from Ella in response, and my anxiety spikes.

I take a breath, and I stand from my chair, fighting the urge to squeeze my eyes shut. I go to her side, kneel down on the hard tile of the hospital floor. "Ella," I whisper.

She turns her head, drowsily, not opening her eyes.

"Baby, can you hear me?" I stroke her hand.

She yawns. Fights to open her heavy eyelids. "Keith…" she says, turning away.

I turn her back to me. "I'm here."

She forces her eyes open. "What happened?" she asks.

"We're all here, babe," Christina says, and she crawls into bed with her.

She closes her eyes, then they open again. "Where are the babies?"

Anger and sorrow fight inside me, but I push against it.

"Hope's with Daddy," Christina says.

Her limp body stiffens, tightens into a rigid line. Her breathing picks up. "Where's Faith?"

Christina looks to me, and I feel my own breath catch, heave.

"Keith?" Her adrenaline must spike. She's suddenly aware. "Call for the babies, I want to see them."

The door opens, and all of our faces turn. The doctor, Ethan, enters. And despite no words being muttered, despite nothing but vibrating machines and a persistent drip, his face says all the words. His expression delivers the message.

Ella's eyes go wide. "No…*no.*" she cries, her soul sounding like it's breaking open, her tears spilling. "*No!*"

The sound of that word brings chills to my body. She screams it. She cries it. "*No…*"

"Shh." I say, trying to comfort her. "*Shh.*"

"Faith! Where is she?"

I put my arms around her, letting my body claim hers. "Shh…" I whisper.

I have no words. I just close my eyes and picture Hope. Hope, peacefully asleep in the bassinet. Hope, breathing up and down.

How would Faith look in that crib next to her?

Ella is crying so hard, but I can't open my eyes.

Hope is sleeping, peaceful in that crib in my mind. This time, I see Faith. I focus on Faith. I take a breath. I see her. When my eyes are closed, I see her.

I'll have her too. I'm seeing her face, and she is beautiful.

She looks like Hope. I'll get to see Faith, in all the beauty of her sister.

Chapter 7

ope is still wearing the pink and blue cap the nurse put on her. My eyes follow her little head as it moves back and forth with Ella in the maternity ward rocking chair. Hope is quiet, content, but Ella looks like a shell, detached, like she's disassociated from this world as she rocks back and forth, her eyes not reaching or meeting mine. Faith's cap burns in my pocket, I had taken it when they let us see her. My hand goes to it, the soft cotton between my fingers becoming a method of assurance.

Destroyed. Destroyed is how I feel, after sitting here. After being here. After realizing that things like this happen, that life is not guaranteed to anyone. That innocent, angelic little faces can be ripped away just as fast as those granted a life worth of time. Time is not distributed fairly. It's uneven, and just like with most things, some people get more.

Feeling the pain hurts too much, and I feel the urge to push it away, to reach, instead, for the numbness Ella's in and become a hollow shell, empty of everything but blood and bones.

I would like to be the one holding Hope in my arms. I need her heat and closeness to keep my fire burning. To keep the ice building in my body from completely taking over. Because ice...ice is too fragile. It can shatter and break if not handled properly, and I'm starting to freeze.

"Need me to take her?" I offer, my voice hoarse from lack of sleep.

Ella continues rocking, silent, mellow, measured, there, but not.

The frozen ice fractals build in my blood. A knock sounds, the strong wood door opening a crack. Dr. Ethan pokes his head inside and motions me toward the door. Shock and a million stapled-together butterflies flutter in my stomach. We've seen a rotation of doctors, an endless stream of nurses, but it's been two days since…and Ethan hasn't shown his face.

I look to Ella. She seems unaffected, uninterrupted, so I stand from the chair that's been home, fingering the stiffness that lingers in my lower back. "Coffee, babe?" I say to her, but she remains quiet. "I'll be back."

Moving toward the door, I nod a silent hello as I approach the doctor…Ethan. He nods back, the smile I remember from before nowhere on his face. We're both silent, some sort of unspoken agreement in place that we wait for the door to be shut behind us before speaking.

His first words are still a whisper. "Let's use the consultation room."

I nod again, follow him, as we move through the maze of the hospital, stopping at what seems like a private coffee bar to get coffee.

I take a sip as we finish the walk, the coffee hot and nearly burning my tongue, but settling at the same time. Like a hug in a mug.

Once inside the room, Ethan motions for me to sit.

"I'll stand. I've been in that chair for too long now," I say.

Ethan remains standing too. He nods. "Ella?" he says, her name like a question, the blood draining from his face. His color changing like a hole was punctured inside him and his entire life is being sucked from within.

"She hasn't spoken in days," I say.

He breathes out. "I'm sorry." He paces back and forth. "I was forced to take some time off. I want to be there for her, and you. For whatever you need."

I take a sip of the coffee, then set it on the table. I move to the window and look out at the cluttered traffic of Boston.

"I want to offer my support to you and your family," he continues.

This blast of heat surges inside me, and I curl my lip, anger taking hold. I storm toward him. "What more could you possibly do?"

His puppy-dog eyes shift to the floor. The dark circles under them highlighted by fluorescent lights. It's the first time I notice his hair's a mess, and his clothes are wrinkled. "Ella's my friend, and Faith…Faith's the first baby I've lost." He stops abruptly, his face burning with shame.

I clench my fists, suddenly frustrated. Suddenly unsure what he expects from this conversation. Support us? He fucking broke us, and now he wants us to let him off the hook because he's hurting too. I breathe in and out, try to stop the ice from taking over.

His eyes study me then fall away. "I am here because I thought it might be helpful for Ella," he mutters. "I am here as her doctor, and I'd like to try and speak with her on my own," he says.

The ice in my blood is suddenly liquid, my insides feeling stuck behind my skin. Speak with her on his own? I see a raccoon's muzzle twitching in my mind's eye. I remember the damn text. Call me about last night! His name is friggin' Ethan.

"About last night?" I ask. It just pops out, unintended.

"What?" He seems confused. His eyebrows furrow.

"Did you text Ella the morning her water broke asking to talk about 'last night'?" I ask, moving my hands in air quotes.

He raises his eyes to mine, and I can see something there. "Of course not." His eyes try to hold my stare, but they shift, break away.

"You're lying."

His eyes widen, shock coming to his mouth. He takes a step back. He moves to deflect. "No…No, of course, I'm not," he says. He says it, just *says* it. Just speaks the words without any feeling.

"Don't lie to me!"

"Mr. Higgins, you need—"

"Please," I whisper. "Just tell me the truth. I won't be upset."

He slumps, shrugs his shoulders, biting down on his lip. Breathes heavily, his attempt at retaining his professionalism gone. "Yes. Yes," he says shakily, "I texted her."

My body reacts. Before any words come, my right fist is driving hard and fast into his chin. Pain ripples through my knuckles, then up my arm. My body shakes violently away. He falls to the ground, and I shake my hand, trying to rid the pain.

"Jesus Christ, that hurt!" I say rubbing my knuckles, jumping up and down. "Are you stupid? You must be pretty stupid! That's my wife! Shit, man!"

"You wanted the truth!" he hollers, looking up from the floor.

"No, I wanted you to lie again." I take a deep breath, my anger lessened after one punch. I hesitate, but then walk over to him. He looks defeated. He looks like a child. A child crumbled on the ground with no more fight. I reach my hand down to help him up. He flinches, submissive, then looks at me, puzzled. He looks *like* me. He looks like every kid who has fallen on the ground at the foot of an abuser.

He takes my hand, getting to his feet.

"Shit. I suppose…I'm heading to prison now." A sick feeling twists in my stomach. I just hit another person, and it was so easy…too easy.

"You're stronger than you look," he says, rubbing his jaw.

I rub my palms on my slacks. "I'm sorry. That was un… But what happened that night? What went down that you needed to talk about?"

"No…" he says, holding up his hands, the guilt making him shut his eyes. "Nope, I can't. You have to talk to her about this. I can't. You're already twisting this into something it's not. I made the rooky mistake of getting involved in something that's not mine."

He moves away, shaking his head like he's stupid, like he regrets his decision to be here.

"Were you sleeping with her?" My voice breaks, catches.

Ethan studies me, the vulnerability in my voice making him stop. "No, never…that never happened," he says.

"Then what?"

I see him swallow, clench his jaw. "Words happened. That's all. Words you need to hear from her. But she's in pain right now, I don't think it's the right time."

"You think I don't know that?" I look to the window again, the ugly gray blanket that covers the sky feeling like a punch. I stay still, an urge to sleep right here on the cold hard floor growing.

Faith is dead, she really is dead, and I just want to sleep that away. Right here, right now. All my fears, all my dread...it all just came unleashed with that one punch.

I force the weakness of sleep away. I steady my hands. "So, what do I do?" I ask. "What do we do? You want to call the cops?" I say, and I feel like I'm in quicksand. I hit him. Just like Frank would. "I *am* sorry."

He puts a hand to his forehead, sighs. "It's unethical." He rolls his neck. "But...I'll forget this happened. And you...we...can do what we can to help Ella. She needs support right now."

"And you can do that?"

I study his reaction and see nothing. I don't know what I'm looking for. Maybe some spark to ignite in his eyes, a strange purpose to live again lighting its way through his veins? He just looks removed.

"I can try."

I want to hit him in the face and hug him at the same time. Because Faith is dead, and that's now my excuse for all irrational behavior. I nod instead.

Words happened, yet her pain is too real to explore, it's all too fresh to ask for clarification. Is that right? Is it brave to ignore the hanging piano? Or is it better to cut it down and face the repercussions?

I don't know, but this pain already hurts, and I can't bear salting my own wounds.

"I just need everyone to remember that this is not my story to tell. It's Ella's—I'm just...her doctor," he says. He moves for the door and closes it hard behind him.

"Thank you," I say to the empty room.

<h1 style="text-align:center">Chapter 8</h1>

Winding the hospital halls, shame for hitting Ethan still burning my insides, I reach in my pocket and feel the cap. I feel Faith's cap between my fingers. Faith's dead. She's dead, but…she can't be gone. She's somewhere, reflecting her light down on us, like the reflection of a mountain on a shimmering lake: beautiful, yet untouchable. To touch it would mean to break its beauty with our ripples.

The car is ready, the car seat is secure, and today we take Hope home. Nervous butterflies make my stomach tighten.

As I walk into the hospital room, ready to proclaim we are set for departure, I shift my eyes looking for Ella. I find Christina instead, standing at the foot of the bed holding Hope. As I approach, she points me toward the connecting bathroom. Her face is pale, worried, and my anxiety picks up.

I open the bathroom door. Ella's face is buried in Paul's lap, and he is humming and stroking her hair.

"Everything… alright?" I ask, closing the door behind me.

Paul nods. "Just having a few jitters about going home."

I kneel down in front of Ella. Try to make her look at me. "It'll be okay."

Ella shakes her head no.

"It's scary leaving, I know," I whisper.

She shakes her head no again.

I think about the car seat, the remembrance that we are leaving without Faith.

"I think I'm crazy…" she says, her voice light and unrecognizable. They're the first words she's spoken in days.

I find my eyes locking onto Paul's, a bit of hope tugging at my heart.

"You're not crazy—"

"I want to cry all day!" she bellows, interrupting. "I want to fall, fall until there is nowhere left to fall, until I fall into myself. I want to rip my skin off and itch until I bleed. I want to yank my hair out. I want to run away from you and everyone I've ever known. I want to hurt something, anything, until life actually makes sense again. Is that crazy? Does that make me crazy, Keith?"

I stumble backward, taken by surprise. It's like my heart is being hit over and over again by a meat tenderizer. But the truth is, it doesn't make her crazy—or if it does, it makes me crazy too. Seeing her, like this— wounded—it makes me want to run too. Makes me want to get away, just so I don't have to see her pain. I feel a tingle in my bones, a rushing in my blood. A need, so natural it's terrifying, to run fast and far until everything is behind me. Until my lungs collapse and my legs break off. Until the external pain finally outweighs the internal pain. Until I taste the final breath on my lips and know that this is over.

Run…I need to run away. I need to run until nowhere meets somewhere. I need to push the earth away with my legs. I need to escape her, this woman who I love, but I don't even know. I need to run, because if I stay, I'll only break her more. Because, somehow, my mess is now hers. Somehow, we've turned into two scrambled eggs fighting to unscramble.

What kind of man wants to run away from a broken person? What kind of husband doesn't know how to help his wife?

Frank…

Losing Faith was like an explosion of macrocosm proportions, and now I need to be the one to put the mess back together. And I don't know how.

The only thing I know is that she needs me. She needs me more now than she ever did before. I try to talk, but I have a mouth full of something that can't be chewed. I can't swallow. "Ella..." I mutter. Her name is the only thing able to escape the glue holding my teeth together.

"I'm crazy!" she screams.

"No... No. We lost Faith," I cry, her name making my voice catch. "We lost one of our little girls," I say. "And now we don't know what we're doing. That doesn't make you crazy."

Her tears bubble out and over her eyes.

This is Ella. This is my wife. This is the woman I love, suffering in front of me. This is a mother with postpartum depression. She is a person, a person who needs me.

"Everything will be okay," I tell her.

I reach for her, but she doesn't let me touch her, instead her arms clutch tighter around her dad. I stare. Not speaking, just sitting and trying to turn to stone. Because stone is too heavy to move. If I'm concrete hardened to the surface, if I'm a tree rooted to the ground, then nothing can make me run.

Part 2

Late February

Chapter 9

The electric heater whirs, spins manufactured heat into the neutral-toned office in an effort to cover the intruding draft. My eyes move to the crystals on the end table.

"Why raccoons?" Dr. Samantha Ryder asks, perched in her mahogany leather chair, legs crossed, and glasses balanced on the edge of her nose.

"I don't know. Ever since the day…that we lost…Faith…I feel like they're haunting me, like it's some inane cosmic sign."

She jots something on her yellow legal pad, her eyes temporarily glancing to the page. "Sign of what?"

"That's what I want to figure out. Google's no help."

"Have you heard of confirmation bias?" she asks.

I shake my head. I haven't.

"Humans have this tendency to look for information that confirms their own perceived notions." She taps the pen on the page. "What do raccoons mean to you?"

"Nothing," I say, but hesitate to consider it deeper.

"The mind is a powerful tool and can do some unimaginable things when you go through tragedy like your family has experienced," she says. "You noticed the first one in a state of heightened stress, and now your mind is hyper-focused on finding all signs of them in your daily life. I can assure you, they were always there. You're just noticing them now for a particular reason. What's the first thing that comes to mind when you think of a raccoon?"

"Rabies."

"Are you afraid of sickness?" She glances at the door, and I wonder if maybe she's already classified me as crazy and is looking for her escape route.

This entire thing is new for me. To be here, in a psychologist's office, of my own free will, it's a big deal. Ethan arranged for Ella to speak with Dr. Fletcher through multiple channels, but I called Dr. Ryder on my own, because… I can't be losing my mind too. Yesterday, as I was backing from the garage, I had another encounter with a raccoon. He was resting on his haunches, staring from the end of the driveway with his curious beady little eyes.

"I don't feel like I put much focus on disease," I finally answer.

"Well, what's another thing you associate them with?" she asks.

"Theft. They steal their food."

"Think about what that means on various levels. What could theft mean to you?"

I swallow and try to joke. "I've never stolen a thing, scouts honor."

The joke falls flat, the electronic heat sucking the humor from the room. "It doesn't have to be so literal. It can be a broad feeling. Maybe you feel someone has taken from you?"

A ripple of meaning sparks in me, but as I try to grab it, as I try to examine it for understanding, it disappears. I go with the obvious. "What if it was a sign that Faith was going to be stolen from me?"

She uncrosses her legs, adjusts flipping to the other end of the chair. "Maybe. It's possible that's how you explain the first encounter to yourself, but what about all the others?"

I unzip my coat further, pull at the collar of my shirt. The room suddenly feels stuffy, the damn heater claiming the breathable air. "Sometimes I worry I'm stealing Ella's time."

Samantha shifts again, eyeing me. "How are you stealing her time?"

I move to pull my jacket off. "Can we turn that heater off?"

She's quick to reach forward and hit the button, a five-beep countdown warns of its shutdown. "How are you stealing Ella's time?" she asks again, before the final beep even clears.

I struggle feeling like I'm worthy of Ella, it's true, but there's something else. A deeper truth to assign to the word "theft" than I was planning to go in this session. In fact, I had no intention at all to mention Frank, to mention Mom. This was to talk about Faith, to figure out why I'm being plagued by raccoons. My eyes must register shock, my body must show something because Dr. Ryder seems to straighten further. "What are you thinking?" she asks.

What am I thinking? That spark bursts into flames.

Frank. I'm thinking of Frank. Frank stole from Mom. He stole her entire life, locked her happiness away and put her on a shelf, separate from the rest of this world.

But me, what about me? I abandoned her there with him, left her to fend for herself against a brutal man. My breath constricts, tightens. My brother died—her son—and I still left. I picked up and moved on without them. How does that make me any better than Frank? I hit Ethan.

I've spent the last ten years angry with her for not choosing me, for not coming to find me in this world, and now I have a child, I am a father, but I still need her here. I still want her to come through the door and wrap me in her arms.

"Keith? I'm here to listen if there is anything you want to share, but you're in control here. If you want to talk about something else, that's fine too."

I nod.

"Do you want to move on?"

I nod again.

"Do you want to talk about your relationship with your wife?"

I close my eyes, regretting the decision to come here. What was I thinking? How can I possibly avoid all the bombs from blowing with topics like these?

"Fine," I lie.

"How is she coping with Faith?

"She's…she's terribly sad," I admit. "Sad to the point where she doesn't eat. Doesn't sleep."

"Does that scare you?" she asks.

"Yes. I'm scared for her. I wish I could do something to lessen her pain. And our daughter. I…I worry she blames Hope."

Dr. Ryder sighs. "I don't mean to frighten you, but, in all reality, she might. It's not uncommon with postpartum," she admits.

"I'm trying to be strong for my family, but I don't know how. I don't know how to be…dependable. I don't know how to be reliable. I want to be understanding of her recovery, but I'm angry all the time. I'm angry at Ella for being broken. She's so broken that she doesn't see how much I'm hurting for Faith, too, and even that makes me angry, but at myself. I'm a selfish, self-absorbed person."

I take a breath; I am a failure.

"Despite this being our initial conversation, I can assure you that what you're feeling is completely normal. All of your emotions are completely valid."

"I lost Faith too."

"I know you did, and I'm sorry for your loss."

"I don't know how to be a dad, and I feel like I've been doing it on my own the last few weeks."

"I imagine that's stressful. Do you have any help?"

"My mother-law, Christina, she's been great. She's there every day, helping with the baby. I'm grateful. I've been working remotely, from home, which I still can't believe my boss allowed, and Christina's the one who makes that possible. Oh, and the new girl at the office, Jenny—Jennifer—she has really helped me get to be with my family."

"I'm glad you have a support team." Her eyebrows lift, she picks up her notepad and starts scribbling. My eyes watch her pen move on the page, and I try to visualize what she's scripting.

"How long are you planning to work from home?"

"I'm supposed to go back to the office tomorrow."

"On a Thursday?"

I shrug. "Figured it would be easier to start with a short week."

"And Ella?"

And Ella…her name's a question now. Ella will be Ella. She'll stay lying in her sadness, stuck.

Chapter 10

Whiteness blinds, the snow-covered world glistens under the unexpected February sun. My cheeks are only now starting to feel the cold. It's taken the entire ride home for me to cool off from Dr. Ryder's blistering office.

"Beatles day here at 95.5. A little Rocky Raccoon to get your afternoon underway," the radio DJ says as I pull into the driveway.

The guitar strings strum, eerily.

"Now somewhere in the black mining hills of Dakota

There lived a young boy named Rocky Raccoon

And one day his woman ran off with another guy

Hit young Rocky in the eye

Rocky didn't like that

He said, 'I'm gonna get that boy.'

I hit the power button, flushing the car of noise.

"Dammit!"

I maneuver the car next to Christina's, leave space for her to pull out when she leaves. Trudging inside, I'm thinking about raccoons again.

Rabies. Theft. Frank.

A rabid Frank stole my mother's life. Alcohol stole his…and Scott's. Have I stolen mine back? What about Dr. Ethan Stacey? Did he steal from me? Did he take Faith, and as a result, Ella too?

Nothing happened, only words.

Home is quiet, and warm, and I move gently to keep that energy unbroken, although I feel the tightness, the unanswered questions, and the lingering text message from Ethan. I've avoided the conversation for weeks, because Ella, she's hurting, but for me, too, because I'm hurting and scared.

Maybe that's the raccoon's message? I'm terrified to face the truth of the daylight, so I hide in the darkness.

I find Christina lounging on the sofa with Hope nestled against her. I make my way closer, kiss Hope, and smile at Christina.

"Where's Ella?"

Shrugging, Christina answers, "Bedroom." She yawns, arches her back in a stretch. "I have to head home. Paulie—the lazy bastard— probably hasn't fed himself all day."

I laugh. "Thank you. For being here, for…all of us."

Her face is serious, like that was unexpected, then soft. "I'd do anything…for any of you." She stands and hands me Hope.

Taking her, I kiss the baby-soft rosy cheeks again, her newborn smell filling my nose. "She's so cute."

Christina chuckles, pulling on her coat. "She really is an angel."

Hope wiggles and squirms in my arms. "I think I could hold her all day, and not do anything else."

Christina's face pales. "Hold them while you can, because soon they grow, and the world tries to hurt them." Her eyes mist, and she scurries for the door.

Something was stolen from her too.

"See you in the morning," she says. She pulls her coat on, wraps a scarf around her neck. "Take care of my girls. And if Ella…" Her words fall off.

And if Ella... I nod. "Of course."

She nods back. And if Ella...

The Ella of today is not drastically different from the Ella I first met. I've always sensed she's carried a sadness inside her. It's that sadness that links us. Ella went to Northeastern University, an upscale private school in the Fenway Cultural District of Boston. I was broke and working for M & M's Landscaping, the company that serviced her school. I spent hours at that school, mowing the grass, planting flowers, and re-mulching the gardens. The campus had beautiful grounds that traced the full outline of the open court.

I had seen Ella before. She would study in the grass with a few of her girlfriends. So much beauty in only one soul. Friendly and magnetic, she would wave when I was staring.

On that day, the scorching heat melted our minds, drenched our clothing with sweat. My sticky shirt clung to me, the faint abs under my thin layer of chub clenching tight to impress. The campus was quiet, most students were home for summer break. Soiled, covered in sweat and dirt, I wanted nothing more than to take a shower. I looked around, but didn't see anyone standing by, so I stripped off my shirt, started spraying myself with the icy hose. I washed my face and wet my hair, embarrassing groans escaping my lips.

"You bathe outside often?"

Shuttering, shutting the hose off, I wiped the water droplets from my eyes, thinking I was in trouble.

It was Ella, smiling. Her long raven hair was tied up in a braid, her eyes two buckets filled with all the stars and blue of the ocean. Her legs were long and slender in her cut-off jean shorts, an inch of her torso poking out below her white cropped tank top. Sweat balled at the base of her hair, making something inside me give way.

"Occasionally," I muttered, managing to smile back.

"That water must be freezing. You have goose bumps," she said. "Have you seen a tall girl, blond hair, probably wearing jeans and a hoodie despite the heat?" she asked.

"No, I'm sorry, I haven't."

"No worries," she said. She turned her back to leave, scanned the area, looking for the mentioned girl.

"What's your name?" I asked.

She didn't answer right away, instead pretended to keep looking for her friend. Then she turned, looking at me again. Her eyes connecting with mine like two windows illuminated in the dark. "Ella," she said, smiling slightly.

"Keith."

"You're always working. We waved a few times, but you never waved back. Are you in school here?"

"I'm shy, I guess. I go to Boston College...just work here."

"Shy? I don't believe it for the world. You were just bathing in public," she said and laughed. "Besides, guys who look like you don't get shy."

I creased my brow. "What? You mean sweaty guys with grubby faces and dirty fingernails?" I held up my hand to show the soil packed under each nail.

"That's a fashion statement. Girls go wild for a dirty boy."

I laughed, feeling slightly awkward, wondered if that was flirting. After a moment without words, I asked, "What do you study?"

"Chemistry," she said. She smiled, but it didn't reach her eyes. "Sometimes I'd rather be out here, planting flowers."

"No," I said. "You wouldn't."

She gave me a look like I couldn't possibly understand. "What about you? What do you study?" she said.

"Marketing."

"What are you doing right now?"

I hesitated, confused. "Well, besides bathing in public, I have to plant all of these flowers before I can call it a day." I pointed to the pile of daisies and irises waiting on the sidewalk. "Why?"

"I've read the same chapter five times, trying to understand it, but can't, and Tonya is apparently being a bitch and standing me up." Her smile faltered for a second. She looked like she needed one good reason to keep from disappearing.

"I'm sorry, but I'm horrible at chemistry. I don't think I can help," I said, feeling like I was about to let her down.

"Everyone's horrible at chemistry; its fine," she answered. "I need a distraction. Want some help?"

"Huh?"

"Can I help you?" she asked again.

I was confused. I started thinking maybe this was some kind of cruel joke. "Why?"

"Why not?" She shrugged her shoulders.

"Well, if you don't mind getting all dirty. Do you like, need money?" I asked, hoping that wasn't the case because, shit, I'd have to pay her from my own paycheck.

"No. I'm just bored and curious."

"Are you nuts? Are you some sort of crazy person?"

"Maybe?" Her eyes seemed sad.

I shook my head, still confused. "If you really want to," I said. "We need to plant these Gerbera daisies outside of the administration building." I bent down and grabbed two shovels and put them in the wheelbarrow, then I loaded the remaining space with the flowers.

I made my way toward the administrative garden, thinking she would follow, but she stayed back, lingering around the hose.

"Over it already?" I asked.

"You want me to follow you? Got it. Straight to business!"

I smiled, shaking my head.

She was oddly competitive, had this drive to make everything into a race. She was beyond determined to beat me, even though I was not contending. She worked on the right side of the garden, and I worked on the left. Our eyes darted back and forth, our smiles flirting. We met in the middle, after an hour in the sun. By the end, she was covered in soil and sweat, too, her skin burned red from the exposure, her smile seeming genuine.

Our hands touched as I helped her to her feet, her thumb brushed across my knuckles. My eyes couldn't stop themselves from seeing what our entwined fingers looked like. We studied each other, looked away, broke away, and then headed back to the hose.

"I totally beat you," she said, pushing her shoulder into mine. She had dirt all over her face, and for some reason, it was the most beautiful thing I'd ever seen.

"I let you win, but thanks for the help."

"I feel alive," she said.

I just laughed, passing her the hose to wash her hands.

"It's so cold," she chattered, a mischievous grin forking at her lips. She turned the hose on me, spraying me in the face. I coughed, choked, rushed her, grabbing the nozzle to turn on her.

"Ah!" she screamed as she tried to wrestle me to the ground. Her arms went around my torso, and mine around her shoulders. I bear-hugged her, rolled her to the ground on top of me.

"Do you think I can help again sometime?" she asked. She was still on top of me, and I didn't think I could answer. My eyes flicked to her lips.

"Really?" I said to her mouth. We were so close; I could have touched her with my mouth. So close, and I wanted to touch her with my lips.

"Yeah, I had fun." She rolled off of me, stumbling to her feet. I stood, too, brushing the dirt from my already soiled shirt.

"I had fun too," I said. "I just feel like I'm taking advantage if I don't pay you."

"Hmm, you can buy me an ice cream sometime, if it makes you feel better."

"It would." Our eyes met again, and I studied the crisp sharp color of them. Dark blue, almost black, with waves of white stars. I bit my lip, pushing the urge to kiss her away.

"I better get going," she said, breaking our eye contact. "I'll see you soon, and I'll be ready for my paycheck then."

She got up and walked away. I stared as she walked, watching the way her hips swayed back and forth, mesmerized by the way she flipped her hair out of the braid and around her shoulders. She stopped abruptly and spun around. "Keith," she yelled, as if she needed to get my attention again. "There's a movie playing tonight outside on the court. You should come," she said.

"Okay." I smiled.

After cleaning up the tools, I rushed back to my studio above Mike and Meredith's garage and showered. I must have tried on all ten of my t-shirts before deciding on one. I combed my hair and sprayed some cologne. It was only on the drive back to Northeastern that the nerves came. I started thinking that maybe she wouldn't show up. Or, if she did show up, it would be with her boyfriend.

When I got there, she was plopped cross-legged on a blanket, only a few other people scattered across the grass. A massive white screen was set up at the front of the court, illuminating the shadowy figures. She was looking around for someone, and it made my stomach dance. I wanted her to be looking for me.

She smiled when our eyes met, waved me over. I sat down, letting my shoulder press into hers.

"How's my favorite employee?"

She laughed sweetly, and words were meaningless in the ocean of feelings. Her being there, her looking at me, her lips close enough for me to kiss—trumped words.

"So, what are we watching?" I eventually asked.

"*The Little Mermaid*," she cooed excitedly.

I furrowed my brow. "*The Little Mermaid*? Like, the children's movie?"

"Yes, it's a classic!" she said. "It's an epic love story in its own right, so don't tease."

I nodded. "Never seen it."

"You've never seen it?"

"Right, I've never seen it!"

"Well…I'll have you know that it just happens to be my all-time favorite movie," she admitted.

"I'm sure I'll love it then," I said.

She told me that she really wanted to study history and become a teacher, but her mom had convinced her to take up chemistry. How she wanted to inspire children and help the ones who were behind. She told me about her parents and their enormous house. About how she wanted to travel the world and feed the poor. How she wanted to skinny-dip in the ocean, and how she wanted to go hiking in the mountains. She told me she broke both of her wrists when she was younger. And that she played the piano. She told me she wasn't sure if she had ever been in love.

We whispered back and forth through the entire movie and kept talking even after the screen shut off and everyone cleared out. I told her about Mom, how she was the first and only person I'd ever loved.

I explained Mom differently that night. Described her as her young, youthful, and happy self. Instead of the beaten-down mother she became, I used the hidden picture she kept under her dresser as a reference: fresh, beautiful, and cheerful. Smiling ear to ear with her friend Meredith, this life-full-of-hopes-and-dreams-before-Frank glow to her.

Frank tore that up for her, stole it like a thief. He beat and slapped her silly, until she was submissive and vacant. Until all she had left was that stupid picture to remind herself that she'd let a man ruin her.

Ella has always carried a sadness, and I haven't fixed that. Instead, in a way, I've ruined Ella—just like Dad ruined Mom. There was a time when I looked at Ella and the words in my head stopped screaming to get out. There was a vastness to her, like the ocean: beautiful and frightening. Now I've become an active participant in sucking her dry. I've planted seeds in her head, and instead of flowers, cancer has spread.

Chapter 11

For a while, it's just darkness, a black emptiness that consumes the world. But then, muffled words creep inside and pull me from the shadows. Soft whispers—soothing and comforting—in the midst of the black cloud. Whispers that promise safety and warmth, even in a haunted world. The blackness crackles to a startling white light, my hands move reflexively to shield my eyes. The empty words shift into empty phrases that shift into recollection: Ella's voice, singing.

"When the blazing sun is gone,
When he nothing shines upon,
Then you show your little light,
Twinkle, twinkle, all the night."

I turn in bed, squinting against the hallway light spilling into the bedroom. The clock says 3:00 a.m.—only two hours until my alarm for work sounds. Yawning, I push up to my elbow and see Ella rocking in the corner chair, Hope bundled in her arms. Tired from getting Hope back to sleep when she last woke at 1:00 a.m., I must not have heard her stirring.

Despite my sleep-fogged brain, happiness makes me smile at the sight of Ella holding Hope. "Need me to take her?" I whisper.

"Shhh," she mouths, shaking her head no. She stands and heads for the hall, plunges the world back into darkness. The hallway floorboards creak under her feet, followed by a soft *pitter-patter* crackling through the baby monitor.

My eyes are heavy, starry from the sudden re-absence of light. I look to the window to readjust. What's visible of the Martian moon pokes around the blinds, the ruthless wind whistles and whips in rapid, ragged procession, and I shiver, pulling the cover tighter around me. Laying back down, I rearrange to cool the aching in my lower back.

Sometime later, Ella tiptoes back into the room, makes a wide arc around the bed, and heads to the end table. She grabs her phone, and as I go to speak, I realize she's planning to leave the room again.

I hesitate, suddenly unsure if I should say something or pretend I'm sleeping. I hate that we don't know how to talk to each other. There's me, there's her, and there's this heavy unspoken truth that we damaged something we were meant to protect. Resentment floats in the air between us, strapping on to our heels. I want to fix that, so I say, "Thanks for getting her back to sleep."

She stops midstride toward the door. "You're awake?"

"Yeah," I whisper. "Are you coming back to bed?"

Her shadow turns. "I was going to go lay on the couch and watch TV. I don't feel like I can sleep now."

"Okay."

"Okay." She starts moving for the door again, and this irrational idea that maybe she'll be texting Ethan makes me sit up.

"Come lay with me, for just a little."

It's stupid, I know. I should trust her, I should accept that whatever went down with them doesn't concern me, but something in me is still jealous of him, despite the fact he is the last name she wants to hear.

She doesn't move, and for a second I think maybe she'll walk away, but then her shadow moves to her side of the bed, and she slips under the covers. She turns her back to me, and I move to put my arm around her.

She tenses at my touch.

"You are gentle, just like the sunset. You are alive, just like raging fire. You are careful and kind. You are reckless and passionate. You teach me. You show me. You are a champion. My champion," I whisper to her.

She stiffens more. "Those are just words, ya know? Not a magical spell to get you sex."

I keep my arms around her letting the warmth of my body envelope her. I hug her tight. I just hold her, not knowing where to go or what to say to make us better.

I rub her back trying to comfort her, trying to be there. She loosens, so I hold on.

"Everything will be okay," I mutter.

She tenses again but turns toward me. Her hand moves up and tangles in my hair, her nose pressing against the inside of my neck. I feel a small tinge of guilt for wanting her, but then she's kissing me, pressing her lips into me.

She moves on top, spreads her legs over mine, and pushes her body against me, erasing that guilt. Her warm skin makes me arch into her, and I heave forward with lust, wrapping my arms around her tighter. Her fingertips brush across the skin of my chest and goose bumps cover my body. She presses her pelvis into mine, and I thicken under her.

"Ella?" I whisper, feeling ashamed.

"Shh…" she mutters against my lips.

Her touch feeds something inside me, I kiss her back harder, and deeper. It's painful, but I don't want it to stop. She pushes my head back and kisses down my jaw to my neck, traces down my body with her tongue and circles my nipple.

I unwrap us from our tangled clothing, needing to be closer to her. Her body is sharp curves and angles against the plush comforter. I trace her scar from the C-section and push back the thoughts of that day.

Her tongue moves inside my mouth—slow, deep, and deliberate. She presses it against the inside of my teeth, and I surge with need on her taste. I flip her under me. Butterflies dance in my stomach as we lock our hands and collide, letting our desires put those thoughts on hold.

She winces when I first go in, and I pull back. "No, don't stop," she demands. I slide back on top, covering every inch of her with my quaking body, then back inside. She drags her fingernails down my back, each muscle tightening around her touch. I thrust silently and demandingly into her, letting the fever of the moment carry the reminders of verity away.

Chapter 12

My body, tacky with sweat, shivers against the cold draft snaking in from the window. The whipping wind barks like the hounds of hell. I reach with shaking limbs for the cotton sheet and cover our naked bodies.

"Thank you," I mutter, sleepy, yet satisfied.

Her hands come up in the darkness and cover her face. A sniffle escapes from under her hands, then she turns in the bed, away from me. Another hiccup of a sob sneaks out.

I sit up, feeling guilty, feeling stupid, and feeling like I just forced her to take a step she wasn't ready to take. "I'm sorry. That's not where I wanted it to go when I said 'lay with me.' I mean, I liked it, but I just wanted to hold you."

I move to her, put my arm around her for comfort.

She pops up. "No. Don't." She exits the bed, turning the light on in the attached bathroom and pulling on her robe, the tears shining on her face.

I reach for my shorts and pull them on. "I'm sorry."

"Faith. Faith is dead." Her tears come harder, her hands moving to wipe at her eyes.

"Ella." I move toward her, my own throat closing up. "I know." I reach for her, wanting to put my arms around her.

"Do you? Do you know?" she asks, her sadness showing hints of anger. "Because, to me, it seems like you just picked up and moved on without issue. Like life got easier, because now you just have one kid to deal with."

I stumble, visibly pull my arms back and away from her. "You can't possible think that?"

Her eyes shift, snap onto mine. "I can't do this anymore."

"It's hard, I get it. It hurts. You're questioning everything, and so am I."

"No," she says. "No, Keith. I can't be here anymore. I can't be in this place and be the person you want me to be." She tightens her robe.

"What? I want you to be yourself. Nothing else."

The words seem to make her angrier, her hands move to her hips. "You don't even know me."

I fish for my shirt on the floor and pause to pull it on. "What don't I know? If this has anything to do with Ethan, it's fine. I don't care what happened. I don't ever need to know."

I realize as I say it that I believe it. I don't need to know. I don't want to know, I'm okay pretending nothing is there, if it means we can avoid this.

Her face falters, shows shock and disbelief, and then she stares at me, eyes shifting between confusion and fury. "What the hell are you talking about?"

I should say nothing, backtrack and make this go away. "Nothing…a silly text message. Never mind. It's fine."

It's like my words are gas being thrown on a fire. Her body lights into a ball of heat. "No. No. No. You obviously care, the way you just brought that up? You think…you think because another man texts me that it means I'm cheating on you?" She runs her hands through her hair. "That girl Jennifer—she texted you on *my* phone…are you screwing *her*, Keith?"

"No. Gosh! We just work together—"

"Exactly! And Ethan was my doctor—our doctor. He delivered our babies." Her voice catches at this, the tears from before starting to leak again.

I'm suddenly thinking more clearly: I'm an idiot. I'm…Frank. "I'm an idiot," I tell her. "I'm sorry." The text had said *Call me about last night*. Ethan had implied I hold off on asking her about it, that it would only make her more upset. If she wasn't interested in him, then what was it? What did they need to talk about? "I'm not assuming anything. I'm just saying its fine. Whatever was said, or whatever happened, it's all fine. It's over and done, water under the bridge."

"Whatever was said?" she asks, her eyes search mine for an answer.

I try to make mine say, *Everything is okay.*

"It's really none of your business, Keith." Anger, sorrow, and defiance twist her face. She fidgets in annoyance and tugs at her hair.

I cross the room and put my hand over her clenched fist, wanting more than anything to curl into her.

"Please don't touch me!" she shouts, a patch of red flaring up her neck.

"Shh," I say, moving away, raising my hands in surrender. "Okay. Don't wake up Hope."

Her lip trembles.

"Ella." It comes out soft, almost like she's a child. "Ella, it's—"

"Stop saying my name!" It's like the volcano inside of her has finally erupted. Her sadness is closed, her anger opened and in need of release. "Stop! Just stop! Shut up, Keith! Please, can you just shut up and let me think?" she hollers. The veins in her neck pop out, reach like venomous fingers.

"Ella," I whisper again, ignoring her request. It's the only word that comes out, like, if I say it enough, this tension will magically disappear. Like maybe her name is the spell to erase us from our nightmare.

"Jesus Christ! I said stop saying my fucking name! Don't you get it? Can't you understand anything?"

I don't say a word, instead fight against the downward pull of my shoulders. Battle against the urge to cower in front of her.

"Have you not wondered why I rarely touch you? Why you're the only one who ever initiates sex?" she asks. "It's because I can't stand it! I hate the thought of you inside of me. It repulses me. I'm disgusted by it! I have to shut myself down and wait for you to get off."

She's crying again.

"The text message from Ethan?" She pushes her tears down and stares at me, her eyes piercing and pinning me in place. "He's gay, Keith, a total gold star, and per usual, you are so goddamned self-absorbed you don't see anything past the story playing in your head."

I let silence cover the room.

Ethan, gay? True, I wouldn't have thought that to be, but that still doesn't answer all of the questions. Her words hurt, and a defense against hurt is rage. I point my anger at her like a knife. "So, what? You wanted him, and he turned you down because you don't have a dick?"

Her face falls, it's like my question is the final straw to break her completely. Her head shakes, her eyes dig in.

"I fucked him anyway," she says. "I screwed him, and all his friends, while I was pregnant with your babies." She shakes her head again, disappointed. "And...and you want to know something?" she asks, pausing like maybe I'll respond. "He was good! Really good. I needed someone to use me for a change. Just use my body, flip me over, push my face into the pillow, and go to town. An actual proper fucking!"

I shake my head no, getting pissed off. "Now you're just lying."

"He fucked the fuck out of me, Keith. So good and so proper...so unlike you in every goddamn way."

Her ugliness is working, the tight shadowy fingers are closing around my neck, pulling me under. My animal instincts are screaming to run and seek shelter, or to man-up and fight back.

"You are pathetic, do you know that? I'm ruined," she cries. "I'm ruined, and you're still so lost in your head that you can't open your eyes and see that I haven't been happy for years. That we go through the motions and pretend to love each other because that's what's expected of us."

"What are you talking about?"

"This is unproductive." She pulls her hair back, moves into the bathroom.

"No! I'm trying to digest what you just said. You don't fucking love me? Is that what you're trying to say?"

She looks so tired. She shakes her head. "Yeah, Keith. That's right. I hate you," she whispers, her lip trembling and her eyes filling.

I suck in a breath, something breaks inside, and I am falling like Alice, falling into myself. I know those words aren't true but pointed. She's purposely hurting me. She's slapping me in the face with hard and dirty blows to project her pain. Like my father, she's hitting me with words. He never needed another weapon to hurt me. He could use his words as a weapon. He could use his voice and tone to beat me, and those words hurt more than his belt or hands ever could. He was his own weapon, and now so is she.

But I'm me, and I, well, I'm used to being slapped. I'm used to being told I'm nothing. I'm used to being called pathetic. I heard it my entire life. I have scars that run up my arms from the cigarette burns to remind me. I have the indents in my back for proof.

Not good enough for Daddy. Not good enough for Ella. *Not good enough.*

I fight to hold back, she's not in her right mind. This isn't really Ella. This is an illness. It's post-traumatic stress, it's depression, and it's the result of my ignorant words. I need to be the strong one right now, because Faith is dead. I know this, yet, I can't.

I mutter the only word that can escape the hollowness in my chest. "Liar." And then the hollowness inside begins to burn a white-hot flame of fury, and all of my pent-up rage demands to be freed. I follow the light and let it consume me. "You're selfish!" I hiss. It's gritty and vicious, her wrath contagious.

She clenches her jaw, a tear spilling from her eye.

I don't care anymore. The flame is in me; I need to strike back. My heart crackles and pops like lightning, flares, and reaches out to burn anything brave enough to stand its ground. This is my storm now...bare my wrath. Feel the rain and face my flood. It's pounding, pounding, pounding, then ripping.

I am opened now. I can never be shut.

"Selfish!" I scream it, and the faucet is on full blast. "You selfish bitch," I say, wishing there was a hesitation. Wishing there was something that could disconnect me from all of the other men who label their wives with harsh words. I'm tarnished—smudged—just as dirty now as every man history has created.

Her face is crimson, heated, and that fuels me.

A chemical burns my senses, tears flow hot and unruly, making the world blur and seem changed. "You're weak!" I snarl, and even though that's what I heard from Frank my entire life, I still don't hesitate. "You're a weak, disgusting, *whore*, Ella."

Then, I break fully. What's left of me bubbles out in sobbing torrents. I double over, because: *whore*. The remembrance of that word being spit at Mom hits me in the face, her weak eyes flashing before me like headlights.

I am Frank now, and Frank is this world. We are all ruined.

I feel sick, but when Ella comes back into focus, she looks nothing like Mom. She doesn't look hurt...she looks pleased. She looks like this is exactly where she wanted this argument to lead. Her justification that she's right to think I'm a piece of shit.

I feel nauseous and dizzy. I want to run and cry and apologize all at the same time. What's worse is the feeling of relief I have. There's relief in showing my unseen pieces.

I study her face, now emotionless and still. Her anger has drained. All that's left is the plastic version of Ella I've known these past weeks. The shutters go up in her eyes as she cuts herself further and further off.

"I'm leaving," she says in a distant voice.

"No, you're not."

"Get out!" Her scream is animal, primal. It's frightening and alarmingly louder than her voice before.

"I'm sorry."

"*I said get out!*" she screams again, cutting me off, her finger pointing to the bedroom door. "Just go, leave, get out of here!" she spits.

My insides quiver, the ending-cracking-breaking of self-worth rippling through me. Guilt grabs me by the heart. I look at her. Really look at her. She's angry and disgusted, but she's sick. She needs me. She needs me now, more than ever because *Faith is dead.*

"I'm sorry, I'm sorry…okay You love me. I love you. Say it…say it now…I need you to say it."

She shouts, "*Get…out!*" at the same time I say it for her, "You are gentle, just like the sunset. You are alive, just like raging fire. You are careful and kind," I recite. "Say it…you have to say it."

She screams, a blood-curdling noise. "Those words mean nothing! They're nothing!"

"Ella!"

"Get out!"

"And Hope?" I question. "And our daughter?"

Her eyes are black and cold, like two pieces of coal waiting for ignition. The pupils have dilated, changing her face into a mask of horrible that I wish I could un-see. The wretched bitter, testament to what we were, what we weren't, what we almost had: it's all filed somewhere, hidden in that blackness.

"My daughter is already dead," she mutters, and then without warning, my mind turns black.

I put a hand over my mouth, not only in shock, but to stop the ugliness from coming out.

The logical me shuts down, an existential meltdown frying my brain. What's worse is this desire I have to hurt her. I want to march over and slap her in the face. Slap her silly, until she realizes what she just did to me—what she just said to me. That's the Frank in me. The part of me that wants to shake her and hurt her just as much as she hurt me. I turn away, scared of her, and even more afraid of myself.

I slam the door behind me, the crack of the wood echoing through the quiet house. Hope is already crying, her call escaping from the open door of the nursery.

I move toward her cry and try to accept the fact that hopes and dreams and wishes don't count for anything, and that love, like life, always dies.

I've been shot. This is what it's like to be shot. I'm bleeding from an invisible bullet-hole. I feel like I'm drowning. Like I'm drinking water, but it's leaking into my lungs. Like I'm six feet underground, still trying to breathe.

I lie on the floor of the nursery, Hope's cries filling the space. "Shh," I whisper.

My thoughts shatter into disconnected words. Words that seem to float freely with no apparent meaning. The words are scrambled and out of order, jutting out in different directions, like winding tree branches. Thousands of little twigs that seem separate and alive, but when you look hard enough, you can decipher that the branches tangle and entwine into one braided base. One trunk to the tree. One reason for the thousand jumbled words branching within my brain. One reason: Ella.

There's a significant moment right before you break. It's the moment you're on the ledge, and there's nothing but you and your wilting character facing the monster in your head. You feel the beast pressuring you, whispering in a soft sing–song voice to jump. He persuades you that, if you leap, if you fall, if you let yourself break, then maybe, just maybe, adversity will surrender, that there's a chance hardship and misfortune will cower.

So, you choose it. You do it. You follow it. You follow the shadow all the way through, till the end, because nothing can feel worse than that ledge, than that pressure, than that monster choking you from the inside out. So, you jump. So, you break, and, when it's done, and you chose it—

your pieces are scattered. Where the pressure lived, a numb-consuming coldness replaces it. A coldness so black, a coldness so overwhelming, that the reminiscence of who you are, or who you were, is forever washed away. Gone. It's gone. So, you regret it. Inevitability, you always regret it. You regret that split-second decision of weakness that you chose to break.

The thing you never realize is, when you're there, when you're on that ledge, you'll choose to jump. No matter what. Every time. No matter how many ways you can imagine it, you'll pick it, and you'll break.

So, I break. Like a good little boy, I jump. I leap off the cliff, headfirst, into this darkness Ella created. I choose to let her words break me. Breaking from the inside out.

Chapter 13

miss my mom.

I've been so self-focused, so sure this world was going to hurt me again, that I failed to remember that my own actions are the catalysts to pain.

Weak. Disgusting. *Whore.*

Chapter 14

look for Frank, but this is now. This is now, so Frank can't be here.

I am Frank.

My legs are lead anchors drudging across the floor. I pull myself to the bathroom. Through the sobs, a string is unwinding, the tethers of fabric pulling apart to change the me from before into the me of now. Gravity is dragging me to the bottom of the ocean.

I peel my clothes off robotically, run the bath as hot as it will go, and step in to burn away the memories, to burn away Frank from my skin.

I settle into the warm water, the sound of the thudding stream filling the tub, the bubbling, burning sensation of freshwater tingles against my toes. The fight with Ella is still fresh, clinging to me, and I wish I could wash it away. I need to wash away the words…the names, the things I've just called her.

I want my mom. The woman who wanted to protect me but couldn't. The person I abandoned at the lowest point in her life—beaten and broken.

Mom…she would take me to upscale neighborhoods around Christmastime every year. We'd take a bus, just me and her, and spend hours bundled up in hats and scarves roaming the streets, looking at the beautiful lights. We didn't have a camera, so we would take imaginary pictures. We'd even make the little shuttering noise when pretending to snap one. She always claimed she was saving it for later, like she was filing the pictures away in her brain, her heart, and calling them up whenever she wanted to see them again.

One house, built completely of stone, became our obsession. The curve of the stone was unique, the design of the house making it feel like a far-off castle in another era. In our heads, we were in another place, far from reality. Beautiful archways, cobblestone driveways, this huge bay-window with the Christmas tree in front of it. Everything laced in gold and red ornaments, white lights that twinkled like fireflies. Icicle lights draped from the roof; wreaths hung from every window. Unrealistic beauty provable by our eyes.

We spent the most time there. I'd have to pull Mom away. "Come on, Mom, my toes are falling off."

She'd smile at that, hold up a finger…*just one more minute.*

I'd smile back, hold up two…*you can have two.*

One night, the moon was high and full. The sky was lit up with stars; the earth was still and quiet. A light dusting of snow coated the imperfections, found the inconsistencies, and sprinkled the dark with white. Smoke bellowed from the chimney, the smell of cedar filling our noses.

Cold and crisp, the air puffed out of us like miniature smokestacks. A few blocks down, the soft murmurs of carolers singing "Silent Night" serenaded the neighbors.

Turning to Mom, I saw a tear running down her cheek. She smiled, shyly, and wiped it away. "There is still so much beauty for you to find," she said.

She turned, grinning, making her hands into the shape of a box and bringing it to her eye. "Click," she said.

I smiled, feeling silly for getting emotional. The thing was, I wanted her to have that picture. I wanted to do whatever I had to, so that she could hold that beauty with her hands. So she could hold hope that one day we would find it.

That's when I decided to start painting.

I would paint that beauty for her. I would show her, create something that gave her the beauty she longed for, the beauty she wanted for me.

That night, when we went home, I stayed up for hours trying to draw that house. From memory, I'd close my eyes, remember, and then work. No special equipment, just a lead pencil and a piece of scrap paper, the motions becoming necessary for my survival.

Every detail of that house was in my brain, and I scratched, scribbled, and fingered that drawing for weeks, until I got every arch of that stone onto paper.

After hours of work, it wasn't perfect. But when I gave it to Mom, I knew I could add meaning to this world.

"Keith…" She clutched her chest, tears filling her eyes. Her lips quivered, her words coming out choked and messy. "Thank you…it's…" She pulled me to her, hugged me in a bear-tight clutch. "I love you, just don't ever forget that."

The next day, I found a sketch pad and drawing pencils under my pillow. Thanking her quietly, so Dad wouldn't hear, she seemed lighter, younger—hopeful.

I drew that house two thousand more times, until every inch was perfect. At school, I found colored pencils and started adding color into the mix. I would draw everything—people, places, animals—you name it. After a while, I started drawing emotions, and my teacher took notice. My teacher persuaded me to take a painting class that the school offered. That class opened my eyes to canvas, and I never looked back.

School went from worn-out clothing and barely there lunches, from being hungry and ashamed of it, from being teased and ridiculed as an underprivileged kid, to someplace I could go to escape. To a place where I could do incredible things with a paintbrush. Where art gave me the hope for better days.

The bathwater reaches my chin, startling me; I flick it off before it overflows.

Mom never came to find me, never called or contacted me. *I love you, just don't ever forget that.*

Has she forgiven me?

Holding my breath, I submerge myself under the water. Bubbles flutter from my nose and mouth, the warm water tightening my skin.

Ten seconds, then fifteen. I come up and wipe the droplets from my eyes.

How can my Mom not forgive me?

A noise breaks the still ripples of darkness to remind me of the dirty truth—the reason she can't forgive me. The front door opens, shuts. The rumble of Ella's car drifts in through the window.

Weak. Disgusting. Whore. I spoke to Mom the same way I just spoke to Ella, spitting pointed words with rage and poison.

Chapter 15

A burning angst lives in my gut, simmering in unending doubt and worry. A bee's nest has filled my lungs.

You are gentle, just like the sunset… That's all bullshit.

The truth is: I'm not essential. I'm replaceable.

How do you become essential to somebody? How do you become everything? Irreplaceable. To the left, to the left. Everything you own in the box to the left. Damn you, Beyoncé, I'm frigging replaceable.

I'm clearly not essential to Ella…and neither is Hope, for that matter.

Christina will be here any minute, and despite the sick feeling I'm carrying after our fight, and from those words I said to Ella, I am supposed to go back to work.

Looking at Hope is the only thing I can do to put some of the broken pieces back where they belong. Hope is clarity. She's the love that makes everything else fall to the side.

The way she looks up, so trustingly, while I'm feeding her, it fixes me. She stares directly into my eyes, stealing my heart. Her soft baby skin and little fingers and toes, the smell of her tender little baby cheeks, and the warmth in the tiny crook of her neck—all of it heals me. When I'm watching her, I can almost forget that Ella left this morning—went off to God knows where. She's not here; nevertheless, her presence is strong and demanding. Her scent is hidden in these walls, her essence forever entwined with this space.

She'll be back, and I'll apologize. I do know she's physically okay—the texts I've sent her say *read*.

"Hello?" Christina yells from somewhere downstairs.

"Christina, I'm upstairs in the nursery," I yell back, startling Hope. "Shh, it's okay," I say rocking her lightly.

Christina's footsteps clatter on the stairs. "Didn't I tell you to call me Mom already? Feels wrong when you call me Christina. You're the father of my granddaughter. Oh, by the way, I've decided I'm going to have Hope call me 'G.' Sounds young and hip, right? I plan on being a young, hip, and fun grandma."

"Okay…G," I say, trying it out.

"Let me see my little cutie. Aww, look at her. She's so stinking sweet." Without warning, she plucks her from my arms. That empty feeling hits me like a sledgehammer.

"She's already had a bottle, and I changed her diaper." I push myself up, move to pick up the room. "She's been up for over an hour, so she may want to nap soon."

Christina nods. "Where's Ella? I didn't see her car in the drive."

I take a breath, not sure how to proceed. "We had a fight."

She moves to sit in the rocking chair, crosses her legs. "It's been tough, I know that. Where'd she go?"

"I was hoping to your house. I said some…hurtful things."

She holds up a hand. "I don't need to hear the details. I'll text Paul, put him on the case. It's possible we just missed one another. I was out of the house early this morning to get my yoga in." She reaches for her phone, texting Paul. "Go drink some coffee and splash your face. You look like shit. Can't go back to the office looking wrecked."

I sigh. "I don't know, maybe I should wait a few more days to go back. We should work this out. It wasn't a normal fight. This was…big."

♊

Standing in front of the elevator doors in the lobby, Life at Your Reach, and its familiar energy, starts rooting in my stomach. My out-of-control hair, my un-ironed clothes, and this shirt that needs to be re-tucked is going to be hard to hide.

I almost push the button, then don't, turning to start back to the car. I should go to Paul and Christina's house. Paul confirmed Ella was there, curled up and sleeping in her old bed. Christina told me to go to work, to let the air settle for a few hours.

"Shit." I twist around, head back to the elevator, throwing my arms in the air.

"Screw it." I turn away again, sighing in exacerbation. I ball my fits, stopping myself, and punching my leg. Turning back, I stand there, physically unable to press the button. I fix my hair in the elevator reflection, try to flatten the wrinkles, and start laughing. "Screw it!"

Still looking at my reflection, a hand appears on my shoulder. It squeezes, and I freeze. "Keith?" The voice is rough and scratchy and sends a chill up my spin.

Sausage-Neck!

"Richard! Hello. Let me press the button for you. Sorry, I'm a few minutes late." I press the button and watch it turn red. "Sorry I've missed, sir. I apologize for my lack of commitment to work recently." The elevator doors growl open, and I watch his stark expression turn red as he enters. I hesitate, don't move to get into the elevator.

He notices my hesitation.

"Keith, get in the elevator," he says in a clear, demanding tone.

"Yes." I do as commanded. And, once I'm in, I'm in. No getting out now. The doors slide closed, and I feel the gentle lift of the elevator as it sails upward. It's so fast, I close my eyes and recenter through the nausea. Richard waits in utter silence, not saying anything, barely breathing. And…this behavior is odd for him. He's a loud man, generally an obnoxious man. Yet, right now, he's silent.

The doors glide open, and we both exit, mutely. We make our way through the lobby and head toward our desks. "Take an hour, then come see me in my office," he says.

"Okay," I say anxiously. My mind starts spinning, as a million reasons for a visit to his office take shape. I duck into the bathroom and splash water on my face.

I make my way through the office, finding small comfort in the fact that the day-to-day activities and faces appear to be the same. Pushing down my anxiety, and putting a brave face on, I wave as heads turn and watch.

At my desk, Ella's smiling face beams down from the cubicle walls. It's like a form of torture in the shape of paper. Rather than having paper cuts, I have a minor meltdown, pulling them down and stuffing them into the drawer.

My attention shifts to the left of the keyboard. Coffee, fresh fruit, and a brown bag, rolled at the top. The renewed scent of the coffee radiates, my eyes closing when the aroma hits my nose. A pink gift bag with pink tissue paper sits next to it. Adjacent to the bag is a pink Post-it note. *Higs, welcome back. I have a feeling you skipped breakfast. — Jenny*

Her writing is pretty, curly and cursive. I poke my head over the divider, but her chair is empty. Reading the note again, I notice a small arrow on the bottom right, and flip it over.

P.S. This paper is rose-scented. Take a whiff.

I do. Pulling the tissue paper from the gift bag, I reach inside. It's a mirror that hooks to the headrest in the backseat of the car, so Hope can see herself, and you can check up on her from the front.

When I go to slide it back into the bag, my eye catches something else. It's a little stuffed panda with buggy eyes.

I write a note back.

Thanks so much. I appreciate how kind you have been to me, and Sasha…

And then I draw a smiley face and a three-dimensional cube, because the paper looked too plain. I place it on her keyboard and notice Sasha isn't on her desk. It's not on mine either. Maybe it's already dead? Of course, it is.

I open the bag and pull out a whole-wheat bagel with jam on the side. Also in the bag is a fun-sized pack of peanut M&M's. Because she's right, and I haven't eaten, I spread the jam and take a bite. The bagel is fresh and delicious. I shove it down and follow it with the coffee.

Some while later, I hear Jenny typing on her computer. I stand up and peek over the wall. "Thanks for breakfast."

"Higs! Yes, hello. You're welcome." She smiles. Her hair is longer, reflecting just how long I've been gone. She's wearing a fitted pantsuit, gray and striped—her makeup dark.

"It was great. Thank you."

"Good. I didn't know what you would like. Or if you prefer cream cheese or jam? See, I don't like cream cheese, but I know most people do. I went with the strawberry jam; that's my favorite," she explains.

"Good choice."

"So, how have you been?" she asks cautiously, her face seeming to soften.

"Well, that depends. Do you mean figuratively?"

"I think I mean literally?" She raises an eyebrow. "Both?"

"Life sucks and then you die," I mutter playfully. "I had a teacher who always said that. Turns out she's right."

"That's awful," Jenny says. "But, true. I'm so sorry. Good listener," she says pointing to herself.

"How are you?"

"Honestly, terrible. I haven't slept in days. I'm having nightmares..." she says, sliding back into her chair. "I've been having these awful dreams about baby orcas being abducted from their parents. They make these haunted screams."

My face must register confusion, she presses on.

"I watched this documentary the other night on Animal Planet about killer whales, and it's dreadful how some people treat them."

Right, kangaroo births. "People are horrible," I tell her, lightly chuckling.

She squishes her face together. "People are trolls. We stroll into their territory, into their homes, and then pluck them out of the water like we have the right? It's wrong."

"Trolls? Maybe you should make t-shirts. You sound passionate about this," I tease.

"That's a great idea, Higs! I'd wear one."

"Me too."

She smiles. "What should the shirts say?"

I think about it for a second, but nothing good comes. I try anyway. "Hi, I'm Keith, and I say 'NO' to whale abductions."

"Ha!" She laughs and covers her mouth, looking around. "You would put all of that on a t-shirt? Don't you work in advertising?"

"I'm a little out of practice. Plus, I think it sends a clear message. The whales would appreciate it."

"Absolutely," she drawls, shaking her head. She giggles again. "In all seriousness, I do feel bad for them. Who are we to take precious animals away from their mothers? We force them to live in an oversized bathtub, and then poke and prod them until they do what we want. It's cruel."

"You're right, people suck. United in our hate for people," I say, holding my hand out to give her a high five.

She smiles and gives me a quick pat. "To be completely honest, it's not the whales keeping me up. There's this rascal of a raccoon getting into my crawl space, and I'm terrified it'll get into my bedroom. I've notified my landlord a hundred times at this point, but now I'm thinking I need my own trap."

My smile falters.

She notices, her face looking concerned.

"Raccoon?" I ask.

"It's a cute little fat thing, but I'd prefer it stop breaking into my personal space."

I close my eyes because…why? More raccoons? Of course.

Dr. Ryder said it's just me noticing what's always been there, but it all feels targeted; it all feels purposeful. It all feels like the universe is fucking with me.

Raccoons really are thieves, and this morning I stole something. The way I spoke to Ella…I stole her trust for me. Snatched it back with my raccoon paws and broke it over my knee.

Chapter 16

Richard's metallic office is noticeably cooler, the smooth silvery surfaces shining like ice. The hairs on my neck stand on entry, the bleak gray of winter oozing in through his floor-to-ceiling windows.

His attention shifts, and I move deeper into his den, heart hammering in my chest. "Sorry to interrupt, but you asked me to stop by, and I didn't want to keep you waiting," I say, rambling. "I have seven possible leads, four of them seem legitimate, and we've contracted prior business in the past. I've reached out and set up calls to discuss initial tactics and will set up face-to-face meetings when it seems likely to move a strategy forward."

He nods, despite the cold air, and sweat pebbles the crown of his head.

"I plan on working very hard to catch up. I know I'm behind, but that won't be the case for long. I'm prepared to work as many hours as needed..."

As if on cue, my phone starts vibrating to contradict me. I fumble to find it in my pants pocket, cursing myself for not shutting vibration off. "Sorry. So sorry."

"Keith," he interrupts. "I fully understand your commitment to work, and I'm not worried about you falling behind. You've delivered solid content working remotely."

"Oh…" I can't help it, a small gasp escapes my mouth.

I don't know how to arrange my face. This surely is not the same Richard I know. The man I know would never compliment me. The man I know has always blocked me from moving to the design department.

"If needed, I'm comfortable extending your time. If you feel it's still essential, I'm okay with you working from home."

Since when is Richard an understanding boss? I shift my eyes to the window, confused. He had threatened to move my desk to the mailroom the morning Hope was born, the morning Faith was stolen.

I go to respond, but my cell phone buzzes again, the vibration shaking the air and seeming to make the decision for me.

My eyes slide to his. I force myself to not look away. He fidgets under my gaze, like being this nice makes him uncomfortable too. For a second, a part of me misses the mean Richard. At least I knew what to expect. I'm completely lost here. Responding to a nice Richard is harder than responding to a mean Richard.

"Seems like you should answer that," he says.

"I'm sorry," I mutter again, pulling out the phone to silence it. I see the display screen, notice that it says Christina, and my mind goes directly to Hope.

"You're dismissed," Richard says.

I nod, shimmying backward and out of the office. I miss the call, and when I hit redial, her number is busy. My stomach flips, my mind slipping to the worst-case scenario.

Something happened to Hope, something hurt my baby, and this something stole her from me too.

I call again. This time Christina's voice answers in a panic. "Keith… Keith, can you hear me? I was wrong, I was wrong, Keith. You should have gone to her, you should have gone and patched things up with Ella this morning. I'm stupid, so stupid. She's gone, Keith. She's gone!"

There's a split second of relief. My baby is fine, Hope is okay. But then the guilt washes in because Ella is gone. She's gone.

"What do you mean by gone?"

Chapter 17

The warm air of the hospital suffocates me, sucks the air from my lungs and makes me crave the way the wind whipped and called from outside. There's a knock at the door; it's slow and soft at first, then harder and more prominent, like whoever it is fears the noise will be carried away.

"Come in," I say.

"Hello," says Dr. Ethan. He's noticeably more put together than the last time I saw him. His white jacket pressed, and his hair cut short and combed close.

"Hi," I say back. "Thanks for agreeing to see me."

He nods, semi-confusion pooling at his mouth. "What can I do you for?"

I take a breath, try to think of how to word what I need to ask. "Ella's gone," I explain, blunt. "She left a note for her parents that said she was going to see her friend Tonya in California."

"Okay," he mutters, his eyebrows colliding together. "What does this have to do with me?"

Sighing, I fight the burning desire to ask him if he had sex with Ella. I know she only said those hurtful things to punish me, but I also know something happened. I know there was something that needed to be discussed between these two.

Eventually, he breaks the silence. "You're still curious about the text?"

I nod. "It's stupid. It makes me mad at myself that I can't trust her, but I know something happened between the two of you."

He looks uncomfortable. "Keith," he says. "I'm sorry, but, like I said before, nothing physical happened, okay? There was nothing, just some words. Just something she felt comfortable admitting to me, but this is crossing a line. This whole situation has crossed a line."

"My dad was an alcoholic. The bad kind," I say, cringing. "So bad that I can't trust myself," I explain, shivering.

Frank is alive. He is somewhere out there, hurting someone else. Breaking some other innocent soul, and I still can't escape. "I can't be him. I can't become that man, and not knowing the truth is making me doubt everything I've built for myself."

Ethan sighs, crossing his arms. He moves for the window, draws a circle on the fogged glass. "I sympathize with you, I do, but this is not something I could ever say for another person. This is Ella's story to tell."

His words spark the burner, a low flame ignites in my gut. "She's told me plenty, but it's not aligning with your story. For all I know, you were the best she ever had. You screwed her good and proper."

The vulgarity of those words feels like a violation of a safe space, feels violent.

"What?" He pivots on his heels, chest heaving, annoyance turning to anger with a snap.

"Yeah, according to Ella, you were, and I quote, 'good and proper.' That's not true?" I ask, knowing in my gut that it's not, but feeling like this is the only way to get him to admit something. To speak an ounce of Ella's truth for her.

He shakes his head. "She said that?" His chest is rising and falling so fast.

"Yes," I say. "Tell me it's not true."

"It's not. That's not true. Not that it's any of your business, but…I have…a partner," he declares. "I've never laid a hand on her. I can't believe I'm even explaining myself." His hand moves to his head; his fingers drag through his combed chocolate hair, messing it up.

Ella had said he was gay. If…if Ethan is gay, and he didn't sleep with Ella, then what happened?

Words were shared. I get that, but I just want to know.

"I'm sorry." I sigh. "This is nuts, I know. I need to know the truth. I feel like you're the one holding the answers to all of my questions."

His eyes crease at the corners, sparkle defiantly. "You're wrong," he says. "Ella has your answers. Ella, not me. The two of you are a mess."

He crosses the room and exits, closing the door behind him, like the period in his statement. He's right, of course, I know this. As we get older—Ella and I—we grow apart. As I grow into me, into myself, it's like a pit is expanding between us. To grow into me, it means I have to accept the mounting space between us. We've been lonely, yet never alone, suffocating under all of the syntactic layers of who we are supposed to be, instead of what we are. She took her trust for me back long before this morning.

We both have stolen from ourselves.

Chapter 18

Ella's image rises with the sun, yet holds stubborn to the moon, the presence of her memory sets pain to flame. Day, night, and every in between: she's here—but gone—haunting. Her silence is a sword overhead, her striking features chiseled like stone into the canvas of my mind.

She's here, in this house—yet gone.

She hasn't responded. There has been no text or call declaring she's made a mistake and wants to come home. No signs that any of my "I'm sorry, Ella!" messages have put a crack in her hate for me. Tonya called Christina to let her know that Ella made it to Long Beach safely, but she's avoiding the discomfort of her absence. Christina keeps softening the truth: *She's fine, it's all fine! Soaking up that SoCal sun is good for her soul*, she says.

Ella's lack of words has stripped me bare, silence carving rigid streams, burning in twisting rivers down my face. The questions, so many questions, remain.

Relationships take sacrifice, they take communication and compromise. They take maturity. They take a little hope and a whole lot of faith. They take two people willing to drop everything right then and there to run to each other in the middle of the pouring rain. Even if it's the kind of pouring rain that everyone else is running away from, you're supposed to grit your teeth and run face-first into it.

But…she doesn't want me to follow her. What's more heroic? Going anyway or respecting her request for space? Maybe space is what we both need. Space to heal and think, because Ethan's right: we're a mess.

The garage door rumbles to a close, exhaust meeting the crisp winter air in bellowing clouds as I back from the driveway. I ignore the raccoon, pay no attention to its criminal whiskers, because, of course, one is there. Of course, he's waiting to remind me that I'm a thief.

Gone, Ella's gone, yet still in that house. Sometimes God makes it so hard to put our souls in his hands. Sometimes he makes it so easy to blame him. I'm tired of learning the lessons. I'm trying to put the puzzle of Ella together, to study the details of her pieces closer. I blew it when I accused her of betraying me. That accusation hit her like a slap in the face. All I know is, she shared a piece of herself with Ethan, and perhaps it's a piece I'm not meant to know.

I enter the highway, pull to the right lane as the car putters for speed.

She trusted him with something she couldn't trust with me, and I can see why. She's right: I am self-absorbed. Frank's voice lives in my head. Most days, I'm reliving the chaos he brought into this world. His voice slithers from neuron to neuron, lighting my insides like a steady stream of gasoline.

"Well, kid, are you just gonna let 'im talk to you like that?"

Scott. Scott had said awful things, and Frank had heard. A man would do something, a man would fight back. "Pound 'im in his teeth, Keith. Go on, be a man," he told me.

"It's okay," I said.

Frank stood, agitated. "Scott come over here." He motioned for him. Scott moved slowly, obeying. "Now, Keith, take your hand like this," he demonstrated, "and pound your fist into his teeth. That'll teach him to talk to you like that again."

"It's okay, really. I don't want to."

His lip trembled. "Fucking do it, and do it now!" He put his hand on his belt, threatening a much worse punishment if disobeyed.

Scott looked at me, waiting, telling me with his eyes it was okay. I went closer, balling my hand into a fist like Frank had shown me, a pounding fury shaking my insides.

Scott's face up close was handsome, the build and structure strong, his jaw set rigid in determination. I raised my hand in front of his mouth, hesitating.

"Hit 'im. Hit 'im hard, and hit 'im now," Frank commanded me.

I squeezed my eyes shut. I didn't want to. I didn't want to hit him. I didn't care about the awful names he called me; I forgave him. But Frank was there, breathing, panting, and growling behind me. He was in my ear, tormenting me to hit him. Taunting and teasing me into this vortex of emotion and angst that I couldn't escape.

And I knew…I knew that, if I didn't hit him, Frank would. If not me, then Frank's fists or belt would violate Scott's body and then mine.

I wound back.

"Do it!" Frank hissed, and I did.

My fist came back, then rocketed forward, crashing into Scott's closed mouth with a ferocity meant for Frank. I felt a pinch where my flesh met his teeth, and a small bout of pain tickled up my arm.

Scott rubbed his teeth, a small cut on his lip starting to drip with blood.

Frank cackled gleefully in his husky drunkenness. "*That-a-boy.*"

Daddy was proud.

Scott licked embarrassingly at the blood on his lip, rolled his hurt eyes at Dad, and without thought, I spoke words I shouldn't have. "I'm sorry," I muttered.

Frank's hand was on the back of my neck instantaneously, his rough grip squeezing and forcing me to my knees. "Sorry? Sorry! Why the hell would you be sorry? Scott needed a lesson, and you gave it to him. Don't be such a goddamn pussy."

"Sorry, sir."

He smacked the back of my head, then moved around me. He cupped his hand at the base of my chin, squeezing his fingers into my cheeks. "Goddammit!" he bellowed. He shook my face. "Do you understand English? Stop saying you're fucking sorry! Stop being such a weak son of a bitch!"

I nodded, fighting the urge to apologize again. Fighting the urge to speak back.

Later, Mom came and found me, hugged me, whispered, "Life is greater than despair, it's stronger than him. One man's mask should never become your own."

She couldn't protect me physically, yet her words were protection. Her words preserved the fundamental structure of my humanity. *Daddy was proud…* Maybe she'd done more to protect me than I'll ever know? She didn't want me to wear Frank's mask—yet here I am, every day, retreating to the inside of my head to replay his cruelty. Fastening on my disguise to tell the world I am fine—everything is okay.

I pull into the parking garage; claim the same old spot I always do.

Protection. Maybe I need to do more to protect Ella? Maybe that's the lesson in all of this?

Climbing into the elevator, I silently put Mom and Dad into the vault I've built in my head, and file them away for the quiet. With the ding, I exit the elevator, trying to paint on a smile. Before I make it to my desk, I see Jenny—standing, smiling, and talking with Barb from HR. As I work my way closer, she calls out, "Morning, Higs!"

"Morning."

"I have to tell you all about the documentary I watched last night— intense! Remind me later, okay?"

"Okay," I say, forcing a chuckle. I mentally prepare myself for raccoons—it's going to be about raccoons.

Jenny doesn't sit. I see the top of her head still poking over the top as she mutters in conversation with Barb.

I've been thinking about what Richard implied, that he'd be okay with me working from home longer, if needed. Hope's my only hope right now. I should consider it.

Stifling a yawn, my eyes burn with tears. The first email I read forces the idea of working from home away. It's from Richard, addressed to both Jenny and I, about a hot new lead he needs to meet with us on.

"Higs?" Jenny says, her green eyes peeking over the divider. Her hair is pulled into a bun, messy, yet purposeful. "What's good?"

My yawn fully escapes now. "Morning."

"Parent life, huh?" asks Jenny, smiling at my yawn. She rests her satin-covered sleeves on the divider. "I won't tell Richard if you want to close your eyes and catch a few Zs." Her grin is defiant, her eyes shifting in the direction of his office.

"I swear, it's some sort of cosmic karma. She's always sleeping, just never when it's time for *me* to sleep." Hope's tiny face comes to mind, and it steals my sadness. "When she actually *does* sleep, I end up just staring at her face. She's perfect—angelic and still—like, if I don't hold on to her, she'll grow wings and fly away."

"Baby cheeks," she says, creasing her eyebrows together. "Out of this world!"

Hope already has a growing range of emotions, her little face working to express them, the baby chub of her cheeks seeming to roll over her jaw. The pudgy little hands and legs constantly moving. Her smell, the way she snuggles on my shoulder, the genuine trust her eyes give to me…it's all turning me into a dad.

In the mirror, I may see Frank. But, in her eyes, I see only my reflection.

When I hold her, I feel her trust. I feel her comfort. She knows I would never let her down. She knows I would never let her fall, that I would never stop loving her. Something about having someone's full trust helps the absence of Ella sting less. Knowing Hope's mine, knowing, no matter what, that I will love her forever, it restores a piece of faith I was ready to let die.

"What's this new project Richard is putting us on?" I ask.

Jenny shrugs. "I'm not sure; he hasn't stopped by. But exciting, right? We get a project together." She looks to the window, thinking. "You like the color brown?" she asks, confusing me.

"I mean, I don't hate it."

Her face pinches together.

"What's wrong with brown?" I ask.

"It's just such a dead, uninspiring color. Look outside." She points a finger to the window.

I turn, looking past the half-open, dull vinyl shades, and seeing nothing but the gray of winter. Cars move on the highway, and my eyes travel with them to the brown patches of dirt poking through the snow off the shoulder.

"Winter makes me hate brown," she says.

"I get that," I say.

"I miss the blue, the baby blue of the summer sky."

I nod. "Do you get seasonal sadness?"

"No, not really." She shakes her head, her face lighting. "I'm being dramatic. It's just the lack of color in Boston over these winter months is discouraging."

"I've been wanting to paint for that very reason. It gives me the chance to look past the gray."

She shifts, seeming to stand taller, her eyes widening. "You paint?"

"I mean, I try. I enjoy it, but I'm not very good."

"I want to see something! What do you paint?"

"Mostly landscapes, sometimes portraits."

Her eyes sparkle. "Like naked people?"

I laugh. "No. I've never actually painted a naked person."

"Do you paint your wife?"

I crease my eyebrows.

She laughs. "I didn't mean naked, I just meant in the general sense."

"Oddly enough, no. No, I've never painted her. I've been wanting to paint Hope but haven't."

"Then who?"

I bite my cheek. "My mom." An uneasiness builds in my shoulders.

"That's sweet. A momma's boy. Oh! The documentary," she says, reminding me that I forgot to remind her.

I exhale, try to let go off the tension that was building. "It was about raccoons, right? You watched a documentary about raccoons?"

Her face looks confused, falls for a second. My stomach lurches, readying to hear all about the damn coons, but then she laughs. "No! Not about raccoons, although I'm still waiting on my landlord to catch that critter. I switched to the Discovery Channel. Demons! Ghosts!" she says. "The dead are definitely up to something when they depart."

"I don't think I want to know."

"This couple bought a new house, and the chain on the attic door used to swing all by itself," she says, explaining anyway. "Whenever they'd walk by, it'd just be swinging, like something touched it. They were afraid to go up. Always afraid they had a ghost living there. One day, they hear a girl singing, right, and it's coming from there." Her eyes are huge. "Now, picture this grown man with a baseball bat in one hand and a kitchen knife in the other, sneaking up into his attic, ready to pounce on some demon-chick."

"Oh god, did he accidentally kill someone?"

"No, but the singing got louder when he swung the door down. He followed the noise, and eventually, all he found was a radio that was switched on in the far corner."

"Someone was messing with him?"

"No. It was only the man and his wife living there, and she was at the foot of the ladder asking for updates. But I haven't told you the scariest part...he checked the radio. It had no batteries and no cord to even plug in!"

"Shut up!"

"Higs…" she says, and her face ripples with mischief. "I was ready to call my little mask-wearing friend down from his hiding place to cuddle me. I was so freaked out!" she teases, laughter in her voice.

It takes me a second to understand who she means. "Mask-wearing friend?" Then, that fast, there's a flop, heat surges to my face, a tortured uneasiness written into the lines. Raccoons. The memory starts to sharpen and take shape in my mind—significance. It feels like a million shining stars aligning, pointing me to the answer. To the answer I must have always really known: raccoons wear masks.

"But raccoons are thieves," I say out loud, but it's for me. It's to convince me.

Jenny looks confused, her face crumbling. "No," she says. "I don't think they're thieves. Misunderstood? Yes. People think they are bandits because they wear permanent masks, but they aren't like people. Raccoons are *meant* to wear masks, but people, Keith, people are meant to take their masks off."

I close my eyes. "*One man's mask should never become your own,*" Mom had said.

She was talking about the mask that everyone tied to Frank was forced to wear. He manipulated the things around him, made their insides twist until they couldn't align anymore. I said it myself, when I look into the mirror, I don't recognize the man looking back, because of the mask. It defines me.

I shiver. Raccoons wear masks, but people are lucky. People were meant to take their masks off—but I *am* wearing a mask.

And I've been wearing this mask for years, hiding from the light, because that's how you avoid pain. You ignore the truth. You step to the side and hide in the darkness of night. You only face the daylight with the mask, because the mask feels like protection. The mask lets you lie, lets you say, *I'm fine, everything is okay,* despite your world being on fire.

I suddenly can't breathe. The mask tied around my face is so tight; it's blocking my air, and I want to rip it off. I *need* to. I need to rip it off, untie it, and breathe as me.

"Everything okay?" Jenny asks.

How? Where does the mask end, and where do I begin?

Chapter 19

My computer dings. The fifteen-minute reminder for the upcoming project meeting Richard scheduled splashes on the screen. Rolling my neck, I dismiss the notice and start running through my open accounts. I'll probably have to give a brief project update in today's meeting, and I'm always a mumbling idiot unless rehearsed.

Jenny gets up, undocking her laptop. "Want to head over?"

"No," I say. "Need five to prep. I'll meet you there."

She nods, leaving her cubicle, no doubt wondering why I've gone quiet after our earlier discussion, but I can't go there now. I push it until the last second, then make my way to the conference room. Jenny's face smiles a hello; I fall in next to her.

"Higgins," she says.

"No Richard yet?" I ask.

Richard bustles in, as if on cue, looking messy and short-fused. He goes into an overview of our month sales report, our profits, and our objectives before even sitting.

I find my mind wandering, and snap awake when I hear Jenny's voice. She's sharing her project work and discussing ideas for future developments. She speaks so confidently, and I get a twist of nerves when I realize that, after she talks, it's my turn. I list off the bullet points in my head so that I'll be able to get it all out smoothly.

"Excellent, Jennifer. Keith, what's the update with BioBags?"

I shoot off into my explanation about BioBags, and all of my other projects and leads.

He stops me by raising a hand. "I have a hard stop at the half-hour mark, and I want to get you all the details on this new project."

I nod, staying quiet.

"I was recently contacted by Evangeline Iris Reborn. It's a clothing line, made fully out of sustainable resources. The company is relatively new, but growing substantially, thanks to the brand owner and her large social media following. She's the latest influencer with a multi-million-dollar-company, praise Jesus."

Jenny and I chuckle.

"They're only domestic at the moment," he continues, "but she's looking to expand into the global market. The brand is querying agencies to pick their brains, and I want our name associated as quickly as possible."

Jenny leans forward, her face excited. "I follow Evangeline. I've been wanting to get my hands on her romper for some time!"

Richard nods, and I try not to let my face show that, once again, I'm out of the loop. I have never heard of her.

"I want the both of you to work together on a variety of proposals—entry gate to fully stacked. And then meet with her team to present the options."

"Did they mention any dates yet?" I ask.

"That's the catch," Richard says. "They aren't local to Boston, and I prefer you make the presentation in person, before next Friday. I'd want you to develop the presentations together, and then Jenny could do the traveling." He looks at me, preparing for push back.

He's already mentioned I can take more time. He's already made it clear I don't need to rush back in, and now he's giving me an out from traveling. His kindness puts my nerves on edge. "Where's she located?"

"I heard a whisper that she'll be on a ski trip, staying just outside of Ann Arbor, at Mt. Brighton."

"Where's that?" Jenny asks.

No matter how many times I get back up, another wave tries to knock me over. My emotions are waves, cresting and breaking, shifting before the opportunity to settle allows. My head's roaring, spinning. The sound of a slamming door whooshes in my head. I know where Ann Arbor is; I know exactly where it is.

"Michigan. Just outside of…outside of Detroit."

They both look at me, try to figure out why my voice sounds so shaky. My mask was tied into place there. That's where Mom is. Dad too.

I picture all of my raccoon friends. Maybe I need…I need to amend my mistakes, confront what I abandoned, or else I'll be stuck living in the past. I need to start with Mom. I need to fix it, in order to fix myself. In order to trust myself, I need to go to her and fix what I helped break. I need to start with the first knot on my mask, in order to untie the rest. Only then can I truly support Ella. Only after adjusting my own oxygen mask can I offer to help with hers.

And Hope. Loving Hope requires I pick the scabs and continue to bleed. Frank is the world, and the world is cruel, but you can't hide from that.

I need to return, to go back to the place I deserted all those years ago. To evolve, and to stop remaining.

"I'm going with Jenny," I declare.

Richard nods.

Fate. Faith. Faith is dead. Hope. Hope's alive.

Chapter 20

The warm, sudsy bathwater pools in the fiberglass tub, eases the anxiety from my limbs. Hope splashes around, slippery from the water and bubbles. We got in together—me, underwear-clad—out of fear she'd fall beneath the surface.

"Daddy missed you today." I wash Hope with the terrycloth washcloth, the sweet smell of the foaming bubbles dispersed by the spill of the faucet.

She looks at me like she understands.

"Oh, you missed me too?" I lather her hair.

Earlier today, Richard told us that, because the Evangeline Iris brand never flies unless the plane purchases the carbon offset, that we would be driving the 806 miles from Boston to Ann Arbor. He doesn't want any risk of the company not choosing Life at Your Reach, so he's sending us in an electric car, which translates into frequent recharging stops.

"I'm pumped for this trip, Higs!" Jenny had said.

I only smiled, unsure how I was going to be able to sneak in a side trip to Detroit to find Mom. I don't even know where to begin preparing for that.

Now, I sigh, cleaning out the gunk stuck in Hope's baby-chub layers. She wiggles in protest. I lift her up, giving her raspberries on her belly. She giggles.

"Wow!"

She giggles again. It's her first real chuckle, and it sounds so sweet. It's so tender and unspoiled, that I laugh back.

"Your laugh is perfect." I tickle her belly again, watch the way her eyes sparkle.

She squeals.

"That tickles, huh?"

She goes back to focusing on the water, sticking her chubby fist in and out. "I know I have a lot to learn about being a dad, but…I'm trying."

She stares at me, silent and still. Just looking, thinking without sound, taking me in with a seriousness that's beyond her undeveloped age.

Her serious eyes stay on me.

I rinse her peach-fuzz hair, rubbing and washing gently around her soft spot. She's not bald, but she doesn't have much hair left. Her once-full head of chocolate has thinned, replaced, instead by the dark raven hair of her mother. An equally dark complexion and serious eyes make her the shrunk-down, baby-size version of Ella.

Ella. Still no word from Ella. Christina said Paul spoke with her, briefly, and apparently, she sounded lighter already. Suggested that she just needs time. I guess Hope and I are a heavy load for her, if a few days away is all she needed to feel lighter.

Hope wiggles in my grip. I flip the water off, instantly missing the hot water mixing with the lukewarm suds. *Ella.*

"I don't know what to do about Mommy," I say to Hope, breathing out of my mouth heavily. "I don't think dads are supposed to say this, but I will. I'm scared. I'm scared she'll never come home. I'm scared you'll have to grow up without a mom, and that you'll blame me for it."

She looks at me, putting her foot in and out of the water.

Then she farts.

"Hey, you just farted on me, little stinker!" I laugh. "Daddy's sorry. I'll make a promise: I'll never admit I'm scared in front of you again. Okay?"

She giggles.

"You've mastered the art of laughing."

As I'm reaching to pull the plug of the bath, my entire leg vibrates. I jump, startling us both, looking around anxiously, like maybe a bomb had gone off somewhere in the house. "What the…"

I feel this warm sensation spreading down. A new smell hits my nose. A bomb, indeed.

Shit runs down the front of me, oozes out into the bath, surrounding us like oil in a puddle. The water goes murky, the smell changing from pleasant to earthy.

I stand, raising Hope above the mess. "Oh!" I gag unintentionally. I manage to pull the plug of the bath with my toe.

Shit runs down my torso, clings to my underwear. Hope gives me this slightly guilty, yet relieved, look. I'm completely covered from the belly down in a honey mustard, sandy-textured, baby poo. Clumps of it have twisted in my leg hair. My bellybutton is nonexistent, packed full. I look down, trying not to notice the ring of shit circling my feet.

"Oh…" gag "my…" gag "goodness…" gag.

How does it smell so bad? How does a baby, who only eats formula, shit this much? How am I going to get out of here without getting crap all over the bathroom?

The water completely drains, but the bottom of the tub is still speckled with shit particles. I start to laugh, then I get another whiff and have to stop.

I turn the water back on and start shuffling it around with my feet. The shit mixes with the water, making the bottom of the tub look like the start of chicken noodle soup. I gag again.

I test the water and wash her butt off, then I reach for a towel and lay her on the ground. She starts crying, immediately, like she's offended I'm putting her down.

I stand, rushing to clean myself. When I do, I lose my footing, and slip on shit. It's not graceful. I fall hard, smacking my back into the fiberglass tub. Poop fills my ass-crack, and I gag again.

Hope lets out a high-pitched wail. I sit up and try to quiet her. It doesn't work, the smell now volatile. I start the shower with the howls and yowls of Hope in the background. Pulling the curtain closed, trying to wash quickly, I keep pumping as much body wash into my hand as possible, stripping my underwear off and leaving them balled up on the shower floor.

After about a minute, when I'm content that there's absolutely not a speck on me, I turn the water off, opening the curtain in a frenzy to quiet Hope. As I do, a figure comes rushing into the hallway, lurks in the doorway.

It's a man. I scream, naked, and scared that a stranger chooses this moment to rob my home.

The man screams, startled too. "Is everything okay in here?" he shouts, making Hope yell impossibly louder.

"Ethan?" I holler, confused. I remember I'm naked and cover myself with my hands. "Why are you in here?"

His face looks alarmed. "I was at the door, and it sounded like someone was dying!"

"So, you aren't robbing me?"

He semi-chuckles. "No!"

I motion with my head for a towel. He throws me one, and I wrap it around myself. I reach down, wrapping Hope in her frog towel, and try to quiet her down.

"There's something on your face. Right near the corner of your mouth." He motions with his thumb.

I use the back of my hand and wipe across my face. Crap smears across my hand and onto my lips. "Take her! Take her! Take her!" I yell.

I shouldn't talk. Jesus, I should *not* speak. I feel it in my mouth. "Ah…" I start screaming with my mouth open.

He steps in, taking Hope, and I close the curtain. I ditch the towel and flip the shower back on, not worried about the temperature. I flick it to hot and start scrubbing the shit off of my face. Somewhere, in the background of me dangerously drowning myself, I hear Hope still crying.

I wash quickly, turn the water off, and dry off swiftly. "Here! Here, I'll take her," I say to Ethan.

"It's okay. You can go get dressed if you want," he offers generously, his big man-hands cradling her gently. He looks so natural.

"It's okay."

He shrugs, handing her over.

Hope doesn't stop crying, even after she's dressed. I rock, I coo, I try a bottle, I try a pacifier. Nothing works. She screams and cries, and no amount of bouncing stops her.

SD

As I come down the last few steps, I see Ethan waiting. He's still wearing his coat and shoes, as he stares awkwardly from the front door. "Sorry, I thought she'd never go down," I say.

"I apologize for letting myself in," he says.

"Yeah, I thought *I* was the one crossing the line?" I smile to let him know I'm kidding.

"Touché." He chuckles. "So, is that a normal nightly occurrence? I don't see them much past the newborn stage."

"Some nights are easier than others. We were in the bath, and Hope dropped a bomb on me. It was crazy. I'm talking about shit everywhere. Oh, which reminds me, I left my dirty underwear in the shower."

He cracks up. "Gross. You're telling me that was *poop* on your mouth? That's fantastic!"

I fake scowl.

"She may have a gastrointestinal issue. That cry wasn't the normal I-need-attention cry. She sounded like she was in pain."

"Really?"

"Yeah, she seems colicky. You may want to change her formula."

I nod, crossing my arms and studying his face. "Why are you here?

His face gets serious, uncomfortable, but he forces out the words. "I spoke with Ella."

For a second, I'm angry—she trusted him before me again?—but then confusion sweeps in. She seemed equally upset with Ethan, her trust for him fading into raw hatred. To her, he killed Faith.

"She called you?" I ask, my throat scratchy.

Ethan nods.

Chapter 21

I t's like finishing a really good book but hating the ending. Or maybe even like finishing a really good book but loving the ending. Sometimes they leave the same feeling: unhappiness, discontent. Longing: this powerful and emotional urge for more than what was given. The belief that you cannot move forward unless you know every last detail about the characters and how their lives turned out.

Some stories end, and I accept that. But certain stories, they can't end. They ignite a flame inside that can't be put out with the final pages. And sometimes it'd be a crime to say it's over.

I think Ella feels our story is over, and that, if we were a book, the chapter of us has come to an end.

"I can't believe I'm even here, that I am even getting involved, but her voice…" Ethan shakes his head, his eyes seeming to cloud.

"Broken?" I ask.

"Pleading. Vulnerable," he says.

I want to rewrite the ending to our story. Try to extend it, try to fix it, and try to change something about it so that it doesn't end with me and my heart on the floor, but I feel Ethan bracing, readying himself to end another man's marriage.

I steady myself. Square my shoulders. "What did she say?" I ask.

He breathes out, resigned. "When Ella was pregnant with the twins, she would come into the office looking like a person who was hurting but trying not to show it."

My heart hurts, but my head wants to argue. She seemed fine to me...*was* fine. I was the unsteady one: always pulling at the seams of myself, trying to find the answers. Trying to not only convince her I was worthy, but also me.

"She was one of the first patients I had after moving from Florida, and I feel like we connected instantly. I had opened up about why I became an obstetrician. Told her my story."

He turns, putting his back to me, keeping his face hidden.

"And she related?" I ask, fearing my voice may stop him from explaining.

"Well…" he mutters, clearing his throat, "to pieces, yes. It was more about the heaviness of the secret we shared that bonded us."

"Secret?"

"I told her about my mother, how she was a free spirit, that my grandparents just about smothered her. Which backfired, because then she went wild, fell in with the wrong crowd and got pushed into drugs, mostly pills. She met a not-so-nice man, who she let do not-so-nice things to her. She got pregnant. Only, she didn't know she was pregnant. For months, she took pills, did other harder drugs, and got beat around like a battered housewife," he says. His voice shifts just a fraction on the last sentence. Everything else was clear and concise, almost practiced or rehearsed.

He's silent. I clear my throat. "The baby, it was you?"

"Yeah, it was me," he says. "She was already five months pregnant when she finally took a test." A moment passes in silence. "Five months of poisoning that baby in her belly. Poisoning me," he says.

My confusion grows, questions build on the edge of my lips. What does any of this have to do with Ella? How could she relate to this?

"I spent the first few months of my life going through heroin withdrawal. Then the first few years of my life having seizures. The entirety of my life living with a mother who cried and apologized for her mistakes. I tried so hard, for her. So that she knew I didn't blame her," he says.

A hush covers the room, and I think he's done, until he speaks again. "I had to work twice as hard as any other kid. I had to put in double the work. I had to go through hours, days, years of tutoring and summer school and therapy just to keep up. Just to stay on the same track as everyone else."

"I'm sorry for that," I say. "That is heavy."

"I was also—" he pauses, "—gay. I was a gay, underdeveloped kid, who was so afraid to admit that. I was afraid to say it out loud for so long, to confess to all the bullies that, yeah, maybe something really is the matter with me." He finally turns, stares at me. "As a homosexual, you fight yourself for years. You fight the message that gets delivered, on every outlet, that you are wrong, dirty…evil."

His eyes are scary, I see his struggle.

"Ella…" he says.

My stomach lurches, her name making my anxiety spike.

"Ella doesn't know how to accept the fact that these are the cards she was dealt. She can't relax. She can't stop searching for a way to change what can't be changed."

He takes a minute to breathe, and I interrupt. "That Faith is dead?"

He nods and looks at me understandingly. "Partly." His voice is small, his eyes pleading with me to put something together so that he doesn't have too. He sighs, sees I'm not following. "Ella can't change her soul. She can't change who she is on a fundamental level."

"Well, who is she?" I ask, and then a flicker. I think about something, but then feel stupid, because it can't be that. Ethan's eyes note the change, he sees that flicker and fights showing relief. "No. It can't be…Ella…does she like…women?" I ask, feeling silly, feeling certain that I'm missing the mark, as usual. She has a shirtless picture of Justin Bieber on her phone.

Ethan's face freezes, the room steadies, and then he nods. *Yes.*

"That makes zero sense," I say.

Have I been so blindly wearing my own mask that, again, I've failed to see Ella? Has she been waking every morning, raising her hands above her shoulders, and then tying on a mask she felt necessary to survive?

"To you. It makes zero sense to you. But people like us, we've learned how to pretend for the world."

People are meant to take their masks off.

Part 3

March

Chapter 22

"OMG, let's get a Frap," the scantily clad (wannabe) Spice Girl in front of us says to her friend; she's channeling Scary Spice.

"Rena, don't even… You're so bad," her friend says, nudging her. Definitely Baby Spice.

"Whatever… I've done Pilates all week," Scary growls.

"More power to you, girl. I love how bold you are. Fearless," whines Baby.

"Thanks, betch."

They do this weird little wiggling-fingers handshake, a modern-day twist on spice-life.

I turn to Jenny and make a goofy face, trying not to shift into my newly found dad mode.

"What's a Frap?" I whisper in her ear.

We are a few hours into our adventure from Boston to Ann Arbor, thick into the sticks of upstate New York now. We just walked two blocks from the Tesla charging station in Syracuse to the corner Starbucks.

"Ew, WTF? Like, you mean to tell me you don't know what a Frappuccino is?" she says, in a perfect mock of the young girls.

I laugh. "No, but it sounds like it'll go straight to my hips."

"Higs, you need a pick me up. I say you get the most fattening Frap they have, and then ask for extra whipped cream!"

"But I haven't done Pilates this week," I joke.

"Your hips are fine," she says, instantly blushing. She fumbles for words. "For an old man that is…" She tucks a strand of hair behind her ear.

"Hey! I'm not old. I'm only twenty-seven."

"That's old!"

"It is?"

She nods.

"Wait, how old are you?" I ask, my voice going suspiciously lower.

"Twenty and six," she says sarcastically.

"Still a baby," I tease. She chuckles. "How about I let you order for me, and I'll go find us a table? It's filling up quick in here."

"Good idea," she says.

I head for a spot furthest from other people and pick a rounded booth close to the window that seems more private. I slide inside, pulling out my laptop. I log into my email, making my way through some of the messages, trying to find the one I have from Meredith—Mom's old friend in Boston—to find the contact information she forwarded about a woman named Jane. Meredith hasn't heard from Mom in ten years, not since receiving a chased, panicked call, ensuring I'd made it to Boston and, as she puts it, a plea to look over me. Meredith says, if anyone were to know Mom's whereabouts, it'd be Jane.

It's an address and a phone number, although Meredith cautioned not to call in advance, for fear that Jane spooks easily. So, instead, I google the address again.

Google Maps pulls up the grainy image of the corner laundromat—Laundryland—off the dark and dreary Dequindre Street in Forest Park Detroit, and the apartments located above them.

"Those girls make me fear for feminism," Jenny says, startling me.

I feel compelled to close my laptop lid. It's almost like I'm looking at something dangerous and forbidden.

I start mumbling about work. "I thought about the project all night. I think I have some good ideas," I say. "I did a ton of research on the company, and I have some notes that may be helpful, but I know Richard would scream if we made edits to any of the auxiliary documents."

"I still think Pandora, Spotify, and other free music-streaming apps are the way to go. They have ad banners, and brief voiceover snippets every couple of songs. It's relatively inexpensive. The girls who are going to wear this jumpsuit—" she slides into the booth next to me, hands over a dark cookie-laden Frappuccino, "—are going to be edgy, and we've targeted all the angst stations."

I chuckle. "Damn angst stations." I nod toward the drink. "Thank you! This looks delicious."

"This, my friend, is a Double Chocolaty Chip Frappuccino with blended crème and extra whipped cream. Good for the soul."

I take a sip, the rich, bold flavor filling my mouth. The creamy blended liquid tasting like heaven in a cup. "This is ridiculously delicious, thanks."

"Let me know how you feel about it further into the trip. And thank Uncle Richard...he's footing this bill." She laughs, checks her watch. "We're a good twenty minutes into the charge now."

It's going to take an hour to fully charge the car at the Tesla superstation, but we don't want to risk running low on battery in the wide-open land between towns in upstate NY. Taking a big sip, I get an instant brain freeze. My face pulls tight, my hands coming up to my temples.

Jenny grins, giving a half dimple as she pulls out her laptop. Turning back to my computer, I pull up the email and study the address again. There are only forty-two miles between Ann Arbor and Detroit. Do I go to Jane's right away? Do I go at the end of the trip? How do I tell Jenny? It's Saturday, and depending on how fast we make the drive, I might have all of Sunday to find Mom.

"You okay, Higs?" Jenny asks.

Am I okay? I almost laugh. Faith is dead, I'm driving toward my mother, and all I want to do is hug my lesbian wife and tell her it's okay... she's free to take off that mask.

"I'm fine."

"Sad you won't see Hope for the next few days?" she asks.

"Yeah," I say. "I'm missing that little face. Ella's mother has her, so she'll be content."

I realize the slip immediately. Surely that will lead to questions: *Why doesn't* Ella *have her?*

"What is the most awkward thing you've ever experienced?" she asks, interrupting that spiral.

I force a laugh, remembering that Jenny loves random questions, relieved to not explain away Ella's absence. "Like, at work? Or in general?" I ask.

Her typing halts. She smiles, glad to have gotten me to bite. "The *most* awkward, so anywhere, anything," she says.

"I…I don't know," I say, my mind going blank, with nothing coming. "I have nothing."

"Quit stalling, Higs, and say the first thing that comes to mind."

"Okay…" I laugh, again. "Maybe in college? There was this girl, her name was Courtney. I think she was a teen mother. She would bring this little boy with her to classes, sometimes leave him out near the decorative pond to go…fishing. I tried to befriend her, just to be nice, but she couldn't seem to learn my name. Always called me…Carl."

Jenny starts laughing, her hands coming to her mouth. "Carl?" she questions.

I feel my cheeks turn pink. "Yeah, she couldn't get my name right. But one day, I tried to stop her little boy from taking the koi fish from the pond. The fish was wiggling, almost falling from his hands, and I said something like, 'Be careful that fish doesn't jump from your hands. Those things are slimy,' and that kid wasn't having it."

"How so?" Jenny asks, her eyes laughing.

"He had a southern accent and told me: 'I knocked 'em out. I hate it when they splash the water from my bucket. So, I hit 'em over the head with a stick. Makes 'em go stupid for a bit.' I just tried to tell him that *these* fish were more pet-like, and less knock-them-dead-type of fish."

I take another sip from my drink. "He thought I was questioning his ability, so he ran and got his mother."

"Oh no!"

"She accused me of heckling her kid and questioning her parenting skills. And when I went back to class the next day, my professor scowled at me and told me my seat had been moved to the back."

"You mean man! Stopping kids from hitting fish. So, did you ever see her again? Or try to explain yourself?"

"I kept my distance." I shake my head. "I would hide if I ever saw her or the kid around campus."

"I wonder what she told your professor?"

"Maybe he was the dad," I tease. "I hate the name Carl, anyway. It was best to keep my distance."

"Carl, you're right. Horrible name." She looks me in the eyes, seeming to go serious. "My favorite part of that story was watching your face. Your facial expressions when you talk…kill me."

I try to process what she means, but nothing comes. Her eyes are still on me. "What does that mean?"

"You're so into what you're saying, and every face you make perfectly captures how you must have looked and felt when it was actually happening. Your emotions are just there, and as long as people see you, like, actually open their eyes and pay attention, they'll know how you feel. I like that about you."

I hesitate. "I'm readable?"

"Very."

My stomach flips. "That's a scary thought. I think a lot of things I don't want other people to know."

She laughs. "Maybe not everyone can read you," she says, but her tone implies *she* can.

An invisible hand closes around my stomach, nerves making me avert my eyes.

"Well, that leads me to *my* awkward moment," she says, moving the conversation forward. "I guess college is a time for awkward encounters." She laughs. "But mine is not nearly as good as yours. No judgments, okay?"

"On my honor."

"I took organic chemistry to fill a science credit—stupid move—and it was impossible. My professor was a jerk, and the textbook looked like a foreign language. I just wanted to pass the class, and it completely stressed me out that it didn't come easily to me. During finals week, I didn't do anything but study chemistry. I never showered, not once! The day of the test, I got there first to go over my flash cards. When people walked in, they were covering their noses with their shirts, but I didn't think anything of it. I didn't smell anything weird or gross. When the professor walked in, he started practically gagging. He made some calls and had us moved to another testing room. When we moved into the new room, everyone still smelled the smell. Everyone but me."

"Please, oh, please tell me that it was you they smelled?"

"It was," she says, covering her face. "The professor walked around the entire room sniffing like a bloodhound. When he got to me, he stopped and glared. 'Ms. Clark, is this some sort of prank you're pulling?' I was mortified. Beyond embarrassed. I stood up and said, 'That awkward moment when you eat garlic and don't shower.' I laughed, like it was funny, but everyone just stared."

I chuckle. "You poor girl! I would have laughed with you. Did you at least pass the test?"

"He made me leave! He said I needed to shower if I wanted to pass, and that I could take it the next day with another section of the class. It kind of worked out better. I got an extra full day to study. I never got my test grade, but I ended up pulling a B- in the class."

"I can't really imagine you being stinky. You always smell nice."

"Well, I do try and shower regularly nowadays," she jokes.

We fall silent for a minute, staring. Then we fall back into our laptops, fall back into distraction. I pull up the Google tab again, study the laundromat, and think of every possible outcome of what life would become if I found Mom there.

Chapter 23

The car hugs the road, the engine so discreet that only the hum of tires against asphalt wakes the dead air. Jenny's driving. We've been taking turns behind the wheel. I wouldn't mind driving the entire way, as I'd appreciate the distraction. I'd appreciate having something to do with my hands and mind instead of sitting and spinning about what to do about Mom, but Jenny seemed eager for her turn. Her previous chatterbox tendencies have since gone silent.

When I can't take it any longer, I break the quiet. "Where's home for you? Are you a Boston native?" I ask, not remembering if she mentioned this before, but certain her accent isn't local.

"A teeny-tiny town in Pennsylvania. Middle of know where USA." She chuckles. "A place called Troy. Not unlike this…" She motions to the world outside, the open fields of dead weeds and bare trees on distant mountains.

"A country girl turned big city?" I ask.

"Something like that."

Her eyes track the road, her easy energy not looking to elaborate any further.

"Do you miss it?"

She sighs. "Parts. Only parts."

"I get that." I miss the good parts of Detroit—like how it was a melting pot. The way you could get on a bus and drive through various sections of culture, the bus ticket offering a magic trip to far-off countries and places. There were complete neighborhoods for everything. Irish, Italian, and Asian regions with different art and history to get lost in.

I miss Mom too.

"And you?" Jenny asks. "You don't speak like Richard."

I chuckle and fake the accent. "Dickie's got that wicked pissa accent like he's hanging on the corner with his scratchies, but we all know he's a born Yuppie."

She laughs. "You sound like a natural! When I first moved here, I loved making U-turns just so I could bust out the: I'm bangin' a u-ie."

"That one sticks with you, for sure. And *whip it*. Whenever someone's making a turn, I feel compelled to shout, 'Whip that car for all it's worth.'"

"Don't give me any new material!"

"I'm not a Boston local either. Detroit, Michigan," I tell her.

She nods. "Ahhh, so we are heading toward your roots. When did you make the move?"

"When I was fifteen. How about you?"

"Came here for college and fell in love with the place. Never wanted to go back home," she says. "Were you excited for the move or was it something that your parents forced?"

"Umm…" I hesitate again. "I actually…I moved on my own."

Her mouth shifts into a line. "Huh? What? How? At fifteen?"

"That was a lot of questions." I chuckle, taking a deep breath. "Yeah, I really had no other option."

She seems to hesitate, wanting to ask, but unsure if it's appropriate.

There's a tickle inside of me, a tickle that wants to tell her the entire story. That wants to tell her every detail dand admit things and truths I've never admitted to anyone. But when I go to speak, my programming doesn't allow it. The years of quiet and avoidance are too strong to circumvent in an instance. I settle on Meredith, Mom's friend with the landscaping husband, who offered me solace and a safe space to garner my independence.

"Your parents were just okay with you leaving and traveling to a far-off city to live with a family friend?" Her voice sounds skeptical.

I give half-truths, gaslight, let her think that it's not as crazy as it sounds. "My dad was happy for less responsibility. My mom…she just wanted me to be happy."

And safe.

"Well, if we have time, we should go see your parents! How far from Ann Arbor is Detroit?"

My stomach drops, a part of me grateful for that recommendation, the other half frantic at the word we. *We should go see your parents.* I would never willingly see Frank again, and the idea of Jenny being present if and when I get the chance to see Mom feels intrusive. There's a childhood vulnerability in me still, and I can't share that.

"They're close—under an hour depending on traffic." My voice seems to croak, she notices, so I turn and study the cold outside world. Gray sky and dead brown earth. "Still brown outside."

"Yeah," she sighs. "Thankfully, I have Sasha in my apartment to offer some greenery."

I crease my brow. "Wait? Sasha the plant? Like my plant?"

She laughs. "Yes! Sorry, I'm a thief."

"Sasha's still alive? I thought it was dead!"

"How dare you insult me like that!" She laughs, her chuckle deep and amused.

"I didn't see it on your desk, and you haven't mentioned it. I thought it died."

"Sasha's not an *it*. That's why you kill plants!" She makes a silly face. "I water her frequently and tell her how special she is. That's what every woman needs!"

I laugh. "So, it is a woman now too?"

She rolls her eyes, as if caught in the act. "I did have plans on giving her back to you, promise, but I've delayed, because I love her. She looks beautiful on my coffee table."

"I don't think she brought me much luck anyway, so she's where she belongs."

"Really?"

I nod.

"Good, because I was joking, you weren't getting her back anyway."

The car falls quiet again, nothing but the empty highway and cold winter air. I lean back, stretch my already stiffening back. It's a nearly thirteen-hour drive, with the GPS claiming eight hours remain. We're getting closer to Lake Erie, and that's the one physical memory I have from my previous bus ride to Boston; every other memory is emotional.

"I want to ask, Higs," Jenny says. "I want to bombard you with questions about how and why you moved to Boston, but I have a past too. I have things that hurt in my history, and I know how it feels to have someone ask you to drudge those traumas up."

I turn to take her in. Her face is serious. Sincere and open.

I clear my throat. A piece of truth falls out. "Sometimes I want to talk about it, but it's like I don't know how."

She nods. "It'd be hypocritical of me to ask anyway, because I wouldn't be able to share my scars either."

I have *then*—the past—but I also have *now*. It almost feels easier to talk about the now, but how can I? Is it appropriate to out my own wife? I see now why Ethan weighed his words so heavily, not wanting to cross the line between doctor and friend. It's her identity in question, and I want to respect that.

How can she be a lesbian? I've never once suspected it. We've discussed LGBTQ+ topics, we've both always been in support of letting people love who they love. Her friend, Tonya, the one in Long Beach, she is also gay. I've known that for years; I've accepted that for years. My only guess is that she learned who she was later in life, after me, and maybe she loved me at one point, and maybe that love made her question why life wasn't ever good enough for her.

"I'm worried I'm going to mess up Hope. That I'm going to do everything wrong, and screw up this precious, perfect kid. I want her to have a normal life, but I don't know what I'm doing. My dad…" I fumble, another truth spilling out that I wasn't intending to share. "My dad, he is not good. What if I'm not good?"

"Higs!" She shrieks and I startle, surprised at the sudden volume of her voice. "You're a person. You're a person, Keith, and you're doing nothing wrong. You'll be a great father, who will do the best he can. You're not going to mess Hope up. You couldn't. She only needs to be loved—unconditionally—to be okay. She has love, and that's more than enough," she says.

"I don't know if that's true," I say.

"Well, it is! Emotions are complicated and painful, but necessary. Everyone is twisted and tangled together, and families are never perfect," she says. She looks at me like her own heart is aching. Her face is tight, and her mouth is a firm line. "Ella…she isn't doing well, is she?"

I clear my throat. Both afraid and unafraid to tell her everything. "No—" I choke trying to say her name, "—since Faith. She's not okay."

Her eyes go wet. "I can't imagine her pain."

"She's in California. Long Beach actually. Needed a change of scenery."

She looks at me again, hesitantly. "She just needs space to heal herself," she says, trying to make me feel better. "She's trying—don't put that blame on you."

"Yeah."

Ella isn't coming back for me. The only question is: will she come back for Hope?

Jenny sighs, takes a deep breath. "You shared a scar. Does that mean I should?" she asks, seeming suddenly delicate, fragile.

"Do you want to?"

"I don't know just yet," she answers.

"So…let's just drive."

Chapter 24

"I don't think we realistically considered the possibility of a snowstorm occurring. I mean, it's March, and Richard has us in this little toy, electric car," Jenny says, concern on her face. She's staring out the windshield, trying to see not only past the swiping wiper blades, but also through the thick snowflakes.

"Weren't you just saying an hour ago that this is the best car you've ever driven?" I tease.

"Higs, that was before the sun started setting and the outside world became the night sky. I feel like I'm wielding a rocket ship through space."

She isn't wrong. The heavy snowflakes are pegging the car, tunneling our vision, like we are flying through a wormhole at top speed. I start chuckling. "I didn't even give snow a single thought. Not one little brain cell even suggested to check the weather." I laugh harder.

"Why is that funny? We should be ashamed of ourselves!"

The GPS says we have six hours to go. Now, with the sun gone and a storm brewing, it seems foolish to trade off driving through the night. "Should we stop somewhere?" I ask. "Evangeline will be on her ski trip until Tuesday, so if we get there tomorrow, we'll still have plenty of time to talk to her."

"Yeah, but where? We need to be able to charge this stupid car."

I laugh. "So now the car is stupid?"

She puts a hand to her temples. "This snowstorm stress has me knocking environmentally friendly transportation."

"There's the Jenny I know!"

She chuckles. "Come on, Higs. Get on that phone and find us a place to stay!"

$\mathcal{SD}$

Jenny pulls into the Holiday Inn on the outskirts of Buffalo, the twenty minutes of driving taking over an hour in the now-blistering winter storm. The GPS still reports six hours.

We find the EV charging station and get the car plugged in. The windshield is already burying under the heavy white snow. The parking lot is coated, white like sugar.

"Initial snowfall is so pretty—like icing," Jenny says.

"Covers all the brown you love so dearly," I say. "Won't be fun digging this car out tomorrow."

Inside, we attempt to reserve two rooms, but have to settle for one with two double beds. Jenny seems hesitant at first but hides her frustration swiftly.

We take the stairs up two floors, both of us seeming to prefer the struggle of carrying luggage in wet boots over the cage of the elevator. The room is dark, but warm, and Jenny makes haste to flip on the lights. I change and brush my teeth in the bathroom, and when I exit, Jenny's studying the contents of the mini-fridge.

"Looks like dinner is a bottle of water and the leftover dried edamame in my purse."

"Delicious," I say, sitting down on the edge of the seemingly unclaimed bed. I lose my self in my phone, checking in on Hope with Christina, and then sending a text to Ella. *It's OK, I'm sorry. Take your mask off, but don't lose Hope.*

"Most of the time, Disney sequels are horrible! Originals are best. Like, everyone loves *The Lion King*, but who enjoyed the *Lion King* sequel? No one, because the first one can't be topped!" Jenny says, remote in hand and staring at the muted TV.

"I loved the *Lion King* sequel! Kovu and Zira had a great little love story going on," I muse, dropping my phone to the side and reaching for a pillow.

"Wait! You know their names?" Her eyes bulge, her teeth showing big and white.

"So, you've never seen *Simba's Pride* is what you're saying to me?"

"Oh, I've seen it," she teases. "But I can't claim to remember their names."

"So, you didn't like *Simba's Pride* is what you're saying to me?"

She laughs, falling over on her bed. Her hands come up over her face.

"I may have to go sleep in the car," I joke. "This realization is making me start to question your character."

We both look to the window, where the flurries are still coming down. I shiver, clutching the pillow closer. The smell of Jenny's nighttime lotion fills the air.

"Hopefully, it slows, and they can clear the roads, so we can get an early start tomorrow."

She nods, looking from the window and back to me. "Higs, do you believe in the law of attraction?" she asks. "Like when you believe in positivity, so everything around you is positive," she says, her voice lowering, her tone shifting.

"Maybe," I say. I fall back on my bed, look to the off-white popcorn ceiling. "Maybe that's why shit happens to me. I think shit-like thoughts."

She chuckles softly. From the corner of my eye, I see her inch up the bed, pull the comforter down sleeping crawl inside. "I think I believe it," she whispers.

I do the same, move up the bed and take refuge under the covers. "I think there are times we get to choose, instances where we are free to steer our lives. But other times, the heart takes what it needs. A heart goes where it belongs."

The wall-hung heating unit kicks on, rattles softly. "Hmm. Profound," Jenny whispers.

"I had a teacher once who always shouted, 'Life sucks and then you die.' Even with all the painful bits, I don't want to believe that."

She chuckles at this.

I turn in bed to look at her, the heat of the room making my eyes heavy.

"You've told me that before, Higs." She sighs, comfortable, but something seems unspoken.

I look at the clock, stifle my yawn. "It's only 8:42 p.m. You know you're getting old when you're fighting sleep prior to 9:00 p.m."

"Well, we could always unmute *Simba's Pride*."

"I knew you lived life dangerously."

She laughs. "Can I ask something?"

I nod.

"Can you tell Ella we're sharing a room, please? I know she's in California, but I'm worried about this. I don't think she'd be comfortable with this set up; I know I wouldn't."

I hesitate, consider how to respond. "I told her," I lie. "I just texted her and let her know the situation. I don't…I don't think she cares."

She seems to breathe a sigh of relief, and I wonder if I should tell her—explain to her that Ella made it clear with her words, with her disappearing, with using Ethan to reveal her secret, that she couldn't care less about me and what I do.

"I've had people convince me that I can trust them and open up. Friends that have made me feel like it's okay to show scars, but then steal that ammo and use it against me. I always dodge the bullets, but then my heart gets tougher, and worthy people have to fight that wall built by the hands of liars," she says, her eyes not looking at me. "I see your pain, and I want you to know I'm not a person who collects stories as ammo. If you ever need to talk…" She seems to trail off, lose her way. She shakes her head. "God…what you went through with Faith, it's just… What I'm trying to say is, you can trust me, but also I understand if you don't. I've regretted giving my trust away too easily before."

The room falls quiet, the hum of the heater clicking off right when she finishes speaking.

I don't respond right away, unsure what—if anything—can be said.

I have then, and I have now. I'm two very different people, yet still the same me that gets used by this world, who can't figure out how to love. Hurt can only be felt for so long before you get mixed up and lost in the poetic line of this mess. We all hurt, but this is where and when it's your choice.

"We can make a rule," I say.

"A rule?"

"Yeah, a rule. A rule that allows us to make the rules about what we share. You don't ever have to share your truth. You can hold it, or you can let it go, or you can *decide* to talk about it until you're blue in the face— but only you matter in this situation. You say what you feel, whenever you feel it," I tell her.

She reaches for the lamp, plunging the room into darkness. "A rule." She's quiet for a moment, contemplating. "If I tell you something, can you not ask why? Can that be a part of the rule?"

"The rule says we make the rules."

"My stepfather, I hate him, and people like him," she says, then she's silent as she unmutes the TV, *Simba's Pride* letting us go back to pretending that life isn't messy and full of hurt.

Chapter 25

Outside, the morning surge of March wind violates my body. It manages to touch all of me with a single spin, the fooling streams of light holding pseudo-cordiality.

Jenny's face beams underneath her winter hat, her petite body surrounded by the immense fabric of her coat. She's enjoying the dig-out more than what's socially acceptable, holding a Thermos in one gloved hand.

"It's freezing out here, but I love it!" She smiles.

"Yeah, yeah, yeah, we all know you're a nut." I hustle, my bare hand tucked into my sleeve, as I brush the snow away on my side of the car. Unlike Jenny, I did not have the sense to pack appropriately. She mentioned this morning that she actually plans on skiing at the resort we're meeting Evangeline at.

"It's perfect! Probably one of the last snow days of the year!" She grins, waving the Thermos at me.

"Yesterday, you called this car stupid and seemed mighty concerned about the roads."

She gestures around her. "Look around, Higs. It's beautiful. The roads are cleared, and the sun is shining. Besides, the law of attraction— remember? Only positivity, Higgins."

The sun glints, bounces off the snowy surfaces in prisms, our breaths reaching out in wispy smoke signals. The cold stings my eyes, my cheeks turning to porcelain.

"So, in this Thermos is boiling-hot water!" Jenny says, a grin on her face. "I'm going to throw it up, and the freezing air will mix with the hot contents of the Thermos and create a beautiful transcendental snowfall."

"Transcendental? Isn't there enough snow on the ground already?" I laugh out loud, and she scowls.

"Trust me, Higs. I just watched this the other day on the Discovery Channel."

"That teasing-smile on your face makes me question this entire thing," I say.

She chuckles, coming around to stand near me on the driver's side of the Tesla. "Okay, crouch down."

I obey.

She unscrews the cap, counts to three, and then tosses the water into the air with a huge, joyful grin on her face. She crouches down next to me, our faces turning to the sky searching for the snow.

I'm smiling, a big dopey grin consuming my frowns. Jenny's laughing, her teeth sparkling in the sun.

Happiness, excitement, then, suddenly, alarmingly, something else. The boiling liquid comes back with the whistling wind, burning my neck and face with fierce little bee stings. Jenny lets out a scream, takes off running.

The vicious stinging persists. I lunge to follow her, falling instead, laughing. I cover my face, deep, hard laughter at Jenny running for the sidewalk taking control. The image of her small frame bobbing under her oversized coat, one hand holding her hat on, embeds into my brain. The childish holler echoing in her wake making me laugh harder.

After a safe amount of time, I poke my head out, as Jenny runs back, gasping for air. The cold strips away the monotony, letting us forget who we are supposed to be.

She's laughing, too, half a frown on her face. "Sorry!"

"No more Discovery Channel for you!"

She smiles fully, reaches down to help me up. Little red burns in the shape of tiny Hershey's kisses speckle her exposed skin. Her eyelashes are cocooned like frozen trees, crystalized and sugared. I point out the little blisters. She turns, scrutinizes me. Says my face is the same.

"Stop! Don't move, Higs!" she demands. Her face is serious as she squints and inspects my complexion.

She takes off her glove, and a smirk consumes her face. The light bellows around her, and happiness radiates out of her pores in palpable waves. She slides her soft finger over my cheek. She laughs and pulls back her finger. "It worked," she says, holding a tiny snowflake on the tip of her finger. "It really worked!"

"You're crazy!"

The stinging ache from the burns is poked by the wind. I reach out with the spilling light, rub my fingers over her slightly raised skin, where the water burned her, my fingers touching her marks. Jenny is still, unmoving, as my thumb rubs over three, then four of the little kisses.

"You have so many blisters."

She deep chuckles, moving away. "This will make quite an impression on Evangeline. We roll in all burnt and blistered, crash her ski vacation, and talk business. Let's do this!" She walks to the passenger side and pulls the door open. "You get three hours, Higs! The last three are mine."

Chapter 26

We arrive at the Candlewood Suites—just outside of Mt. Brighton, Michigan—right after 3:00 p.m. on Sunday. Prior to arrival, we were already confirmed for two rooms, and sent two one-day passes for the ski resort. Jenny convinced me to stop off at Old Navy to get half-priced winter wear, so that I can actually make use of the ski pass tomorrow. She thinks being up for the adventure will resonate with Evangeline.

I've decided that going to find Mom will have to wait until after this business is handled. I push down and ignore that whisper. The whisper that screams, "Now! Go now!" A whisper can scream all it wants. That doesn't change the fact that it's still a whisper.

After we get settled in the room and I Facetime with Christina and Hope, Jenny convinces me to travel to the ski resort, where we can get dinner at the grill, go over the project pitch, and scope out Evangeline, because Jenny thinks she'll surely be there.

The lodge is warm, rustic, and woodsy. The air occasionally catches the cold off the skiers who pass by the rugged hand-carved pinewood tables in the mountain-inspired dining area. The foyer is home to a stuffed raccoon, its furry black mask secured around its eyes, offering a sign of peace now, fear no longer holding power.

The fish tacos that are served contradict the mountain scene, the taste of shrimp triggering hints of beach among a diamond-dusted landscape of ice.

Jenny, discussing who is going to say what and when tomorrow, freezes. Her body stays motionless, but her eyes track across the room. Turning to see what she is looking at, I notice a pretty young girl with thick, wavy, brown hair, under a powder pink ski cap, making her way through the lodge.

"Don't turn!" Jenny whisper chastises. "That's her. That's friggin' Evangeline Iris. My word, she's beautiful."

I turn back to look at Jenny. She's like a deer trapped in the headlights. I laugh. "You have a girl crush?"

"Let's follow her!" She jumps up, her eyes seeming to point.

"No, we can't just follow her. Our tacos!" I say, too late. Abruptly, Jenny's mobile, moving through the lodge and toward a hallway. I follow her—Jenny, who is stalking Evangeline—though a door and down a hall.

"You're a stalker," I whisper. "What if she thinks we're psychos?"

"Shh," she hushes, heading through another door and then picking up the pace as she pivots up a set of carpeted stairs.

We run up three flights, exit the stairwell into an open space filled with windows looking out onto the mountain. Thickly trimmed glass, sliced at various angles, looks out onto a world of snow and ice.

"There she is!" Jenny whispers, pointing. She's further down the lodge, moving toward the furthest windows, overlooking a lake.

We slip into two of the sofa chairs facing out toward the windows. I look toward Evangeline, see her on her phone.

"What's the plan?" I ask. "Approach her now? I thought we'd wait till tomorrow."

Jenny suddenly jumps up, moves behind me, and puts her hands over my eyes.

"Stand up," she says. "I have an idea."

"Okay," I mutter, standing slowly, and moving awkwardly, so she can continue to reach my eyes. "What *is* this plan?" I ask, grinning.

She giggles. "*Eww*, stop smiling, it tickles my hand."

I try my best to pull my face back together.

We walk a couple paces, and then Jenny speaks. "Buford, you have to see this view, the sunset is exquisite. The way the oranges and yellows melt with the reds, well, it's enough to take your breath away." She positions me and instructs me to close my eyes. I keep them closed as told. "Okay, now open."

I do, and as they open, I prepare myself to laugh, to question my new name. Buford? But as my eyes meet the sunset, it's all I can do not to shudder at the beauty in front of me. The sun is melting into the horizon, like she said. Dripping with shimmering rays that bounce on the rippling water of the lake, lighting the sky in a warming haze.

Evangeline is taking a selfie, probably for her Instagram page.

The colors of the sunset blend together stunningly in a way that seems to fill the sky with an explosion of passion and heat. Shades of blue lick through the strokes of pink and yellow. The sun crests dangerously on the water's edge. The sky is cloudless and still, like the gates of heaven are open, and we're staring straight into its beauty.

Something inside me is begging for absolution, to take me with it, wherever it's going. I want to fly into it and make my home in it. I want to paint it.

"What do you think, Buford?" Jenny asks. "Should we ask this kind lady to take our picture?"

"It's...It's amazing. It's beautiful," I manage to say. I want to say it's so much more. That it's heaven. That it's my mother, and all of the beautiful things about life combined. That it's Hope, that it's Faith.

Jenny's silhouette shadows my face, the light pouring around her and then into me. The freckles and dimples highlighted only by the mask of the shadows. Her skin is perfect like porcelain in the fragile fading light, the blisters from earlier now faded.

The sky is an alarming shade of blue smeared with deep tones of pink, purple, and orange, all blending and mixing effortlessly until its core, where light and heat are exploding outward like a message from above. It's like a puffy bowl of rainbow sherbet ice cream with a scoop of sunny-side-up egg yolk in the middle, and all I want to do is find a spoon. Find a spoon so I can reach up, dip in, and fill my mouth with the taste of it. So, I can experience what it's like to fill myself with perfection.

I'm dying. And I'm dying. My heart is spilling over, and I'm drowning in its wake. It's killing me. The beauty before me is killing me, and I think I want it to. My body is screaming for oxygen, but I've forgotten how to breathe…because this beauty. This beauty in front of me matches the beauty next to me, and my body doesn't want to fight it. Ella has abandoned me.

I reach out, unable to stop myself, and I touch Jenny's hair. It's so soft and falls through my hands like water. I shiver, and she turns her eyes on me. Eyes that are filled with shock and curiosity, and I shudder open.

Her face is a light. Her eyes two candles of hope, quivering in dispute, and she ignites me. I catch on fire. I am a shivering flame.

There's a clatter behind us, a man dropping his ski poles. "Hey! Why are you freaks following her?" he asks.

We jump simultaneously, and then Jenny grabs my hand, and pulls me toward a door down a hallway, and then into an office. There's a wooden coat closet. We climb in quickly, shutting the doors behind us, and move toward the back.

"I might have to dye my hair and change my name for tomorrow now," she whispers. "Unless Narnia is on the other side of this wardrobe."

"Do you think she'll remember our faces?" I ask.

"I can feel your heart," she murmurs. I think I hear her smile. "It's beating so fast. And yeah, she'll remember. I should have thought that Buford name through a little longer. I couldn't remember what that college girl called you. We can just say you go by Keith, but on your birth certificate, it's Buford. People do that when they have weird names."

I chuckle. "It was Carl," I say.

My hands are awkwardly pressed to the wood of the closet, unsure where to rest.

"Buford Carl Keith Higgins—it's fine," she whispers. "I don't think he followed us."

"Me either," I say.

"Should we get out?"

"I think we should."

Jenny opens the door, spilling out of the closet and hitting the ground with a thud. Two faces, one with wavy brown hair and a pink ski cap, stare at us, their hands on their hips.

SD

The March wind whips outside, whistles against the shutters of the lodge, and chases the remaining skiers indoors. Evangeline sits with us at our table, late afternoon coffee in hand, a curious grin painted on her face.

"You are insane," she says to Jenny, smiling. She finally takes that pink cap off her head, tussles her hair. "Where did you come from?"

"Thank you," I interject. "I've been saying this for weeks now. A total nut."

"Buford!" Jenny chastises. Evangeline laughs.

Somehow, Jenny has not only managed to keep us from prison time on stalker charges, but has also managed to win Evangeline over, all while dropping subtle figures about sales and projections, going over details on rebranding and strengthening her established brand on the global market.

Jenny cradles the neatly constructed portfolio in her hands, pats it, and then places it on the table in front of Evangeline.

"Not to kill the ambiance, but we've got great ideas. If you want, take a look at this tonight, and if anything tickles your fancy, maybe we can chat about it between slopes tomorrow," she says, chill now, like she's just one of the kids.

Evangeline takes the folder, moves to open it, but is halted when Jenny stops her with a hand. "I've got to know if that cutie who called me a freak is your boyfriend?"

Evangeline turns, looks across the room at the boy who confronted us earlier. "Just a good friend, but he is cute, right?"

"Totally," Jenny says.

She catches me studying her, and I give her a look like, *What the hell? She was about to read that thing.*

"After you read the proposal, if there is a direction or suggestion on where you want to focus, just let us know. If there is something in this copy you want to see particularly revised, don't hesitate to ask," I say.

Evangeline's smile loosens, her eyes get smaller. She shrugs. "Yeah, man. I've caught Jenny's vibe."

Chapter 27

Cold bites at my cheeks, the wind wiggling into and around my scarf-less neck and down into my cheap coat. I clutch the metal of the ski lift, hug the poles to me, wondering how many people lose them while traveling up the mountain. Looking down, my feet dangle heavy with skis over snowcapped pines.

Jenny hollers, "I'm the king of the world!" The echo mocks her.

"I think I should have stayed inside and waited for Evangeline to show face," I say, wondering why in the world I let Jenny talk me into this. "I can't believe people just do this, like, for fun."

"Higs, she's nineteen. No way we see her for at least another two hours. Besides, at this hour, we'll have the mountain to ourselves!" Smoke signals from her mouth, the smell of her minty breath intensifying the crisp air. Despite the Earl Grey morning light starting its due, the Martian moon continues its beam from behind the trees. The Earth is shadowed, illuminated only enough to shut the mounted slope lights off for the day.

"There is no way in hell I can be out here all day. Old Navy snow gear is doing little to protect me from the elements."

"Mind over matter, Higgins. This is going to be a blast. After a run or two, you'll be crooning a different tune," she says, surveying the open air around us. "Now prep yourself. When we reach the top, we'll need to be ready to slide off."

I shuffle the poles, mimic her hands and feet, and ready myself as suggested. Before it seems time, Jenny's sliding off the seat, landing with a jump and shouting, "Whooo hooooooo!"

I hesitate. The white, hard cold of winter sprays upward in Jenny's wake, the Earth shaken in a majestic globe. The freezing, howling wind whips in rapid, ragged procession, barks like the hounds of hell. The sharp smell of frozen air burns hot in conflicting sensations, and then I do it. I leap from the bench after Jenny, chest heavy and eyes watering. I shout, too, breaking the air with my, "Whooo hooooo!" to match that of Jenny's.

I coast forward, digging my poles into the snow to stop myself.

"Don't use your sticks," Jenny shouts. "Use your skis; turn them inward."

"Don't use my poles? Then what the hell are these things good for?"

"Balance!" she says, perched on the edge of the mountain, taking in the stark, stern beauty of the rolling passage that waits before us.

"Is there another way down? I don't think I'm ready for this."

Jenny chuckles. "It's a rite of passage! You'll fall. We all do. But, like my daddy taught me, we get up, and we persist."

My dad taught me the gift of persistence too. "I'm persistently disappointed in my dad!" I yell to her over the wind.

"Leave that all out on the mountain," she says, going into a brief ski demo. Always land with your skis on the ground. Fall onto your side or back, not elbow, wrist, or hands. Protect your neck. Use the damn poles to get back up. Avoid the trees and the gnarled roots standing guard around them. "And Higs," she says, "have some fun."

She seems to conjure goggles from nowhere. She secures them over her eyes and then pulls out second pair, handing them to me. "Let's do this!" She pushes off and then screams her way downward. I take a deep breath, count to three, and then I do the same.

I try to slow myself at first, try to tense and tighten against the feeling that I'm falling—that I'm losing control—but you can't fight a mountain, because if you try, if you battle against the mountain, it'll hit you with its full force. Survival requires you to ride the mountain. It requires you to relinquish your control—free yourself—surrender to the natural wave of it, and I do. Suddenly, I'm swimming, and like in life, I'm following the only path the current allows, because swimming upstream is impossible to endure long-term.

I let it move me, laughing at the joyful screams of Jenny before me.

SD

"The implementation phase...it's too long. I need this implemented much sooner than outlined. I like the idea for billboards, but not that quote. The number is too high. If you can get this lowered, I think this proposal's perfect," Evangeline says, surprising me.

How can a nineteen-year-old kid be so self-assured? So confident and ready to take on the business world? It seems easy for her, natural in a way that I've had to fake my entire life.

I think of the mountain and how I had to follow it. My bones are sore and tired from riding, but my heart is lighter. Maybe this isn't what I should be doing. Maybe I've been writing with my left hand, when I've never needed a pencil, only a paintbrush. That thought sets my nerves on fire.

"That went well," Jenny says, Evangeline tramping through the snow back to the lift behind her.

"Yeah, thanks to you."

"No, thanks to our great proposal," she says, smiling.

"Mmm-hmm," I say, not so sure anymore.

Jenny's eyes grow serious. "Don't forget the rule, Higs."

I nod, let my face go slack, as if to say everything is okay.

The mountain controls the flow, demands you feel its pull and give way. But what about life? Why is there such a wide berth for interpretation?

What is life asking of me? What do I do when I get to Detroit and find Mom? What do I say?

What if she doesn't know me?

What if she doesn't want to know me?

What if…what if I don't know me?

𝒮𝒟

The warm hotel feels like a haven. I want to crawl under the covers and not move until the ice inside my blood sufficiently thaws out, but I persist, pulling on my jacket and boots again and grabbing my keys. I move for the door. On my cell phone, I pull up the map and punch in the address to the laundromat—Laundryland. Traffic is light, and it says I should be there within the hour.

Jenny and I discussed heading home first thing in the morning. Tonight is all I have to get in contact with Jane, in hopes of finding Mom.

I pull the door shut, and head to the far end of the hallway to find the stairs. The stairs have a musty smell, the years of snow-soaked patterns leaving their mark forever. Jenny seemed confused about why I couldn't join her for dinner, but she didn't ask why I needed the car.

My phone vibrates, then it rings loudly in the enclosed staircase. I pull up the screen and read the name on the display: Ella. Confusion makes me silence the call, makes me end it, a new anxiousness replacing what was already lingering with the thought of driving to Detroit.

Ella's calling…finally.

She calls again. I don't answer, too stunned, too unsure what to say. The phone goes still, a missed call, and instant regret makes me pull up the screen to dial her back. Before I press send, the phone vibrates again, the screen displaying Ella's name.

I take a deep breath. "Hello?" I say, my voice thick and strangled. There's a long silence, but I hear her hurried breathing. "Ella?"

"Hi," she says, her voice small and unsure. "Didn't think you would answer. Third time's a charm."

157

I turn around and climb back up the few stairs I mounted, abandon the stairs altogether for the hallway, and then head back toward the room. "How are you? How's California? Are you okay?" I say, reaching my room, and painfully aware that Jenny is one room down.

"Yeah," she says. "I'm doing…better. You talked to Ethan," she says, not asking, but stating.

I pull my key from my pocket, press it to the door. It swings open, and I hurry through it, the heat welcoming me. Inside, I kick off my boots and move to sit on the bed. "I did."

"And?"

I clear my throat. "And I wish I had the right words to say. I get it would be hard, but I wish you could have told me yourself."

"That would have been impossible."

"You hurt me," I say, and against my will, there's a tremble. "You hurt me worse by not telling me yourself."

"I know," she says. "I hurt myself too."

I hear her sigh into the phone, and I crawl into the bed with my coat still on. "What do we do?"

"You hurt me too," she says, catching me off guard.

I consider it, and I know that I did, but my arms cross, shield, and protect for battle. "I'm sorry," I whisper.

"I know."

"Did you love me?" I ask.

"Of course. That's why it's so hard. I don't want to hurt you. I thought I'd pretend forever, if it meant I didn't have to break your heart."

The word—pretend—makes me shiver. The darkness of winter, and our past, making it feel like midnight. "I've avoided my own pain. I think I would have been understanding."

Life is difficult, it hurts. That's the lesson I've learned from a young age.

"Pretending is making me sick, Keith. There is a great pain in not being known, and I was stifling myself, shielding who I was, and not to protect me, but…for you."

I sink further into the bed, reach for a pillow. "I never asked you to do that."

"The world asked, Keith! The goddamn world asked!" she snaps, but then she clears her throat. "I don't want to fight. I'm sorry. I just called to say…hello."

"I've got thick skin; I can take it. Say whatever needs to be said. Just get it all out now. Let's get it over with. This world is shit—I know that."

She steadies her voice. "I don't want to pretend I'm not gay anymore," she says.

I sigh. "I'm not asking you to pretend."

"That's why I left, Keith. How can I not pretend there? Being around you and my family. It's all I know how to do—pretend!"

"You're missing Hope's life. If you make this choice, that's what you're choosing. You walked away… You didn't just leave me, but you left *her*. Your daughter won't know you, because you turned your back on her."

Her composure breaks, and she sobs into the phone. "I was scared—I *am* scared. Losing Faith broke me. I have to heal. I have to figure myself out. I don't want to abandon Hope, but I also can't abandon myself anymore."

Her sob breaks open. She chokes, crying harder.

The air feels cold now, so I crawl under the covers, wrap myself deeper. Tears are threatening to spill from my eyes, too, but I choke them down. "Please, please don't cry," I whisper. "Our family is special…we are all deeply feeling people in a messy world. Hope's going to have struggles and pain that we can't understand. She'll love you, even if you love another woman. But…she can't love you if you aren't here."

"I'm sorry…" she wheezes. "I just can't be there, at least not now."

She's quiet for a long while. I reach and hit the lamp light off, plunge the room into darkness.

"But maybe…maybe Hope could come and be here with me?"

I close my eyes. Fear and dread spiking in my blood. You can't dive from a tree and then expect to not feel the fall. You just can't. I don't even speak; I don't even react for her to hear.

No. Never. Hope will never be taken away. I hang up the phone.

Chapter 28

Avoidance is a survival technique. For thousands of years, people have been surviving by fighting or fleeing. Avoidance is an act of fleeing, it's running from the threat of pain and heartache by ignoring, by avoiding, by delaying it, until you've talk yourself out of it all together.

I've been uncomfortable for so long that the thought of making changes to improve that is scary.

I feel my mask, but fear untying it. I struggle writing left-handed, but abandon my paintbrush. I sense the flow of water and feel its gentle whispers, yet continue swimming upstream.

"Morning," Jenny sings, getting to her desk back in Boston, perky and seemingly un-phased by our anxious, quiet trip back from Ann Arbor. "Isn't it a beautiful day?"

"America sucks!" I grumble from behind the cubicle divider, fake mirth.

Upon our arrival home, I cried so hard that breath wouldn't come. Like a hurt child at the onset of sobbing, breath held, that conditioned reflux of breathing an afterthought, my mouth wide open, lips turning purple, trying to remember to breathe. I was hurt. I hurt myself. And

160

I was angry. Angry at my weakness, at my wasted opportunity to find Mom.

But Ella spooked me. Her call rattled the confidence I'd mustered, her proposal looming like a threat. I needed to get home, I needed to have Hope with me and know she's mine.

"Already singing the blues, Higs?"

"I say we quit our jobs and open a daycare facility. All we need to do is rope in six kids, tie them to the wall, and throw them some chocolate every few hours. We'd be set for life. You in?"

"You had me at *America sucks*. Of course, I'm in, but we need to hand this overture into Richard first. We worked too hard on this Evangeline deal."

"Right! We'll hand it in, and then ride whimsically off into the sunrise…to our future in child rearing!" I say, managing to pull off the happy, light tone it required.

"Perfect. What exactly will we be riding? Just so I can prepare accordingly. I wore six-inch pumps today that wouldn't work too well if it were on horseback."

"Motorcycles?" I question.

"These will work. Been there, done that! Why exactly are we starting a daycare service?" she asks. I hear her unpacking her backpack, taking things out and moving them around the desk.

"I need to put Hope in daycare, and the average price for daycares around here is $2,000 a month."

"Wait, what? $2,000 a *month*? That's more than my rent!"

"Tell me about it! I don't know. I have to get something worked out."

She clears her throat. "What happened with Ella's mother?"

"She can do it part time, but she'll be returning to work, and it won't be consistent."

"Daycare service it is," she says. There's a moment of silence. "In all seriousness, Debbie in Contracts—she helped with reducing the quote for the billboards—she mentioned her kids go to daycare…here. I think there's one in this building, for employees only, but I'll ask her. She's a sweet lady, and I'll pump her for the deets, Higs."

"You'd…do that?"

"Of course! Now, should we hand this contract into Richard or what?" she asks.

We move toward Richard's office, our project binders in hand. The reminder that I failed my mother again still knocks around like a stone in my stomach. The thought that Ella could decide—just decide—to show up and take Hope from my everyday life, like it's no big deal, makes me physically sick.

They say it's easier to just rip the Band-Aid off, to get it all over with, using one quick and brutal strip, so that you can feel all the pain at once. They say that peeling the Band-Aid back slowly hurts more, that, in a way, it's a cruel punishment. But what if it's not only about your pain? What if slowly ripping the Band-Aid off lets you control the bleed? Lets you stop it from getting all over someone else?

What if that's the responsible route? Sometimes burying your problems isn't weak; sometimes it's survival.

My hand slips into my jacket and rubs the familiar cotton of the little pink cap, the beanie from the hospital, the one that was meant to be Faith's.

Maybe…in a way, I'm still riding the mountain.

Part 4

October, Seven Months Later

Chapter 29

"You seem distracted," Ethan says, hands tight on the steering wheel of his too-clean SUV. "Why are you distracted?" His brown hair is less formal, finger-brushed to the side. The car smells strongly of his cologne.

I've somehow let him convince me to go to the bar—Westies, in Harvard Square—with him and his boyfriend, Jason. Jason will meet us there, his apartment supposedly around the corner from the square.

Ethan's been poking around the house as of late, making me his charity case. I've become accustomed to his random visits. The food he brings when he's just stopping by, and the laughs we share over garbage TV. I suppose, since he stepped across the line with one foot, to spill Ella's secret, there was nothing left to stop him from jumping across with both feet.

"I'm not. Just missing Hope. But you're right, I need to loosen up," I say, putting on my smile.

"You're a great dad. Don't sweat leaving her for one night." He pivots, looks over his shoulder to parallel park. "You're all in with her! Hell, I wish I had a dad as devoted as you."

He mentioned that he never had a dad growing up, and I told him about mine. *Frank.* I guess it's different, but the same. He didn't have a dad, and I had a bad one. This somehow makes us both broken in a way I can't explain.

"You're nice."

He puts the car in park and shuts the engine off. "You catch more flies with honey than you do with vinegar," he says. "At least that's what Mama says."

"These phrases." I laugh. "Where are you from again?"

"I was born in Kentucky, but we moved to Melbourne, Florida when I was two. I fancy myself a southern gentleman."

"Gay *and* from the south? You hit the jackpot."

He laughs, unbuckling his seatbelt and arching up to stash his keys in his pocket. "The gays are everywhere, trust me."

"Yeah, sometimes even secretly under the same roof," I say. I mean it as a joke, but it's too harsh, and it unsettles the playful vibe of the conversation.

"You know, she didn't want to hurt you," he says. "That's why it was so hard for her to say it."

"I know," I mutter. "I've been told. Although—" I unbuckle my seatbelt, too, reach for the door handle, "—for someone who was so afraid of hurting me, she sure did not go about it in the best manner."

He clears his throat, nodding. His discomfort noticeable, his knuckles reaching and tightening on the stirring wheel. "Well…Faith," he says.

Right, either way. I lost them both.

Nodding, swinging the door open, I step out into the night. "Let's do this."

The bar is packed, a mixture of race, color, and gender swimming together under the dim lights and thundering music. People stand shoulder to shoulder, shouting over the melody to be heard. The air's thick with a sour alcohol must.

I follow Ethan closely. He weaves and ducks, zigzagging his way toward the counter of the bar.

The wood is sticky, but Ethan leans on it to shout his drink order anyway. "I'll take a Sam Adams—the Octoberfest," he says to the bartender, then motions at me for my order.

"I…" I hesitate. "Nothing for me, I'm good."

The bartender seems unbothered, turns and heads to collect Ethan's order. "Are you sure you don't want anything?" Ethan asks. He furrows his brow in question but doesn't push. "It's socially acceptable nowadays to order water or soda."

"I'll take a water then," I say.

When the bartender returns with the beer, Ethan slips him money. The change is returned with a plastic cup of warm tap water. I take it, thanking Ethan and the bartender.

"Let's head to the tables," Ethan says. "Jason already has a booth."

I nod, again, following his lead and mazing my way through the crowd of people. It takes longer than it should to move the short distance to the seating area, but soon enough, we reach a back booth with a young guy, perhaps early twenties, sitting with two girls.

My stomach drops, the sour smell of the room making me miss Hope and the smell of her baby breath. I'm starting to wonder if this is a lame attempt on Ethan's part to match me up with a nice girl.

Jason stands, moves to Ethan. He's shorter than Ethan—coming only to his shoulders—slim and dressed in all black. I'm mildly shocked to see them kiss on the mouth, but only because it's a new sight. The kiss makes me think of Ella. Has she kissed another girl in the months she's been away?

The two women—girls—are dressed provocatively, with dark make-up covering their eyes, their lips pouted like fish. One is dressed in a tight red dress, the other in a white dress that has cutout patterns exposing her shoulders. They squeeze together so that we fit, and we shimmy our way into the booth.

"That's Rochelle," Ethan says. Red-Dress gives a wave. "And that's Hedi." White-Dress smiles. "This handsome devil is Jason." He squeezes his cheeks.

Jason pulls away. "And you must be the straight man with the missing lesbian wife," he says.

The two girls chuckle.

"Babe," Ethan says.

I shrug, laughing it off. "I generally go by Keith, but 'straight man with the missing lesbian wife' works too."

This seems to please Jason. He laughs, his eyes sparkling with mischief. Ethan's normal and natural confidence seems to waver, his face becoming a mask of insecurity.

"Lighten up, Eth," Jason mutters.

The conversation moves toward work, the four of them talking about an orderly at their hospital. I focus on my water, drinking the heavy-filtered liquid only to appear busy. The music shifts to something techno, the frantic beat making my heart rate pick up. A waiter appears at the table, holding a tray of several test tubes, a blood red liquid filling them.

"Shots!" Jason exclaims. The girls squeal in excitement. He rises to take the tubes and passes them amongst the party. He hands one to me, and I suddenly feel like I can't refuse it. How lame would I be to say no, to pass, and let them fight over mine?

It's cold in my hand, the pungent smell oozing from the tube.

Jason raises his hand, smiles at the group. "To a night off!" he exclaims. "May it lead to drunken madness and flirty fortunes!"

"Flirty *mis*fortunes!" White-Dress says.

"Here! Here!" says Red-Dress.

Ethan looks at me. "It's cool if you don't want it."

Jason notices this exchange, and despite there being zero reason for concern, something like the look of jealousy fills his eyes. His mouth gets pointy. "Ethan don't be silly!" He clanks his tube into mine. "Cheers! Here's to Keith joining the squad!"

The girls thrust their tubes forward, wait for me to meet them halfway. I don't want it. I shouldn't feel pressured to take. Yet, my hand moves forward, clinks into each of their tubes, as I say, "Bottoms up!"

I chug it, the burn tickling in a frighteningly good way at first, then a chemical aftertaste scorching my throat and nose, making me cough.

"That's what Ethan was saying last night!" Jason says, laughing, initiating more chuckles from the girls, and a slight grin from Ethan himself. It takes me a second to catch on.

A second server appears at the table, this time with blue test tubes resting on her tray. My empty stomach gurgles in revolt. How can I possibly put anything but food into it at this point?

"Jesus, you ordered round two already?" Ethan asks.

"Round three is shortly after," Jason quips, proud of himself. "Pineapple. We haven't had an entire weekend off with each other in, like, months. Let's enjoy it!"

My anxiety grows. "I'll skip the next shots until I secure some food," I say, forcing a laugh.

"Nonsense," Jason insists, forcing the tube into my hand.

I take it, unsure why I feel like I can't decline. They count to three, and this time I try sipping it instead of throwing it back. The burn makes me pucker my face.

Red-Dress—Rochelle—laughs. "It's been a while since you hit the party scene, huh?" she asks. "It's like riding a bike; it'll come right back to you. Shoot it back, don't let it touch your tongue."

I follow her advice, tip it back, and drop it in. It still burns, but the aftertaste passes quickly. I nod.

"How old are you? You still seem pretty young to be out of the game," she asks.

"Twenty-seven," I say.

"Same," she says. She takes a swig of her chaser drink, winks behind the glass.

"Let's dance!" White-Dress exclaims.

Jason and Red-Dress seem excited about this. They thrust their arms into the air, hollering.

Okay, Keith, I say to myself. Now you are back in control, no more drinks. No more pressure.

"If we all go dance, we'll lose the table," Ethan says.

"It's fine," Jason says, pulling at Ethan to get up.

I offer to stay back, but then Red-Dress—Rochelle—starts pulling me to the floor. As we make our way into the dance thrum, the pulsing music makes my head start throbbing. I feel a tad lightheaded and wonder if the drink is hitting me that fast.

We all start dancing, me awkwardly trying to avoid touching Red-Dress, this weird little sadness bundling into my gut. I miss Hope. I'm worried for Ella, still, after all this time. But a strange new thought is rooting in my brain. *Where's Jenny?*

I wish Jenny were here. I'd love to dance with her, hear her laugh, feeling safe knowing she wouldn't pressure me into Daddy's demons.

I shiver.

White-Dress dances over, a drink in hand. She passes it to me. I shake my head no.

"Vodka Cranberry," she says. "Try it. It's sweeter than the shots."

I take a hesitant sip, surprised to find that she's right. It's delicious. Sweet and easy to knock back, almost like there's no alcohol in it at all.

Maybe that's her cover. She's just drinking juice in the pathetic way we pressure ourselves to fit in. Like it'd be weird and shameful for her to have a good time without a cup of poison in hand. My dancing becomes more natural, moving seeming to become more fluid.

"I'm getting another," White-Dress says. "You want one?"

"Why the hell not?" I tell her, letting my reservations go. Why the hell not…

SD

I focus on the disco ball and realize the room is spinning. I laugh, because, for some reason, this is hysterical. Rochelle grinds her backside into me. A light giddiness fogs my mind. Ethan turns to me, slumped onto the top of a booth.

"Who are you looking for?" he asks. "You keep studying the room like you're on the hunt for someone, or maybe you're just forming an exit strategy."

I smile a lopsided grin. "You have great pores. Do you moisturize?"

"Are you looking for someone?" he asks again, slurring and slapping my hand from his face.

"Shh," I say putting a finger to his mouth. "Richard can't know."

Ethan pulls away, smiling, "Who is Richard?"

"Richard can't know I think Jenny is beautiful," I slur, wiggling my eyebrows up and down.

"Jenny? Text this Jenny!"

"She's too good at life," I say, and get the urge to hug him. I don't realize I'm doing it, but then Ethan says, "Okay, cool guy!" as he peels himself from me.

"Did you ever notice that we have a day, or a week, or a month for everything? A Donut Day. A National Haircut Day. Basketball Week. Gallbladder and Bile Duct Cancer Awareness month! I mean, Jesus, when does it end?" I ask him. He says nothing, shaking his head, so I go on in an old man voice. "Today is a serious day, it's Traffic Awareness Day," I say. Then I switch to a girly voice, "I'm sad, it's Middle Child Day."

"Ya done?" Ethan asks.

"We should go for a walk. It's Skyscraper Appreciation Day! Look, here's my new kitty, it's Adopt-a-Cat Month. Did you get pasta? It's Noodle Day."

"Now are you done?"

"I'm sick of it. Sick of it, I tell you! So sick of it, in fact, that I declare today Keith Day. A national holiday to celebrate the fact that there is absolutely nothing else to celebrate."

"Dude, declare it *Jenny Day*, and text her."

I start shaking my head, but before I can respond, Jason appears. "Shh…he's here," I say.

"What?" Jason asks. "You talking about me?"

"No."

Jason creases his eyebrows, and Ethan tries not to laugh.

"I think you need to take it a little slower," Ethan says, taking away my drink. "It's a bit early to be this wasted."

I take my drink back, downing it. "Fries! Order me fries," I yell, wondering why the room is swaying.

He laughs, leaving, maybe to order the food, maybe to do something else. Jason hands me a shot of something else. "Don't listen to Ethan. Drink up!"

I take it, the taste no longer burning.

"You're fun," he says, proudly.

So, I take another and then another. Pounding them down just like Dad—the pecker-head.

SD

"Teach him a lesson," I say.

"Huh?" Jason asks.

"I should have taught that pussy a lesson. A man stands up for himself," I mutter. Something snaps inside of me, this itching making me pissed off and violent. My tongue twitching for more of whatever Jason keeps feeding me.

I scan the room for him, for Frank.

"Frank, let's teach Scott a lesson," I holler.

"What the hell are you talking about?" asks Jason.

I look for Frank again. In the sea of unfamiliar faces, a familiar one rains down. I point it out and Jason turns. "Look, it's Scott," I say.

Jason chuckles. "Who's Scott?"

"My asshole brother. I wanna go kick his ass."

"Don't be a pansy!" he laughs. "Go fuck him up!"

Jason's low gravel voice makes my insides splinter. I feel angry. So angry and pissed off that my brother had the audacity to die, a lesson should be served. "Fucker totally blamed me for Dad being a cunt. The asshole!"

Jason laughs, giddy and drunk. He turns back, talking to Red-Dress.

My fries come, and I inhale them, feeling less sober by the minute. Feeling like I want to do something. I get up for the bathroom, my eyes looking for Scott—shit, wait, no, Scott's dead. I stumble, righting myself on the wall.

"Scott!" I call.

I make an uneven lap around the entire bar, not seeing Scott anywhere. I head to the bathroom, splash some water on my face, and take a piss. The room is spinning, the mirrors jumpy. For a second, I see Frank's face in it, so I shatter the glass with my fist.

When I head out, I make a loop, looking for Scott again. I find him talking to an attractive woman with long black hair. When she pulls up, her ocean blue eyes bore into me. My heartbeat picks up, and for a hot second, I swear it's Ella. Disgusting rage fills me…*Lesson. Teach him a lesson!*

I shake my head. *Get it together, Frank…*

Keith. I'm, Keith.

I move back toward the table, scowling. The problem with people like me is that we are always seeking approval. That's all I've wanted my entire life. To have done something that resulted in acceptance and approval. Mostly, from Frank. I tried so hard to please him. To find a way for him to be proud of me. But that's a joke. Nothing I ever did was good enough for him. I could never make him happy. And now, today, it's his fault that I walk around with my bones weighing me down, just trying to please everyone. Just searching for approval and acceptance any place I can get it.

I need to be liked. I need to be loved. I need to be told I've done a good job, and that's just stupid. I shouldn't care. I shouldn't worry. I shouldn't try so damned hard to do what everyone else wants me to do. I should…I should accept the fact that I'm not great. I should accept the fact that I'm not special. I should forget about pleasing everyone and just do whatever the hell I want.

Screw, everyone!

I sigh, alone, drunk, and pissed off. *Let's start shit. Slapping your hand into something will help you feel again.*

I'm Frank. I'm drunk, and I'm Frank.

Lesson. Teach that boy a fucking lesson.

I move for him—Scott—right toward him. I barrel right into the wall of man he's become. The creature turns, baring his ravenous teeth.

"Scott!"

"It's Jim," he mutters. He gets this drunken glint in his eye that makes my stomach do a little flip.

"Fuck you!" I say, wanting to hit him for Frank.

"What's your problem, man? Pathetic drunk," he says.

Years of Frank calling me pathetic swell to a dangerous level in my head. White hot anger blazes inside me. "What's pathetic?" I ask. "The size of your dick?"

He's confused for a second, not expecting a fight. He recovers fast, equally hardened and ready with his fists. "Say that again to my face."

I laugh, because I did, in fact, just say that to his face.

Idiot, teach this shit a lesson.

I can't tell if it's him saying it or Frank. More anger comes. More memories of Frank saying the same thing on replay.

Pound him. Pound him in the fucking teeth.

I lash out, but falter.

I am not Frank. I am not him. I take a breath and reach for control.

"Scott, I'm sorry. I'm sorry." I go to hug him, move to put my arms around him. "I miss you. I love you. I don't want to hurt you."

"Faggot!" he spits, pushing me with the palms of his hands.

Lesson. Lesson!

"What?" I ask, feeling like a sob wants to break from my chest.

"You heard me. You're *pathetic!*" he says. "You're a fag," he says, face pinched and eyes drunk. "You're here with the faggots."

Rage, and this need to hurt him, overwhelms me. Daddy taught me well. It doesn't bother me that he's bigger, and probably even stronger. I have years of experience being hit.

I ball my fist, like Daddy showed me, and thrust it upward into his chin making his teeth slam together with an awful, ear-piercing crack. His eyes go wide, and blood drips and squirts down the edges of his lips.

He shrinks back, trying to hide his face, but people are hooting and hollering and thrusting their fists into the air yelling. "Fight!"

We're all animals. It's like in middle school, when a fight would break out in the play-yard and everyone would gather around chanting, "Fight. Fight. Fight." People worry about the apocalypse coming. Well, this is it, people. We *are* the apocalypse. It's already here. We are what's wrong. We are the end.

He gains confidence from the audience's chants. His face contorts, and the veins in his neck bulge out. He doesn't know me. He doesn't know what I'm feeling right now. He doesn't know that, when I'm drunk, I feel nothing at all.

"You'll be sorry you did that," he says.

I don't regret it, and I'm not sorry. I'd do it again if I had to. Even if he kills me, I wouldn't be sorry. Lessons need to be taught. So, I just raise my eyebrow. It's a small expression change, but it gets my point across. Someone needs to teach this boy how to behave like a man.

"Fucker!" Out of nowhere, a wild, screaming woman lurches from the crowd and slaps me. "That's my boyfriend!"

Her foot moves, up, then down, and suddenly I'm falling, going limp to the ground, a piercing throb hitting my temple.

I get a look at the barbed wire tattoo on the woman's arm. "Pamela Anderson?" I ask. Then blackness swallows me.

Chapter 30

Crawling out of the darkness of sleep, back into reality, back into consciousness, I realize I'm home. My comfortable bed and soft sheets cocoon me, offer a hug against the harsh light infiltrating the window blinds. The punitive smell of body odor and sour breath makes my stomach feel flimsy, ready to break open. My head pounds.

"What happened?" I groan.

The sun is shining through the windows, and the rays feel pointed, feel like they were sent just to punish me. I reach to remember something, anything, and then the mental image of getting my ass kicked by a Pamela Anderson wannabe makes my urge to vomit stronger.

Shit…

I hit him—Scott—but not Scott.

The guilt feels like a slap, and I close my eyes to stop from spinning.

Frank, I remember thinking like Frank. I remember wanting to start trouble, wanting to hurt.

I try to sit up, but something heavy keeps me down. Then, pain throbs through my head, forces me to slow my breathing and take deep breaths. *What the hell happened to me last night?*

A guttural, throaty snort sounds to my left, followed by the smacking of dry thirsty lips. I jump, unsure what type of animal to expect in my bed. "Christ!" I shout, ready to be attacked by some hideous creature.

I turn to see the animal, a hideous thing, indeed—the question is better phrased as *who*…who to expect in my bed. Ethan is lying adjacent to me, his face relaxed, his open mouth releasing hot air that hits me in the face, makes my stomach lurch. He's under my covers, the top part of his body—also known as the chest—naked and exposed. His tan shoulder jutting out like a tree limb.

Shirtless? He's just shirtless. He's in my bed, shirtless.

I better have pants on. I go to check. Then, like a dummy, I realize why I can't sit up. The heaviness isn't only from my head. My eyes follow his shoulder down his hairy man arm. It's draped across me, around me.

"What the hell, Ethan? Get off of me!" I shout, tossing his arm away as hurriedly as possible.

He groans and stirs, coming to, ever so slowly. He yawns and scratches his head, his eyes sleepy and distant. "Morning, princess," he mutters, yawning. "Singing a different tune this morning, are we? What happened to Poo-key Bear?"

"What the hell happened?"

"You're a nut case, that's what happened." He yawns again. "You were out cold for a good ten minutes after that kick. It was wild. As a person of medicine, I could not, in good conscience, leave you alone for the night. Someone needed to keep an eye on you—and Rochelle and Hedi would have taken advantage of you."

"Such a gentleman," I mutter. "And you didn't?"

He rolls his eyes. "I considered taking you to the hospital, but I didn't know if the cops would show up asking questions. That was my first time trying to control an uncontrollable drunk."

I think back, slowly remembering bits and pieces of me singing at the top of my lungs.

"I was worried. You get a little…a little dark. And we need to work on you thinking you can just hit people. I thought I was just a one-off case."

I close my eyes. "Was I singing Alanis Morissette?" I ask, groaning.

"It was Meredith Brooks, and it was unfortunate." He rolls over, pulling the covers with him, and I realize I'm still in bed with him. Then, I see his exposed back. "Jesus, you're not naked, right?"

"Maybe!" He laughs.

I stand from the bed, moving to the nightstand to study my face. It's pale, drained, and lifeless, but undamaged. I finger my temple. A lightning bolt of pain shoots, and I jump, pulling my fingers back.

"I'm not naked. I have boxers on. Plus, even if you wanted something from me, it doesn't mean I want anything from you," he says, rolling back over and pulling up the covers to confirm. "I'm a happily committed man."

I think back. "Your boyfriend's a bit of a dick."

"Well, he's never provoked a violent altercation."

I'm silent for a moment at that. "I think I'm still drunk. My head is spinning," I say. "I'm sorry I ruined the night.

"Jason," he sighs. "Jason will be pissed I didn't spend the night with him. But he'll get over it."

"I'm sorry. Should we never speak of this again?"

"That's probably for the best," he mutters.

I go to leave the room, but then hesitate. Something inside me feels weird, different. I'm regressing. I'm getting worse. I've tried so hard to make positive changes, to notice what I'm feeling and deal with it, but now my fears are coming to roost. I felt Frank inside of me last night, even though he's still somewhere in this world, causing trouble of his own.

"Last night is exactly why I don't drink."

He doesn't acknowledge me at first. How would anyone else understand how much I felt like Frank last night? How would anyone else understand why that's my biggest fear? They couldn't. But then he says, "You were seeing Dr. Ryder right after…Faith. There's nothing shameful about continuing therapy, Keith."

He sounds so clinical, medical, and professional again. Like he has two hats that he's switching between, and it makes my head swim.

"Yeah, maybe."

"We all have people in our pasts we can blame for why we are messed up today. Who are you blaming?"

I blame…Frank…I blame him for everything. I go around harvesting every negative feeling and emotion, and then I trace it back to him. I bring him into every experience with me. I remember the horrible things he did and said on a daily basis. I blame him for the pain in my past, I blame him for the pain my mother endured. I blame him for every shitty memory I have growing up. I blame him. I do. I blame him for everything bad in my life.

I cover my face.

I blame him, no one else. I blame him, because what else is there to do but blame?

I blame him, because if I didn't, I'd have to own up to my own mistakes. I blame him, because if I didn't, I'd have to accept the fact that things are the way they are. I blame him, because it makes it easier to think about the feelings that well up inside me. It makes it easier to accept that I'm insecure, that I'm scared, that I'm alone, and that I don't have the answers. Blaming him puts all of that on him and it takes it away from me.

Frank is always to blame.

Chapter 31

"Dada," Hope says, her cheeks red and rosy. The outside air is warm for October, the sun shining in bright rays. She teeters on chubby toddler legs, taking a step, then bouncing on her bum in the well-manicured grass, the grass now browner than green.

A pale-yellow rose rests on Faith's gravestone, a rose I didn't put there. A rose rests on every tombstone of a child under three in this cemetery. A rose put there by someone who must be hurting as much as me.

After last night's shameful display, I needed to be with both my girls. I stand, silent and thinking. Thinking of everything I'm grateful for, and everything I'm not. I've blamed Frank because he is ruthless, yes, but *I've* let his poison become my crutch. *I've* let avoidance become my song.

Hope trying to walk is almost like a dance. She's dancing around her sister's headstone, as if she weren't dancing alone. She smiles and laughs and calls for me with her beautiful voice.

How can a heart be full and broken at the same time? How can you smile and cry? The only answer seems to be you just can.

I rub my fingers on the worn cotton of Faith's cap, as I watch Hope play in the murmuring breeze. Today, this year, is nothing like the today of last year. I try to picture what it could be like. I try to imagine the differences that could have changed everything.

Would Faith be like Hope?

I can't seem to straighten and organize as fast as Hope manages to untangle and scatter. She is like a wave that rushes through the room, littering the floor with toys and debris. Cute face, but don't let that fool you. She'll tear the room limb by limb. It's movies pulled from the cases and pages missing from books. It's strawberries mashed into the carpets, and marker scribbled on walls. It's cell phones in the toilet and Cheerios in my briefcase. It's bubbles poured in shoes and fruit snacks under pillows. If Faith were here, would that all double?

Hope. Hope's my life, and Ella's missing it.

It's my thoughts of Hope that bring this smile to my face. I follow her with my eyes, then with my ears. Now, she's singing. She's singing, "Maisy Mouse," as she wobbles her way around the dead grass in the cemetery.

Maisy Mouse is her new favorite book series. Maisy has a panda, and Hope's favorite toy is her stuffed panda from Jenny. I think that's why she loves the Maisy stories.

Hope's favorite spot to read or sing about Maisy is her fort. She pulls me into our hallway with her little hands and closes all of the doors. We have four rooms adjoining a short hallway, and if you close all of them at the same time, it creates a fortress. Sometimes, she likes to turn all the lights off and sit in the dark. She makes me sit down too. Refusing to let me leave, she leads us in a chorus of "Maisy Mouse." We sit in there, for what feels like hours, as she continually opens and closes the doors to let the light flutter in and out at her will. Silent streams of golden light pouring onto her face and then disappearing as fast as they come.

As she hums and sings "Maisy Mouse" now, I watch as the light dances on her face just like it does in our fort. Just like it does when she cracks open the door. An inspiration of life and hope shining its way through the darkness. Exactly what she is for me too.

I smile, and then I chase after her. "I'm going to get you," I yell.

She falls, crawls, and squeals her cute little squeal. "No," she giggles back. "No."

"Oh, yes I am." I blow a kiss to the tombstone—to Faith—as I chase Hope back in the direction of the car. I scoop her up and blow raspberries in the crook of her neck. She shrills and arches backward, trying to escape my embrace. I do it again, and she laughs harder. It's that laugh that fills me inside. It's her voice, and love, that hold the pieces of me together. She's my glue. She's the thing that makes me hit play in the morning when it'd be easier to pause. The person who makes stop impossible.

I squeeze her.

"Dada?" she whispers.

Love. Love is raw and dangerous. It can make people do incredible or awful things. It's the easiest thing that manages to be equally difficult. It's confusing and complicated. It's wrong when it's right. It's everything around you saying no, but the universe screaming yes. It's all of that, till it's not. Then it's love, and love is love. It's a whisper that you shout. It's a beating of your heart. It's the flutter from within. It's pure. It's simple. It's love.

A driving emotion that changes you. A filling that wipes away the bad. Love is different. It is shifting. It's weird and sometimes irrational, but it's love.

How is it possible to love someone the way that I love Hope? Love, to me, was always complicated. It was always messy. Always a fight till the bitter end. But, loving Hope, well, it's clean. It's a fresh and free start. It's this feeling that pumps through my blood, telling every fiber of my being to live for love. Pure, simple, primal. This protective instinct to paint the world I want her to see. This immense pressure to laugh and cry when I see her smile. The tenderness one word whispered can mean.

"Dada," she whispers again.

"Hope," I whisper back. She smiles, and I do too.

Chapter 32

"Keith…Keith? Earth to Keith."

My foggy, still hungover, mind snaps to attention. "Huh?"

"Are you okay? You've been washing the same coffee mug for the last ten minutes," says Christina, crossing her arms.

The hot water bubbles under the spout, warmth emanating at the source, then fading as my distorted reflection stares back.

I was thinking about the way you look when you stand over a puddle, your reflection distant and rippled. Wondering what it would be like to be that Keith, to be the Keith on the other side of the pool. The self-contained Keith, who doesn't have to force a mirrored smile. The untouchable one who's safely locked away, only needing to exist. You can stay there, safe and frozen, but okay.

"Yeah, I'm fine," I say. "Daydreaming, I guess."

She looks at me wearily, and I turn back to the sink, shutting the faucet off and holding back my sigh. What sort of person wants to live in a puddle?

She stays planted, rooted at the counter, arms still fastened, looking at me intensely, like she has something heavy to say.

"Is there something I can help you with?" I ask, moving toward the Crockpot to stir the pork roast that's been simmering on low for the last six hours. The smell fills the room, and I poke a fork in to check the status.

She shrugs. "No," she says, sighing. "It's just…" she starts, but is interrupted by my phone. It rings and buzzes enthusiastically, the screen illuminated, reading "Jenny." I move to silence it, but Christina shakes her head. "Go ahead, you can get that."

"It's fine, you were about to say something."

She nods, her shoulders seeming to loosen. "Get it. I'll check on Paul and Hope in the living room. It was nothing important."

I dry my hands on the kitchen towel and bring the phone to my ear. "Hello?"

"Higs!" Jenny says, her voice a tad different on the phone. "Sorry to bother you over the weekend." I hear something clatter, then what sounds like a car door closes in the background.

"No worries, what's up?"

"I've been in the office, working on the Solvent case, to finalize the contract. Richard was pretty adamant that it be closed yesterday."

"That makes for a horrible Sunday."

She chuckles. "Yeah, I'm really living life." Her car starts, and there's a moment where the audio changes, distorts. "Can you still hear me?" she asks, tinny.

"Sure can."

"Anyway, I'm sorry to be a pain, but I was wondering if I could have you look at the contract? I need another set of eyes on it. I could swing over, and I promise I only need like fifteen minutes of your time."

"Ahh," I say, and my mind goes to Christina and Paul who are here for dinner. But it's Jenny, and if I know anything about her, it's that she would drop everything to help me. "Of course," I say. "I live in Mission Hills though; it'll take a good thirty-five minutes to drive here from the office—fifty if there's traffic."

She sighs, relieved. "Thanks, Higs. That's fine, I don't mind a drive. Back home, the nearest grocery store was a good half hour."

"Right, you're a country girl. I've seen what your neck of the woods looks like on our Detroit trip."

After hanging up, I send her my address, and an unexplained nervousness builds in my stomach. I wind my way to the living room, suddenly super aware of the toys and laundry that should be put away.

Christina and Paul are sitting with Hope on the carpeted floor, a sea of different toys surrounding them. Hope notices me, her smile lighting her face. She teeters, and then drops to her knees, crawling for me. I swoop in, making an airplane noise and pulling her to my hip.

She nuzzles into my side, giving me a squeeze before stiff arming me and wiggling back down to the ground.

"Hope, come over here and show Daddy what you've learned," Paul says. He looks at me, making sure that I'm paying attention, that I'm ready, and then focuses on Hope. "Okay, Hope, say 'Pop.'" He exaggerates the pronunciation. "Pop!"

Hope smiles, her toothy grin on display. "Pop!" she says, her little voice proud.

Paul laughs, ecstatic, starts clapping. Christina and I join in, and Hope laughs, enjoying the praise.

"Now she needs to learn to say 'G,'" Christina says. "If she can say Pop, she should be able to say G."

"You're trying too hard to be hip, darling," Paul says. "I bet if you try to get her to say—" he pauses, then whispers, "—Nana—" Christina purses her lips, "—then she'd already know how."

"I'm not old enough to be a Nana!" Christina says, but she scoots closer to Hope, holds her hand. "Say Nana."

"Nana!" Hope says.

Paul laughs, and I snort. Christina's eyes go wide.

"Nana!" Hope says again.

"Oh, my word, it's actually adorable! Okay, I'm Nana." She points at herself, like Hope speaks sign language. "Nana!"

We all laugh, and Hope shows off proudly. After some time playing, Christina asks, "Who was on the phone?"

That nervousness builds in my stomach again. "A work colleague. She's actually coming here now. She needs me to review a contract for work."

Christina's eyebrows collide. "On a Sunday? At dinnertime? Why can't it wait till Monday?"

"Our boss is relentless—she's feeling pressured to submit it today."

Christina's face doesn't seem to buy that response.

"It should only be for a few minutes."

"It's fine," Paul says. "It's no issue—just stinks anyone has to work on a Sunday."

Christina seems annoyed by that, but then adjusts her face to look uninterested. "Well, on that note, I guess I'll just ask what I wanted to ask before any new guests arrive."

Paul grows anxious. He moves from the relaxed, lying down position he was in, to a seated position, his back pressed into the couch.

"Yeah?" I ask.

Christina puts her hands into her pockets. "I talked to Ella. She finally answered one of my phone calls."

My stomach drops to the floor, the room suddenly gets warmer.

"How is she? Is she coming home?" I ask, the words rushing in a flurry.

"No," she says, and her eyes lose something, her shoulders looking defeated. "She asked about Hope, misses her."

I nod.

"She said…she said that you know why she left. She was sure that you would have told me—so that maybe I could understand." Her hands pull from her pockets, go to her hips. "Funny thing is, you haven't said anything, Keith."

I feel heat on my face. "We got into that fight before she left. I said horrible things, I told you that."

She shakes her head. "She assured me it wasn't something you did, because I asked. My mind jumped right to the worst-case scenarios, but she shut that down. She said it's not that, she said it's something she's battling. Something she has had to live with and carry on her own. And it sounds like it's not only about losing Faith."

"Yeah," I say, but there is an anger growing in me. Say it! Why can't she just come out and say it? Does she think they'd somehow stop loving her? Her parents live and breathe Ella.

"I'm spinning. In my head, I'm spinning for an answer," Christina says, pausing. "I hurt, Ella…somehow. People damage each other," she says. "Sometimes intentionally, but mostly unintentionally. Somewhere along the line, she learned how to hold her emotions back, and I let her."

"Honey," Paul says. "There's nothing—"

"How can we fix it? How?" asks Christina, her serious eyes boring into mine.

"I don't know," I whisper, pinching my mouth together. "I *really* don't know."

"Can you please just tell us what you do know?" It's Paul speaking this time.

I shake my head. "It doesn't feel right to say it for her."

"Please," Paul says, pleading.

My breath catches, Hope tugs on my pant leg, and I reach to pick her up. I tell it like I understand it. "She's hurt and confused. She loves you both so much, but because life is life, she's felt like she's had to wear a mask her entire life. She's felt like she had to wake up every day and play a part that society was forcing her to play, and she didn't know how to communicate her needs. Or maybe she even felt guilty about having those needs at all. But when Faith died…her mask started to suffocate her; it felt impossible for her to untie it."

"I'm not following. What mask? What do you mean?" Christina asks.

"Ella thinks…she feels like she might be…she's…she's gay."

❧

"She's here," I say, startled by the doorbell.

"Well, let her in!" Paul chuckles.

We walk to the living room, leaving Christina in the kitchen to finish setting the table. Hope is on my hip, and I'm holding her close against me, feeling her wiggle beneath my arms.

I grab the door and swing it open to meet Jenny.

She's smiling, her energy like a light. I have a weird thought that she's like the light that trickles in through the cracked door. A shining to chase away darkness.

She smiles at Paul, and he smiles back, ushering her in and asking for her coat. He takes it and she sets her briefcase down next to the door.

She's dressed in her work clothes still, yet alarmingly relaxed. Her hair's tousled, a few more buttons undone on her blouse than normal. She's calm, her cheeks rosy from the breeze, her eyes happy and clear.

They meet mine, smile, but then she moves on, looking past me to Hope.

Hope's foot goes out, her leg raising and wiggling to show off her new pink shoes.

"Hey, you! Are those new shoes? I love them." Jenny laughs, inspecting them closer. "You'll be all the rage at daycare!"

Hope wiggles and twists, kicking her way to the floor. I put her down, and she tumbles to Jenny.

Jenny crouches down to her knees, opening her arms for Hope to waddle into. She stands up, swinging Hope to her hip, blushing under her blush.

"Forgive me!" she says. "I'm Jennifer…Jennifer Clark. I work with Keith."

She moves toward Christina, putting her hand out, offering a hello. Christina paints on a smile and offers her hand. "Hi. I'm Christina. Keith's…Keith's…" she stammers. "Hope's grandmother. You've meet Hope before?"

There's an awkward silence I jump to fill it. "Hope goes to daycare at my office. We've both stopped by at lunch to see her."

"Keith's told me so many great things about you!" Jenny says.

Christina gives me a quick, pointed look. "And…I, you," she lies.

Paul moves to stand next to his wife. He tickles Hope with one hand and reaches to shake Jenny's other hand. "I'm Paul," he says, and I appreciate his lack of assigning a title.

I move to her, closer. I haven't said hi, officially, and it feels awkward.

"Hi! Come in! Let's get away from the door."

"I'm sorry to crash the evening. I just need, like, ten minutes, and I'll be out of the way." She returns to the briefcase, grabbing it with one hand. "Although, I am happy I got to see this cutie," she says making a face at Hope.

Hope smiles, wiggles down, and then crawls for the toy box and starts ripping everything out. She holds her favorites up for Jenny to see. She doesn't hold Panda up. She tucks him under her arm, already sure that Jenny knows of him.

"Nonsense," Paul says. "Dinner is on the table. Why don't you join us first?"

"Oh, I'm so sorry. I didn't realize the time. I can't intrude on your dinner." Her face turns red.

"It's no problem," I tell her.

Jenny's hesitant. She looks at me for a second, then sits on the floor next to Hope. "Are you sure?"

"Absolutely," Paul says.

Chapter 33

Christina and Paul are gone, splitting soon after dinner, Paul dragging a puffy-eyed Christina to the car. Christina visible wrestling with the idea of Ella being a lesbian, and her face showing the proof. It's new for her. Or maybe it's the fact that we ate dinner at the sturdy mahogany dining room table, the one Christina and Paul had purchased as a gift for Ella and me. Something about that meal made me feel like it was less mine and more their table.

Jenny is at that table now, still. Marking her papers with red pen in the places I suggested changes in the contract.

At dinner, everyone talked except Christina. She stayed quiet and reserved, studying everything that came from Jenny's mouth. Jenny seems to have passed the acceptance test with flying colors for Paul. But, with Christina, I felt the need to remind her that there is no test. That we are only friends. Every once in a while, I glimpsed Christina's eyes, and I swore it was Ella looking at me. My stomach would flip, but then I would push that ridiculousness away, and I would focus on the sun, and the sun is Hope. How she would laugh and giggle in her highchair. How she watched Jenny talk with a sparkle in her eye. How she made sour, pouty faces at Paul and how he made them back.

She is the sun, radiant and brilliant, her smile like the streams of light poking through the clouds. She's beautiful.

If I'm honest, Jenny is beautiful too. Is that wrong? Would it be wrong to admit that I think she's beautiful, despite still loving Ella? I once was told that the best people in this world know how to love other people. But how can love be so thick, so tangled, so twisted into a ball sometimes that it's almost impossible to understand?

"It's sort of hot in here," I say. It's probably the last mild night for a while. "When you're done, want to bring Hope out back before bed?"

"Sure," she says, shuffling her papers. "I'm all done. Let's do it, Higs." She secures her paper bundle with a clip and then tucks them into her bag.

I get Hope bundled up in a coat and hat, and we make our way to the back yard. It's a gorgeous night, the fresh air is crisp, and it wakes my sleepy brain. The moon is full, beautiful, the clouds dabbing the darkened sky around the reflected light. That same light echoing off the swing set, illuminating our faces.

Hope's little face—round and smiling—is tilted toward the sky, beaming, as her eyes take in the hugeness of the consuming moon.

"Moon," I tell her.

"Moon!" she shouts, parroting me.

"Yes, isn't it pretty?"

Jenny glides across the backyard, stops and sits on the swing with her eyes smiling.

Hope reaches up, grunts and groans with exaggerated effort, in an attempt to grab the moon and hold it in her arms. "Ah. Ah. Ah," she grunts, reaching above her head.

Jenny snickers. "I think she wants to touch the moon."

Hope continues reaching, her frustration starting to reach her face. Jenny stands from the swing, puts her hands up, and goes up on her tippy toes as she's reaching too. "Ah," she says, reaching.

Hope hears the noise, stops reaching, and studies Jenny with a serious look.

"I'm reaching too, Hope," she says, jumping now, dramatically.

Hope tries to jump but doesn't get far from my grip. Jenny leaps, and it sends Hope into a fit of laughter.

I move her to my shoulders, and she raises her arms to try again, giggling. Then, she goes quiet. "Dada," she whispers. She rests her head on my head, kisses me on the forehead.

Her voice is different—in a bittersweet way—little, but big, as if blossoming. It's the first time she's sounded like someone new to me, like a little girl just flowered in front of my eyes, my baby now slowly, little by little, growing into a beautiful little girl. A smart, witty, gentle little lady.

"Moon," Hope says again.

Jenny moves back toward the swings and sits down, pushing off. "You have such a cute backyard."

"Benefit of being out here in Mission Hills," I say, crossing the yard and putting Hope into the baby swing. I count off and then give her a swing, making rocket swishing noises and pushing her closer to the moon.

"I love it. The houses are adorable, and you have great outdoor space," she says.

"Are you right in the city?"

She nods.

Suddenly, Hope screams at the top of her lungs—loud and high-pitched—making me jump. She screams, again, equally loud and terrifying. "Hope? What? What's wrong?" I start panicking, stopping the swing to inspect her.

She screams again, and just as I think something seriously wrong is happening, a belly-rolling laughter follows.

"Are you kidding me?" I ask. She screams louder, in a girly high-pitched squeal that makes me cover my ears. She screams one more time, laughing and giggling afterward, like screaming as loud as possible is the funniest thing you can do. "You're naughty!"

Another scream breaks the air next to me. Equally as loud, but not quite as startling. I turn, catching Jenny throwing her head back, laughing after her scream.

"What the heck…"

Jenny screams again. Hope laughs hysterically, then screams back. It goes on and on, both of them screaming and laughing so hard until I'm laughing. I let out a scream, as high and as loud as possible. My voice breaks, and Jenny snorts. "Stop, stop, stop!" Jenny says. "I'm going to pee myself."

This provokes me to scream again, and Hope giggles into a fit.

"Hey! Keep it down over there," comes from somewhere in the darkness. Then I laugh again, guttural and deep. It's so hard, it's almost ridiculous.

"Sorry," Jenny yells. "Shh. Shh," she says, trying not to laugh.

I clamp my hand over my mouth, still silly with laughter. I grab Hope from the swing and run for the house.

Inside, we all laugh again. Out of breath, I say to Jenny, "You're naughty too."

"So, I'm told," she says, giggling more.

I put Hope on the ground, and she crawls with lightning speed for the bin of toys in the living room. She starts pulling out toys and books, turning the room into another mess.

"Oh, no, no, little girl. It's past your bedtime!" I chase after her, catching her quick, and jiggling her. "I have to lay with her, or she won't go to sleep," I say.

Jenny jumps to her feet. "Oh! I should get going, it's getting late."

"Oh, I didn't mean…I wasn't trying to kick you out…"

Jenny laughs. "I've stayed longer than I was intending. Thanks for the contract help."

Something in me wants to thank her. I want to say, *no*, thank *you*. Thank you for making tonight a little different. For bringing extra laughter into our little world.

She moves for her stuff, grabs her bag and slings it over her shoulder, her coat still on from before. "Well, I'll see you tomorrow then," she says. She crosses over and strokes Hope's head. "Good night, cutie," she whispers. "Gosh, she is just beautiful. Her dark hair and crystal blue eyes."

"Yeah," I say.

"It's not my business…" she starts, then sighs. "Sorry, I know it's not my business, but how is she? How is Ella?"

"The rule, Jenny!" I smile.

"I know, I know."

The words dangle on my tongue. "Fine," I say, breathing out. "She's fine."

She nods, moving away toward the door, not wanting to pressure a further response. Hope wiggles trying to get down, but I fight her.

"Well, thanks again," Jenny says. "Don't make her wait any longer. Poor thing's tired," she says, nodding to Hope.

Except she's not. She's nodding toward my crazy child—who is five seconds away from rampaging the house—because she's nice and wants to give me an easy out.

"Ella's gone, she's not coming back. She's left me because she's... she's gay," I say in a rush. It's like all the air has rushed from the room, but with it, a weight, a weight and a pretense that's been resting on my shoulders for so long.

"Oh, Keith," she says, and there's a conflicting tension in her face. Maybe relief and pain washing over her in an instance of pity.

"The damn rule," I say. "It's fine really, the hardest part's been not saying it. Now I've said it, and it's out there, and I'm still breathing."

Her hand comes up to the strap of her backpack. "I'm proud of you, Higs," she says. "For sharing another scar."

"Yeah, I'm an open book, remember?" I ask, chuckling at the remembrance of our Michigan carpool.

"Hey, you invented the rule, remember?" she says. "Would it help if I gave you a hug?"

My stomach twists, because, yes, I want that, but then it settles like a stone, because I've already been close enough to smell her tonight—that floral scent endearing and enticing—and I don't think I'm strong enough to be surrounded by it and then let go.

"I don't think it's a good idea," I tell her.

She nods, backing closer to the door, her eyes steady on me. "Then, on that note," she says. "Happy sleeping for all, and to all a good night." She smiles, big and emphatically. "I'll see you tomorrow, Higs."

"Tomorrow," I say.

She glides out the door, and I hesitate to close it. Watch her walk for the car and look back up at the moon. There's a tickle in my stomach.

I close the door, lock it, rest my head on the wood door.

"Dada," Hope says.

I take a breath, then move to pick her up from the floor. Shutting the lights off around the house, we make our way to the bedroom. Dressing Hope in jammies, and then brushing her few budding teeth, we start the tedious bedtime routine. The monotonous changing and brushing, closing and settling.

There was once a simpler time, when I could just feel tired and go to bed, but now there are tasks upon tasks. Routines that have to happen for sleep to be granted.

I pull down the sheets, settle into the clean, cool bed like a sigh. Exhaustion making me want to close my eyes as soon as my head hits the pillow, but Hope jibber jabbers and talks to her panda, making him jump on the bed. "Bedtime, sweetie," I whisper.

"No," Hope says.

I yawn. Hope sits up with Panda, tossing him into the air, laughing. "Lay down."

She pops up, bouncing on the bed. I take her, lay her down, but she giggles more, bouncing higher and harder into the air.

The night feels heavy. Without Jenny here, my mind's back on last year. Back on the day where everything changed. Back on the day where I lost Faith, then I lost Ella. The sadness washes over me, even though I don't want it to.

Hope jumps again, landing on my head now, laughing.

"Ouch," I holler, grumpily. I grunt, covering my arms over my face, sighing. "Jesus, just lay down."

I decide to fall asleep anyway, to drift off and let Hope figure it out on her own. *Nothing is ever easy, and nothing ever will be.* But then I'm startled. Warm, wet lips are pressed into my exposed cheek, a heat and warmth coursing my veins, instantly filling me.

I pull my arms away. Hope's smiling face beams at me, with all the answers I never knew I had the questions to.

Love. I love this little monster more than life itself. More than the sea of words in the dictionary could ever define. The reason for my life...is her. As peculiar as it sounds, I feel like Sleeping Beauty. Like, true love's kiss just woke me up. I'm Sleeping Daddy.

"Want to hear a story?" I ask.

Hope settles into me. I tuck her under my arm, holding the hand that isn't holding Panda. I close my eyes, and talk, the words soft and mumbled.

"Once upon a time there lived a handsome King,
Who loved his Princess even more than the flowers of spring.
That King worked hard all day and all night,
To run his kingdom without a fight.
The wind blew heavy, and it was hard to dream,
But the Princess could always find a way to make him beam.
The sky tumbled and rumbled as he fell asleep,
No noise could wake him from counting sheep.
All the land could hear those snores,
They were loud and rumbling like the mighty shores.
He became known as *Sleeping Daddy* by all,
Because no one could wake him, no noise big or small.
Then, one day, his Princess came along,
She gave him a kiss that made him feel strong.
The King awoke with no more fright,
And smiled always, day and night.
So, every day from that day on,
The Princess scurried to that sleepy King at dawn.
She was fast and speedy, and never late,
For she knew her kiss would decide his fate."

She breathes, still. Fast asleep... forever protected by me: Sleeping Daddy.

Part 5

December

Chapter 34

The monstrous tree, green and glittering, fills the noisy space with its scent, the fresh pine mixing with what must be synthetically infused wisps of peppermint bark. Fake foil-wrapped gifts clutter the ground at the base, blinking lights alternating between red and green. Chatter competes with the festive tunes of Christmas.

On the tree, I search for my ornament, pull it off, and go in search of Jenny's too. When I find hers, I inspect it closely—a wooden reindeer with her name scrawled in cursive, the yearly memento from Life at Your Reach for signing your life over to the devil.

Tucking it into my pocket, I duck and weave through the meticulously strung-together people, avoiding eye contact and willing the clock to tick faster, questioning why? Why? Why, am I here at a company Christmas party anyway?

Scratch that. I suppose I know the why. Jenny! The only reason I'm here is because Jenny asked me to come. The only reason I decided to leave Hope for the night was to see Jenny.

At the bar, I order the signature drink—spiced cocoa—but I ask them to make it without the alcohol. "So, you want hot chocolate?" the bartender asks, and I nod.

He hands me an oversized red mug, my hands warming at the touch. The drifting smell corresponding with the taste, chocolate and sweet.

I'm missing Hope, and I'm doing it because…because Jenny.

Scanning the room, my nerves zing, and I check the clock again.

I'm anxious, but maybe it's not all about Jenny. There is a thought that's been wiggling its way into my brain. The approaching holiday has me thinking about the Christmas house—the one Mom and I would go and see every year. We'd take a bus, just me and her, and spend hours bundled up in hats and scarves, roaming the streets, looking at the beautiful lights. I think of it every year, but, this year, I want to go back. I want to see if the magic in my head meets reality. But then, there's still Mom. I couldn't work up the nerve to find her when I was last there, and my heart would want to go find her after seeing that house again.

Downing the drink, I find the dessert table and load up on overly sweet treats. Eating one and then another, I wander the room awkwardly. *Should I leave?* I bite into another piece of candy, my stomach aching and head pounding, Jenny's laugh plays like a song.

I see her, perched, studying the giant candy canes surrounding the entry. Massive and glossy red-and-white plastic that marks the path forward.

"These are fantastic," she says to someone I don't know.

The unknown person mumbles a response I don't catch. I wind my way through the stuffy room to get closer to Candy Cane Lane, a new take on "Santa Baby" beating through the speakers, making the room feel more confined.

Jenny's wearing tight, black leggings with high-heeled leather boots that roam to her knees. Her sweater is red and oversized, acting more like a dress than a shirt. It buckles around the waist and buttons high around her collar. Dark red lips rim her mouth, her light complexion standing out in comparison. She moves in slow motion.

Disconcerted, I move closer. I cross the room in great strides, maneuvering through the cluttered space. As I approach, her eyes catch mine, her mouth smiling. She does this little wave that makes me smile back.

She's moving toward me now, too, but before she reaches me, Rebecca, her friend from the accounting group, steps right in front of us, cutting us off. I stop abruptly, almost crashing into the back of her, trying to slow my barely halting gate.

Jenny giggles, giving another little wave. I return it awkwardly.

"You look great," Rebecca squeals, leaning forward and hugging her. "Doesn't she look great, Keith? Tell her!"

Oh, so you did see me. "You look great," I say, and Jenny giggles again.

"Stop," she whispers, giving a silly spin. "So do you!" she tells Rebecca. "And you, too, Higs."

"You've got to go sit on Santa's lap. He's giving out free socks. They're fuzzy and so cute," Rebecca whines.

"Okay," Jenny says.

Her smell strengthens as she steps around Rebecca and closer to me. "Hi, Keith," she says, nudging me with her elbow.

"Hi." I nudge her back.

Rebecca leads us toward the bar.

"So…" Jenny says.

"So…" I say.

"So…you came! I'm glad."

"Yeah…I'm happy you're here. I've determined I'm lame." I smile and it feels silly. I try to stop it.

"Higs, you're not lame! Crazy, yes, but not lame."

"How's it back to me being the crazy?" I ask.

"Lest we not forget thee who mumbles to himself."

I chuckle, shimmying up to the counter next to her and snatching up a festive-looking cake ball.

"What should I get?" she asks.

"I had the hot chocolate. It was good, but I'll be in a sugar coma soon," I say, mouth full of cake.

She laughs. "It's Christmas, the time to indulge. What are you getting?" she asks Rebecca.

"Vodka tonic for me," Rebecca says. "I don't do the fufu holiday specials."

"Well, I'm joining Keith in the sugar coma," Jenny says, ordering a candy cane mocha drink. We wait for the drinks, then the three of us make our way to a standing table on the far side of the giant Christmas tree.

"Does Richard come to these things?" I ask, looking to see if he's around.

"This is my first holiday party," Jenny says.

"He was here last year," Rebecca says. "Let's avoid that hot mess at all costs."

I chuckle. That's the first sound thing Rebecca has said.

"I see Charlotte in line to meet Santa," she says. "BRB."

Jenny nods.

When she's out of earshot, I say, "You may want to avoid taking advice from Rebecca."

"Why is that?" Jenny asks, taking a sip of her drink. The white, frothy, whipped cream leaves a spot on her nose.

"I don't think she has your best interests in mind."

Her face lights. "Why?" She laughs.

"You've got…" I say, using my finger to scoop the foamy whipped cream from her nose.

She raises her hand and wipes at her face.

"She thinks sitting on Santa's lap is a good call, but I'm warning you, because that guy's a total pervert. He's copped a feel on every girl in here," I say, shrugging. "I mean, Rebecca claimed they were fuzzy socks, but they looked pretty basic to me."

"Basic socks are the worst," Jenny agrees.

"I think they say 'Life at Your Reach' too. People can't be that proud of where they work."

Jenny laughs. "People love free stuff. We work in marketing, and we know these things, Higs."

"We work in sustainable marketing. Nonetheless, here we are, entertaining the idea of futile consumerism."

"The irony!" she teases. She pivots, moving the conversation along. "Are you almost ready for Christmas, Higs? Did you spoil Hope?"

"Are you trying to catch my hypocrisy?" I laugh. "The amount of shit and unrecycled wrapping paper I have under my tree is enough to get me fired on the spot."

"Self-awareness is an important quality," she teases. "I respect that in you."

"What about you?" I ask. "All your shopping done?"

"I was an eco-friendly little elf this year and sent wool dryer balls to the entire family. I'm sure that's exactly what they had at the top of their lists."

"Self-awareness is an important quality," I tease.

"Mm-hmmm," she says, taking another sip and wiping her face as a reflex.

"Are you heading to the mountain for Christmas?" I ask.

"Not this year!" she says. "I'm horrible, I know, but this year, I just wanted to try it out on my own. How about you? Are you Michigan-bound?"

The nervousness from earlier is back, swimming in my stomach. "Actually, yeah, I think I might be making a trip."

"Jenny!" interrupts Rebecca.

Jenny turns at hearing her name.

Rebecca's not speaking. Instead, she's laughing and pointing up.

Jenny gazes up, then covers her face, so my eyes follow the same path. Ceiling. Ceiling and something green and leafy hanging overhead.

I squint, confused, before the word comes to mind: mistletoe. It's mistletoe.

"Come on, you two. You have to kiss!" says Rebecca.

"It's a work party," Jenny says. She looks at me. Her face smiling and beautiful, and so close. What is she thinking? She goes to laugh, goes to joke, goes to deflect, and I suddenly just can't. I can't live with the fact that we've gone our entire lives under the same sun—under the same stars—and my lips haven't touched hers. My cheeks heat, and then my hands are on the base of her neck, pulling her to me, seizing the moment, and crashing onto her lips, while my body clumsily fumbles to catch up.

Her hands move to my shoulders, and I am kissing her, connecting our mouths in feverish need. Her soft lips shut around mine, her lipstick smearing, edges breaking and parting in rhythmic dance, and for that moment, it's just me and her—her and me—the sweet taste of chocolate between us. Breaths exchanging fast and hungrily, then slowing to a simmering, steadying burn.

We break apart, gasping, our faces only inches apart. My eyes open, fall upon Jenny's vulnerable shut eyes, and I'm failing, stumbling, forgetting to stop myself, as I pull her back to my lips. Her beautiful face—innocent and pure—open for me to take. I pull her into me, her hands clutching around my neck to hold on. Her lips parting for my tongue to push inside and explore. Her body resting against me, leaning, and my hands travel.

My heart races, clarity and insanity mixing together as time quickens and slows in unison. Life, it's rushing and roaring around us, but we are static. I am breathing air. My mouth is making love to hers in endless and fruitful swipes, and I am breathing all of the air in this universe. I'd been breathing under water my entire life.

I slow the kiss, pulling away only enough to give her upper lip another nudge with mine.

I wait, dizzy, panting, whirling in a windstorm of heat and passion.

She stays in my arms, pressed against me, and all I do is breathe.

Her eyes open and lock onto mine. A moment of need fills me, tightens my body to iron, and I study her face, perfect and there, warm and heated under the dim lights. My lips still tingle, urging me to go back for more. The colors in her eyes chipping and shattering in hues of green that flicker and break like candlelight.

"What the hell?" asks Rebecca, breaking the moment, stealing our quiet.

My heart drops.

Jenny wiggles, moving away, and the noise around us clangs back into focus. Music and laughter and motion swirling where it doesn't belong.

"I've never seen a mistletoe-kiss like that. Hell, a peck on the lips would have sufficed, Keith," Rebecca scolds.

I chuckle, but my stomach flips—an apprehensive haze tainting the beauty from before. Worry rushes in. Worry that our kiss will be the muttered secret, passed around the office. Our first kiss, and everyone has seen it.

Rebecca laughs, starts pulling Jenny away. "Girl, you need to touch up your lipstick now," she says.

Jenny turns back only once as she's dragged away. Our eyes meet, almost longingly. Then she's gone, and I'm left standing alone. Confused, excited, nervous—everything all at once. I reach up and drag my hand across my mouth. Red lipstick smears.

A chill snakes up my back, and without comprehension…I run.

Chapter 35

The darkness can't find a space amongst the midnight sky. The glowing of the moon in assistance with the twinkling houses of the December night make the presence of dawn seem closer. The shadows from the branches of the trees etch and reach inside the bedroom in consequence. Christmas is coming, and the world is pretending to be joyful.

The quiet house creaks, moans in defense of the blustering winds. The clock says 12:23 a.m., and my mind spins with her taste. Dizzy with the sweetness of chocolate and Jenny.

I abandoned the party tonight, abandoned her there, after what had to be the best kiss of my life. The bed dips as I roll, reaching for my phone. I fumble, check for a message, anything, looking for a reason to call her so late.

We have the next week off; work can't be my motive. And I've already decided, we're leaving tomorrow, Hope and me, taking off on our Christmas adventure. Driving out to Michigan to see that house, to see our Christmas house, and take a real picture. And after I show Hope that house, I'll go to Jane's with the address Meredith gave, and call her. I'll ask for Mom, and I'll see what happens.

I climb out of bed, weary, but not able to sleep. I make my way down the stairs. Fidgeting, I curl up on the sofa, try to blink rapidly to force sleep.

Jenny's eyes, her lips, the sweet taste of her, the curve of her body as it arched and dipped into mine—it's on an endless loop in my mind. How could I be so stupid as to leave?

I sit up again, this time flicking the TV on and looking toward the kitchen. Maybe one drink? It won't be a problem if I just have one. Just a glass of wine, focus on the TV, and lock Frank in the vault.

I can do one; one isn't a problem. It's fine. I don't drink the hard stuff anyway, so just wine. One glass, that's it.

I stand, the cold of the hardwood leaching into my bare feet. I walk two steps, hesitate, but then keep shuffling.

One glass. One glass is fine. I'm home, not out at the bar. No hard stuff.

I fumble around the kitchen in the dark, knocking over the salt and pepper as I search for the light switch. Flicking it on, the loud brightness makes me squint.

I retrieve a glass and find a bottle of wine, oddly hidden behind the cereal. Corkscrew in hand, I dig the metal tool into the soft, durable cork.

A knock.

My hand stills on the glass, stops with the turning of the screw.

Silence, only the sounds of my breath wheezing. I listen closer.

Nothing. No sound, but I swear I heard a knock. Swear that I heard something knocking on the strong wooden door. Or someone.

I cross the kitchen, turn through the family room and to the entryway. At the door, I flick the outside light on.

Another knock.

Hesitant and moderately alarmed, I look into the peephole.

Her face is flushed, red, and filled with tears. Her arms are wrapped around herself, hugging in tight unsure vice. Her beautiful face isn't like I remember, isn't as soft and sure as it always was.

I open the door, anxious and confused but pleased.

She sees me. A bark of pain wretches from her mouth. Her eyes wet with tears that lean toward painful sobs. She moves into me, folding herself into my arms, small and fragile in the night. "Keith," she cries.

I hug her, wrap my body around hers. "Come in…come in…"

She moves in, shuffles, and I guide her into the house, closing the door, then bringing her to the sofa. I sit her down, fetch a blanket, and wrap it around her shoulders.

"Jenny…Jenny what's wrong?"

She looks at me, hiccups trying to stifle her cry. Reaching forward, I wipe at her tears, stroke her cheek. It's freezing cold, like ice under my hand. "You're so cold."

I put my arms around her, hold her, and rub my hands up and down her arms.

"I've been outside…" She sniffles. "I saw the light turn on. I didn't want to wake you."

"What happened?" I ask again. Her lip quivers, her mouth not wanting to cry. "Are you hurt? Did somebody hurt you?"

She nods her head yes, then shakes no, unclear with the answer.

I hold onto her, hug her, fill her with my heat. She makes no move to talk, so I do the same. We stay there, her locked within my arms, her small soft sobs making me ache inside.

I move, lie back, pulling her onto me, resting all of her blanket-covered body against me. We stay tangled, twisted in heat and limbs. Until her sobbing diminishes, until her cries turn to breathing, until her mind comes to still.

Tonight, her scars are open.

SD

The morning light streams in gentle strokes through the shaded window. The soft hum of movement evident in the outside world. Jenny still sleeps, her body motionless in my arms, the blanket cocooning her from whatever made her hurt last night. The warmth between us helps me forget the persistent urge I have to pee.

I stroke her hair, moving my hand in soft motions. "Jenny…"

She's still, her face soft and finally back at peace.

"Jenny," I whisper again.

Her eyelids flutter. Her body trembles, shutters, and then her eyelids quiver open. She stares for a second, confused, then she closes her eyes, brings her hand to her forehead, and tries to shimmy out of my grip.

I hold onto her, keeping her from moving away. "Don't go…"

She stills, her head turning, eyes opening, flicking back and forth between my eyes and my mouth. "I'm sorry," she whispers. "This is uncomfortable, I embarrassed myself last night."

"No…you didn't."

"I did. I shouldn't have come here." She looks away, her eyes filling with tears again.

"I wanted you here…"

Her eyes come back to mine, scared and reckless, a brief spark igniting.

"What happened?" I ask.

Her spark is gone again. She stiffens, then pulls away, tries to stand up. I attempt to hold on to her, but let her go as she persists. She gets to her feet, hands me the blanket. "I'm sorry I came here. I should have known better." She flattens the wrinkles in her outfit, runs her hands through her hair.

"I'm not. I wanted you to come. I regretted leaving the party."

Her eyes dart back and lock onto mine. She goes to say something and hesitates. She tightens her face. "Everything in this world is made to be broken," she murmurs.

I stand, too, reach out and grab her hand. This is not Jenny. Jenny is endlessly optimistic. The light. "Don't be like me. Not everything has to break."

She starts crying again. Her normal smile nowhere on her face. "But it always does! Everything always breaks! I don't want you to break me. I don't want to break you." Her words come out in a hushed rush. "I break everything, Keith." She looks away, defeat filling her eyes. "Trust me."

"I do trust you."

"That's not what I meant… You're still married," she says, disappointment on her face.

"And she's been gone almost a year."

"It doesn't change the truth!" she barks.

"The truth is, she's a lesbian."

Her eyes sharpen to take me in. I rub circles with my thumb on her wrist.

"Last night, when I kissed you…it scared the hell out of me too."

"Don't," she pleads, eyes filling, last night's mascara running down her face.

"It scared the hell out of me because I've wanted it for so long—I just couldn't admit it. I know I should mourn Ella longer—I should feel ashamed. But I don't. I knew that, after it happened—kissing you—it would change everything. I knew that, after it happened, it'd have to change everything, because kissing you once could never be enough. It's not enough."

Her lips move a fraction, and my eyes are on them.

"I'd really like to kiss you…again," I say. "We're all a little broken. We all have flaws. Scars, as you like to say. It'll always be hard, but that's life. That's feeling. They're the symptoms of living and feeling the world around you."

She trembles.

"What happened last night?" I ask again.

"I'm scared," she whispers.

I pull her close to me, and it's like that's where she belongs. "Of what?" I whisper.

"Losing myself again. Falling back into the person I used to be."

I squeeze her. "We all live with that." I think of the wine I wanted last night. I think of the night out with Ethan, my drunken meanness.

She sighs, breathing, contemplating. "Last night, I embarrassed my-self. Made a complete scene at the party, because that Santa touched me. He grabbed me like you warned me he would, and I lost it on him. Slapped him and went berserk." Her face pinches, tears welling, and threatening to spill again. "Rebecca got so mad. Didn't understand why I was making it such a big deal. But it wasn't right, it's *not* right. He shouldn't be able to touch me if I don't allow it."

I tighten, angry not only with the Santa, but with me.

"I'll beat the bastard," I say. "I wish I would have stayed. I wish I would have been there to stop him. I'm so sorry."

She hugs me tighter. "Don't apologize for him," she whispers.

"I'm leaving today. Come with me."

She sniffles. "Where?"

"Michigan."

Her eyebrows come together. "What's in Michigan?"

"Detroit."

A tear falls on her cheek. "What's in Detroit?"

"Answers."

She hesitates. "You expect me to go all the way to Detroit with you, when all you'll tell me is 'answers'?"

"Yes."

"Will Hope be going too?" Her mouth twists, almost smiles.

"Yes."

She leans in, hugs me, rests her head back on my chest. "I'll go, Higs."

"Thank you," I whisper.

"When?"

"This afternoon."

"Today?" she says, shocked, but amused.

"Tomorrow?"

"Today is fine," she whispers.

I smile harder. She rests her chin below the hollow of my neck and looks up. I stare at her, running my thumb across her face, under her eyes, then down to her lips. She shivers. I want to tell her that, even though her eyes are puffy, and even though her makeup is smeared down her face, she looks more beautiful than ever before. Instead, I shiver, too, and kiss her again.

It's a soft and gentle kiss that seems to calm the chaos in our minds. Her lips part around mine, and my heartbeat marches in frantic beats against time.

Pulling back, Jenny whispers, "Now what?"

"We go to Detroit."

"And then?"

"We come back."

"And then?"

"We figure it out."

Chapter 36

"This is exciting," Jenny whispers, relaxed, comfortable, leaning against the armrest. "Another thirteen-hour car ride to Michigan, with the threat of snow, plus, this time, with a toddler!"

The worry of waiting for Jenny was torture, yet she'd needed to talk to Richard, needed to formally file a complaint against that bastard Santa, and I was willing to wait as long as it took, if it meant she was still coming with us.

The sun is resting low in the sky, flame dwindling as we get closer and closer to the night. "It is," I say. "At least, this time, we aren't in a Tesla, and we have the *Frozen* soundtrack to play on a loop. 'Let It Go' isn't getting old at all," I tease.

"I prefer 'Do You Want to Build a Snowman?'" she says.

"I have a secret," I whisper, signaling for her to inch in closer. "'Let It Go' is going to be the death of me."

She laughs, biting her lip, leans forward, and hits repeat. "I think we should enjoy this a few more times."

"You devil!"

"What? I don't want to deny Hope her favorite song. She deserves to enjoy herself on this long…scratch that…very, *very* long trip."

Hope chuckles after hearing her name, lifts her toy, and shakes it.

"So…do you want to tell me what's on the agenda in Michigan?" Jenny asks, adjusting her seatbelt and unzipping her purse to dig inside.

I tighten my grip on the steering wheel, keeping my eyes trained on the road. "Don't get mad," I say. "I want to take Hope to see Christmas lights." Boston is filled with beautiful lights this time of year, so I rush to explain. "Not just any Christmas lights, but…lights that were really important to my mom and me as a kid."

"Why would I be mad at that? I'm excited to see that part of your life. Is your mom…has she passed on?" she asks, her hands stilling and no longer rooting through her bag.

"No—she's alive."

"Thank god," she says, seeming relieved. "Is she coming to see the lights with us?"

Snow flurries have started outside, so I hit the wiper blades. "I'd really like that."

Jenny goes back to rooting in her bag. "I'm excited to meet her then, Higs."

The song ends, and I see Hope start to get restless, but then repeat strikes and the chords of "Let it Go" start back up settling her.

I sigh, anxiously. "Yeah…"

"Are you worried about me being there? Does she know about Ella's… departure?" she asks, finding a tube of ChapStick and saying, "Ah-ha!"

She smears it on her lips, the scent of cherry filling the space.

"'No," I say. "I'm not worried about you. I'm worried about me."

"Why do you say that?"

I check the rearview mirror again, see Hope content and playing with Panda. "When I was young, Mom and I would take a bus to this neighborhood on the outskirts of Detroit. It's called Sherwood Forest," I tell her. "We were really poor. Not just poor in the sense that we did without luxuries, but poor in the sense that we did without necessities."

She reaches out and puts her hand on my arm.

"For us, wasting money to get all the way out there was a huge deal. We had nothing to waste. But, somehow, every year on Christmas, she found a way to get us there."

"So, it's very bittersweet—a pleasant, but painful, memory."

"I guess."

She rubs circles on my arm, and I realize I haven't been completely forthcoming with the details. "Jenny—I haven't seen my mom in ten years."

Her hand stills, stops doing the circles. I run the wiper blades again. Jenny breathes out.

"Does she know we are coming?"

I look over at her, then down at her hand on my arm. "I haven't talked to her in years."

She sits up taller, adjusts herself in the seat. "Okay," she says. "I wasn't expecting that." She pauses. "Are we seeing her?"

Hope's eyes are looking heavy in the mirror. I lower the volume a notch. "I don't know. I mean, I want to. I don't know. I wanted to on our last trip, and I couldn't."

"Sherwood Forest?" she asks. "That's where this house is?"

I nod. "It's a historic neighborhood, filled with unbelievable houses. They're incredible. Back then...to us..." I stumble, looking for words. "It was a lifestyle we could only dream about. These houses were massive pieces of cultural art that brought us—Mom and me—to another place. It got us away from Dad," I tell her.

I feel her tighten, so I pause, but then the words rush from me, needing to be shared. "There was one house in particular we loved. It'd be the last house we'd go see at the end of the night. Mom would spend hours there, if I'd let her. It was made of stone and had massive archways. It looked like a castle, and we'd pretend we were royalty. We'd talk in fake British accents and contemplate how life on the other side of the wall was," I tell her. "They covered everything with lights, and you could see their tree in the front window. It was massive and golden."

"It sounds lovely. I'm assuming you haven't seen the house in years either?"

I nod, notice Hope's eyes close further, her lips press into the sleepy duck face she always makes. I lower the music so that it's barely audible. I think of how much I love Hope, how much my chest aches when I look at her.

"How can my mom not miss me? How can she not know that I need her? I left her behind with my dad. I was selfish, and I left her on her own, when I could have helped her," I say, my voice shaking. "I know that, but she can't blame me for my dad being an asshole." I mutter, a lump growing in my chest. "I'm sorry, I don't know why I'm drudging this up."

She pats my arm again. "Do not apologize, Higs. From what you've told me, from what I've put together, your mother, she let you go for a reason. A reason that may not make sense to you or me, but a reason that made sense to her. She loved you and wanted your happiness over hers, which meant she was willing to let you start over. She was strong and brave, just like you. Your mom doesn't think you left her behind. To her, she was with you. She was living a better life with you in Boston. She is there, even if she isn't."

I feel her eyes on me, but mine stay on the road. Mom always tried to protect me at the detriment of her own needs. "How could you possibly know that?"

"Well, I can't…but I do."

"So, tomorrow, I show you this house, and then what?" I ask.

"We figure it out."

SD

The clock shows after 10:00 p.m., the night sky, the lack of traffic on the road, and the soft hum of tires on blacktop is rocking Hope into a deeper, dreamy sleep. Jenny turns, takes her in, and whispers, "How is she this cute?" She shakes her head and yawns. "Talk about something,

I'm getting sleepy too."

"I took your ornament, the one they gave out at the Christmas party. It's on our tree."

She smiles, her head leaning in to rest on my shoulder. "Can you drive with my head like that?" she asks.

"Mm-hmm. You don't have to stay up, you can nap. Last night was a rough night for you."

She doesn't say anything, but her head moves, nods to acknowledge the comment.

"Should we talk about that, actually? Why it upset you so much?"

She's silent for a long time. So long, I think she might be sleeping. Then, she sighs. "I was mad and hurt."

"With Santa?"

She tenses, her hand squeezing my arm. Her voice comes out timid, low, unsure. "And someone else."

"Who?"

She lets the murmuring motor fill the silence, breathing in uncomfortable patterns.

"It's okay," I say. "We don't have to talk about it."

"I mentioned it—him—before. On our last trip out west."

I think back to our time in the Tesla, to her nervousness at the mention of scars. "Your stepdad?"

"And people like him," she says.

I shiver, flicking from low to high beams, and then back again. "I'm sorry."

"I don't want your apology."

"Did he…hurt you?" I ask.

Jenny sucks in her breath. "Let's…not," she says, her hand moving to her face. Hope's eyes open for a second, so we go still, silent. Hope looks around, then closes her eyes again.

After a beat in silence, Jenny leans over the center console and rests her head on my shoulder again. She whispers in my ear, "I'm sorry. I'm not ready, okay? I just want to enjoy our Christmas adventure."

"Okay," I say.

Quiet fills the space again, and dread hits my gut. There is a sad reality to this world: it hurts us all. Something about Jenny's hurt ignites my anxiety. The world has stolen my innocence once before, what's to stop it from doing it again?

Jenny seems to doze off, her head still resting on my shoulder, and I wish there was more I could do to support her. I look to Hope, and my anxieties become exothermic. How can I protect her from this world? How can I protect her from the hurt that seems to come along with being human?

It nearly makes me want to curl into a ball and never move.

SD

2:00 a.m., the cold and crisp frost eats its way across the grass of the Holiday Inn. I grab our bags and Hope, as we huddle together, shuffling into the lobby.

The king room seems just big enough for the three of us, and my bones feel tired and sore. I settle Hope into the bed. "More than halfway." I yawn. "Should get there tomorrow afternoon."

Jenny nods and yawns too. She looks around the room at the dated curtains, and dark-colored floors. "Our old digs, remember? We should watch *Simba's Pride* again."

We laugh, then look at each other awkwardly before shifting our eyes down at Hope.

"I'm going to clean up," she says, disappearing behind the bathroom door.

I change quickly, then settle back on the edge of the bed. Afraid to fall asleep before she emerges. A new nervousness dances inside me.

The door swings open slowly, the bathroom light already turned off. She steps into the low light of the room, and there's something so beautiful about seeing her stripped down. She's wearing plain, powder blue pajamas, face clean of makeup, hair brushed straight. She moves closer, smelling like a mixture of mint and flowers, a delicious combination of her toothpaste and lotion.

She comes to my side, sits next to me on the bed, her beauty radiating, captivating me.

She puts her hand on mine and looks me in the eyes. My hand comes to her face and touches the soft skin. She turns her head into my palm. We sit there like that until I have nothing but my desire to fall to. I pull her to me and kiss her. Soft. Slow. Passionately…then fiercely. My tongue explores the sweet remnants of her mouth; my hand moves down her back.

When the kiss slows, I pull back, studying the mole above her eyebrow, and she turns, smiling shyly. Her dimples show; I trace kisses over her eyes and nose, my lips tickled by the fluttering of her eyelashes.

"You are beautiful," I whisper.

She smiles that shy smile again. Her hands come around mine, eyes opening with a question. I move to kiss her again, but before our lips can touch, I hear Hope moan. I stop and lay down, putting my arm around her to comfort her.

"Dada?" she mumbles half asleep.

"Yes, baby," I say, stoking her hair.

Jenny touches my arm, then crawls across the bed to the other side of Hope. She finds my hand and laces her fingers through mine. She puts her feet on top of mine and places a kiss on Hope's forehead.

I tell the story again. The story that Hope loves, and neither of us can now sleep without. "Sleeping Daddy," I whisper. Jenny rubs her thumb over mine. "Once upon a time, there lived a handsome King, who loved his Princess even more than the flowers of spring…"

I whisper the last of the story and watch as both Hope and Jenny drift into sleep. Tonight, I get to hold both of them.

Chapter 37

Detroit—cold and brisk— hits us with thick strands of winter sun. Pulling into the Hilton Garden Inn in downtown center city, the hotel is huge and plain compared to the colorful Motown mural flanking the inn.

Hope squeals. "No!" she shouts, squirmy and ready to run after being cooped up. She wiggles impatiently against her safety harness straps.

Inside, the lobby is warm, brightly lit, and decorated chaotically for Christmas. Santa figurines in every shape and size are scattered around, snowmen mixed in between, holding puppies and kittens.

The room is cozy, clean. A king bed—the frame made of wood—is turned down. The window shade is open, letting the sun trickle in, and the city stretches out in front of us. I let Hope down, and she crawls through the room in a rush, exploring every inch.

Jenny hangs her coat in the closet and tucks her bag at the bottom. "I always find it strange that road-tripping can be so exhausting. I've been sitting for hours, yet I'm so tired."

"There's no rush to go anywhere. You can nap if you need."

"I'm down for whatever. Ready to head out and explore whenever you are," she says. She kicks her boots off and sits with Hope.

I still don't know what I want to do—or rather, how I should go about doing it. Jane, the woman whose address and phone number I have to find Mom, lives above a laundromat in a part of town I don't want to be walking around in after dark, especially with Hope and Jenny. It took us a better part of the day to make it here. At best, we have a good two hours before sunset, but Hope's been in the car and won't be too eager to be strapped back in.

I feel myself wanting to push off going to find Mom till tomorrow. It just makes more sense, but I know if I wait, my anxiety will only begin to boil. It'll boil and boil, until the rapid simmer burns all of my courage into avoidance.

"Maybe you could stay with Hope, and I could go and talk to Mom?" I ask, shoving the room key into my pocket.

Jenny's eyes travel to me, her smile warm. "Sure," she says.

"It's just—"

"Don't even explain—go!" she tells me. "We'll be fine. We'll go down to the lobby and get some snacks, and then I'll introduce Hope to hot chocolate."

"Thank you, Jenny."

SD

Laundryland is a twenty-seven-minute drive, situated on the corner of Dequindre Street in Forest Park Detroit. On the drive, I find myself rehearsing what I should say, but then it raises my apprehension, so I decide to focus on the radio instead.

On Mack Avenue, my unease spikes again, as the neighborhood turns darker, more run-down and littered with gratified walls. To my surprise, as I get closer to Dequindre Street, the neighborhood improves, and I'm pleased to see recently renovated buildings and clean streets.

The laundromat is freshly painted, gray, with a neon sign flashing. Laundryland.

221

Parking, I climb from the car and fish for the number to call Jane. Three—no four—people shuffling about with laundry can be seen through the hefty windows of the laundromat front. Another woman, with long gray hair, waits outside on a metal bench, a magazine in hand, and a cigarette puffed back to mostly ash hanging from her mouth. She looks me over and gives a smile.

I punch the number for Jane into the phone, the smell of cigarette smoke burning my nostrils and reminding me of the nights I'd wake up, needing to cover my face and block the smell of Frank's late-night cigarettes from reaching my lungs. It rings, but Jane doesn't answer. It goes to an automated message stating the voicemail box is full, try again later.

I breathe out, feeling like I'm smoking the same cigarette as the stranger on the bench. "Excuse me. How do I get up to the apartments above the laundromat?" I ask.

She draws on her cigarette, the end turning red, and the ash quivering, threatening to spill. She exhales, blowing the smoke to the sky, and then licks her cracked lips. "Entrance is on the far side of the building, sweetheart. Can't get to it from the Dequindre side, but there's an alley right over there that lets you cut around." She points it out.

"Thank you," I say. "Happy Holidays."

"Who you tryin' to see? I know everyone up there, and I ain't ever seen none of them with a pretty white boy like you." She chuckles.

"I'm trying to find Jane...I don't know her last name."

"You sellin' somethin'?" she asks.

"No, I'm—"

"'Cause she'd be real mad if I send you her way and you're tryna sell her something she don't want." She flicks the expired cigarette, goes back to her magazine. "She ain't friendly. Don't like no one."

"I'm not selling anything, I can promise you that. Just looking for someone she might know," I say.

She puts the magazine down. "And who's that?"

"My mom."

The woman studies me, crinkles her eyes. She shuffles into her purse and pulls out another cigarette and fumbles with the lighter. "2A, sweetheart, but you didn't hear that from me," she mutters around the cigarette.

"Thank you."

She waves me off, and I follow the alleyway around the building, the smell of fabric sheets wafting from the dryer vents. The thought of Frank lingers, and I wonder, suddenly, how close he is. I hustle faster.

On the far side of the building, I find an unlatched door leading up a set of stairs. At the top of the stairs is a hallway, five off-white wooden doors lining the space.

I find 2A, nerves dancing in my gut. I hear a TV on inside, the sound of syntactic voices and music. I think about calling the number again, but then I knock instead. I knock three times, and wait, the sounds of the TV still blaring.

When nobody comes to the door, I knock again. "Hello! Anyone home?"

There's no answer, but I hear movement, sense a degree of irritation coming my way. I go to knock again, but the door opens a crack, swings only partway open, while still chain-locked.

"Who are you?" a stern voice growls, still hidden behind the door.

An older female hand flashes in the open space, shows she's holding a wooden bat, just in case I've came with malicious intent.

"Jane? Are you Jane? I tried calling," I say, making my voice friendly.

"And did I answer?" she asks, sarcastic, her voice thick and hard, like life has had a thing or two to teach her.

"I'm sorry to bother you, I really am. I'm looking for Lily Higgins." I wait, giving her a moment to talk. She doesn't respond. "Please," I say.

"I don't know a Lily Higgins, never heard that name," she says.

Dread fills my body, and a panic makes me fidget. "Are you Jane? I got your name and number from Meredith Dorse—in Boston. Lily is my mother, and I'm looking for her, I just need to talk."

She closes the door. "I told you; I don't know who that is. You shouldn't have come here."

The door is riddled with black scuffs and scraps, so, instead of pounding, I rest my hand on the battered door. I wonder, if I use the name Frank, if that will garner any remembrance. "Please. Lily is my mom—I need to find her," I plead.

There's another long pause, then a bang on the door. I jump back, startled.

"Are you stupid or something? I told you, I don't know that name. Now stop harassing me before I call the police."

My bravery from before fades, my hope and determination now unsettled. I'm unclear how to respond. I slink away, feeling like my only lead is losing steam.

At the bottom of the steps, I pull my phone out, dial Meredith. She answers fast, after only one ring. She's excited and happy, eager for Christmas, and I move the conversation past pleasantries.

"Jane won't talk to me—she won't even open the door. If that's even her at all."

"You're in Detroit?" Her voice is concerned, surprised. "Why?"

"I'm trying to find her, Mere."

She sighs heavily. "Let me try and call Jane myself. Maybe she'll talk to me. Give me two?" she asks.

"Thanks," I say, hanging up. I turn and look back up the steps, through the window in the door, and spot a woman at the top. She's crouching, straining to study me. Her hair is pulled back, tight and black, in a bun at the base of her skull. Her face is hard, yet pretty and makeup-free. Her clothes are plain and basic, but clean and wrinkle-free.

When our eyes connect, she startles, eyes widening. Then her pocket erupts with sound, her phone ringing, and she leaps forward out of my view. The last thing I see is her trailing hand, holding a sturdy wooden bat.

SD

"She just wouldn't answer?" asks Jenny, her puffy coat zipped to her neck. Hope is bundled up, too, curious and excited, with all the lights and festive decorations draped down Centre Street. The air is piercing, and the sidewalks—lit with white Christmas lights—aren't helping to ease the disappointment of not talking with Jane.

"I know it was her. I mean, her phone rang. She was spooked, didn't even come back to the door when I went back up."

We duck into a sock shop, wandering our way through the various aisles to enjoy the wacky patterns.

"Maybe it'd be better to go back with Hope and me. It might seem like less of a threat," Jenny says, holding up a pair of socks that say "Take No Shit."

"You need those," I say, smiling. "And…it's not a bad idea. Maybe that's what we try tomorrow?"

"I think I may be able to make her feel safe, Higs."

Hope shrieks, excited at the pair of rainbow socks.

"She's hyper. How much cocoa did she have?" I chuckle.

Jenny laughs. "That's between us ladies." She puts a hand out, grabbing my arm, and I look at it. It feels natural, not new or weird at all for Jenny to be touching me. If I'm honest, I have always had an attraction to Jenny, but when and where did that attraction turn into feelings? A part of me may have pretended to be only friends forever, if that mistletoe hadn't given me wings.

I grab Hope the rainbow socks, think of Ella. "Do you want to find someplace to get dinner?"

"I'm down for whatever, Higs. I'm surprised how beautiful Detroit is. It has a bad rep, but I'm loving this downtown area."

"Wait till you see the Christmas house; it's really something amazing."

"Do you want to go tonight?" Jenny asks, dropping my arm and grabbing a pair of Gilmore Girls socks. "OMG, need!" she says, her face excited.

I am worried about seeing it—the house. Sometimes, the anticipation of doing something special trumps the actual experience. What if the house is a disappointment? I want it to be extraordinary. I want it to be incredible, just like I remember it feeling with Mom.

"We don't have to go tonight. Another night is fine."

Jenny grabs another pair of socks, her *need* collection growing. "I probably should have asked this before getting in the car back in Boston, but how long are we staying?"

I laugh, finding wiener-dog socks and handing them to Jenny. "Need," I say. "And you just trusted me. Got in the car with zero reservations and no questions."

"I came for Hope." Jenny giggles.

Hope wiggles in my arms, and I pick up a pair of panda socks and give them to her. She puts them in her mouth, which equates to *OMG, need* in baby.

I laugh. "We went from colleagues, to friends, to now I really want to kiss you every chance I get."

She stops moving, her eye meeting mine, intense and sweet. She smiles, then gives a quirky grin. "Higs, not in front of the kid."

I laugh again.

Jenny starts walking, browsing. "You never answered the question, Higs. Do you want to go see that house tonight?"

A part of me doesn't want to face it tonight, wants to avoid and delay. But a bigger part can't wait another moment, wants to abandon everything to see it. "I...do."

Chapter 38

ulling into Sherwood Forest, I'm struck immediately with how
familiar it is. The big, beautiful houses are decorated from head to
toe, dressed in lights and color like no time has passed. The quaint
still of the neighborhood mixes with the night and mood to make the
perfect Christmas escape.

Jenny's breath rushes out. "It's incredible," she says. "These houses
are stunning."

Big and stone, each house stands like a pillar in the night. I pull off
the street and park. This is already closer than Mom and I would get
taking the bus, and I feel unsure how to navigate to the house by car and
not on foot.

Rebundling, I hold a sleepy Hope, and the three of us make our way
through the neighborhood. The air is perfect, crisp and cold, but clear.
The night sky is brightly lit by the moon, the smell of cedar tickles my
nose, our breaths smoke out in front of our faces.

Various people are walking the sidewalks, taking in the houses and
lights. I think of Mom and me, how we mazed our way through the
town, toes numb.

Jenny smiles, and so I smile back. "It's amazing," she says.

I nod, pointing out a house I recognize, and we walk, first side by side, then gloved hand in hand. It feels like Christmas, like the first real Christmas I've had in years.

Anxiety is strange. Some days, I feel like my emotions are tied to a trigger, and if the rope is pulled, I'll fire. It's always scared me to recognize that I hold anger and sadness inside, so much of it that I worry that, if I allowed myself, I'd start crying and never stop.

Walking faster now, we move almost like we are drawn to a destination, like the house is calling us.

In this moment, that anxiety has decided to loosen. It's decided to let the loops and loops of words and thoughts settle and sit, to stop the toxins from oozing from me in waves. I'm closer to Mom.

We stop on the corner.

"It's there," I say, pointing. "That's the one."

There, just up ahead, is the house. Huge and massive and shining like a beacon, it sings. Every inch is laced with twinkling lights, every window offering the tender glow of a candle, every arch and peak sagging with garland and tinsel. It outshines even the toughest of competitors, as not even a fragment of the home is lacking in stunning design.

It's perfect. Even sections without lights manage to shimmer under unseen laser lights. It is glowing, humming, with power and beauty. I stare so hard that the blinding white lights start to look blue in the night sky. Then, like magic, a sparkle of light twinkles across the house, and my eyes weren't lying. The light shifts to a deep blue.

I turn to Jenny, seeing her face illuminated by the light. She's smiling. "It's blue now," she says, excited.

And as she speaks, the lights fade to darkness. The house shuts down, the air turning black. Faint whispers of music stream from the house. Christmas music, a guitar, and the start of a violin softly playing the "Carol of Bells." The house begins to glow softly again and then gets brighter as the music grows louder. There's an explosion of light and sound that rockets the night sky, heavy electric guitars filling the area, and lights dancing rhythmically to the music. Not just one color, but all colors, twinkle and blast at sporadic intervals to the beat of the music. It's the most rocking version of a Christmas song I've ever heard.

Jenny squeals. "Whoo!" she yells. And Hope follows, laughing as she yells.

The front of the house is all blinking lights, and other lights are projecting a keyboard onto the roof. The keys shift and illuminate like they are being played. The guitar screams. The lights blaze, heavy and hard. With every beat of the drum, the lights surge harder—brighter, making the smiles permanent on our faces.

It's magic.

Minutes later, as the song comes to an end, the lights shatter out of the house, blinding us back into the darkness. We scream at the finish. "Yes!" we yell.

"Again!" Jenny screams.

The lights emerge, slowly, the house returning to the stunning white and gold streams that made the house heavenly upon our arrival. It stays illuminated, still, beautiful like the night belongs to it and not the other way around.

A subtle sound taps behind us—a *click*.

I turn to see, examine, and I hear it again, the faint *click*. I know that click. A woman, dressed in a dark coat, her hair spilling out in winglets around her winter hat, stands, taking a picture—our picture, the house standing in the background.

Another *click*, and then the camera comes down. There's a tear streaming down the soft face behind it.

The click, *this time, was real.* My voice almost doesn't come, but then it finds its way out, thick and tangled. "Mom?"

Chapter 39

The night is still, calm, yet my blood is roaring and rushing through my veins. There's a pulsing in my ears.

"Keith?" Jenny asks. "Are you alright?"

Mom is a statue, motionless and beautiful, a mute figure, and for a second, I wonder if it's real. If it's true.

"Mom?" I say again.

Her lip quivers, she doesn't move, and I wonder if part of her is tempted to run in the other direction.

"Hi," she finally whispers, and then she's crying. Tears are streaming down her face in a torrent, her emotions hitting her like a storm. She moves toward us. "Can I hug you? Can I hug you?" her voice asks, thick and heavy.

I crash into her, my arms the answer. Hugging her, and hugging Hope, and my eyes are spilling, and I can't remember how to breathe, but I don't care…I don't care. She's speaking, muttering, and I can't think, I can't understand the words.

"Is this your baby?" she's asking, and she's kissing Hope. "My God, it is, it is. Her face is yours."

I'm crying, sobbing, and I don't know if I can stop. It's finally happened, the rope, the trigger, it was pulled, and now I am tears. It's scaring Hope. She's crying now, and Mom's crying, and Jenny is taking Hope, but she's crying too. Her face is wet.

"I'm sorry," I tell Jenny. And then I'm crying harder, impossibly harder. "I'm sorry," I tell Mom. "I'm so sorry I left you."

Chapter 40

My head aches. It feels like a thousand pounds after exerting all the emotions I hold.

Jenny drives the car back to the hotel, Mom and me sitting in the back with Hope. We whisper only, trying to control our passions for the sake of Hope.

"How did you know to go there?" I asked.

"Jane found me. She mentioned you were poking around, asking questions," she whispers. "I had a feeling you might go to our spot. I've been walking around the last two hours, hoping."

Her voice makes me shiver. It's hers, and it's like the last ten years never happened, like we were never really apart. Only the lines in her face say otherwise.

"Jane wouldn't tell me anything."

She pats my hand. "She's a good friend, she means well. Frank has been looking for me."

His name chokes me into silence, and we ride, feeling the gentle rumble of the engine.

At the hotel, Mom waits in the hall as I put Hope in the bed, and Jenny, graciously, crawls next to her, whispering, "Go. Talk and catch up." She smiles, and so much has happened, so much has changed, that I feel myself wanting to say the words, but know it's too soon.

I…love you.

Instead, I am quiet, nod, return the smile, then I slip from the door and join Mom in the hallway. It's bright, and I see her, *really* see her. She's older, but still so pretty, a spark in her eye that wasn't there the night I left her. The night Scott died.

We move toward the elevator, toward a section of cheap lobby furniture, and we seat ourselves there. The stiff couches are uncomfortable and unforgiving. She takes her gloves off, and her hands are still hard, still abused from the cleaning products she must be using.

"You're still cleaning?" I ask.

She nods, averting her eyes.

"And you're not with Frank?"

She nods again.

Relief feels me. "Scott," I say, my voice breaking. "I'm sorry…I just left."

Her lip quivers. "Don't say sorry—*I'm* sorry." She clears her throat, looks around, and pulls off her hat. Her hair is still dark, brown, and wavy, with little gray. "You had a rough start in life, and I carry a lot of that blame on my shoulders," she says.

I shake my head. "I don't—"

"I've been scared that I'll die before you ever forgive me," she whispers, her voice small.

I move toward her, sit on the sofa nearest, and reach out a hand. "I don't blame you. There's nothing to forgive."

She moves her free hand to my face. "You've turned into a man," she says. "Made something for yourself, of yourself, and that's something I could have never given you. You're the one thing that turned out good, and that makes my life seem meaningful."

My cheeks heat, embarrassed. "I have so much to tell you, and so much to ask."

She smiles suddenly, her face looking lighter. "I read a story the other day by Loren Eiseley, and it made me think of you. It was about a young man and starfish. It was talking about how an older, wise man was walking on the beach, enjoying the sunset, and along the beach were hundreds of washed-up starfish that the waves from the stormy weather had carried ashore. He then saw a young boy picking up the starfish and putting them back into the ocean. The wise man called to him, 'What are you doing?' The young man responded, 'The sun is coming up and the tide is going out; if I don't throw them in they'll die.' The older man responded, 'But, young man, there are miles and miles of beach with starfish all along it—you can't possibly make a difference.' The young boy then bent back down and put another starfish back into the ocean and replied, 'Well, it made a difference for that one.'" She chuckles. "I like that story."

"I do too," I say.

"Isn't that true, though? How we lose sight of how pure life can be? How genuine it is to be a child? The boy in the story was doing something that he believed in. He knew he was doing better than doing nothing at all. He listened to himself and believed. I never allowed you to have that youthful wisdom. I was scared of it."

I breathe heavy. "I don't need you to explain a thing to me. I want us both to let it go and move on, fresh."

She clears her throat. "It's been a long time, Keith. I need to say this…please."

I nod.

"I pictured you as that kid. I pictured you as a child, fighting for what you believe in. Fighting for the ones who couldn't fight for themselves. I can still picture you as a boy: spunky and determined to make things right. Passionate about your ideas, and willing to take the initiative to go after them." She steadies herself, looks at me seriously. "Sometimes, when you were a kid, I wished you weren't like that," she says, and her voice cracks.

"It's fine," I say.

"I wished you were agreeable, so that your father wouldn't be so hard on you." She looks me in the eyes. "That was wrong. It was wrong of me to think that, to want to limit you, in order to appease Frank. I'm so proud...that you didn't settle for what you had here, in Detroit. That you were brave enough to leave what little bit of comfort you had in this world behind. You made a difference for yourself, for your future, and I could never be upset with you for that."

I don't know how, but I start crying again, and Mom hugs me.

"I'm so glad you have a baby girl," she says. "She's a smart, sassy little girl, I can tell already. A fighter that will drive you crazy in the best way possible."

I smile, compose myself and wipe at my nose. "Hope's amazing."

"And Jenny," Mom says. "Her eyes tell me she loves you."

"Jenny's amazing too."

"Keith—don't make the same mistakes I've made," she says in a rush. "Never let the person who matters the most to you walk out of your life. No matter what, you follow your baby. You follow her as far as she needs to go, and you make it right." She's crying again, and so now I'm hugging her, reassuring her that it's fine. Everything is fine.

After she settles, we sit in silence for a while, taking each other in, wiping tears from our eyes.

"We are a mess," she says, chuckling.

I laugh, too, halfheartedly. "I've realized that for some time now."

She laughs for real now.

"Move to Boston," I tell her. It slips out unintended. "Live with us. I have room. I need help."

She shakes her head—no. Instant shock twists my insides, and I feel my face shatter into confusion.

"No," she whispers, her face suddenly serious.

"Why?" I plead.

"I never can," she says, and I can see she believes her words with ferocity.

"I thought..." I lose my words.

"I'd only bring hardship into your life. I can only bring negativity, and I won't do that to you," she says, clearing her face. "You've worked damn hard for what you have, and I won't jeopardize that."

I stand up, move to the window, and press my face to the cool glass. "You'd jeopardize it more staying here," I whisper.

I turn and catch her face fall, but she shakes her head again, pushes emotion from her mouth. "No, Jane is right, this is the only way. Where I go, your father goes. He has a way of tracking me. He finds me, Keith."

For a sick second, I want to vomit, and then I want to scream. This cements the fact that Frank is alive, that he's still hurting everyone around him.

How often does he find her? How afraid is she walking down the street? Does he hit her still?

"Do you call the police?" I ask.

"Every time, but that doesn't stop Frank. As soon as he's out, he's back."

I force a laugh, the thought giving me chills. "He doesn't know where I live. Boston's far. That man could never make it there alive. If he had the drive or funds to travel, then he'd be dead already. Any money he has will go toward his booze."

Her mask falls, concern written on her face.

I'm untying my mask too. "Please," I beg.

She covers her face with her hands. "It feels safer to dream about how your life unfolds and not dragging you down with me. He's worse, Keith. He didn't get any better with age. He's cruel, and he'll hurt your family."

My eyes lock on hers, and I tighten my jaw. Anger grows in me, not fear. "Then I'll buy a gun."

Chapter 41

"What if he's watching us load my bags right now? What if he sees the Massachusetts plates on your car? I should have met you back at the hotel—this is a mistake." Mom shakes her head, her eyes panicked and wild. She starts pacing around the car, the midday sky a menacing gray. "It's a mistake, Keith. I should stay. You should go without me." Steam flows from her mouth, her warmth hitting the cold air.

She's starting to sound paranoid. Frank couldn't be here, looking on with calculated intent. That's not his gimmick. He makes his presence known, his anger flowing out of him in waves that can't be stanched, torrents that demand instant expulsion. But I know this fear, I understand it on an intimate level, and I want to be a conflicting force. I want to be kinder than before, gentler than she's accustomed to. I want to be everything she's deserved her entire life, but still hasn't received.

"Mom, sit in the car with Jenny and Hope. Get warm and comfortable—I'll grab the last few bags, and then we will bolt." I reach out, rest my hand on her shoulder. "Frank's not here, and even if he was somehow watching us. Massachusetts is big, he won't be able to find where we're heading off the plates alone."

She settles, wanting to believe me. "What about the plate number? Can he track them? What if he gets someone who can run them through the registration database?" Her eyes are still concerned, but she furrows her brow humorlessly. "Have I watched too many crime shows?"

Anger grows in me, and I try to hide it so that Mom doesn't think it's for her. Frank—I'm pissed at Frank for making Mom so afraid to live her life. Instead, I soften my face, and smile. I go around and open the front passenger door. "Get in, Mom. Frank doesn't have those kinds of resources. Trust me."

She wraps her coat around her and takes a deep breath. She nods. She tucks her head into the door. "Jenny, honey, you can sit up front. I'd like to sit in the back with Hope."

Jenny's face pops forward. "Of course, Mrs. Higgins. Come in out of the cold, get warm. You're going to love Keith's house."

Jenny jumps out of the car, sans jacket, and does a little wiggle. "Brrrr." She hurries into the front seat and closes the door, her hands going to the heater vents.

Mom starts sliding into the car.

"Just the two bags left on the kitchen floor? Nothing else?" I ask.

She nods. "The rest is Jane's. She'll put someone else here that needs a safe space."

I close the door and make my way back to Mom's tiny studio apartment above the antique store, not far from Jane's place at the laundromat. I hear the doors lock in my wake, and I wonder if that's something Jenny did as a precaution, or something Mom asked of her.

I climb the old mildewy wooden stairs to Mom's sanctuary. Inside, the space is clean, basic, with white tile floors and off-white walls, but cozy, and I'm grateful she had a warm place to call her own. I suppose I have a great deal to thank Jane for, if she'd ever allow that conversation to happen.

Inside, I grab the two bags and take in the place. There's a cute tabletop Christmas tree on an oak dresser near the front of the studio; it could be something of Jane's or something Mom bought to make it feel more festive. A futon serves as the bed and a couch, so I drop the bags, cross the room and sit down to test its comfort. It's soft, not excessively bumpy, and it faces a small, outdated, flat-screen TV.

She has four bags. All of her belongings could be packed in a single night. Or does she leave them packed, just in case she needs to run? *There are more locks on her door than bags, five different bolts.*

That fact makes me shiver, so I stand, grab the bags, and close the door behind me.

SD

"Proposition," Jenny whispers. She leans into the door, her head on the window. Hope's finally sleeping in the back seat, Mom's hand holding hers. Hope had cried for a good hour. She's over her harness and seat and done with the car. "Next time we travel to Michigan, we fly."

Mom chuckles at this, softly. "I think I'm fine with never returning."

I turn to Jenny. "You won't miss all of the quality time these hours have brought us?"

"I'd laugh, but I don't want to wake Hope up," she says.

"We could stop by your hometown," I offer. "We get pretty close to your stomping grounds. How would your family feel with an impromptu Christmas visit? You show up with a boyfriend, a kid, and his mother, just in time for Christmas dinner."

Mom finds it funny, chuckles, but Jenny's face falls, loses colors, and she sits up fast. "I'd rather not," she says, adjusting her seatbelt.

I think of her stepdad and the bastard Santa, and guilt washes over me. "I'm sorry, I was only kidding. I didn't mean…"

She recovers, smiling. "It's fine, but, yeah, no, we shouldn't do that," she says. She rumbles through her purse and pulls out a package of peanut M&M's. She opens them and hands them to me.

"Are you trying to give me a sausage-neck?"

"Huh?" she asks, confused.

"You're always giving me these candies," I say. "You must love peanut

M&M's."

She whisper-chuckles, her cheeks turning pink. "Yeah…no…"

"You just always have them with you?"

"Well, my Gran—she thinks I love them. It'd break her heart if I told her I didn't anymore. She sends me a package once a month, and it's always stuffed full of fun-sized peanut M&M's. I have one full cabinet at home that's overflowing. Before you came along, I had two full cabinets."

"Jenny," I scoff. "Are you using me, just so you don't have to admit to your grandmother that you don't love peanut M&M's?"

She smiles, nods. She opens another package and turns. "Do you want any, Mrs. Higgins?"

Mom smiles and takes them. "Thank you! You can call me Lily, if you want."

"I've been making a conscious effort not to call you Mama Higs just yet. Don't want to scare you right off the bat."

Mom chuckles again.

"I have more," Jenny says. "If anyone wants them." She digs through her purse, pulls out not six, not seven, but eight additional mini-sized bags of peanut M&M's. She piles them in the front cup holder. "A whole stash."

"You carry all of those around with you, and you don't even like them?" I ask. "I thought I was special. Like I was the only recipient who got a special treat."

"You *are* special," she says, patting my arm. "You, and every homeless person I encounter," she says.

Mom laughs. "Weird people are my favorite type of people."

Jenny turns dramatically. "I take that as the biggest compliment, Lily."

"Well, what's your favorite candy?" I ask. "Because, obviously, I know nothing about you."

"Hmm…I'd say dark chocolate."

"Okay, that's acceptable. I love me some dark chocolate," I tell her, and a yawn escapes, big and exaggerated. Between last night's dramatic reunion, the late-night conversation, and persuading Mom to come with us, I didn't sleep at all. Not even an hour.

The sun is starting to get low in the sky, the winter twilight making darkness take the sky faster. I look at the clock, already almost 5:00 p.m.

"I think it's my turn to drive, Higs," Jenny says. "I've been waiting for my chance to get behind the wheel of this beast for hours."

I chuckle again, but it's broken by another yawn. "You're right," I admit.

We make a pit stop, fueling the car, and purchasing snacks and supplies for when Hope decides to wake back up. Jenny climbs into the driver's seat, and Mom takes the passenger seat. She directs me into the backseat with Hope, and I feel sleep claim me before the car even pulls from the lot.

Chapter 42

A bump jostles the car, and my mind makes a journey toward wakefulness, unsure if the last twenty-four hours is real or a dream. The hum of the car lulls me, and I want to succumb back into sleep, but I turn my head to check Hope. She's sleeping still, peacefully in her car seat, so my eyes roam to the clock: 7:00 p.m. I've only been out for two hours.

There is low music playing, an unrecognizable song.

"In the early years, I would come up with fake stories to explain why he was such a bastard. I went around and around in my head, trying to understand how a person could be the way he was," Mom whispers.

My mind wakens quickly, wanting to join the conservation, but I stay slumped over like I'm still sleeping.

"One time, I made up a little sister," Mom explains, "a little sister that he loved. I was giving him a pass, because, in my head, he was the older, broody brother of a sister—a little sister—that he loved and lost. I told one of my friends that, one day, Frank was coming home from school, and his sister wanted to ride her bike next to him, but he didn't want the other kids to think he was lame, so he yelled at her and told her to get lost. She went off crying," Mom says.

I'm confused, but don't want her to stop sharing, so I stay rooted.

"She never made it home," Mom says, continuing the story. "I told my friend that she was hit by a truck and left on the side of the road like an animal. That she was gone, and this killed Frank, broke his insides to pieces, because, of course, he blamed himself. If only he would have let her ride home with him, she'd be safe now, so this was his fault, and nothing could bring her back. He started drinking to mask the pain. Started getting drunk and liking that he couldn't remember his *shit*-life anymore. At first, he'd only get drunk on the bad days, and the rest of the time, he was manageable. Then we met and fell in love, and he was better, happy. Then something triggered his depression. Somewhere along the way, he became an alcoholic, and stopped realizing that he hurt everything around him," she says.

Mom sighs, and then the car is silent for a minute.

"We all convince ourselves it's human," Jenny whispers.

"I made it up, Jenny. What kind of story that ends with the innocent little sister dying sounds better than reality? It's sick, right? But what's worse is the truth. The truth that there was never any reason for him to be the way he was—at least that I know of." She pauses, takes a breath and then rushes on. "There was no reason for him to lash out at us like he did. He liked power. He liked to deliver pain, and that's all it was."

"I'm sorry you've had to endure him all these years," Jenny says.

"And that's what I hate most: he's become my existence. My whole world spins around a man I can't escape. Even if he never finds me again, how do I get him to leave me alone?" Mom asks. "When I was a kid, I would have this dream about a snake coiling around my neck, taking my air, and the harder I fought, the tighter the snake would pull. I think that dream was warning me of the future. Frank is like a snake that won't let go.

"Mmm," Jenny sighs. "I can relate to that."

The GPS chimes. Our exit is in two miles.

"I assumed you could relate. My friend Jane taught me to recognize signs of other survivors. You want to share your story?"

I hear Jenny swallow. Hope moves in the car seat, but only slightly.

"No," Jenny whispers. "I haven't even told Keith yet."

"Keith's a survivor too. He'd understand."

I close my eyes tight and wish for sleep, because I do—I understand. Sometimes, I feel like I give all of myself away. Like I break off pieces and leave them behind, a breadcrumb stream of me littering my wake. I've been blaming Frank my entire life, running from him within myself and failing to escape.

Who would I even be if I'd never been hit?

The thing is, I think I'm starting to win. I have Hope, I have Jenny, and now I even have Mom back. My mask is unraveling, and I can't allow Frank to force it back on my face.

All this time, I thought I was being selfish for wanting to live my life, but, no, I've just been conditioned to think I deserved less.

Suddenly something makes sense, it all just makes perfect sense. *There will always be moments of weakness.* There will always be moments where I'm not good enough, or strong enough, or wise enough, but there will be moments where I am. There will be times when I'm the strength, where my words or arms will do the fixing.

Chapter 43

Boston greets us with sweet sunshine, rays of it breaking through the trees like fingers. Pulling into the driveway, a scowling Christina, her arms crossed dubiously—her energy demanding to know where in "God's hell" I ran off to with her grandbaby before Christmas, evident in her posture—stands in wait.

"Who's that woman?" Mom asks. "She seems disturbed."

Jenny chuckles, in the passenger seat. "She's fun."

"It's my mother-in-law—Christina," I say. I slide toward the window, roll it down. "Hi, Christina," I yell.

Christina blinks in response, her face hardening. I pull into the drive, transition into park, and shut the car down.

I hop from the car, and she's on me in seconds.

"Not even a warning? You just up and bolt, and I'm supposed to be okay hearing about it via text?"

Mom slides from the backseat, and I see Christina's eyes shift to take her in, confusion washing across her face.

"I'm sorry," I say. "This…This is my mother."

Her eyebrows raise. "Oh!"

Mom takes a few steps forward, reaches out her hand. "Lily."

Christina takes her hand, her words no longer pointed. "Christina." Tears rush to her eyes. "Oh, my." She pulls her in, hugging her, Mom looking awkward and rigid. "I'm sorry, I just…I never thought I'd get to meet you…I'm just so…glad." Her voice breaks.

Mom noticeably straightens her shoulders. "Thank you for being here for Keith, when I wasn't."

Jenny comes around the car, Hope on her hip.

"Hope!" Christina says.

"Nana!" Hope squeals.

Mom watches them interact—Hope and Christina—taking in the familiar relationship the two of them have built over the year, then Christina's ushering us inside the warm house that she helped put a down payment on back when Ella and I first started a life together.

"Christmas is nearly here! I would have been beside myself if Hope wasn't back home." She pulls her coat off, her angry energy from before nowhere in sight.

Mom stands off to the side, her eyes wandering the space.

I move to stand closer. "Welcome home, Mom."

She seems unsure, hesitant. "It's…beautiful."

"It's so cozy here. We'll give you a tour," Jenny says, yawning. "It'll feel like home in no time."

Mom smiles, looking exhausted too.

Jenny moves to my side, rubbing my back in a sweet reassuring sentiment. The fatigue from the trip hits me, and I want Jenny to unfold me. I want her to unravel me. I want her to smooth out my crumbled heart and unwrap me from myself. I need her to unwrap me. I need her to envelop me in her arms and flatten the crinkles that have creased my surface. To redraw me. To remake me. To rewrite the old story that balled my paper in the first place. I want her. I want her to take me higher, further, deeper than we've ever gone.

I breathe her in, closing my eyes, enjoying her flowery scent that has such power over me.

Jenny…Jenny, she's love. She's real. She makes me feel so incredibly strong and wanted—she makes me feel like me. Jenny and I—well, we are messy and tangled and braided together by something I can't put into words. It's like we were twisted together by our separate pasts, an attraction of need pulling us from where we were to where we are. We need the other's arms to make the world okay again. We need to be hinged. We are each other's hinges.

"Tour!" I say, pushing forward.

Hope giggles and tries to say it too. "Tor," she says.

We move throughout the house, Mom seeming enamored by every room. She's particularly taken by the studio, where she looks though some of my past works. Her cheeks flush with warmth, and her eyes look more and more alive.

The afternoon air is soft and still, everything around quiet and tranquil. I sigh, because everything is like it should be. Just like it was before it was bursting with chaos, just like it was before we filled the world with never-ending noise and confusion.

"I love them all," Mom says, holding the painting of the sunset from the previous time Jenny and I had visited Michigan.

I get an idea. Christmas is in two days, and I have nothing for Mom. I haven't painted in too long, and my fingers are itching. I will paint what the picture on her camera missed.

The picture that she took of Hope, Jenny, and me in front of the shining Christmas house. Hope cradled in my arms, the tear on my face, the house beaming in the background. The picture is missing something—someone. It's missing Mom. It's missing her standing there, watching us, loving us, and protecting us, as she takes the picture. The click of the camera missed her, but my brain didn't. She was there, and I still see it…and I will create it. For all it's worth, I will create that for her. Because all of these years she's protected me, and it's time I start protecting her.

I settle Mom into the guest room—her room—show her how to work the TV and the shower. There are so many things she needs to hear about: work, Ella, and life these past years, but those can wait for later. For now, we will all just breathe and smile.

This is it. My mask is broken on the floor.

"Let me know whatever you need, Mom," I say. "Anything, okay?"

She turns, her face seeming to go pale, losing blood.

"What?" I ask.

"I'm sorry, Keith," she says. "But I can't sleep here until…until you buy that gun."

Chapter 44

Obtaining a gun in Massachusetts is an unsettlingly fast process. We applied for the license and registration online and set up the required safety and training course for tomorrow already. I looked it all up, with Mom hovering over my shoulder, filled and submitted all the forms and paperwork. I'll be a gun owner before Christmas.

I had a baseball bat in the basement, so I moved it to the front door. Jenny ran to Costco and bought a pack of wireless safety cameras, and some self-set-up alarm systems. Hope went and spent the night with Christina. Then we pulled the car into the garage, and I reassured Mom that I had plans to be awake for hours. That I had a lot of painting to catch up on and would watch and listen.

"Sleep, Mom," I said, "you're safe now."

"When it's just me, I'm not this worried. But I can't have him finding you again. I won't have him near your baby."

"Everything is going to be fine."

She went to bed, reluctantly, and I've honored my word, staying awake and painting late into the night. The canvas seems to hum under my brush, the Christmas house coming to life, Mom's capped ringlets the focal point to the piece.

SD

The night is quiet, still, and the moments I do hear noise, I worry Mom is not able to sleep. But every time I creep past her room, it's dark and quiet.

I want her to sleep soundly, to be still and content for once in her life. She's been stuck in the "on" position for too long. It can't be healthy to be in constant fight or flight mode. I suppose that's what life has become though. The world is violent, dangerous, and every second upon every minute something new is trying to hurt the things we love.

I take in my mostly completed piece, feeling satisfied that Mom will appreciate it. She always loved when I drew that house for her. Tiptoeing up the stairs, the house is quiet, but a faint glow is coming from under my bedroom door. On entry, I see Jenny, the room dimly lit, a soft glow dusted on her cheeks from the flickering candle on the nightstand.

"Couldn't sleep?" I ask.

"Higs," she says, a hesitant smile on her face. "I think I went to bed a little too early."

"I've been painting—"

"Mama Higgin's still doing okay?"

"She hasn't come out. I hope that means she's getting some sleep. I understand her fear. I just wish I could hold it for her."

"'Cause that's what you do. You try to hold things for the people you love. She'll settle in," she says. "Come cuddle with me a little?"

I move to the bed, slipping under the covers, and putting my arms around her. I sense a heaviness in the room, so I stroke her hair. "I can be strong for you," I whisper.

I feel her tense at that. She turns her eyes on mine in the soft light.

"For a while, I was fragile, broken," I say. "I couldn't handle anyone else's pain, but I'm okay for now. I feel rooted. You were always so strong for me. I can be strong for you."

She closes her eyes, hugs me tighter. "I'm scared, confused, and far from perfect, Higs."

Jenny has alluded to things…about her stepdad, but for the longest time, everything has been about me. Everything is spinning around

Hope and I, and I haven't dug into that part of her. I haven't asked the questions that have been there...just threw dirt over them, so they didn't infect this thing we've started. It seemed to be what she wanted. That, plus it seemed easier. Easier isn't necessarily right.

Some people go their entire lives pretending to be someone else, afraid to be themselves. I tried it, but I can't do it. I can't let Jenny do that either.

"Jenny?" I whisper. "You can tell me. I know we have the rule, but..."

She's breathing steadily, but I feel her presence, know she isn't sleeping.

"Are you awake?"

"Yeah..."

"You can trust me," I say.

"I..." she croaks, then clears her throat. "I know and I do. It's just not easy for me to talk about. It's not easy for me to admit this part of me," she says. "Can you blow the candle out? It might be easier in the dark."

My heart throbs, a new sadness building, but I do it.

I feel her suck in a breath, so I match my breathing to hers.

"I've mentioned before that, when I was young, Mom and I moved in with my Gran?"

"Yeah..."

"I thought I'd dealt with it, that I had it buried deep enough to never resurface..."

I think of Frank. I think of everything I tried to bury that *always* comes back.

"But...being with you has reopened this door. I don't mean to put any blame on you. It's just, I've never trusted anyone the way I trust you. Never cared for anyone like I care for you. It's the first time in my life that I've felt safe enough not to live with this all alone. And that scares me. It's like a shovel, digging up my past. All of my old insecurities have been fighting to take over. This feeling inside, this feeling that I need to be perfect for you, is overwhelming."

"Jenny..." I breathe her name, not knowing what to say.

"When I was a sophomore in high school, I was in a really low place," she says. "We were poor, and I was overweight. I would wear a lot of colorful makeup to hide myself. It was my war paint. I liked hiding what was underneath, didn't want anyone to truly see me. Girls at school would write nasty messages on my books, boys would laugh at me in gym class," she explains.

I stroke her shoulder.

She flinches away. "Please, don't. Just let me think that I'm alone. Don't talk, don't…touch me," she whispers.

"Okay," I breathe.

"I could tolerate the teasing," she continues. "But then Mom married Dale…after my dad…died. Dale was…bad."

Dale—the stepdad. The one who makes her mad. The one who is not a good person.

"Another reason I wore so much makeup." She pauses, then goes on. "At the time, I'd rather get teased for wearing makeup than get teased for having a drug-dealing stepdaddy," she says. "And kids are cruel. They use anything they can against you, even the fact that you have no control over what a man does to you."

I feel sick instantly, remembering my childhood and my father and my struggles. Remembering how it felt to be hit, then picturing her being treated the same. "Did he hit you?" I ask, disobeying the request for silence.

"Not really, only once, when he was high. Mom made him apologize afterward, made him buy me something we couldn't afford. But another time…I got home from school, and no one was around. It was the beginning of summer, and we lived in a tin can; it was stifling."

She pauses to wipe at her nose and face.

"I opened all of the windows, turned the fans on, but it was still an oven, so…I decided to put on one of Mom's dresses to cool down. The dress felt light, and it was the first time that day I felt comfortable. After ten minutes of me twirling around, Dale walked in. He was drunk and high and aggressive, saw me in Mom's dress, and laughed. 'Pudgy little thing,' he said. Ignoring him, I retreated to my room. That's when he reached out and grabbed my…my bottom. I quickened the pace, but I could feel him following me down the hall. I could smell him: sweat, grease, and booze, on top of whatever chemicals he had been cooking with. I turned my head to look over my shoulder, and I could tell by the look on his face what he was planning. He started licking his lips and grabbing his crotch. He was making these noises, god-awful noises."

"No." My voice pleads with her in the darkness, *tell me he didn't touch you*. This was supposed to be a story about how he hit her—not this, please not this. I think about that bastard Santa who grabbed her at the Christmas party, and my nausea doubles. But I told her I could be strong, I told her I could help her hold this.

So I don't say anything else, I stay there, not touching her, like she asked, letting her speak.

"He grabbed me by the hair and then tossed me on the bed. I was screaming and crying for him to stop. Thrashing and fighting and trying everything I could to get away, but I just wasn't strong enough. He pushed my face into the bed so that he couldn't hear me anymore, and I could barely breathe. I thought I would die, so I stopped fighting. I felt more pressure on my back and then heard the ripping of my panties. I just kept crying. I couldn't do anything…I couldn't get him off me."

No. No. No…

"He…raped me," Jenny says, the shadow of her hand coming to her mouth. "It hurt…he was rough. I…I went numb. I just shut down. When he was done, he left me draped across the bed, smacked me, and told me it was 'the best cherry he'd ever popped.' I heard the shower start, but I couldn't move. I laid there, so scared…shaking and whimpering. I didn't even try to run. I didn't even try to fight back when he came back to do it again. He grabbed me and threw me in the shower. He told me to clean myself off. He told me that, if I ever expected to be with him again, I had to clean myself properly. He made me feel like I was the dirty one. I was ashamed of myself," she cries.

I want her to stop, need her to stop! I close my eyes, wanting it to go away, but her words flow forward.

"When I wouldn't clean myself, he pushed me to the floor. He opened my mouth and told me if I tried anything he'd kill me and my mother. He forced himself into my mouth, over and over again, until he had enough. Then he turned the shower back on and put me under it. He said he needed to be back inside of me, and that if I couldn't clean myself properly, he'd show me how. He washed me. Then he raped me again," she said. Her sobs grew louder in between words. "I didn't know if it would ever end. It just went on and on."

I need to vomit, want to cry. I want to scream, need to kill this man.

"After he finished the second time, I heard him go to the fridge for a beer. Then, he left the trailer, and I laid there, wondering if I was even a person anymore. Eventually, Mom got home. I went to her, confused, ashamed, embarrassed…his semen still running down my leg. It was almost like I was to blame. A silly girl in a big girl dress, what should I expect?" She breaks into sobs, her shoulders bouncing up and down.

I want to reach for her, but, again, respect her need not to be touched.

"I didn't try and hide it. I just lost it and grabbed her, crying. I was hoping she could make it all better. That she could erase everything that just happened." She took a second, forcing the words out, steady and controlled. "Mom broke down, went after him, trying to kill him with a butcher knife."

My body shakes in anger and heartbreak for her. The truth, the past, the frigging awfulness of it all, it's nearly impossible to hear. This is the real world. We are all broken. I want to take it away from her, to make it better. I want to go find Dale and kill him myself.

We all have pasts. We all have shit. We are all damaged in some way. My tears are broken; I'm aching from her hurt.

"We moved in with Gran, but never told her. I made Mom promise," she says. Then she starts crying again. "I felt like it was my fault. Like I provoked him. I didn't want to go to the police. I didn't want anyone to know. I was depressed for a long time, and it got worse when I found out that I was pregnant." She stilled, waiting for my reaction.

"You have a baby?" I ask, shakily.

"No…I…I couldn't go through with it. I terminated it." She starts sobbing even louder. "I know it's awful. But how could I live my life, taking care of a baby that reminded me of him?" She hiccups, sobs, and I sense her getting ready to run in the darkness.

"Shh… Don't say anything. Don't explain yourself—"

"Mom made me go to the police anyway, but they said it was too late. There was no evidence of that day anymore, and I had already had…" She trails off.

She chokes and lets out a cough. Sitting forward, she heaves, sobbing, crying, hyperventilating, and trying not to. The heat suddenly feels like it's on full blast, like the air was stolen from the room with my ignorance of Jenny's past.

I break, needing to comfort her, or comfort myself. I wrap my arms around her, pulling her against me, fitting her inside of me, where no one can hurt her. Where nothing can reach her except me. "I have you…I have you…"

She clutches on to me, tight and needy. Wanting my embrace now. Needing my comfort, and I give it. I hug her. I hold her. And I don't let go.

"Jenny…I won't let anything happen to you." I feel her head nod. "What happened in the past…it's over…it's done. You're not alone anymore. You're not in that house. You'll never have to go through it again…I promise."

It's quiet, then she clears her throat. "You can't promise that, because I just went through it now," her broken, trembling voice whispers. "Explaining it, well, it brings it back. I was there again, back in the trailer, feeling him touch me. I heard the noises again, I smelled the smells again, and I felt it. I felt it all again—just now. The details…they're just, they're just always there."

I squeeze her, harder, closing my eyes. "Jesus…" I mutter. I can't promise her it won't happen again. I can't make it go away, because it's there, somewhere in her. It happened. And now, she'll live with that the rest of her life. She'll remember it forever, no matter how hard she works to forget. There's someplace that's smudged inside of her. It's like a nail hole left in the wall—the nail itself is gone, but the hole is forever with her.

"There's more. God…" She sighs. "There's more."

More? More than this? What else could there be? I squeeze her hand again, somehow feeling silly for the things I've cried about in the past.

"About a year after the incident…junior year…I became anorexic. It started slowly, but then grew worse as time went on. Five years of my life. Five years…" She sighs, pain switching to anger and regret and then back to pain again. "I was just so tired of being called fat. Tired of the word 'ugly.' Tired of being a cow. So, I started starving myself, restricted everything, and I loved it. Fought for it, starved for it…for perfection. The perfect look, the perfect grades, the perfect life…

"It was an addiction, gave me something to focus on, gave me something to think about, and when you're starving, all that's left to do is think. It clarifies everything. My mind was focused, completely aware. When you're hungry, you get cloudy, but when you're famished…when you're on the brink of starvation, there's this sharp pinpoint of precision. You feel like you have all the answers. You feel clean and light for the first time. You feel powerful. That false sense of power, to someone as broken as me…it felt liberating. After I would eat again, I'd feel dirty and fat. I'd get sleepy and foggy and feel like a person who deserved to be hurt. Then, when I'd stop eating, I'd feel clean. I'd feel pretty and in control. I'd feel *perfect*," she says.

The word *perfect* sounds dirty and tainted coming from her mouth.

"On my quest for perfection, I lost all sense of originality. I hated myself. I needed a way to take back control, needed a way to force Dale out of my head." She pauses for a second, not wavering, but breathing. "I took it too far. It got even worse in college, after moving away. My cheeks were hollow, my ribs protruded, my chest was tight. I started losing my hair, passing out all the time. I would run seven miles in a day and then eat only crackers for dinner. I was slowly killing myself, and what makes me sick is that I didn't even care. I liked how clean and perfect it made me feel. I liked the attention…loved it. It was the first time anyone had ever noticed me, the first time a guy called me beautiful.

"The control over what entered my body, and the result of how I looked, was a nasty mixture. I lost control of my control. Starvation started owning me, my soul. It turned into a back-and-forth battle of bingeing and then purging. Then I would stop and starve myself again. I'd starve myself to the brink of death, until human instinct to survive would kick in, and I would find myself eating an entire refrigerator of food, before throwing it back up. I wouldn't eat around other people, and that clean, in-control feeling became unreachable. I felt ashamed," she says, crossing her arms around herself, taking a breath. "I wanted to die," she whispers. "I wanted to die, so I would pick a target weight, and once I'd reach it, I'd pick an even smaller weight. I got down to eighty pounds and realized I would win…"

I wrap my arms around her tighter, kiss her forehead. But her words keep flowing like a river.

"It's called body dysmorphic disorder—there was no such thing as skinny enough. A part of me knew I was acting crazy, but it had such a powerful grasp on my life that it seemed too hard to fight off. I couldn't sleep, I had no period…I was alone. What I didn't know is how much I was actually screaming for help inside. I never heard the voice, but I know now it was there. Now that I'm better, I can recognize my cries for help."

She stops, stills. I start stroking her hair. Feeling like my words would mean nothing, but my hands can fix this.

She sniffles. "Gran and Mom came here for a visit, took one look, and put me into a treatment facility. I'm…better, but it will never truly be gone. Anorexia is a coping mechanism for being raped, I've learned that. I also know I'm not the one to blame for it. He was wrong, not me. He was dirty, not me. I've learned that, but that still won't erase the constant need for control."

She slows, waits for words, but I can't speak. Instead, I rub her back and rock her. Searching and mumbling things I know won't fix this. "I'm sorry, I'm just so sorry."

She's been through so much and that hurts me for her. We live in a world where people shove their fists in your face because you're different. Where people kick you in the ribs because of your skin color. Where they call you fat for being bigger than a size zero. We live in a world where so many people think it's okay to abuse you—whether it's physically, verbally, or sexually. We judge people on their appearance and ridicule them for their faults. We knock people down. We push them over. We judge everyone, including ourselves.

Jenny was punched, pushed, and slapped down her whole life—just like me. She almost let that define her. She almost let that claim her, until she didn't. Until she stopped listening to the judgments of others and started trusting in herself.

We humans, we're brutal, and we insistent on attacking each other for every flaw, bringing down the things we can't accept and raising ourselves up in their place.

Why can't we accept women as equals? Why can't same-sex couples ever catch a break? Why can't someone be taller or shorter or fatter than another person? Why can't we stop people from hurting other people? Why does skin color or religion matter? Why? Why do any of those things continue to matter?

The questions are endless. The answers...vast. The truth...love. Loving the people around you, and accepting them for who they are, is the only way to stop it. Breaking cycles and opening your mind is the only thing that can save us.

"I have no words. You...you...you're powerful. I'm in awe...of you...of how far you've come. How you fought back and kept your spirit. You're a light. You...define yourself," I say. "Our world is backward. You shouldn't have to be brave to be yourself, but you do. Life beats you into a mold, but you've fought against that."

I pull her into my chest. Seeing her tears, and knowing her story, helps me know the realest parts of her. The parts she hides from the rest of the world. She doesn't have to hide from me.

Life is a battlefield. Every day, I put on my armor, and go to war with my own insecurities. War is unpredictable and new battles arise every day. We need allies. We need each other. So, I whisper into her ear, "Don't let me be the one that unhinges you. Let me be the one that catches you before you fall. The one that tightens your hinges. Let me be the one that has you."

The beautiful thing about life is that it's never the same. It's full of surprises. Some of which are good and others that are bad. There's always a new challenge or a new obstacle to slow you down. What was once easy becomes hard. What was hard becomes easy. We learn and grow every day, and all we can do is keep pushing forward. Keep reaching for the next peg and keep passing the tests. *Because that's what life is about.* It's about letting the past make you better for the future. It's about getting up when it's easier to stay down. It's about doing the right thing, even if that means taking the long way around. Embrace the challenge of tomorrow, because if you don't, and you run from it, it will catch you. It will catch you when you're already winded and tired, and it will demand that you fight. Deal with it now. Feel it now. And defeat it now. So that way it's over and you are ready for what's to come next.

We are survivors, but we are so much more.

Chapter 45

The sun is bright, almost cheery, as it tumbles in through the blinds of the conference room. The office is still littered with Christmas decorations, the energy in the room unsettled and annoyed, now that the holiday is a day off. Jenny taps her foot, distracting me from the monotone lull of Richard's voice. Sales ratios, division statics, yada-yada-yada, the typical department meeting overture, but during an emergency meeting he called during a holiday shutdown.

My phone vibrates, shakes the table. It's a message from Christina: *I'm planning a pre-Christmas Eve dinner at our house tonight. Can you come after work? We'll need to establish Christmas morning plans.*

Mom and I are completing our gun safety training later today. Once that's done, we'll be able to take the proper paperwork to a gun seller and pick one out.

I text Christina and let her know that Mom and I will be there for dinner later.

Richard's voice grows louder. "The time has come for us to make some department changes," he bellows, and the air seems to buzz back to life amongst the sleepy worker bees.

"Changes?" someone asks.

"We all know that, a few months ago, we closed our biggest account yet with the Evangeline Iris group." He briefly eyes Jenny and me.

"I received word from the upper-level executives last night that, because of the success of that deal, they want to expand Life at Your Reach." He smiles, almost gleefully, his face looking more boyish.

Murmuring voices fill the silence.

"Sometimes growth doesn't only involve new additions to the team, it involves departmental mergers instead," he says over the whispers.

Then noise erupts, questions are shouted.

"What does this mean?" Jenny asks me.

I shrug.

"People! People, let me finish." He holds a hand up, silencing the room. "The plan is to merge our office with the global sales representatives, led by Teddy Stevens."

Jenny turns, whispering, "Maybe we can move up to the twenty-ninth floor?" She wiggles her eyebrows.

"Now, because of this merger, we are doing a bit of an office renovation and relocation."

"Fingers crossed," she murmurs.

"We'll be keeping our office here but moving the design department up to Teddy's domain. We'll then refurbish that section of offices to house the employees coming down from Global Contracts."

"How will everyone from Contracts fit in that space?" Jenny asks.

Richard's face constricts. "Well, we *are* expanding people, but…we are also tightening some loose ends."

"Loose ends?" someone snaps.

"Teddy has been asked to retire, and we will merge a portion of our team with the top portion of their team," he says.

"So…we're getting fired, people are losing their jobs? You called us back from a holiday shutdown to fire us? What a great Christmas gift."

Barb from HR kicks in. "Richard will work with Teddy on selecting employees that align with the new mission and departmental values. The others will be placed in supplementary departments throughout

Beltwhile Enterprises. No one is getting let go, but a total of ten people, five from here and five from Teddy's catalog, will be relocated."

A collective breath is released, everyone except me seemingly placated by HR's smooth reassurance.

My breathing is shrill, piercing. The room swings, starts spinning. *Moved? To a new department?* It's silent all around me now, but not within. The words are screaming inside, burning, swirling, tumbling into a frenzy.

I think about how far I've come, about the obstacles the past year has thrown at me, about what I've learned from Jenny…from Mom… and more so, from me.

I am the hurdle, the obstacle in the way: it's me. Frank can no longer bear the blame. It's me. It's my faults, the collection of my weaknesses that have stood in my way…it's…me.

"I'll volunteer!" I stand, shouting, words tumbling free.

Jenny seems alarmed, then chuckles. Richard's boyish face turns back into a scowl.

"I'll move to the design department," I say.

Richards's eyes blaze. "We are not hashing this out in a public area. Teddy and I will meet to discuss particulars later this afternoon."

"Hey, but if I volunteer, doesn't that make it easier? I want this, Richard, I can do it. I'm good," I tell him.

Richard's jaw tightens. "Sit down, Katniss!"

A giggle fills the static air.

"He's astounding. I've seen his work," interjects Jenny. "Consider it when you meet with Teddy. Why not give him the chance?"

Richard turns on her. "Jennifer, please! I've made myself clear. I'll discuss this with Teddy, and we can reconvene later."

I sit, letting out a heated sigh.

"And if anyone else has any issues with what's decided, think twice before sharing. We can change the rules and let people go, if that's the way you want to play."

If that's the way you want to play? Like people's lives are a game? An anger grows in me—I think of that little boy with the starfish. I think about how Mom wanted to believe that I was anything like him. That I was wise beyond my years and willing to stand up in the face of adversity. That has never been me.

I have gone crazy, pushed myself to the brink with this unknown need for perfection, so strong that it's unattainable. This ruthless all-consuming anxiety telling me it's not okay to fall, it's not okay to lose. A snicker inside, telling me that I have to keep my head down and my mouth shut, if there is any chance of winning.

And of winning what?

I have an inability to own my faults, an embarrassment to feeling alone. Because…I'm different. A different breed. And is different wrong? Because, sometimes, I feel wrong, like I bleed deeper, feel deeper, hurt deeper than every other man. A man who never says what he wants, never takes what he wants, never does what he wants. Just picks and pokes at this reflection that's not even him.

And again, to win what? I think of Evangeline, how young she is, but how sure and confident she is with her decisions.

"Move me to the design team...or I'll find another job," I say.

"Huh?"

"Have me moved...or consider this my two weeks' notice."

Richard's face stiffens, shoulders growing tight. "So, you're just going to throw this in my face? You're just going to demand what you want?" he asks, dumbfounded.

"Yes."

"You aren't serious?"

Jenny fidgets next to me.

"I am. I won't do this anymore. I'm not going to stay…I'm not going to keep…wasting time."

"Wasting time? You do your job to get paid, that's all."

"I want to paint," I say "I want to draw, want to create things with my hands, want to make something special from nothing. And, if you can't support that—if you can't accept that—then I have to leave. It's not personal."

"No!" he hollers. "You have no qualifications to demand your placement. I've given you more *slack* than I've ever given anyone else, and all you've done is choke me with it."

A moment of silence, his face hard and eyes dangerous.

I shrug.

"You'll go where I put you, and that's the end of that."

Swallowing hard, I mutter, "Then, I guess this is goodbye."

He erupts, spits. "Okay! Fine! Goodbye, Keith! Be out of here within the hour!" he shouts.

I falter, hesitate, but then stand. Squaring my shoulders, I whisper, "Sure. I only need ten minutes."

I feel powerful. Like I'm finally riding the mountain, instead of fighting against it. I stand, moving for the door. Think about Mom and how, when I get home, we are heading to a gun range to take back our safety.

I've seen Frank abuse alcohol my entire life. I watched him, observed him, learned from him, as he pounded drink after drink into his body. Watched his blood mix, then dilute itself into alcohol. Learned through his actions what's normal and healthy, while I was growing and changing on some fundamental level that we, as adults, can't even begin to comprehend.

I've seen too much.

Binge drinking is like a gun. *It's not the weapon that's killing; it's the person behind it.* It's a cycle, it's a circle, and it's a wheel that's going to keep spinning. And as it spins, it will only continue to get faster and faster until there's nothing left to do but crash. *Unless I stop it.*

I am the hurdle; I am the obstacle.

Together, Mom and I are taking our own control back.

Chapter 46

Mom stands, stoic, her feet planted, her shoulders squared and her jaw tight. Her brow is serious under the safety glasses, her hair tucked behind bright orange earmuffs. The instructor flashes the green light, and Mom's face doesn't falter. She squeezes the trigger on the deadly Glock 19. *Pop. Pop. Pop.* One after another, the paper target shatters.

I hoot and holler, cheer from the safety zone. After her round of firing finishes, the red light goes on, and Mom's hands fall, like we were taught. She engages the safety and beams.

There's a series of clicks. A new paper comes into her path, and our instructor, Harrison—tall and handsome in an orange jumpsuit—leans forward from the safety booth and hits a green button labeled *speak.* "Gnarly, Lily! Let's see you give those skills another go."

Mom assumes the planted stance. The gleaming black gun, powerful in appearance, stands at the ready. Harrison counts down into the microphone, and then, again, there's a green light.

Pop. Pop. Pop.

The light turns red, and Mom drops her hands again, engages the safety. Harrison speaks into the microphone. "Leave the gun on the stand, and I'll buzz you into the safety box."

She deposits the gun on the stand and approaches the box, smiling. Harrison presses another button, which initiates a buzz, and Mom opens the door.

Harrison gives a "woot!"

"You're better at that than me," I tell her.

"I feel alive." She giggles.

"Ms. Higgins passed with flying colors. You," Harrison says to me, "I'll pass you if you sign up for the monthly range practice."

We laugh, and then a second employee retrieves our target papers and brings them to us as trophies. Each round, we were allowed three shots. Mom, equally as new at this as me, managed six deadly shots to my two.

Regardless, we both end up signing up for the range practice, and the instructor presents us with certificates and a list of approved and recommended guns for first-time weapon owners.

"Come back after you find a weapon that fits your needs, and we'll get you familiar with it," Harrison says. "But don't forget that's exactly what it is: a deadly weapon...a weapon that requires an abundance of safety and responsibility when storing and handling."

SD

The damp air of the basement won't pose a threat to the safety of our new firearm. The cool, slick, black aesthetic of the SIG P226 9mm will be tucked and locked into the all-weather protective vault. The gun doesn't look as shiny and procedural in the safety of my home. It looks like a new threat, hard and cruel, the all-steel construction looking like a piece of machinery normal pedestrians shouldn't yield.

"It's kind of scary," I say, shivering.

Mom looks at me, nods. "It stays down here, only you and I know the passcode, Keith. Not Jenny or Christina—you and I, Keith. Got it?"

I nod, swinging the vault door closed, and punching in the code to lock it.

"We don't open it when Hope is home, ever. She'll go to Christina's, and then we'll take our lessons. Besides that, it stays locked, here, untouched."

I nod again.

"Unless…" she says. Her words fall flat, and her eyes bore into mine. Then she turns, crossing her arms, and jogs her way up the stairs.

<h1 style="text-align:center">Chapter 47</h1>

knock, out of habit, on the huge, sturdy double door that arms the massive home. A blue-and-gold wreath the size of my body hangs on a durable hook. I ring the doorbell twice, sure that the knock will go unheard if they are in the back of the house.

"This is their house?" Mom asks, her eyes wide.

I nod, remembering my initial shock after seeing Christina and Paul's house. Huge and shingled, it looks like a historic piece of architecture, yet it has a modernized flare. There's a massive stone chimney running up the front, double-paned windows, and multiple balconies opening the castle to the outside. The house sits on a triple lot in North Canton, and despite Ella being an only child, the house is over eight thousand square feet—five bedrooms and six baths throughout.

"Is it only the two of them here?" Mom asks.

I nod. "Seems excessive for two people. Apparently, they bought it way before the housing market blew up."

"The other half," Mom whispers, shaking her head.

"Wait till you get a look at their Christmas tree."

It takes a few minutes, but then Christina opens the door. "Hi," she says, her eyes tight, and her lips puckered. She welcomes us in, and she avoids my eyes, instead settling on Mom.

There's an awkwardness to her still, the same presence I heard in her voice making her shoulders tight.

We follow her through the house, Mom's eyes dancing around the space in wonder.

"Where's Hope?" I ask.

Christina stops walking. "She's out back playing," she says. "It's pretty mild for December, and she had some energy to burn off." She fidgets, fixing her hair. She moves to the kitchen, and we follow.

In the kitchen, she gets us two glasses, fills them with ice and water, and hands them to us. "Shit," she says, her hands coming up to her temples.

"What?" I ask, confusion making me snap.

"You're going to be mad, but it just happened, okay?"

Mom's face tightens, and I imagine mine doing the same. "What is it? Is Hope alright?

Christina waves her hands at this. "Fine, she's just fine. It's just…" She sighs again, moving toward the back door. "I'll show you."

She pulls a coat from the hook, puts it on. She opens the door and slips out first. Then Mom follows. I close the door behind me, turning. And there, standing in front of me, in Christina and Paul's backyard, playing on the swing set I built, playing with Hope, is…

"Ella?"

Her big blue eyes are nervous as they survey me. Her hair is black and long, resting straight on her shoulders. Time slows, freezes, and my eyes refuse to blink. The breeze blows against my cheeks. Hope turns in slow motion, seeing me and smiling.

"Dada!" she yells.

She's there still—Ella—and beautiful. Thin and pale, but her. I feel Christina turn to look at me, but my eyes stay on Ella.

All I can think about is what she said the last time we spoke, when I hung up on her. *Maybe Hope could come and be here with me.*

Chapter 48

"Keith?" It's Christina's voice now. "Keith, she's home for the holidays," she says.

Standing here, silent and weary. Standing here, stuck. My eyes break from Ella, move to Christina. Her words make this her fault. "When did you plan on telling me she was back in town?"

The level of my voice makes her take a step back. "Tonight," she says. "At dinner." She looks at Ella. My eyes don't follow hers.

"Give me her!" I demand, thrusting my arms out for Hope.

Mom's hand squeezes my shoulder. "Keith, just—"

I shake her off, interrupting. "Hope—I want my daughter!" I wave frantically.

Christina's eyes are back, digging. She moves between us and takes Hope. She carries her to me.

"You were just going to let Hope play with her all day without saying a thing to me?" I feel heat on my face. "Shame on you!"

"Keith?" Christina tries.

"It's not...right."

"She's my daughter too," Ella mutters.

I cover Hope reflexively. "She's not! She's *not* yours!"

Ella's tight face doesn't falter. She stares with mysterious eyes. Hope tightens, clutches her little arms around my neck.

Fumbling, moving, I turn away from Ella, take a breath to calm down. "I'm sorry, sweetie. Daddy's sorry. I didn't mean to scare you. Here… go—" I peel her fingers from around my neck, "—go to Grandma," I say, handing her to Mom.

Mom takes her, stealing shocked glances at Ella.

"Take her inside?"

She nods, looking at Christina and Paul, then Ella again. Moving slowly, they go inside, and I take a breath before turning around.

Christina talks first. "Keith, give her a chance. She's sorry, okay? She's doing well now, she's here to make things right. This…this is *my* baby and my Christmas wish."

"Make things right? You let her see Hope behind my back. I can't trust you! She can't storm in here and take her away from me. It doesn't work that way, and you know it. She left us!" I turn on Ella. "The day you gave up on us is the day you gave up the opportunity to be her mother!"

She wraps her arms around herself, the settling sun bringing a new chill to the air.

"Keith, let's all just calm down and talk about this," says Paul. "She's not here to take Hope away from you. She's not here to take anything away from you. She's just here, back, trying to make amends for what happened in the past. You can be pissed, angry, hurt, or whatever you are, but Ella—" he points to her, "—she's that little girl's mother. She'll always have a right to see her. So, let's talk about it. Let's figure this out rationally, with our little princess in mind."

Something inside me quivers, then my lip does. I understand. I understand his words, but I don't want to. This was wrong. I should have been here. I should have known.

Looking at Ella, I get this fear in my gut. Would she try and take Hope away from me? It's been months since she mentioned bringing Hope to California. Months, and she hasn't tried to reach out or make good on that request. I take a deep breath.

"Mom, Dad, can I have a minute alone with Keith?" says Ella, her voice steady.

I turn, seeing her, and it hurts my eyes. She's still beautiful, and I don't want her to be.

Paul nods. He takes Christina's arm. She's reluctant to go, but follows. The door shuts, and Ella and I are left alone.

Watching her, she makes no move to come closer, but instead, sits on the swing and pushes off with her legs. It's weird to see the person I once knew so well. Forcing rational thoughts into my head, I speak. "I'm glad you're doing better."

She nods. "Me too," she whispers. She's quiet again, kicking her feet and swinging higher. Her sweater, oversized, hangs around her like a blanket. "I missed home."

I nod, thinking of everything that has changed. Thinking of everything that happened in life that she doesn't know about. "The weather?" I say, trying to joke, and against my will, there's a tremble.

She stops swinging, using her feet to slow herself down. Her eyes study me. "Not the weather," she says, a light humor to her words. She kicks at the mulch. "Hope. Mom and Dad. You."

I shove my hands into my pockets, look to the sky. "She's cute, isn't she?"

Ella smiles. "The cutest thing I have ever seen."

Something inside me weakens, softens, and I feel tears come to my eyes. "She's not leaving me."

"I'm not here to take her away from you," Ella says. "You're her dad, I know that. I'd just like…I'd like to be a friend to her, if I could. Maybe, one day, a mother." Her voice trembles on the word "mother," and I feel my eyes start to spill over. I nod, the anger in me extinguished.

"I quit my job today," I say.

Ella laughs. "That's good. You've hated it there for years."

"I'm in love with a girl named Jenny."

"Ah-ha! The one that texted!" She chuckles.

I raise my eyebrows at that. "It just happened."

"I'm in love with a girl named Sabrina," Ella says.

I laugh, wiping at my face. "I'm glad."

She nods. Her hand moves to her pocket. She shoves it inside and pulls out a folded piece of paper. "It's awkward, but I wrote a letter to God. It's what's been helping me come out to everyone." She unfolds the paper. "Can I read some of it to you?"

I nod, move, and sit on the swing next to her.

"It's long. I don't have to read the entire thing." She sighs.

"I'd really like to hear it," I say.

She clears her throat, looks down at her page. "Dear God," she says, shyly. "I've spent the last 26 years making demands of you. *This isn't the real me! Make me different!* But you've remained persistent: *This is you! You know who you are!* Yet, every time I start believing you, every time life grants those small moments of clarity, the weight of society bears down with its heavy fist. And you, sir—or madam—created this society!"

She looks at me hesitantly, and I nod for her to continue. She looks to the paper, a tremor in her voice. "Maybe you can just read it…to yourself?"

I chuckle, taking the paper. It's warm, and despite paper being light, I know how heavy this was for her. I start from the top.

Dear God,

I've spent the last 26 years making demands of you. *This isn't the real me! Make me different!*

But you've remained persistent: *This is you! You know who you are!*

Yet, every time I start believing you, every time life grants those small moments of clarity, the weight of society bears down with its heavy fist. And you, sir—or madam—created this society! Now, that's not me pointing a finger, it's just my thoughts getting tangled on your message. I know that you know that I am scared. Sick to my stomach at what will happen when I learn to accept who I am. You, dude, created this world that frowns upon weakness, and now I have this urgency inside, almost like some clock is ticking. It feels like time is disappearing, and that if I don't figure out the end game, an explosion will sound.

I am…gay.

You know this, because you made me this way. Didn't you?

We've already covered that marrying a man to fix what I thought was broken wasn't the intended message; we've also covered how I spent my entire life running away, convincing myself I wasn't queer. We've dealt with that, mostly, but why do I still feel wrong? I have felt wrong my entire life.

I should mention—to your credit—you've continued telling me the opposite. You tell me that you made me this way, that you love me this way. But, then the world spits another definition onto me—dike!—and I hate to break it to you, but you made them too.

So, naturally, I have questions: Why? Why did you make them see me as wrong?

I was damaged by a family who loves me, but never understood the power of their words. Damaged by "gay," because it always reminded that a core piece of me was built incorrectly. Did you intend for that? Was it some test I needed to overcome?

I've been thinking about that time I started weeping—spilling and shattering so completely that I couldn't help but speak truth—were you proud of me? Part of me looks back and can see the strength it took to bare that weakness, but another part is stuck digging for the bigger picture. What I think you want for me is always shifting, the puzzle pieces not seeming to fit together in the order I was working toward.

I am gay. Yet, I married a man who you made headstrong and stubborn.

I never wanted to cause pain. I never wanted to cause grief or shame. It was never my intention to hide myself so completely. I loved him, and I think you wanted that, because so many of the good things in my life have come from the roots we've planted together. From the life we've built.

How can it be both things?

Was I pretending? Am I pretending? My entire life, I've pretended I am not afraid. You gave us two beautiful children, but then took one of them away. Was that my punishment for lying? And then you made me destroy my family in order to save myself. Why is that true? Did you think I was strong enough to handle that?

I know a husband deserves to be cherished by a wife, but then I hear the flicker of what your voice might be: *yes, he does deserve that, but not at the expense of who you are.*

Is that you? Are you saying what I think you're saying?

I hate the fact that I have to hurt someone in order to be myself. I'd like an easy button. I want him to say the hard stuff and connect the dots, so I don't have to say it all again, but that doesn't seem to be what you want for me. It's not the lesson you set in motion.

I believe the solution is to say what I feel, to feel something and say it. But it's not easy! It's not simple for a woman who has been frightened her entire life. It's not simple for a person who has spent every day covering herself with shields, digging herself into holes in an attempt to hide. I have always believed I was broken. That somehow YOU screwed up when making me, and I don't want to feel like that anymore.

Why do you need bravery to be yourself? Does the courage come from gritting down and staying the course? Or should one always soar on the wings of their individual truth? Did you paint us all in nuanced strokes for a greater lesson? Why are others hearing a different message from you?

Please, for my sake, let me put this blame onto you. It's too damn heavy for me to hold. Let me point all ten fingers and curse your name, because without hope that this is all a part of your greater strategy, I may fully turn to stone.

Can you be my target?

Yours, Ella.

Part 6

December, Christmas Eve

Chapter 49

'm just a modern-day archaeologist digging for myself in this pile of bones. I keep finding something new every day.

I dreamed of Mom last night, her long hair fluid around her face. Her worried shoulders tight, eyes swirling with fear, muttering, "Everything will be okay," rocking back and forth in a ball on the floor. She was frightened of something, but I was steady, sturdy for once in my life. I comforted her, whispered the same four words back.

When we woke this morning, I hugged her again, assured her that my life is always better with her in it. Mom went out, reluctantly, with Christina and Ella on a girls' trip, lunch, and nails. Later today, I'll have everyone here for Christmas Eve dinner. Since Hope is napping, now is the perfect time to catch up on cleaning and wrapping.

My cell phone rings. My eyes strain for focus, pull up and measure my reflection in the pale-light bathroom. "Yeah," I say, answering the unknown caller.

"Hello, Keith," the familiar voice rasps, fumbles for a second.

"Richard?"

"Jennifer sent me a few snippets of your work. Have a few minutes to talk?"

"Snippets of work? Not following, Richard."

"Your paintings, you idiot! I have a scanned copy of something you've painted," he says, voice rising in annoyance, but steadying almost instantly. "The one of a house, with you holding the baby. It's not horrible."

Jenny was shocked to hear of Ella's triumphant return, giddy, but trying to contain her concern for the fact that our life is a soap opera.

"You shittin' me, Rich?"

"You want the meeting or not? Don't call me Rich! One offer, Keith! Just one!" he barks, the clatter of a car door outside echoing through the house.

"You're here?"

I move from the mirror, peer out through the bathroom window to the driveway below. A rusted Pontiac rests, lights still on, driver seat now empty.

"No! Why would I be there?"

"There's a car—never mind… Okay. Yes! I want the meeting! Thank you…Richard."

"Yeah, yeah. Don't be all grateful just yet. I'll have something set up for after the new year."

I hear the *click* of the phone and stifle my laugh as I make my way from the bathroom. Holding my breath, tiptoeing closer, I check on Hope, who is still napping peacefully in her crib, lips pursed, cheeks pink from the comfortable room.

I close the door, quiet and with care, and move for the stairs to peek out at the unknown car. The visitor knocks on the door, the racket making me pause in my footsteps and listen for a crying Hope.

Nothing.

Then again, booming at the front door. *BANG. BANG. BANG.* The violent thuds thwack into the door: one, two, three, shaking my insides, stealing the still silence of the midmorning calm. I pick up the pace, not wanting the noise to wake Hope.

In the corridor, I ask, "Who is it?"

Listening, hearing nothing, feeling the presence on the other side of the door instead of seeing it, the air starts to feel disproportionate. "Hello?"

"I hear it from my sources that I have a grandson?" The harshly cruel voice behind the door growls.

The bony scrape of fingernails slashes into skin, my fingers nervously cutting their way up in anxious horror. A weak, jittering moan comes from my lips. The disgusting remembrance of how pathetic I am freezes me, slaps me across the face, with an immensity I can't even dare to consider. A weight strapping to my ankles, something pulling at my neck, another thing eating at my innards.

Frank. Frank? Frank, is here? In Boston? On my steps?

I take slow, shallow breaths, not answering, every feeling I've ever had hitting me at once.

He bangs on the door again. *BANG. BANG. BANG.* "I know you're in there. I heard your voice."

My pulse quickens, climbs, beats its way into my ears, and squeezes my eyes shut. Daddy's here. Mom was…her hesitation, her worries, she was right…

"Keith!" he hollers, and I know it's him.

His voice is the same, only rougher. Gruff and aged from substance abuse, but *his* just the same. For a second, I think of running. I think of hiding under the bathroom sink, just like I did as a boy. Years of panic and anxiety I'd pushed away, now standing on my doorstep. *How is he here? There is no way! I'm not a kid! I'm not a kid! I'm not a naive kid anymore!*

I am the hurdle!

"Coming," I mutter, haunted and afraid and sounding just like a child. "One second." I look around the room, panic taking over in my gut. I grab my cell phone and dial 911, but slip it into my pocket without pressing send.

Hand shaking, it travels without prompting to the brass door handle, cold, heavy. It's mockingly secure as it taunts, and my hand wants to come back, wants to wrap around myself.

He's here and he'll leave. I'm a man now…he can't hurt us! My eyes find that hand… My hand, which is on the knob. Why is it on the knob?

Run? Open? Hide? Confront?

Rooted in indecision, I manage to turn it anyway. The door swings, creaks, moans on its hinges, as if to protest. The abrupt deluge of his scent—sour and musty, a delicate concoction of alcohol, vomit, and piss—violates the doorjamb, crosses into my home before being asked.

Open now, fully open, the same fierce eyes from my childhood peel away the walls I spent years building. Suddenly, I'm a boy in front of his father.

His skin is wrinkled, blemished, and damaged by time and substance. Parts of him glow green, the onset of liver failure a daunting promise. His frame is slim and gaunt. His hair stringy and long, but just as dark as I remember. His clothes are torn and ragged. Dark circles ring his eyes, and his toothy grin smiles at me.

A small part of me almost misses that smile, still longs for that acceptance.

"Hello, my boy," he says, the smell of liquor on his breath.

"Frank," I say as a greeting. I stare at him, pondering what's next. Why is he here? And then again, Mom's voice. *Frank isn't right, he'll take what he wants.* He's here for my mother.

"What are you doing here?"

"Came to see my grandson," he says, shaking a grainy picture of Mom and Hope in my car outside her Detroit studio apartment. "Wanted to wish you a Merry Christmas in person."

My insides scream. Mom was right. Jesus, Mom was always right. "How'd you get that?" I ask.

His face gets tight, pinched in calculation. If he's here for her, then maybe I need to convince him Mom's somewhere else. I left her in Detroit, just helped her move, yeah…

"I was helping Mom move to a new place. Nice two-bedroom in Auburn Hills," I mutter.

His teeth show, his eyes dig, chastise me, as if he knows I'm lying. "Right..." he drawls. "Because she's in Michigan still. She'll love to see a picture with me and my grandson," he says, winking like he's playing along with some game.

"It's actually a granddaughter," I bark, and my tone is too sharp, angry for no reason other than the fact that he's here, drunk, and will never give a shit about Hope, that he's still looking to hurt Mom, even after all this time.

He laughs a little. "Figures."

"What's that supposed to mean?"

He puts his hands into his oversized coat. "Weaker men have weaker sperm," he says, looking around me to peer inside.

Moving to block the doorway, I laugh, just to make him feel like an idiot. "Right, Dr. Dad. I forgot how wise you are."

His nostrils flare, a blind rage demanding to be extinguished. His coat pulls taut, tightening around him, as if to cage that wrath. "Aren't you going to offer your old man a drink?" he asks, voice raw and damaged.

Panic slaps me again, my face falling flat, that questioning attitude feeling like regret. What will he do if I say no? What happens if I slam the door in his face?

His mouth quirks to the side, and in that moment, I see a small hint of Scott.

"Sure," I say. "Sure... Come in..."

I move, letting him enter, the door closing without me telling it to. The phrase, "Why am I letting him in?" playing on repeat. Then, that smell again, hitting me, smacking me back into someone I've outgrown. Something else starts to echo in my mind, sinister and disturbing. *Gun... gun... gun,* whispering, derisive and demanding, again and again. *Gun!*

Our gun—Mom's gun—is in the safe downstairs.

The thought is utterly ridiculous, but then I hear my voice say, "I keep the good stuff down in the basement. I'll have to run down and get that. Is that what you're drinking—bourbon, vodka, scotch still?"

"You know me well, son," he mutters through cracked lips.

"Sit here," I tell him pointing to the sofa. "I'll be right back."

Running, fleeing, I bound down the stairs to the basement, no fear of it anymore. The real fear is already here, on my sofa. I go to the gun safe. Opening it, I grab it, fumble, making a muffled noise while loading it, my insides sticking together.

The cold steel of the pistol screams in my hands, forces me to shove it, slip it into the back of my pants, under my shirt, away from my dangerous fingers. It teases, heavy and threatening against me. I take a deep breath. *Run, now, run.*

Hope…Hope is still sleeping upstairs.

Rushing, flying back up the steps, grabbing a bottle of wine on my way up, my mind goes black, starts painting images of him taking her, stealing her, punishing me in the way he used to punish Mom.

Bounding to the top, his tattered ensemble comes into sight, just as his smell does—seated exactly where placed. I slow my gait.

"Looks like I'm out of the hard stuff, but I have this wine," I stammer, calming myself. I take forced breaths.

He chuckles that Frank chuckle, making me shiver. "Is it at least dry?" he asks.

Nodding, pouring him a glass, I'm careful to keep my back to him. Not just because I'm nervous he'll see the gun, but because I remember who he is. If he wants to hit me, he'll do it when I'm not looking, and I don't know a father who doesn't try to hit me.

He takes the glass, pounds it back into his gullet, without even glancing at it first. I sit on the arm of the sofa across from him.

"So, why are you here?" I ask again. I'm too aggressive, and my fear isn't fear anymore; it's just anger. He's not bigger than me. He can't hurt me anymore. Gun… "Why are you here, Dad? Don't tell me you're full of regret and you came to make amends?"

He coughs, rough and gruff. "No. That's not it." He looks at me spitefully. "Why, you have regret, boy?" He gives me this stupid look. A look that's supposed to make me feel inferior. A look that should make me feel less—because, hell, only weak people have regrets.

I scoff. Years of taking his abuse, of letting him define me, years spent in fear because of him, it all melts into one colossal heap of anger and disgust. "Yeah…I mean, sure."

He looks at me, then tilts his head, downing his glass. His hazy eyes fall back down, expecting an answer.

I can't hold back my snarky remark. "About the only thing I regret is that choice I made in fourth grade, when I chose to write an essay about you. The teacher said to write a one-page paper on who our hero was. Every boy in class picked their daddy to write about. So, naturally, when it was my turn, I picked you too. I mean, I was embarrassed not to. If my father wasn't my hero, then surely, I was queer, and you always made sure I knew how wrong it was to be queer. I was too naive then to bullshit my reasons. I wrote, *Today my daddy is my hero, because he didn't hit me, which I liked. He's my hero when he sleeps at the bar, because Mommy doesn't have to cry. On Monday, Mommy hid the money, so I had a Pop-Tart for lunch—Daddy's my hero for not checking under the garbage bag.*"

I laugh now, fake. "You were never one to take out the trash. Only one to bring it in and dish it out," I spit.

His eyes blaze to life. His lip curls. He wants to remain calm, but I'm giving him no reason to. "Your mouth…you never did know when to shut it!" he snarls.

"Well, the truth hurts, doesn't it?"

He shakes his head, disgusted. "You were always looking for pity. Always expecting things you didn't deserve." He tries to drink again, even though the glass is empty.

"Yeah, I guess it's too much to ask for basic compassion, basic acceptance, and basic humanity. You're right, it's my fault," I say, and it's stupid. My attitude is stupid.

He slams his fists into the table, roaring, "Shut your mouth!"

It snaps shut, gluing itself closed, my body sinking down into the couch.

The house is quiet, no sounds of Hope waking up. *Sleep baby, stay asleep.*

He's breathing fast and measured, working to control his usually uncontrollable outbursts. I go to speak, then stop myself. *Stop provoking him, just stop. Give him whatever he wants and get him to leave.*

I wait until he looks calm before speaking again. "What brings you to town, Dad?" I ask more evenly now.

"To see my son," he says, eyes snapping back to me. "And to meet my granddaughter. It's Christmas. You want me to spend it alone?"

"Well, she's out of town," I lie. "And I'm heading out soon too. Is there something you need before you're on your way?" I say it calmly, sweetly, but even I can hear the anxiousness.

He tightens his jaw. "I thought I raised you better than that, boy? Going to kick me out that fast?"

I can't stop myself. "You didn't raise me at all," I say evenly, no cracking or wavering.

I've turned into a man who isn't scared of his daddy anymore.

He stands from the sofa, his bottom teeth protruding from his face, and his fists clenched. Snarling, spittle flying from his muzzle and wetting his war-chapped lips, he shouts, "Fuck!"

I recoil immediately, involuntarily.

I guess that's a lie, I am still scared of Daddy. I taste the fear, the fear I've always known, coming back and mixing with that anger. Then I feel the adrenaline start seeping from my kidneys, shouting at my heart to run and to run fast. Get Hope and run.

He notices my fear, smiles, enjoying his power over me. "You haven't changed at all, son," he says. He wobbles over to the bottle of wine, already filling his glass.

But I have. I'm not just scared now. I'm angry. I'm angry as hell, and I'm strong.

"No, I have," I say. After a minute or so of silence I say, "You haven't changed at all, Dad." I smile and eye his glass.

He chugs the liquid inside, fills it again. "Nope...I haven't."

I look away, fearing the coldness in his eyes and hating myself for it.

"I've actually got to get going. Where are you staying? Maybe we can meet up some other time? Grab lunch."

His face turns red, and he takes a step toward me. I hop off of the sofa, and he stops.

"Boy, you really let money ruin you, didn't you? Treating your own dad like a criminal. Do I have to ask you to stay here? Your own father has to ask to stay with his son? You'd let me sleep on the street, wouldn't you? Should I pretend you aren't disrespecting me? You must think you're privileged and better than folks like me, because you have a nice house and fancy clothes. You're still nothing but a boy who needs to be taught a few lessons."

"There is nothing valuable you can teach me," I mutter, shocked with my own words. Physically unable to not fight back anymore.

His face shakes a little from clenching his teeth.

I shift my feet, feeling the gun on my back again. I take a deep breath. I can't shoot him, and if I keep provoking him, he might give me a reason to. I need to get him to leave.

"Frank, is there something you need?" I ask, again. "Money? Booze? What?"

He points a finger at me. "You call me sir!" he screams.

I take a step away, wanting to scream back, wanting to shout, but not. Instead, I nod, and my agreement puts him back in control. He calms down. He goes back to the wine and fills his glass, even though it's not completely empty.

"Are you hungry?" I ask him.

"No," he snarls. "I didn't come looking for a handout, Keith. I came to see you."

"I didn't mean it as a handout. It's a long trip, I figured—"

"Quiet, boy. There you go again, answering me back!"

I hush, nod. Jesus, how do I get out of here? I feel my phone vibrate in my pocket, so I slip it out. It's a message from Jenny, *Word on the street is that Richard's caving to your demands.*

I fake a sigh.

"What is it?" Frank asks.

"Oh, nothing. Just the person waiting for me," I lie. "They're wondering where I'm at."

"Tell them your dad is in town, and you need to cancel. Is that so goddamn hard?" he spits.

"Sending it now," I say. *EMERGENCY*, I send to Jenny. *Send Help.*

There's no delay, the screen lights and vibrates with her call. I silence it and slip the phone back into my pocket.

Frank sits again on the sofa, scratching his face and unbuttoning his jacket. "On second thought, I am pretty hungry," he says.

I nod, instantly backing toward the kitchen. I grab a block of cheese from the fridge and arrange it with some grapes and crackers on a plate.

I carry the plate and set it on the coffee table in front of him. He's quiet as he eats.

"Well, how was the trip?" I ask, making small conversation, wondering how he has a car.

"Long," he hisses, his eyes already looking drunk. "Mighty fucked up that you make an old man come all the way to see his granddaughter. It would have been easy to find me." His words slur, and the distant drunk look in his eyes makes me look away. I've seen that look too many times in my life. "Disappointed in your daddy?" he asks. He stands back up, swaying slightly before moving to a picture on the wall. Looking for pictures with her—with Mom—in them.

"No," I lie.

"Dammit, Keith," he snarls. "Manners."

"No, sir," I say.

He stops at a picture I've painted, a sloppy, nostalgic look covering his face. "You still wasting your time coloring?"

"No, sir," I say.

"You lying, boy?" he screams, turning to me.

"No, Dad, I don't have any time for it."

He senses my fear and likes it, so he lets my lie slip. He passes the living room, then looks around the kitchen.

"Looking for something?" I ask. *Run, I should run.* Get Hope and run, but how?

He glares at me. "I told you I didn't want any handouts," he hollers. "You keep disrespecting me, I'll teach you a lesson for old time's sake."

I bite my lip and clench my jaw shut, focus on breathing to keep my words in. Slowly and drunkenly, he searches for something. He searches for her.

"What's this room?" he asks, pointing to the closed studio door.

"My office."

"Can I see it?"

After a second, I stand back up. "She's not in there," I tell him.

He smiles. "Who's not in there?"

"Whoever you're here to find," I say, calm and steady. Staring at him, silence covers the room, and the sound of a ticking clock fills my ears.

He huffs. "I told you I was here to see my granddaughter, goddammit!"

His hand moves to his belt to threaten me, and I lose it, scream at him. "You'll never meet her! You'll never be a part of our life! You'll never be welcomed here!"

He curls his lip into a snarl, his face red and blotchy in seconds.

"You coming here was a mistake. Mom's in Michigan! She's hundreds of miles away, and you're crazy if you think she isn't. And me, well, I'll never trust you. That's impossible, because you're a weed, a pesticide, a poison designed to ruin everything around you, and you do a damned good job at it. So just leave…just get the hell out of my house!" I ball my fists, waiting for him to come at me.

A snarl tears out of him, but instead of charging me, he moves toward the studio, kicking the door open with an alarming amount of power.

"Where is she?" he yells. "Where's my wife?" His voice is rough and guttural.

I race in after him. "She's not here, Frank! She's not fucking here!" I yell.

He rips through the studio, breaking everything in his wake, hollering, hooting, and jittering like some kind of animal. "Lily!" he bellows.

A startling clarity hits me: It *was* Frank. He caused all of this. He ruined everything. I am the obstacle, yes, but only now, because of Frank.

"She'll never be yours, Frank. She'll live her life in fear of you, but she'll still never be yours!"

He stills, turning for me. His bloodshot eyes screaming murder as his hands move for me. He's at me fast, throwing his fists at my face. I duck and move around him, just missing the blow. He tries again, dripping with anger now.

"I'll kill you!" he screams. "Tell me where she is, or I'll kill you!"

His fists come at me again, this time making contact with my shoulder, sending me backward on my ass. As he moves to cover me, I kick out, sending him into the wall. I jump up and, without warning or thought, the gun is in my hand and pointed at him.

He slows, eyeing me. Shock covers his drunk face, breath hitching raggedly.

"You won't pull the trigger. You can't pull it. You're too weak. You've always been too weak," he hisses. He lets out another throaty cackle.

I point the gun at his head. "Test me, Dad," I growl back. "I'll pull the trigger. You don't know me anymore."

"Do it. I want you to," he says, no fear crossing over him. No jest. He welcomes the gun, pleading for me to put him down.

I put my finger on the trigger, a whisper of tension flutters. I'm breathing heavily, shaking, trembling, in and out, in and out, and I just can't pull it. I try, but everything inside me shudders to a stop.

My eyes catch a glimpse of her behind him. The painting of us at the Christmas house, Mom, hanging there hauntingly, watching me through her painted camera lens. I can't do this. I can't. I can't kill him in front of her.

He laughs. He laughs the ugliest, most evil, laugh, and I shiver. *A monster*. He's a monster, and I've been right to blame him for everything, only wrong to let it change me.

I lower the gun. "I could kill you," I say, choking a bit on my words. "I *would* kill you," I clarify. "But I just can't give you the pleasure of making me into a monster. I'm not a monster. I'm not you." I stare at him, backing away. "Now leave. Mom is in Auburn Hills. She isn't here. I wish she were, but she's not. So, leave my house, and never come back."

He stares me down for a moment, then he nods his head in agreement, the hint of a smile pulling at his lips. His eyes are black and cold. I turn to leave the room.

I turn my back to him—*on him*.

Stupid.

His fist crashes into the back of my skull, and the burning, blinding pain sends me flying to the ground. I scurry forward, flip on to my back, and try to push myself up. He's on me fast, his fists in my eyes, in my nose, and in my mouth. Repeatedly, over and over again, his fists drilling into my head. Reminding me of all the times I was on some floor, screaming, begging, and pleading for him to stop hitting me.

Just like before, my pleads don't work.

No doesn't mean no to a monster.

He hits me again, and again, and again. And as his fist is repeatedly boring into my head, all I can think about is how his hands were made to hurt. His fists were made to punch. He was made to deliver pain.

Everything slows down. The movements, the noise, the light.

I see his fist coming toward me again, arching for a blow to the temple, and I think: *weak.* This man is weak. This man is the weak one, not me.

I turn my head, moving just in time for his bloody fist to slam hard into the wood floor.

He pulls back, bellowing in a gargling growl. "Fuck!" he screams, and I bury my fist into his gut, knocking the wind out of him.

Then, my fist finally connects with his face—hard against his mouth. I push him off of me with all my might. He tumbles to the ground, laying on his side, and I'm on my feet.

He laughs. "So, you're finally going to fight back?" He tastes the blood on his lip, and I can feel his anger grow. My eyes don't leave him as I pant for breath. His eyes flick to the floor in front of him, and I follow his gaze to the gun.

I dropped it.

"Going to shoot me, Dad?" I ask, but before he can answer, I'm running and kicking it out the open door of the studio. I hear it slide out of the room, and then bounce down every step of the basement stairs.

He laughs again. "Don't trust your old man?" he asks.

I wind back, kicking him hard in the stomach as my response. He curls into a ball.

"Get up and get out of here. That's your last warning!" I ball my fists hard, holding myself back from pounding his face until nothing but bloody remains are left—because I'm strong. I am strong enough to know better.

The words scream in my head, *"Look what you made me do! Don't make me do this. You made me do this!"* They're Frank's words, not mine. They're the words of a weak man, who took out his frustrations on things that couldn't fight back. *Don't make me break your arm, boy. Don't make me come in there and shut you up. Don't make me hit your mother again.* His weak words, his weakness, not mine, and it's taken me my entire life to see that.

I am strong enough.

He pulls himself to all fours, coughing blood. For a quick second, I feel powerful, but it turns into disgust even faster. That's how he'd felt standing over his child. Standing over his beaten and battered wife—shit, standing over his bloody children. He felt powerful.

He gets to his feet slowly, a sly grin on his face. If it weren't my dad, I'd assume he'd leave. But this is Frank. Frank won't leave. He'll have to show me who's boss.

True to form, he reaches for his belt. The cruel, malicious snarl consuming his face.

"Fight me like a man," I growl, spitting my blood at his feet. I swallow back the taste of metallic liquid.

He raises his eyebrows, pleased with my offering, and lets the belt go.

"Do you know that I hate you?" I ask him. "I hate you more than anything else in this world."

He charges me, fists balled, and evil in his face. The smell of bourbon and cigarettes reaches my noise just before him. I don't flinch. I let him barrel into me. Attacking him, as fast and as hard as he's attacking me. I punch him hard. So hard. Harder than I'd ever imagined I could hit anyone.

He grunts, and I wind back, bringing my fist into his jaw. I strike. Pain shoots up my hand and he stumbles back.

"I hate you!" I yell. "I hate you!" I scream again, my voice catches, and the trembling tension in my chest makes me sob.

He eats it. He lets that fuel him. "So pathetic. So fucking weak. Crying like a pussy-ridden baby," he mutters.

I jump at him, and he moves to the side. This puts me further into the studio. This puts him in between me and the door. I feel my mother's painted eyes boring into the back of me now.

I'm done running away.

"Why, Dad? Why do you hurt us? Why do you want to cause us pain?" I ask. "You've ripped this family apart. You've hurt us all. You've scarred me as a person," I say. "Why are you back? To finish killing everything you've ever touched?"

"I was correcting you. I was making you a man!" He spits blood, wiping at his mouth with the back of his hand. "I was teaching you exactly what my daddy taught me. At least I wasn't a pervert, like my old man. I taught you what was right, but I obviously failed as a man. Look at the pansy I've raised. A cock-sucking pussy. A father's worse nightmare."

"You were never a *man*, let alone a father," I snarl. "A person who hits an innocent woman and her children will never be considered a man."

He clenches his teeth, pissed off and violent. All my father has left in this world is his idea of what a man should be. The fact that I am questioning that must be downright insulting.

"You weren't innocent, you little shit. I saw the way your faggot eyes looked at me. Judging me. Ridiculing me for my problems. You and your mother judged my addiction. You laughed behind my back. You tested my authority as a father."

"You were never a father!"

His eyes go wide, and he makes a run at me, full force. I jump back, kicking my leg out and connecting with his knee. He buckles forward, and I strike out with my fist, connecting loosely with his ear.

He lets out a scream, falling into a pile of paintings and canvases. I stumble sideways, pain stabbing in my own leg from the kick. I fall into an upright easel, lose my balance further, and tumble to the floor, the easel shattering under me. I yelp in pain.

When I get back to my feet, Dad's coming at me with the belt. He couldn't handle his own son getting any hits in. The bastard had to go for the belt.

He whips the metal buckle at me, and it wraps around my arm. The pain stabs into the bone, vibrates pugnaciously. With an aggressive twist of the arm, the belt loops around further, and I pull him forward.

Instead of plummeting into me, he lets the belt go, and I fall to the floor alone. Before he gets the chance to jump on me, I'm up.

Shock registers on his face for a brief second as I hold up the belt.

"I'm not a helpless little boy anymore, Frank," I growl. "I know how to fight back. You won't win," I say. "Now come here and let me teach *you* a few lessons," I mutter, glaring at him, wiggling the belt.

He looks at me stupidly, drunkenly, the evil in him pouring out of every expression. The disgusting whiskey-soaked air lingers between us, and I can't get his words out of my head.

I was teaching you exactly what my daddy taught me. At least I wasn't a pervert like my old man.

The cycle of abuse. The wheel of violence. Where does it start? Where does it end? Who is to blame? I start thinking about what's next. What *is* next? How will this end?

"I'll kill you, boy," he whispers again.

I stare into his cold eyes. "Go ahead and try," I dare him.

A sharp noise breaks past the rushing in my ears. A wailing, crying. The pleading cry of a child, of a baby.

Hope…

Dad hears it, too, eyes going wide. He runs. Not toward me, but away from me. Leaving the room in a whirling rush.

Hope, no, no, not Hope.

Confusion lingers for only a second, clarity hitting home when the sound of his feet hit the basement stairs. He's not going for Hope. No, he's going for the gun.

He's going for the gun!

I run for him, not knowing if I'm fast enough to get to Hope and flee for safety before he gets the 9mm. At the top of the basement stairs, I see him already midway down, and I'm not fast enough. We can't escape. He'll be up and back before we can get out.

Thinking, not thinking, I throw myself at him, soar through the air, down the stairs, and for a second, it's like I'm flying.

Then I smack into him, and we become a ball of twisted legs and arms plunging down the wooden stairs. Adrenaline makes every stair-thrust into my back unsensational.

He lands first, and I hear the rush of air smack out of him. Then, momentum keeps me spinning, and I flip, landing hard and cracking my head on the concrete floor. Stars dance and my vision blurs.

I look over at him—he's still.

I try and sit up, but my head spins dangerously. I lay back down, still hearing Hope's faint cry.

"Congratulations," I mutter. "Way to mess everything up, just like you've always done."

Then, he's looming over me, sitting on my stomach. Sitting on my stomach, and stealing the air from my lungs, making me heave. His fingers—like concrete—around my neck. Laced heavily, thickly, around my neck, cutting off the nourishing air.

I try to pry off his fingers, fail, realize it's not just his hands, but it's his belt. He is strangling me with his belt. I can't breathe. I'm crying, and kicking, and spitting, and I can't move. I can't breathe!

Move, move, I have to move. Red!

Blood pouring from my eyes and my mouth, and I can't breathe. I can't breathe! I can't breathe, and his face is set in a snarl that tells me he's not going to stop.

"You took my life…my wife. You took everything!" he hollers. "You left me with nothing!"

His fingers and belt around my neck, squeezing. The breath leaving me, the air harder and harder to pull in. He came to destroy me. To destroy a life he created, and for what purpose? Because he has nothing left to do? No one else to hurt? Because he thinks Mom's his property?

I scrape and claw at his dirty hands, trying to peel them away, bits and pieces of his flesh pooling under my fingernails, turning his skin red and raw. I push and pull, then buck, but I still can't move him.

His eyes are like black holes boring into me, cutting my insides open. His spit mixes with his blood and smacks me in the face. I try to scream, but I can't. A pounding pulse ripples through my head, under his thumbs, and through my ears. Pulse. Pulse. Blood rushing from my heart, trying to make it to my brain. Oxygen trying it's damnedest to get to my lungs.

I feel my eyes bulge. I pull at his hands again, but his grip doesn't falter. He grunts, squeezing harder.

"Bitch," he snarls. "You ungrateful, bitch." His teeth curl, and his veins pound out of his temples. "You ain't never treated me proper. You ain't never done a damn thing for me," he spits. "Dammit, Lily," his drunk voice slurs, and I realize, in his head, that now he's choking her—

Mom. Then he shakes his head, confused. "Faggot! Faggot…" he yells. "I should have gotten rid of you years ago."

I push up with my hips, trying to make him unsteady, trying to toss him forward. His emaciated, disgusting body not moving. I gasp for air, but none comes.

Dark black stars dance in my vision. It's like dancing shadows in the night, skipping and scattering across my eyes, making me clutch for my pillow with tight fists. Except, this time, it's not a pillow. It's my father's rat-pissed shirt. Pain fills me, sorrow clouds me.

I hear a *pop*, and I can't breathe.

"You had to be a tough guy, huh? You had to make me do this?" he yells. His words. His weak words. "All I wanted was to meet my grandbaby and get my wife back, and you, you made me do this."

Maybe it's true. Maybe he did want to meet Hope. Maybe he came all this way to see her. But I didn't make him do this.

I stop fighting. I go limp, lifeless under his grip. The man I've feared, the man I've feared I'd become, he's squatting forcefully on my chest, draining the life from me. Sucking out everything pure and clean I have. Numbness and blackness remain. No fear. No fear in giving up. I give up. I can't fight back. I can't win.

"Weak! Weak! Weak!" he yells, and I feel it.

I see the end, but I don't feel weak, I feel something else. Smooth, cold metal, pressing into my side. Cool, cold metal biting me, whispering everything will be okay.

"I loved her!" he yells. "You took her from me. You turned her against me."

My hands move down my body and rest at my side without prompting.

His heavy figure crushing me into the earth, my fingers lace around the handle of the gun—cold and heavy. I slip the safety off.

Dying. I'm dying. He is killing me. Me, he is killing *me*. He will take my life, and I will leave Hope. I will leave Jenny. I will leave everyone. Dying.

Hope…

We live and then we die. I think that's as profound as it gets. But… isn't that a miracle in and of itself? You never know when it is your time. It just…comes.

I am the hurdle, the obstacle.

A single tear runs from the corner of my eye, down the side of my face. I hear the drop as it hits the floor.

He hisses one last time, "Weak!"

Then I press the gun to his heart, to his chest, and I pull the trigger. An explosion of noise, and I feel the release instantly.

He slumps to the floor, landing on my face, smothering me more.

Panic makes me push his still body violently. I rip at the belt, freeing my neck and gasping for air. I cough and choke, trying to breathe in all of the air around me. Pain throbs deep inside with every breath.

"Keith!"

I hear my name yelled, and jump, firing the gun again, straight into an already motionless Frank's back. I look at the gun, shaking and trembling in my bloody hand. I turn the safety on, let it fall to the ground.

Fighting to pull in air, my muscles quiver with the aftershock of the fight. Blood runs down my face and into my eyes. My body pounds to life in countless places.

"Keith!" Mom screams again, panicked.

I reach for Frank, for my dad. The rigid lips of the exit wound is like a sight from a nightmare. I turn him over on his back, shake him.

"Frank?" My horse voice croaks a painful jab. He doesn't move, but his bloodied mouth sags open. "Frank!" I shake him more violently, pull him into my arms, hugging him.

I've never hugged my father before.

I feel for a pulse and feel one. He's still alive. "I'm sorry. I'm so sorry." I clutch onto him, tears—confusing tears—blazing a trail down my face. I press on one of the wounds and try to stop the blood. It's pooling, it's starting to pool.

Even though I hated him, even though everything in me feared him, even though he took every opportunity to hurt me, I can't stop myself from loving him. I can't stop myself from *wanting* to love him.

I cry for him, or for what should have been him. I hug him, or what should have been him. Hurt, deep sadness pools inside of me, but no regret comes.

Mom's here now, face pale and sick. Looking at me with large, troubled eyes. "Keith…Keith, I had a feeling. Jenny called Christina, she said you texted—"

"I…" I try to talk, but my voice is gone. I put my hands to my neck and grimace.

Mom crouches down, feeling my neck. "Jesus," she says. "Dear Jesus. Is he dead?"

I shake my head no, tears spilling out.

Her hand goes to her mouth, and she turns her head gagging. "We need help! We have to call for help!"

I nod, going still. Staring blankly off into the darkness of the basement. *I hate basements.*

She points to the belt and back to my neck. "Did he strangle you?"

"Ye…" I try but can't manage.

"Don't talk. Don't talk! Just nod. Did he strangle you?"

I nod.

Mom's face drops into her hands again. "Okay. It's okay. I'm going to take care of this. Don't worry."

"Hope…" I try.

"She'll be fine." She reaches for the body, pulling him off of me. I clutch to keep him, but she shakes her head.

Letting him go, she lays Frank in the pile of blood and pulls me to the stairs. She goes back to Frank, searching the floor for something. I try to ask what, but no words come. Her eyes find what they were looking for when they fall onto the gun. She takes it, slipping the safety off, and standing over Frank.

Panic wells inside of me, but I'm unable to move. "No…" I croak.

She fires a single shot into his chest, and I jump, tears flowing from my eyes again. She was always a better shot.

She comes to me, finds my cell phone and dials 911. Her voice is shaky and heavy, filled with wet tears. "We have an emergency," she croaks, looking the strongest I have ever seen her. "My ex-husband was strangling my son, and I shot him. He's dead. I killed him," she cries into the phone.

I shiver. No. No! Don't do this. Why are you doing this? I did this. I did this.

She hangs up the phone, putting the gun down. Her face tightens and tears fall out.

"Why?"

"Because now he'll never hurt you again," she says.

She comes to my side, falling to the ground next to me, grabbing me and hugging me, weeping. We sit there, next to a dead Frank, honoring him by disgracing him. Crying weakly, just like he would have wanted.

Chapter 50

My dad tried to kill me. *Mom killed him.* Or maybe I did. He's dead, his blood is on my hands.

Flashbacks of him in my house, choking me, keep filling my vision. One minute, I'm getting a glass of water, and the next I see him on me. I've already made the appointment to see Dr. Ryder. It was a requirement to leave the hospital.

Mom's been glued to my side, not leaving, even when the police probe. We told them the truth, mostly, leaving out my two shots, Mom claiming she was the one to pull all three of the fatal triggers.

I shot Frank, too. I did it, and I'm fine sharing the blame. But changing my story now will throw red flags. Self-defense potentially shifting into murder. So, Mom bears the title of killer alone. It's her way of continuing to protect me.

They found samples of his flesh under my nails, the damage done to my throat was substantial, and Frank's violent record is on file with the Detroit police. To Jane's credit, Mom had prepared. She had reported Frank over eight times within the last five years, and a call to the police station returned fruitful reports on Frank and his violent manner.

We arrived home only a few hours ago, Jenny meeting me here with Hope. Hope not understanding why I look the way I do—red and purple bruises covering my face, my throat. Yet, that didn't stop her from snuggling me. She's still mine.

"One sleep till Santa's here."

After the stress of the day, I need something to help me unwind. Something that will help me let it go. Let the darkness and bitterness wash away. Because, holding onto this pain will consume me. It's trying to take all of me in its grasp, but I'm not letting it. I'm letting it go, because I am the hurdle—it's me.

Hope and I hop into some comfy pajamas, meet Mom and Jenny downstairs, as we veg-out to *Frozen*. Our favorite. I still can't get over the fact that they make the prince be a total douchebag in the end. I mean, why does he look at Anna so genuinely then? Where are the hints that he's a dick?

Every time we watch this movie, I think maybe this time the ending will be different. That maybe he'll actually kiss her and melt her frozen heart. The asshole never does. It's always the same painful ending. You'd think, after the millionth time watching it, I'd learn. But, no, I never do.

It's hard to stop falling for the same old tricks. It's hard to break the ease of a familiar routine. It's hard to break how you were conditioned to think. It's hard to forget that your father tried to kill you. It's even harder to forget that you played a part in killing him.

Anyway, Elsa just ran off, so Hope and I are getting ready to belt "Let It Go." I'm on the road to recovery, and this is a free therapy session.

I look at Hope, and she looks at me. At the end of the day, I can't even count on always having her to make me happy. Life will always be filled with things that try to break our happiness. It will always be filled with the unknown, the things standing in our way. It's just the way the world works.

As a father, love is terror. The unpleasant truth being: parenthood exposes you. Opens you, makes you vulnerable to the darkness in this world. Love becomes selfish. Selfish because you protect your kids to protect yourself. Because their safety and well-being is truly your own. Because their pain hurts you worse than anything else.

Love is terrifying, but the closed off loneliness of isolated safety… it's worse.

So, I'm going to hold her hand now. Going to smile and tell her I love her every chance I get. Going to keep living and fighting to survive every minute of the craziness. Because…I don't know what comes next.

The piano chords play, the song starts up, and as always, we commit to our performance. Spinning, jumping, twirling through the air, screaming at the top of our lungs, we shout, "Let it go, let it go!" And I'm really trying to let it go. I'm whirling and laughing, singing through all the aches and pains. Free! Free, just like I've felt these past few months. I pick up Hope, and she giggles as I spin her in circles.

When I put her down, she points to the screen and shouts, "Olaf!"

I jump onto the couch to prep for the finale, the final high note we love to deliver. I'm panting, sweating, and smiling, and I can't help but think that, no matter what, Hope is my one true soul mate.

As I'm bending at the knees to pirouette off of the sofa, I notice movement out of the corner of my eye. It's Ella. She's there watching. Sitting at the dining room table, smiling.

When it's over, I kiss Hope on the head, squeeze her. I feel like the squeeze is so much more than the hug. I bring her to Ella, because…I have to. Because, as angry and as hurt as I could ever be with Ella, she will always be Hope's mother. She will always be a part of our lives.

Ella and I were two kids, caught up in a swirl of emotions, pretending that what we had was a fairytale.

Have you ever loved something so much that it hurt? That it made something ache inside of you? It's just so weird to me that you can love someone, truly and entirely, so much that it hurts. Physical pain manifests in your chest, because you love them so hard. *I love Hope,* so hard, and so much, that, some days, it hurts in the best way possible. And that kind of love, it changes you. It shows you how to be a better person.

Life was so different only a year ago. It changed when we lost Faith. A life so ready to touch others was abandoned, and that damaged us all. But sometimes when things break, they get put back together differently. I found out that *differently* doesn't have to be bad. I've managed to find truth and happiness with different. I've managed to find more of myself—to find the better me, to accept my past and live for the future. As much as it kills me that I never got to hold Faith, I'm thankful for all of the power and wisdom she was able to share with me, just by being mine. Because I did get to love her, and I'll always love her.

I take Faith's worn cap from my pocket, my trembling hand shaking as I reach out. I hesitate, then I hand it to Ella.

A part of me has felt like Faith was with me when I touched the hat, but the truth is, she'll always be with me, no matter what.

"I've been holding onto this for a while. It's helped me. I want you to have it."

Tears spring into her eyes.

Do you think everything is mapped out for us before we're even born? Like the road map of life is concise and clear and every detail is finely printed and noted? The wrong decisions are actually right, because that's the way it was drawn in our plan. Or, do you believe, as the saying goes, *It is, what it is?* Maybe what *is* has no plan. It just is what it is at that moment in time. There's no way to know what the *is*…is. It just *is* because it *is.* Any small obstacle can change our direction.

If I turn left, what is to the right? What's the *is* that's to the right? It isn't the same *is* that's to the left. That makes the right the "*isn't.*" Couldn't we say that the right or the *isn't* wasn't meant to be ours? That what's meant to be ours is the *is?* And why is the *is* meant to be ours?

I got you, huh? It's this logic, or lack thereof, that makes me believe in fate. I believe it's all drawn out perfectly imperfect. That things happen when they happen, because that's what's needed. We need our challenges to push us to be better. To send us on our way to learn the real lesson.

Being a father taught me to break down the walls around me, and to keep breaking down the new walls that pop up. *And that's the thing,* there are always new walls. Every day is a new struggle, a new wall, a new box. You can escape one box, only to jump right into another. That's the journey of life: to keep breaking out of the boxes you put yourself in and to keep feeling.

Relationships force us to take a step back and realize how strong we can be. Every relationship has a purpose on our road map. Our mothers and fathers. Our siblings. Our friends and lovers. And, even more importantly, our children. Our children are the meaning of true love. You love them with everything you have, from the tips of your fingers to the very ends of your toes. With every distant speck of your body, you love them. You burn for them.

When life spins out of control, and you feel an insurmountable amount of pressure to hide away in a box, remember those relationships that changed you. Remember the love worth living for. Remember the words worth fighting for. And if that's not enough, remember it's never too late to create new relationships. To find new love. Connections can be formed with the simplest of smiles and with the kindest of words. It's always possible to fight your way out of the box with love. You just have to push away the fear and open your heart.

I move to Jenny, tucked into a blanket on the couch, her eyes unsettled at seeing my wounds.

"Jenny…I…love you," I whisper.

Her voice is small, but not quiet. "I love you, too, Higs."

Love.

It will find you; it always does. *Just remember, if you lose Faith… find Hope.*

Epilogue—Present Day

Life is a labyrinth of twisted emotions, lessons yearning to be learned the hard way, right from wrong clarified only at the hand of experience.

Nestled into bed, reflecting back on almost seventy-one years of life, the only thing left to realize, that couldn't be realized before, is that life is beautiful, even when it's ugly. The ugliness and the scars only help to define the beauty.

Do you think, right before you die, that you figure out all of life's unanswered questions? The secrets of the universe get whispered in your ear, and contemplations, along with past quests, liquefy into an absorbable matter? You leave with the knowledge only meant to be held by the departed?

I hope it works like that. There are things I'd still like the answers to.

What if God is all of us? What if the collection of all souls is the sum of Him?

Questions, without answers. What if death gives us the gift of knowledge? What if we only die to be awoken by the truth?

I'm dying. I'm dying, and I don't know what comes next, so forgive me for trying to convince myself that the unknown is beautiful.

I've lived a good life—hard, but rich and meaningful. Like Mom, I have cancer, mine attacking the prostate.

I've had the pleasure of learning things that I've realized can't be taught without experience. Some lessons have to be reached. I've learned marriage is like a house—you can't just maintain the surface...everything, down to the pipes and wires, matters. Small breaks and clogs can unsettle even the sturdiest of homes. I've learned that parenting is a lot like riding the mountain, that you can't force a circle into a square. I've learned that Hope's like the open road, and I've spent many years stuck on the sidewalk.

Replaying Mom's words, I never let anything come between Hope and me. I never let Hope get too far from my life. Even now, with her living in Philadelphia, I find the time to call her every day. Even more so now that I'm in a hospital bed.

It wasn't always easy to be patient, that's for sure. Hope is a smart, witty, powerful girl, who knows what she wants and how to get it.

As a teen she'd say, "Well, I'm going out tonight."

"You are?" I'd ask.

"Yup," she'd say.

"Planning to ask?"

"The concert should be over by 11:00 p.m., but I think we'll just sleep at Nana and Pop's," she'd mumble. *Not planning to ask.*

I'd wrinkle my eyebrows. "You think?"

"I mean, if it's okay with you. Can we?" She'd roll her eyes.

"Well, if they're fine with it. Make sure Bryan's parents know the plan."

"They do. They're fine with it. I talked to his mom yesterday."

"Yesterday!? Why are you just asking me now?"

"It must have slipped my mind." She'd bat her eyelashes.

"It seems an awful lot is slipping your mind lately. Like homework and cleaning your room."

"Dad! Really? Why do you have to ruin everything? You're such a fun-sucker."

"Because that's what dads do. We suck up all the fun, so our daughters have miserable lives," I'd joke.

"Just stay out of my life. I'm not your little girl anymore. I can take care of myself."

That's the hard part, right there, where she said, *"I'm not your little girl anymore."* That always hurt.

"You'll always be my little girl, no matter how old you are," I'd say.

"No," she'd say.

"Yes," I'd say.

"No," she'd say again.

"Yes," I'd say again.

"*Dad!*" she'd shout.

"I win."

Being a dad took everything. Sometimes I had to be strong, and sometimes I had to be weak. I had to say no, when I really wanted to say yes, or yes when I really wanted to say no. I had to be sad, and happy, and proud. I had to be scared, angry, and strict. I had to be everything. I had to be the good and the bad. I had to learn when to be soft and when to be hard. I had to be everything. I had to do everything.

Changing diapers. Giving baths. Reading stories. Softly brushing the knots from her tangled morning hair. Teaching. Mentoring. Bringing her to school. Watching her laugh. Seeing her dance. Kissing her boo-boos. Watching her grow.

Everything.

Trying to explain what her period was and then congratulating her like an idiot afterward. Attempting to give the sex talk and using two Barbies to demonstrate. The time I caught her stuffing her bra. Or, when she went to the gynecologist, and I got the bill for birth control. I found every minute of it amazing. I found every minute of it fulfilling.

The tenderness of a three-year-old explaining love to you. "You just know. You just know, Daddy." The giddy five-year-old with her first crush. Or the gentle, bittersweet kiss on the cheek on prom night. The trembling hand resting on your arm on her wedding day. *It's everything.*

Sometimes, I wake up, and I don't believe in anything. But then I think of her, and it reminds me to believe in everything. That's the prize you get for living; you get to see it. You get to see the world, and if you're lucky enough, you get to feel it. *I was lucky.*

It's true…my soul mate is Hope, my daughter is the love of my life, and I was destined to meet her. But the amazing thing about life is that we've been given the ability to love more than one person with everything we are.

Like Jenny. I love my girl, Jenny-from-the-Block, with everything I am. She carved her name into my surface, permanently marking me as hers. She was a beautifully frustrating, remarkably amazing, incredible blessing in my life, and I'm thankful we've had the opportunity to share these years together. I'm thankful she's sitting in the chair beside me, still holding my old-man hand. Although the years have aged us both, watching her sleep peacefully beside me…it still makes my insides tickle.

It took two years to convince her to marry me, always the stubborn lass. It came down to bribing her with the Discovery Channel. I blocked it and said, "You will marry me, or forego the opportunity to enrich your life with such educational primetime."

She just laughed and called the cable company. They turned it back on, but that night, she woke me up at 1:00 a.m., and said, "Yes."

"Yes?" I asked dazed and sleepy.

"Yes, I'll marry you."

And so we did. It didn't change anything. We were still the same loving and devoted people we always were, but I liked that I could call her Higs too.

"Higs, did you do the laundry?"

"No, Higs, did you?"

Jenny was a wonderful mother to Hope. She loved and cared for her just like she was her own. Ella was an active part of Hope's life, too, but her mom was always Jenny.

We had quite the Thanksgiving gatherings, to say the least. Ethan integrated as an unexpected ally into our little family, and Mom met John, a short, stocky fella, who finally showed her how a man was supposed to love.

Ella eventually remarried too. To a kind woman named Brooke.

Grabbing the remote, I switch the TV to channel forty-two. "Higs, a new episode of *Storm Chasers* is on!" I say to Jenny, who's curled up, sleeping, in the oversized rocking chair.

Her head flies up, her hair now salted. She snorts. "Huh?"

I laugh. After being married this long, it's the little things you learn to enjoy.

"Christ, Higs, turn the volume to thirty. I can't hear it this low," she says.

"Good morning to you too," I mutter. "Give your old man a kiss first."

She smiles that Jenny smile, and I get to see my girl's dimples. She tiptoes over and kisses me on the cheek, and then climbs into bed, resting her head on my shoulder. "How are you feeling?"

"Fine," I tell her. "Better today."

"That's great. A few more days off the medicine, and the chemo will work," she says, optimistically.

I nod. I don't tell her why I feel better: I've accepted the fact that I am going to die. I've accepted it and, somehow, know it won't be long.

"I love you." I kiss her forehead.

"I love you too," she whispers, as I yawn. "Are you tired?"

"A little, but I don't feel like sleeping yet. Let's watch this together." She pats my chest with her fingers.

Jenny wanted another baby. We tried and tried, but it never happened. She carried once for eight weeks but lost the baby soon after. Because of the abortion she had when she was young, her cervix is scarred, and she could never carry a baby full-term. She felt guilty, sad, and angry for a long time, and as much as she'd come to terms with it now, I know she still gets upset.

"Look at the size of that hail," she says, smiling.

I nod, trying to fight back the heaviness in my eyes.

"Take a rest. You look ridiculous fighting sleep," she mutters.

I smile, letting myself relax against her. The gentle sound of her breathing, and the warmth between us, putting me at ease. *Take my hand. Take my promise. Take me, everywhere, with you—forever.*

I reach for the breathing tube, then re-rest my head on the pillow. I take long, shallow breaths of manufactured air, watching Jenny watch the TV. As I'm readying to drift into sleep, the door opens. Hope stands in the doorway, her eyes wet with tears, and her face white like a sheet.

"Hi," Hope whispers, coming to my side. She's scared, so I give her a smile. I remember how it was to lose Mom. It was another moment you can't prepare for, but something you have to endure, nonetheless.

Jenny sits up, and I open my arms to Hope. She puts her arms around my neck, and I stroke her hair.

"It's okay. It's okay," I reassure her. "Hope, I'm here. I'm fine."

"I know you told me not to come all this way, but I couldn't be home," she says, sitting on the edge of the bed.

"I'm glad you came," I tell her.

Hope crawls into bed with us, resting her head on my chest the same way Jenny does. She wraps her arms around me. Jenny leans across and plants a kiss on her forehead.

"You came at the perfect time. I was starting to bore Dad," Jenny says.

Hope chuckles, but tears spring into her eyes. "I still need you…"

"You'll have me."

"I'm pregnant, Dad," she whispers, voice trembling. "I need this baby to know you."

I touch her belly. "That's great, baby. I'm so, so happy for you." I bring her hand to my mouth and kiss it. "You're going to make a great mother," I tell her, my words strong and clear. "You know I'd stay forever if I could, Bubs," I say, and that fast, the trembling creeps into my voice.

She hides her face in my chest, and Jenny strokes her chocolate hair.

"You've made my life…amazing." I reach over and put my hand on her stomach again. I remember doing this very thing when she was in Ella's belly. I tell her what my mom told me, "No matter what, you follow your baby. You follow them as far as they need to go, and you love them with everything you are."

"I don't want to lose you," she whimpers.

In life, I showed Hope everything I was on the inside. I showed her me. She should know all of me. I gave her that. "You can never lose me," I whisper.

Hope nods, tears washing her face.

"Hold my hand until I sleep. Please?"

Hope puts her smooth little hand in mine, and Jenny rests hers on top.

"And..." I murmur, "you know I'm a boy, right?"

Her face looks puzzled, and her eyebrows crinkle. If I were strong enough, that would have made me laugh. I wish I could laugh with her one more time.

"Keith is a good name..." I pause, "...for a boy."

She half laughs, half sobs, and gives me a smile. "You'll never change," she says.

My eyes close for a long minute, and when I open them again. Jenny's soothing Hope. As I close my eyes again, the light from the window reflects onto my eyelids. It looks like shattered stars, twinkling, bright and brilliant.

The world is a beautiful place, and I don't know if I'll ever get to experience it again.

Then among the stars, I see my mother. She's holding a baby. The baby looks like Hope, but I know who it is. The curly dark hair tells me it's Faith, and then I have my answer. The beauty of the world will always be mine to see, because when you love hard, you are tied to the people you leave behind. That tie doesn't sever, it just stretches.

My soul is speckled and dusted with pieces of Hope. Within me, she lives, a part of my bones. Together, we are tangled and twisted, tied as one by the fabrics of love. Forever I'll live, imprinted within her.

"Hope, tell me a story?"

She squeezes my hand. "Okay," she whispers. She takes an unsteady breath.

"Once upon a time there lived a handsome King,

Who loved his Princess even more than the flowers of spring.

That King worked hard all day and all night,

To run his kingdom without a fight.

The wind blew heavy, and it was hard to dream,

But the Princess could always find a way to make him beam.

The sky tumbled and rumbled as he fell asleep,
No noise could wake him from counting sheep.
All the land could hear those snores,
They were loud and rumbling like the mighty shores.
He became known as *Sleeping Daddy* by all,
Because no one could wake him, no noise big or small.
Then, one day, his Princess came along,
She gave him a kiss that made him feel strong.
The King awoke with no more fright,
And smiled always, day and night.
So, every day from that day on,
The Princess scurried to that sleepy King at dawn.
She was fast and speedy, and never late,
For she knew her kiss would decide his fate."

A warm kiss meets my cheek, Jenny's shaky voice murmurs, "I love you."

Then it's Hope's voice, whispering, "I love you, Sleeping Daddy."

About the Author

Nicholas Westerfer is a devoted father of two energetic daughters, Evangeline and Isabelle, and lives in sunny California. Balancing a full-time job with the joys and occasional chaos of family life, Nicholas navigates his days with the kind of grace one might expect from a walrus in a tutu.

His passion for storytelling is deeply rooted in his experiences as a parent and the endless inspiration he finds within his lively, albeit bustling, household. Nicholas writes with a mix of humor and heart, striving to capture both the magic and the messiness of everyday life. His writing reflects the vibrant chaos and profound connections that come with raising a family and managing a busy schedule.

Discover more about Nicholas and his writing journey at www.nickwesterfer.com and join him in exploring the adventures of a life brimming with love, laughter, and a few too many pets.

www.ingramcontent.com/pod-product-compliance
Lightning Source LLC
Chambersburg PA
CBHW022018310726
48972CB00006B/1713